I0647688

Airborne

The Speculative Elements
Volume 2

A Cape Breton Anthology

Edited by:

Sherry D. Ramsey | Julie A. Serroul | Nancy S.M. Waldman

Third Person Press
Cape Breton, NS

First Published in 2010

Compilation © Third Person Press 2010
Introduction © Afra Kavanagh 2010
Cover Artwork © Nancy S.M. Waldman 2010
Copyright in the individual stories remains the property of the
authors.

All rights reserved.

No part of this book may be reproduced, copied, scanned, stored
in a retrieval system, recorded or transmitted, in any form or by
any means, without prior written permission from Third Person
Press.

This book contains works of fiction. Names, characters, places
and incidents are the products of the authors' imaginations. Any
resemblance to actual persons, living or dead, events, entities or
settings is entirely coincidental.

Third Person Press
Email: thirdpersonpress@gmail.com
Web: www.thirdpersonpress.com
Cape Breton, Nova Scotia, Canada

Airborne: The Speculative Elements, v. 2
ISBN: 978-0-9811025-1-1

This book is dedicated to all of the unseen, unknown,
untouched mysteries of the universe,
to those who love to think about them and then write about them,
and, of course, to those who love to read about them...

*The Speculative Elements Series
from Third Person Press*

Undercurrents

Airborne

Contents

Introduction

Speculative fiction (SF) is a relatively new term to describe a variety of fictional genres, such as science fiction, fantasy, horror, and the paranormal. All of these fictions speculate about, envision, and populate worlds with beings and dramas different from but comparable to our own. SF as a result entertains; but SF also has other aims. Sometimes, these worlds and beings are extensions, and other times they are reflections, of our selves. So in fact, SF "holds the mirror up to nature." It depicts "the frighteningly possible" and raises questions about the effect science and technology can have on our personal life and on our transformations—big and small, physical and intellectual. In other words, it expresses our fears about being replaced by machines or about governments or corporations that usurp our freedoms, our very souls. It prepares us for the future.

These are some of the compelling reasons for reading speculative fictions, for no matter how strange their fictional worlds are, they are strikingly familiar. To speculate is to form theories, or to conjecture, without a firm factual basis (Oxford Reference Dictionary). The conjecturing in the stories in this collection engages us with its particular focus and different treatment.

Two of the stories in this collection create the fearful possibility that robots might develop free will, as the renegade helicopters do in "The Wild Helicopters of the Australian Outback" by Katrina Nicholson, and in "Pretty Charlie" by Donna D'Amour. Ken Chisholm's "Canto Paradiso" suggests that even a benign technology such as recorded song can be used to do harm. "Mind Drifter" by Julie Serroul and "Gifts from the North" by Chris Benjamin both dwell on positive aspects of the paranormal phenomenon of mind reading or possession. Interaction, *Twilight* style (love and hate), between humans and vampires is the subject matter in Kerry Anne Fudge's story, "Airborne." Krista Miller in "Colony" and Nancy Waldman in "Dragonfly" predict a time when humans will need to escape a polluted and uninhabitable earth in order to survive. "Unwelcome Visitors" by Peter Andrew Smith proposes a world where the familiar and the bizarre co-exist, and humans cope, business as usual. Bruce V. Miller imagines a hybrid creature, a hacker who exists simultaneously in the world and in cyberspace in "The Icarus in Your Blood," while "Daddy's Story" by Theresa Mac Kay celebrates the half-credible, but delicious bedtime stories that tie together coincidence and superstition, and in "Slipstream," Meg Horne takes her characters on a trip backwards in time. "Laika" by Jill Campbell-Miller, "Unmanned" by Sherry D. Ramsey, and "Is There Anybody Out There?" by Sue McKay Miller, reflect touchingly on the alienating, but strangely humanizing, effect technology can have. The unlikely for-hire spiritual powers of a long-lived seer are the subject of "Her Money's Worth" by Sherry Ramsey, and communication with the dead is the product of messing with out-dated analog radio equipment in "On Air" by D. C. Troicuk.

The stories are told from different viewpoints, interesting perspectives. In "Canto Paradiso," a father observes the effect of the "earworm" on his wife and daughter. A man/robot speaks out in "Unmanned." A high school student tells of his involvement with radio technology in "On Air," and "Airborne" is from the point of view of a sympathetic vampire. "Is There Anybody Out There?" offers us a sweet reminder of what and whom we have failed to acknowledge as "the Other" we seek. Very few of the stories conform to the pessimism associated with SF; in fact, stories such as "Dragonfly" and "The Wild Helicopters..." invoke a romantic paradigm and offer happy resolutions to the conflicts they portray. The stories are also written in a variety of styles. Three stories are presented in poetic form. "The Icarus in Your Blood" uses the language of computer programming and the voice of a computer geek. "Daddy's Story" is told in a Cape Breton dialect.

Writers and readers of SF are passionate about the world they are in and about the ones they write or read about. I remember reading *Stranger in a Strange Land*, *Brave New World* and *1984*, and being so affected by their premises that I accepted them as more than stories. To me they were statements on the human condition and forecasts of trouble to come, each true in its own way. It was obvious to me then, and is obvious again in this new volume, that good SF crosses genre boundaries to be recognized for its true contribution as social and political satire. Ken Chisholm says that he started with the idea of an "earworm," but then his story progressed to be about forcing people to stay awake as a way of killing them. The source of the threat remains vague in order for the story to consider how a person can stay a decent human being when the social order is collapsing around him. There are elements of social criticism throughout the collection, as for example, in Sherry Ramsey's poem-story "Unmanned." Ramsey here portrays the isolation and heartbreak that men employed in the business of killing must feel.

Place has always been a fifth character in Cape Breton fiction, both a presence and a force. Such novels portrayed Cape Breton as the mother-land and described the anguish of the sons and daughters who love it, but often have to leave it. The writers in this anthology, however, do not write in that same anxiety about place. They may set some stories in a recognizable Cape Breton, but they do not dwell on the harsh realities that are specific to this island. Instead, they focus on trans-global issues, such as the problematic advances in computer technology or robotics already mentioned or the necessity for finding new home planets to replace a threatened earth (perhaps echoing the theme of the Diaspora that Cape Bretoners have had to endure). Trans-global concerns are a common component in most speculative fiction, but are a new element in Cape Breton writing. Readers may find this a refreshing change.

The writers of these stories reach across with their stories to connect with us, the readers. We relish that their stories, despite the problems they describe, point to a brighter future than the one that news reports allow us to believe in. And we are happy that as individuals, they are our neighbours and friends. The editors at Third Person Press have created an important venue for new talent, and should be congratulated. In fact, readers can look forward to yet another volume of speculative fiction from Cape Breton; the call for submissions for volume three, "Unearthed," is already out. A fourth volume about fire, the fourth element, is also promised.

~ Afra Kavanagh
August, 2010

Afra Kavanagh is Assistant Professor in the Department of Languages and Letters at Cape Breton University.

Canto Paradiso

On the morning after the second night of no sleep, Rhea cried and fussed and refused to be comforted no matter how long Lori rocked her in her arms and sang to her.

Finally, exhausted, Lori shoved the baby at me and padded into the kitchen, staggering slightly through the living room door.

I gently held my daughter to my chest, coaxing her without success to nestle her little blonde head against my shoulder.

She settled a bit, but I knew she would not fall into sleep.

In her young brain, the melody of a song endlessly replayed itself over and over and over again.

I foolishly wanted her to tell me what that song was. I needed to know. I wanted her agitated grunts and gurgles to form a series of notes, a recognizable melody I could sing along with her. Maybe if we could just sing the same song together, she would find some peace.

Or maybe sharing my baby's pain would console me. And Lori.

The song continuously playing in my head was an old 1970s novelty tune, "The Night Chicago Died," about gangsters and machine guns.

Lori told me the song in her head was "Endless Love" from that 1970s teen movie, but the way her eyes stayed fixed on mine when she talked about it made me suspect the song had some meaning for her that she was keeping from me.

I stared at the television, working hard to focus on the weary looking newsreaders. Their eyes were bleary. They stumbled over the words they read. They had nothing hopeful to report. All over the world no one could sleep, no one could escape the drone of music looping through their brains.

~ Airborne ~

One of the newsreaders, a woman with barely combed hair, lit up a cigarette on camera. The man next to her popped a pill in his mouth. It might have been to help him fall asleep or make him function better as he stayed awake. Pills, like a solid eight hours in bed, were becoming a worldwide scarcity.

I must have zoned out—not asleep, just trapped in the peppy groove of the song—because suddenly I was back on the sofa staring blankly at the TV screen with the smell of burning toast filling our apartment.

"Lori!" I shouted, "Lori! Toast!"

I heard a weak "Yeah, I got it" from the kitchen.

Then, a wave of panic as I realized Rhea hadn't even twitched a muscle when I yelled out to Lori right in her ear.

I held her away from my chest so I could look at her. Her blue eyes were wide open, a little bubble of spit shimmering at the corner of her mouth.

She was breathing, thank God. Like me and Lori, she had drifted into the trance of the song. Then she frowned, my heart broke, and she resumed her squirming and crying.

Lori stalked stiff-legged into the room with a glass of orange juice and blackened toast. Rhea stretched her chubby arms towards her mother but Lori ignored her. Rhea, angry now, kicked her little fat legs harder when I kept her on my lap.

"How long were we gone this time?" Lori asked.

I looked at the time in the bottom corner of the TV screen.

"About three minutes," I said.

"They're getting longer," Lori said.

Rhea let go a howl of frustration and flung her head back, smashing into my chest.

Lori looked at her and said, "I wish there was a way to shut her up for just two minutes."

She saw my expression and said with a trace of exasperation, "You know what I mean."

She picked up a piece of charred toast and bit into it, staring at the television screen.

§

The week before, I stood in Sobeys at the meat counter talking to Lori on my cellphone, asking her if she wanted me to

~ Airborne ~

buy another tray of pork chops because they were on sale two for one.

Before Lori could answer, my cellphone cut out.

So did the phones of the other two people, also in mid-conversation, standing next to me at the meat counter.

So did the cellphones of everyone in the grocery store, in all of the stores up and down the mall, out in the parking lot, all over Sydney, all over Nova Scotia.

That blackout lasted a minute, and, when I arrived home, Lori told me, according to the Canadian Broadcasting Corporation, it affected the entire planet.

She looked scared when she met me at the door, Rhea bouncing on her hip and playing with her little purple plastic pony.

"A glitch," I said. "Hackers." I was worried too, but felt I should reassure her.

"They're saying sunspots on the news channel," she said. I thought she might be bouncing Rhea too hard and too fast, but the baby made happy sounds and looked like she was enjoying herself.

"There you go," I said, taking Rhea from Lori's arms for my welcome-home-Daddy hug.

But then another blackout came exactly forty-seven minutes and twenty-seven seconds later.

I was standing in the kitchen doorway holding Rhea and a wave of nausea made my knees quaver. My vision blurred for a second. When it cleared, I was on my knees, pitching forward with Lori running to catch Rhea before I flung her onto the floor.

"Richard!" Lori said, grabbing Rhea just in time.

"Jesus, what happened?" I said, barely recovering my balance, my heart pounding with terror.

"The radio went all staticky and you tumbled over," Lori said, tickling Rhea's tummy, making her giggle, and distracting her from her close call.

"Jesus," I repeated, steadying myself against the wall as I stood up, "It was like something zapped me."

"Kind of like an electric current passed through you?" she said, turning back to the stove to check the steaming pot of spaghetti sauce. Usually, she would not hold Rhea so close to the stove but she wasn't ready to hand her back to me.

~ Airborne ~

"Is the baby all right?" I said as I plopped down in a chair at the kitchen table.

We both looked at Rhea. She looked at us looking at her. Then she made a big gummy smile at the new game Mommy and Daddy were playing with their little empress.

"She's good. Are you all right?" Lori said, and held the back of her hand against my forehead. "You look pasty."

"No, I'm fine," I said, taking her hand away from my head and kissing the pulse in her wrist. "It's going away."

Lori brushed my cheek. "Supper's ready."

We ate in silence. Rhea sat in her high chair, her tray in front of her, and with a slow and steady beat banged her plastic spoon against her bowl of pureed carrots.

I thought of talking about work, the exciting world of storm windows, but stopped myself. Lori still missed her job at Citizenship and Immigration and every time I mentioned my own work I noticed she became restless.

Lori was at home alone with Rhea all day, except for when either my mother or hers dropped by, and she would get up at least once a night to nurse Rhea. I helped out as much as I could after work, but I knew it wasn't enough and sometimes it caught up to her.

A couple of weeks ago, I ate the last yogurt cup in the fridge and Lori, after finding it gone, exploded, "Can't you think of anyone but yourself for once?"

I thought she was going to slap me. She didn't and instead flung her arms around me in a painful hug. The intensely teary way she kept saying "I'm sorry, I'm sorry, I'm sorry," scared me almost as much as her sudden anger.

Now, with all this craziness in our heads burning everybody's last shreds of patience, I feared Lori had even less strength to hold her back during any more outbursts.

I watched as Lori stood and walked to the window. She pulled the curtain aside and looked down onto the street.

"What?" I said.

"I thought I heard a car stereo outside," she said, turning and giving me a puzzled half smile, "But the street is empty."

"I didn't hear anything," I said, stirring the cream into my coffee. For a second, the lazy swirl hypnotized me. "I can hear it now," I finally said.

~ Airborne ~

"There's nothing to hear now," Lori said, releasing Rhea from her high chair. She held the baby's backside to her nose. "Stinky bum syndrome. Clean nappy, stat, Ms. Rhea." She looked at me again. "You okay, sweetie?"

"I'll be all right," I said, "You take care of stinky bum girl before the paint peels off the walls."

"Maybe it's a flu bug," Lori said, "Take a personal day tomorrow."

I drank my coffee and listened to Lori sing to Rhea as she changed her diaper in the nursery: "Early one morning, just as the sun was rising."

For a second, the hum in my head cleared.

§

The next morning at work, the hum in my head was back. I found myself staring at my computer monitor, unable to concentrate on filling an order form.

I heard the melody more distinctly now, but as familiar as it sounded in my head, I could not pin down the name of it and that drove me crazy.

Then, as I was keying the last specs of a new construction project into the order form, the fluorescent lights of the office flickered, and my computer crashed.

Artie, at his desk on the other side of the room, slammed his hand on his desk.

"Damn," he said, "Three Wittle Fishies."

He caught me staring at him and smiled, his face reddening, "This song—my uncle sang a lot—it's been buzzing in my head all morning—couldn't remember its name. Just now—when the lights went nuts—it came to me. Three Wittle Fishies."

He sang the first couple of lines and laughed.

Penny came in, carrying the morning mail and said, "Me too. But mine was Camptown Races. Doo Dah, Doo Dah. Weird, eh?"

I felt a cold chill. "Whoa."

"What?" Penny said.

"The Night Chicago Died," I confessed, and laughed with my co-workers at the weirdness of it all. "At least that won't be bugging me anymore."

After three more power flickers, Quentin, our supervisor,

~ Airborne ~

stood in the door of his office and announced, "It looks like the world will have to go one day without quality custom-fitted aluminum windows. Go home, folks."

He ambled back into his office humming "I Kissed a Girl And I Liked It."

The humming in my head grew louder and more insistent and I needed a drink. I asked Artie and Penny along.

The beverage room up the road from our office was surprisingly crowded for lunchtime on a weekday. And instead of the usual blare of an all sports channel on each of the three big television screens placed in corners of the room, we had serious-faced news reporters standing in front of jostling crowds in Moscow and New York and other world capitals.

"Signal From Space?" one of the headlines under a female reporter said.

"What's going on?" I asked the server after I ordered a round for the three of us.

"They're saying some weird radiation hit the Earth somewhere over New Zealand," she said. "Like a radio wave or something. That's what they're saying made all those blackouts. They're even saying it's getting in people's heads, you know, making them hear—" she lowered her voice to a whisper, "—music."

"Do you hear music?" I had to ask.

She hesitated before answering. "The Alphabet Song." She rolled her eyes. "It's like I'm back in frigging elementary." She shook her head. "So, do you guys want to see the lunch menu?"

I gave her a bigger than usual tip when she brought our beers and burgers.

The beer tasted good but did nothing to mute the growing hum inside my head. I walked Penny out of the bar to her car. Artie stayed at our table and ordered a triple rum. The bar continued to fill with new customers.

After Penny drove away to pick up her kids at their school, I walked to where I parked my car. A hundred feet down the road, next to the drive-through at the coffee shop, I saw a well-dressed, middle aged woman standing with her forehead against a black metal light pole. Something about the way she was standing there made me concerned. I walked nearer and saw she was knocking her head against the pole.

~ Airborne ~

"Stop it, stop it, stop it," she said in a quiet monotone, her cheeks wet with tears.

"Doctor Sheppard?" I asked, standing about ten feet away from her. She shared an office with the pediatrician who saw Rhea.

She looked at me, not recognizing me at all.

"It won't stop," she said. "Amazing Grace, how sweet the sound."

"Can I drive you home?" I asked. "Can I call someone to come and get you?"

Her eyes focused on me then. She straightened her back and recovered some of her professional demeanour.

"You're...Richard?" she said.

"Yes, that's right. Are you okay?" I moved closer to her.

She smiled weakly, "Rough day. It's something about that space thing, isn't it? Do you think it's true?"

"I don't know. Strange stuff is going on."

"Yes." She smoothed her hair away from her forehead. "Strange stuff." She had a small, barely visible bruise blossoming in the center of her forehead.

I said, "I don't understand how it could be affecting everyone's brains though."

"But that's just it," she said, grabbing my arm, "That's exactly it. Your brain, my brain, everyone's brains—we're all electricity. I've seen it—kids living next to power lines. They say they hear things, they don't learn the way others kids do. We tell the parents whatever's the diagnosis of the day but we don't know what goes on in there." She slammed her palm against her temple. "How it works. Electricity," she said urgently, pointing her finger in my face. "And what are radio waves but a kind of electricity? We used to lobotomize children by sticking a metal probe behind their eyes. Just think what we could do with electricity." She spat out the last word.

I couldn't think what to say other than, "Are you sure I can't help you?"

"Are you an electrician, Richard?"

"No."

She flung up her hands as if to dismiss me.

"I need an electrician," she said emphasizing every word. She turned and walked away from me singing loudly, "I was blind but

~ Airborne ~

now I see."

I sped home, worried about Lori and Rhea. They weren't at the apartment. I called Lori's cell phone.

"I'm at the park," Lori told me. "Rhea was fussing and I thought some sandbox time might cool her out."

"Is it working?"

"Not much. I'll pack her up and head home."

"Stay there. I'll join you."

I walked over to the park in a couple of minutes. Things looked normal. An elderly couple walked a grey muzzled black Labrador retriever. A quartet of teenaged boys practiced their skateboard moves in the bandshell. Ducks paddled around the pond.

I sat down next to Lori on a bench and we watched Rhea crawl around the sandbox. The baby shook her head as if shooing away an invisible fly buzzing her ears. I told Lori about my encounter with Doctor Sheppard.

"God, that poor woman," Lori said. "Do you think she has, you know, some sort of mental condition?"

"She thinks it's that radio wave that's on all the news channels."

"Radio from space," Lori said, shaking her head. "It's insane. Like some sort of stupid conspiracy movie. More like some lab experiment gone wrong. Only they don't have the balls to admit it."

"If there's some scientist behind it maybe there's a cure," I said, watching Rhea grab fistfuls of sand and throw them at a family of ducks poking their bills into the grass blades.

"There's no cure. If there was a cure, we'd be cured," Lori said, her face flushed with anger. "Rhea! Stop that! Leave those goddamn birds alone!" She jumped off the bench and raced over to the sandbox. She grabbed both of Rhea's wrists in one of her hands and began slapping them with her other hand. "Do not hurt the birdies. Bad baby, bad, bad, bad baby."

"Lori!" I said, pulling her away from the sandbox. She kept her grip on Rhea, who wailed in shock and terror, and when Lori almost yanked her off the ground in my attempt to separate them, Rhea wailed even louder.

Lori let go of Rhea and turned, burying her head in my shoulder and sobbing, "Ohmygod." Over her shoulder, I could see the elderly couple frowning at us, the skate board kids laughing, the ducks serenely paddling to the far side of the pond. I put my arms around Lori to comfort her but she broke free from my embrace.

She ran to the sandbox and scooped Rhea up in her arms, gently whispering as she rocked her back and forth, "Oh, baby, Mommy's so sorry. Mommy didn't mean it. Mommy loves her baby Rhea."

I stood in front of her, "Maybe I should take her for a bit."

"I'm all right," Lori said, turning her body to put it between me and my daughter. "Don't look at me like that. You know I would never hurt Rhea—no matter what kind of freaky shit goes down."

I took a step towards her.

"Don't," she said, pleading. Rhea had stopped wailing and had dropped her head against Lori's shoulder, snuggling as if ready to sleep. "See. Rhea knows I'm all right."

§

I slept on the couch that night, listening to Lori groan and turn in our bed, not finding sleep; listening to Rhea, beside her, cry and whimper; listening to that inane Seventies pop tune endlessly loop through my brain.

Just before dawn, the three of us found our sleep. But not for very long and even then my dreams of Lori clutching Rhea to her chest, running away from me, were drowned in that idiotic song.

After we pulled ourselves out of bed and off the sofa, we sat at the kitchen table eating our breakfast of toast and orange juice, barely able to look at each other.

"Are you going to work?" Lori finally asked.

"I'm taking a personal day."

"You can leave me alone with Rhea, you know," she said, staring at her plate and the slice of toast with a single bite eaten out of it.

"It's getting worse," I said.

"I'm fine," she said with heat.

"No, not you." I looked her in the eye for the first time that morning. "That song. In my head. It's really hard to hear anything in my head except for that song. What about you?"

~ Airborne ~

"Yeah, it won't go away. I tried to think of other songs, TV show themes, waves on the beach. Nothing. Nothing worked," Her eyes teared up. "They'll fix it, right? Whatever it is, they'll fix it."

I reached across the table and covered her hand with mine.

"Sure they will," I lied.

That day, the lights stopped flickering. We hoped that was a good sign.

§

We needed diapers and drove to the pharmacy where the brand we used was twenty percent off that week.

We stopped at a red light and I noticed a man in a dark suit squatting on the grass verge next to the street.

"That's Father Anderson. From Saint John The Divine," Lori said, following my gaze. "What's he doing?"

"He's got his pants down around his ankles," I said, watching him closely now. "And he's talking a crap in public."

The light turned green. We drove on.

§

"If you want tranqs or other sleep aids, we're all out," the armed guard with the spaghetti western mustache told us through the glass door of the pharmacy. "But they still got some herbal tea at the Tim's."

"Baby diapers," I said, raising my voice to be heard. Lori raised Rhea a little higher as if to confirm what I said.

The guard looked at the three of us without changing expression but let us in.

"Buy some diapers for yourselves while you're here," he said, directing us to the baby diaper aisle.

"Pardon?" Lori said.

"Losing sleep, right?" he asked. "The whole world is. Was in the armed forces. Had a course in psych-ops, extreme interrogation methods, sleep deprivation. Longer without sleep, more stressed the subject becomes. Hallucinations, emotion swings, depression, suicidal ideations, and muscle control loss. Sphincter opens, and the subject messes themselves like old Aunt Millie."

~ Airborne ~

Lori looked at me and then at the guard. "Then what?"

"Never had a subject stay awake long to find out," he said, "well, except for the rats. And they all died. Pushed that test too far, ask me."

"The debit still working?" I asked.

§

The next two nights, we slept even less, but on the second night Lori let me back into our bed with her.

None of us had an appetite during the day, but we made ourselves eat anyway.

If Lori had Rhea and took her out of my sight I went and found them. At first she was angry, but that went away. Maybe she understood my concern, or maybe like me, the continuous din of unwanted music in her brain sapped the strength of her emotions.

The internet service stopped responding. One after another the cable television channels winked off except for two news stations. The phones worked, but people stopped calling. The power stayed on. We sat in front of the television all night, not talking, just listening to the inside of our brains, not even realizing we had stayed awake all night.

In the morning, because it was sunny and mild, because it seemed better than staying in our apartment, we went out for a walk around the neighbourhood.

People shuffled by us, hollow-eyed, staring, silent or mumbling or singing a snatch of some song only they could hear. Some of them were neighbours, some of them were strangers; none of them acknowledged our presence beside them.

We heard a raised voice around a corner and reflexively walked towards it.

A man with a couple of days growth of beard stood addressing a group of people who stared at him without expression. He smelled bad. The seat of his trousers was soiled.

"Hydrogen jukebox," he said, pointing to the sky with his hand, which held a shiny black revolver. "Want to conquer the universe? Send a death-o-gram. A beam of information full of math. Our brains run on math, all the really smart brains do. Millions of algorithms, like a universal remote for the TV, run them all. Find the one that clicks the channel. But how do you boost the signal? Hydrogen jukebox!

"It's everywhere. All them hydrogen molecules everywhere you want to be. In the air, in the water, we drink them in, we suck them in every breath." He pounded his chest. "Make all those hydrogen balls vibrate like little quantum radios—play the algorithms like the Top Nine at Nine. Make our brains work against us. Make them into little radio receivers. Play the top ten hits of galactic domination." He leaned closer to us, lowering his voice to a conspiratorial whisper, a huge last-word-of-the-crossword smile on his face. "And you know what's coming?" A sudden bang and the top of his head flew off in a red cloud of meat and bone.

The gunshot scared Rhea and she howled in fright but otherwise nobody reacted.

The dead man collapsed onto the pavement; his hand holding the gun fell behind his back. We stood without speaking, watching the pool of blood widen around the blasted top of his skull.

After a minute, someone drifted away, followed by a second person, then most of the others.

A woman wearing a green bathrobe and fuzzy pink slippers walked over and spoke to the corpse, "Listening to the crack of doom on the hydrogen jukebox." She bent down, kissed the man's lips, picked up his gun and walked off down the middle of the street following the painted yellow centerline.

A man in a red checkered shirt and Blue Jays baseball cap turned on Lori and grunted, "Shut her up," and jabbed a greasy finger at the still-howling Rhea.

I punched him in the face and he went down. I grabbed Lori's elbow and led her away towards our apartment.

"Quiet!" she hissed in Rhea's ear, but the baby kept screaming. "What does it take to shut you up?"

§

We stayed inside after that.

I heard what sounded like gunshots a few streets over, and, as the sun set, looking out the window, I saw clouds of smoke over the rooftops from all areas of the city. Down by the harbour,

~ Airborne ~

someone set off fireworks or maybe they were distress flares.

When we returned to the apartment, Lori had put Rhea in her crib and left her alone. Lori sat on the edge of our bed and stared at the floor. When I sat next to her, she stood and shakily walked to the kitchen. I fell back on the covers and stared at the ceiling.

"The Night Chicago Died." Over and over and over and over and over.

I heard the door slam. The apartment was in darkness.

"Lori?" I said, barely able to speak, "Honey?"

I threw back the blanket covering me—I couldn't remember pulling it over me—and unsteadily rose to my feet.

Lori wasn't in the kitchen or the living room. I looked in the nursery and Rhea's crib was empty.

Rhea. She wouldn't.

I grabbed a knife from the kitchen and tumbled down the stairs to the front door of our apartment building. I steadied myself against the bike rack by the door and looked up the road for my wife and daughter.

Empty street. Where? Park.

I clenched my fists, stood up straight, willed my legs to move.

If the park had been a block farther away, I would never have made it.

The streetlights were dark but the moon was full. Dozens of people stood in groups on the paved pathways, on the grass under the trees, in the curved shadow of the bandshell. They stood with their faces turned to the night sky.

I found Lori by the sandbox, sitting by herself on a blanket like she was having a midnight picnic. I fell onto the grass and crawled to her on my hands and knees. Lori watched me impassively as I neared her, the knife in my hand.

"Rhea?" I said.

Lori only smiled.

"Lori," I said, lifting the knife even though it weighed like a bar of lead in my hand.

Lori looked at the knife but said nothing.

Rhea raised her head over the wood frame of the sandbox. She saw me and smiled.

All I could see in the moonlight was how much she resembled her mother.

I dropped the knife in the grass.

~ *Airborne* ~

"Rhea," I said. "Make safe. Rhea."

"No safe," Lori said, still smiling. "Only." She thought for a second. "This." She laid her hand over mine.

She pointed to the sky.

"On. TV. Gov. Ment. Bombs. There. There. There. There. Way up." She pointed to the star-strewn sky. North. West. South. East. "Hydrogen. Jam. Signal. Scram. Ble. Re. Set." She tapped my forehead between my eyes. "Then. Sleep. Maybe. Maybe."

I rolled onto my back on the blanket, looking up at her.

"Your. Song. Story?" I said.

"Can't," she said, looking down. "Stupid."

"Tell," I said. "Best. Now."

"Jack. Jack. Jack Don-don-donelly. First. Mine. Radio. Car. Yuck. Stupid." She shook her head, smiling slightly. "You. Rhea." She laid a shaky hand on each of us and sang, "My endless love."

"Yeah," I said. "Stupid."

When Lori opened her mouth to laugh, a corona of light blossomed behind her head and then it was like dawn was coming at us from every direction.

Rhea giggled and bounced on her bum. She put up her chubby arms as if to grab at the spreading lights like they were dandelion fluff floating by on a breeze.

I saw the people around me more clearly. Their faces turned upwards, eyes wide, mouths agape. Their shadows grew long then shrank and swung around them like the hands of a madly racing clock.

Rhea started singing—it sounded like a gurgle in her throat but it was a melody, one I hadn't heard before but familiar as a lullaby in its simplicity.

The other babies and young children in the park took up Rhea's song and repeated it as "la-la-la" or as a crooning hum or strung together the first words in their heads that fitted to the melody: "lion balloon dingle popsicle".

Then the grown-ups joined in and for a few minutes the whole park was filled with Rhea's song.

The afterglow of the explosions faded but the song continued. Then, in ones and twos, adults and children sank gently to the grass, to the pathways, to the dew-wet concrete of the bandshell.

Rhea crawled between Lori and me and, with an exhausted sigh, fell to sleep. Lori put her head on my shoulder and closed

~ Airborne ~

her eyes. I folded the blanket over my wife and daughter and gently laid my arm under their resting heads.

I struggled to keep my eyes open so I could listen to their steady, deep breathing. I looked up at the stars, thinking their twinkling was a kind of singing.

I finally allowed my eyes to close but I still saw the stars and I still heard the distant echo of Rhea's song.

❧◦❧

K en Chisholm lives in Sydney, Nova Scotia, and has written (by himself or in collaboration) over two dozen one act plays, hundreds of book, movie, and play reviews, and presently writes a weekly arts and culture column for the Cape Breton Post. He has written music and comedy for the *Cape Breton Summertime Revue* and Howie MacDonald's *Celtic Brew*. He is also a longtime member of the local theatre community as a writer, actor, and director. "Canto Paradiso" is his first published short story and has inspired him to think of even more absurd ways to end the world.

On Air

Keigan dropped the needle gently into place and rotated the vinyl platter manually to queue the next track. "Stay tuned for news and weather at the top of the hour. Up next, we're going way back to 1967, before my Mom was born, but it was one of her favourites. This is for you, Mom. If you're listening."

As the strains of *Nights in White Satin* went out over the air waves, Keigan signalled to Phil through the glass panel of the sound booth. "Don't tell me you can't hear that."

It wasn't there all the time, this feedback, distortion, echo— he didn't even know what to call it. It was all of these, and none of them. Listening at home he heard it as a whine and wow as if the radio wasn't quite on the station, as if the signal were reaching out, searching for the right receiver, missing the mark. The joke around the station was that the old Mark V sound board had been salvaged from an alien spacecraft and was sending transmissions to the home planet.

In another minute or two it would be gone. They might not hear it again for days, or even weeks at a stretch. But the technician in Keigan paid attention, wanted to find the cause, even if he couldn't solve the problem.

Phil shrugged. Any real explanation would cost him money.

§

Keigan had started out as a volunteer at the community station, one of the first to answer Phil's appeal to the public to get involved. Back then he wasn't all that interested in radio. His only experience was with the high school radio club, which he had joined to get to know a certain girl who, as he found out, had joined to get closer to a certain science teacher. The same science teacher had forwarded a link to a web page with a special note for Keigan: "Look into this and I just might pass you. (:-)"

Keigan clicked on the icon and navigated through the site, starting with the intro about the proposed station concept, then on to a brief history of radio and a mini-bio of Phil Sterling. This would be Phil's second career in radio. A local boy who had gone to the city to find work, he had spent the last thirty-five years behind the scenes at the CBC and apparently knew everything there was to know about analog broadcasting. While the rest of the world was going digital, he had been dealing with the fact that his heyday—the era of analog—was over. But ten years into the new millennium, it was his wife's losing battle with ovarian cancer that had influenced his decision to retire back to his home town. The move was one last gift he could give Carrie, to bring her back to live out her life in the place she had never stopped being homesick for. In the end, the illness had won out. He had made the move alone.

The website had directed Keigan to a meeting at a Main Street address. He didn't realize until he got there that it was CGBY. The station had long occupied half of the lower floor of a building erected in the year of the town's incorporation. From the street it looked as if not much had changed since then, except for the windows, which had been papered-over in recent years. Keigan entered where the sign was posted—not at the station entrance but at the adjacent storefront, beneath a faded, painted sign which still read "Rosenblum's Ladies' Wear." His Mom had worked there once, part-time. Inside, he wove his way through the dusty shelves and relics—a virtual museum of broadcasting equipment dating, from the look of some of the pieces, as far back as Marconi himself. A scattering of folding chairs was set up in the back.

"So there I am," Phil was saying, eyeing the latecomer as if already recognizing a pain in the neck, "my first morning of real retirement. The boxes are unpacked, I'm sitting on the deck with my feet up, got a cup of fresh-brewed coffee in my hand. It's October—but what a day! The paper boy comes by with The Telegraph and I open it up and I say out loud, 'Aaaah, now *this* is living.'" His voice softened. "Because I can feel my wife, Carrie, over my shoulder. And I feel this...this grief and longing. And

~ Airborne ~

guilt. Because I forgot she wasn't here anymore. How could I forget—even for a second—that the woman who nagged and badgered and nitpicked and supported and loved and put up with me and all my flaws for nearly forty years was no longer with me? Not physically anyway.

"So I went back to the paper. And the front page reads—"

Phil framed the headline with his fingers. "'Broad Street Fire Claims Two Lives.' A woman and her sixteen-year-old son."

Keigan, who had been drifting into boredom, sat bolt upright.

"I suppose," said Phil, unaware of why all eyes were turning to the latecomer, "some of you knew them. You remember: a picture of the charred remains of the house and the firefighters and a little girl sitting on the curb. Well, it's not what I need to see in that moment, right? So I'm just about to toss it aside when something in the right hand column grabs my attention. CGBY— the station I grew up listening to, the place where I cut my broadcasting teeth—is scheduled for demolition.

"Well. That gave me pause." Phil paused now for effect. "So I drain my cup and I pick up the phone. And you know, I could almost hear Carrie's voice echoing from somewhere inside the empty house, saying, 'So much for retirement, Phil.'

"That same afternoon I'm down here trying to hide my enthusiasm from the guy who's going to relieve me of my retirement savings. 'So,' I say, 'How much will you pay me to take this dinosaur off your hands?'"

After the poignant and amusing intro, Phil got down to business. He had a vision. Unlike his predecessor he was not about to be ground into the sand by economics and a rapidly changing technology. He outlined how he was going to have this old building declared a heritage site, how he was going to open a museum dedicated to the Golden Age of radio. Not merely a static display—though that would be part of it—but a functioning community station representative of an earlier era. As far as he knew—and he was correct—CGBY would be the last, the only, working analog broadcaster in the country. But there was much grovelling to be done, funding to be applied for, licenses to be obtained, renovations to be completed. He needed the community behind him. And, most of all, he needed volunteers.

Half the crowd left when he finished. Others made their way to the table where the sign-up sheets were laid out. Keigan sat weighing his options. He'd be expected to put in a lot of hours after class and on weekends. No pay, but free training, his teacher had said. A good opportunity for a kid in his position, just scraping by, problems at home, no money for college.

A few men had cornered Phil, trying to get their bid in for air time. Keigan recognized them as former staff of the station, local personalities who now hosted charity events and emceed banquets. Pale imitations, his teacher called them, next to legends like Peter Gzowsky and Stuart McLean and Wolfman Jack. Names that would mean nothing to Keigan if not for the radio club. Keigan mingled with others who were signing up for the more immediate but mundane tasks like cataloguing and researching artifacts. Seeing that one sheet remained blank, Phil made a final plea. What he really needed, was a technical wiz. Another Phil. A younger version of himself.

What he got was Keigan.

§

Phil was determined to reconstruct the studio as it had been in the early days of radio, as far back as equipment allowed. But the pieces accumulating in the "museum" had been discarded for a reason. Most of them were out of order. Spare parts and compatible, fully analog components were becoming harder to locate. The transmission tower had been badly damaged in a storm and required costly repairs. Then there was the matter of getting the Commission to grant an exception to the ban on analog broadcast signals and issue a license on historic grounds.

The plan was to track down other small stations that, like CGBY, had chosen to sign off permanently rather than come over to "the dark side," as Phil termed digital technology. Most of the owners were glad to donate obsolete equipment from their dismantled studios and dusty storage rooms; others needed little more than a nudge. By taking the junk off their hands, Phil reminded them, he was saving them the hefty environmental disposal fee.

Keigan spent most of his free time that first year riding along with Phil, sometimes skipping out on school, sometimes dragging Stacey along when their dad was late coming home or had forgotten to arrange for a babysitter. Phil's project didn't impress

Keigan. But, ever since the fire, any reason was a good reason not to be home watching his father sink into old addictions and bad behaviours.

Not that he could blame his dad for not wanting to be around —they were alike in that way. He had days like that too, when he missed his mom so badly, when the memories sealed inside the cool, renovated walls of their home grew so hot they burned the inside of his skull. But he blamed him for a lot of other things. Like giving in to his demons. Like being an absentee parent although he lived under the same roof, leaving Keigan to be mother, father and big brother to eight-year-old Stacey, all in one. He blamed him for something else too. Something unthinkable. But he thought about it anyway. He thought about it a lot.

As they barrelled along over the pitted asphalt of secondary highways, Phil taught the history of radio from behind the steering wheel. Keigan caught on fast. And when it came time to apply theory, they were both surprised at his innate feel for the equipment, as if he plugged into it, interacted with it. Phil had found his analog guy after all.

§

In his twenties now, Keigan was a full-time paid employee long overdue for a raise he knew Phil couldn't afford. Sometimes he thought he should move on, that he had outgrown Phil and his project. But something kept him here—pride in what they had accomplished, dedication, or stubbornness. And then there was the little peripheral he had been tinkering away at in his basement workshop, a digital/analog menagerie of spare parts collected from hi-tech junk yards and environmental swap meets, the gadget that was going to solve the station's distortion problem. And after that—after he worked out the kinks—he'd file a patent. In his daydreams he could see his branding on recording devices in studios and movie sets everywhere. But he needed to impress his boss first. Because Phil knew people in the industry. Phil could get his foot in the door.

Crammed into a DVD player housing, the little enhancement unit had an old clunker of a motherboard that was four or five years off the market, but it was showing capabilities that were totally off the grid. Testing it on his home-built recording console

Keigan could manipulate voices, instruments, sound effects to a hundred kinds of noise or, with a push of a slider or a flick of a switch, refine the same sound byte to a level of such clarity he'd swear the source was in the room with him.

The question was, would it work in reverse? Could he make it pick up interference—like off the Mark V at the station—and filter it, refine it like a homeopathic remedy until the noise was undetectable and only the pure sound vibration remained? He itched to test it at the station. The problem was, the user interface was run through his laptop, and Phil was fiercely resistant to integrating anything digital, afraid it would affect his funding status under the heritage programs.

Privately, Keigan schemed. If he could just get it working, then, later on, he could route the interface through a physical control panel with an array of sliders and dials and switches so that no one—not even Phil—would have to know what was going on inside. Either way, before he even mentioned it, he had to work out all the bugs. And in order to do that—there was no getting around it—he needed to get it into the station and test it on the Mark V.

§

At home Stacey was always goofing around in the mirror, belting out classic Lady GaGa take-offs, mostly to annoy him, which it did. It wasn't until she joined Jake's band that he saw she might have something special. The band—Neon Gecko—played this ugly commercial dreck. None of them was old enough to set foot inside a bar so mostly they played school dances and Blackberry raves. Keigan wasn't sure what their relationship was, exactly. In his opinion his baby sister wasn't old enough to have a boyfriend. When Jake came over, Stacey couldn't keep her eyes off him, but mostly they worked on new material or rehearsed the pounding dis-harmonies they called music. Keigan paid just enough attention to make sure they were keeping—remembering his mother's warnings when he was that age—"one foot on the floor at all times." Because, big brother or not, from the age of sixteen he had been effectively the only parent she had, the one who made sure she ate regular meals and got to school on time.

~ *Airborne* ~

The one who actually came home every night.

Keigan was drawn up from the basement, curious about what CD they were playing. The voice sounded vaguely familiar, but he couldn't place it.

And there was Stacey, softly strumming her guitar and serenading Jake with one of her own compositions. The melody was delicate and haunting. Jake was improvising an orchestral arrangement on a portable keyboard, a better musician than Keigan had given him credit for.

Stacey looked up to see Keigan standing in the doorway listening. He cocked his finger. She rolled her eyes and obeyed the summons.

"What?" she spat when they were alone in the kitchen.

Keigan kept going through to the basement stairs. "Bring your guitar," he said. Then, calling over his shoulder, "Go home, Jake."

Stacey stomped down the steps after her brother. "Why can't you just leave us alone? We're not doing anything."

"You were doing something," he said. Downstairs he interrupted her rant, indicating the microphone he'd set up earlier to record test tracks of ambient sounds. "Do it again."

Her resentment dropped. She took the mike hesitantly. Within minutes she was taking direction from her brother.

"Forget about control in that passage, just go with the emotion, really sell it. That's better. Watch your diction in the bridge. Now try a little variation on that last repeat. Yeah, that's good."

Seeing her like this, so eager to please him, Keigan realized she was right to complain that he never took her seriously. Until now.

"Play it back," Stacey said.

She reached past him to do it herself. He snatched her wrist before she could touch the console and, in the playful tussle, one of them skimmed over the controls. The laptop's cursor darted across the peripheral's control panel. When the intro started, something was off. The song played faintly in the distance. In the foreground they could hear Jake snoring on the couch upstairs, a faucet dripping in the kitchen over their heads and, louder, what sounded like a cat purring.

Keigan was thrilled. "Hear that? Talk about fine-tuning."

~ Airborne ~

"Where's my song?" Stacey griped.

"Yeah, yeah, I'll play it back in a minute. I just need to find out where that interference is coming from and get a fix on it so I can tune it out."

As he made incremental adjustments, Stacey perched on the desk, shifting impatiently. "That's all you're ever interested in," she said. "That...K-box thingy."

"K-box?"

"Yeah. Keigan Junior. You spend enough time with it, it's like your kid." And then she was gone, sniping at him as she stomped up the steps. "You never thought I was any good. You just needed a guinea pig for your stupid Frankentech stuff."

It was the cruelest shot of all. Not because it hurt him, but because it reminded him how easily he could hurt her. And because it was true. Instead of tuning out the interference he had tuned out his sister.

The 'K-box.' He liked that.

In the next minute he was engrossed again, replaying the track from the beginning. Nothing. So...he hadn't recorded the sounds. If he had, he'd be hearing them every time.

He went upstairs. Jake was gone. Stacey must have turned off the faucet. As for the cat...? The neighbour's cat must have got in. Maybe Jake let it out when he left.

§

Besides working the evening shift Friday and Saturday on air Keigan took care of most of the technical maintenance and repair, and was pretty much on call twenty-four/seven. Phil had no qualms about calling him in to deal with the station's technical problems any time, day or night. That's what he got for being the analog guy—and for living just down the street.

Like most nights when he was on air, Keigan got home too wired to sleep. He poked his head into his sister's room, gave her half-hearted hell for still being up. The smartphone lay on the pillow singing directly into her ear. It was one of the original models, the only thing of their mother's that had survived the fire, and only because she had left it in the car. He had managed to keep it running on a recharger he'd picked up in his travels, but when the obsolete battery finally died, he'd have to tell her that was it.

"At least use the ear piece. Or do you want to get brain cancer?" Something he felt a responsible parent would say, something he owed their mother. But, really, he understood. He had been a night-owl know-it-all at that age too.

Stacey threw him a look.

"Come downstairs then," he said, an attempt to apologize for the other night. "We'll work on your song."

She flipped over onto her stomach, blew out the candles she had lit next to her bed the way Mom used to. She dropped her head into the pillow, her face turned away from him.

"Okay. Be like that," he said.

Keigan shut the door quietly and went downstairs. He woke the computer and sat there in the desktop's glow. He had lots to do, real work he had been putting off. He needed to rewrite some software code for the K-box and there was some hardware that had to be cannibalized to see what he could salvage. But the anomaly from the other night had him hooked. How had the studio microphone in the basement captured sounds from upstairs through carpet, plywood, and acoustical tiles?

Going upstairs, he adjusted the kitchen faucet to a loud drip, clicked on the TV, then returned to reset the K-box to default mode. He left the mike open to see what it would pick up but on the replay there was nothing but the hiss of dead air—not even street noise or crickets or the patter of rain on the walkway outside the open basement window.

Frustrated and out of ideas, he clicked on Stacey's icon, hit Play, and sat back to listen. They didn't have anything solid yet, one decent run-through from beginning to end, a couple of rough cuts of other compositions she was working on, and a number of experimental guitar riffs and variations. He didn't tell her, but there was one song in particular that really got to him. She wasn't quite there yet. But, boy, one day.

He reached to balance the bass and treble. His sleeve, hanging open at the cuff, grazed the controls, the shirt button clicking lightly over metal and hard plastic. Suddenly the dim light in the dingy basement burst into luminescence with a swirl of—not music, exactly. Sound, but not sound. Something sensory, but ethereal, too. Other-worldly. Something that shocked him to extreme alertness. For a second he could have

~ Airborne ~

sworn he had actually seen it, as if the sound were three-dimensional, prismatic. Like he was inside a soap bubble, he thought, and laughed. And then, just like a soap bubble, it burst with a soft, popping audio spray—and was gone.

His hand froze in place over the mixing board. *What the hell was that?*

He sat there for a long time, reliving those two seconds—was it even that long?—trying to convince himself it was just his imagination.

If it was, he was nuts.

And if it wasn't?

Then it was something in his own brain. A tumour? The residue of a previous high? But he hadn't touched any of the nasty stuff for a long time. These days he didn't have anything stronger than Canadian beer.

Reality settled back into place, making it easier to explain away. It was nothing, a brain fart. A gaseous reminder to clean up his act. Eat better, get to bed at a decent hour, and okay, he could go a little easier on the beer.

But it was more than that; he knew it. And his instincts told him the K-box was only part of it. Otherwise, he'd be hearing, feeling, seeing something every time. It had to be something else. Something on that sector of the hard drive? Or—the music? Could that be it?

He played a number of downloaded selections from some of his favourite artists. Nothing. Then Stacey's song, the one that had been playing when they heard Jake and the cat. More nothing. Music, he thought, letting his mind slip. It was a powerful medium. It could calm your nerves or rev you up; it could change your mood, lift you out of the moment, transport you to another place and time.

There it was again, near the end of Stacey's session. Coming off one take, one riff, a musical phrase that captured the sweetness of her voice and the sentimental longing of the lyrics. He replayed it again and again, and it took him many tries before he realized that it only happened when his mind was focussed on something else. He forced himself to concentrate on the counter but it was like exercising a new muscle, weak at first, and exhausting. But he was determined, and by the end of the week he was able to narrow the sample to eight bars of music, four bars, two bars. When he had isolated the little gem he duplicated and dubbed it in a series of repetitions until the playback sounded like one of the station's vinyl records when it skipped in place. Still, the effect was unsustainable—a flash, like heat lightning, far off, caught in his peripheral vision, while inside his brain a kind of white noise crackled, but with a fullness, an *intention,* as if meaning were coded into it.

He puzzled over how to expand it. What if something was lost in the dubbing? What if he got her to actually record it like that, repeating the phrase without a pause?

He pictured his sister half asleep in her self-styled third floor attic "loft" reaching out to answer Mom's smartphone. She mumbled something nearly inaudible. *Middle of the night. School in the morning.*

He didn't care. "Please, Stace," he said, "Come down here. For just a minute."

She moaned. "Down where?"

"You have to hear this. Listen." Three floors below her in the basement he held his phone to the speaker and ramped up the volume.

"Is that my song? Why is it skipping like that?"

"You don't hear...anything else?"

"What else am I supposed to hear? Was I snoring? Is that it?"

Keigan ignored the sarcasm. Maybe the sound effect was lost in the phone signal; maybe she had to be there. "Come down to the basement," Keigan told her. "I need you to play it like that."

"Get lost, Keigan." She hung up.

Keigan repressed an urge to go up to her room and drag her downstairs bodily. But then, maybe it was for the best. There was no point in scaring the living daylights out of her. At least not until he knew what he was dealing with.

What *was* he dealing with? A new technology? A whole new concept of—

What? Music? Could he even call it that? Notes sliding together like an oil slick on open water, shimmering like sunlight on waves, flaring like sunspots. Crossing-over into other senses, as visceral as a pulsing drumbeat, so close to visual it almost took shape. So meaningful he could almost *understand*—

And then, like a dream, before he could catch it, lock it into memory as a real occurrence—gone!

~ Airborne ~

§

The next evening it took only a little prompting to get Stacey back to the basement.

"When we get a couple of really good takes," Keigan had promised over supper, "I'll transfer your tunes to a cassette, and I'll take it to the station and play it on air one night."

Concentrating on the crucial eight-bar riff, they collaborated on variations and refinements and Stacey transposed them to other keys, unaware of his purpose. Then, late at night, on his own, Keigan worked at expanding the range of musical notation that created or contained the effect, or was susceptible to it. He didn't know which. Playing the results through the K-box filters he could make certain chords practically shine. One fragment in particular, where her voice sustained D flat an octave above middle C, transported him to a momentary state of bliss equalled only by an Eric Clapton phrasing. With each different key signature, the atmosphere in the basement changed—from light and lucid as a summer morning to heavy and thick as a smoker's haze.

Then, every once in a while, some odd occurrence like they'd heard that first night. Odd, because, as he knew now, the snoring was not Jake's: Jake had already gone home. And not Dad's, because he had been at work. Odd, because Stacey swore she had not touched the faucet. Odd, because there was no cat in the house, hadn't been for years, not since their mother died. They had lost the cat in the same fire. Odd, because this time he had moved the K-box out of reach. He couldn't have adjusted it, not even by accident.

So whatever it was—sounds from inside their house, or from the neighbourhood—it wasn't being picked up by the mike during the recording, but filtering from some unknown source through the speakers along with the playback. And only when the K-box was jacked in.

Keigan grabbed a beer from the fridge and took it out on the front porch. He tipped his head back to drink, contemplating the stretch of adjacent lawns, the tree tops and street lights, the starry sky where he imagined the air pulsing with microwave signals—radio, television, cell phones. What about cordless

~ Airborne ~

phones and GPS and Bluetooth? And there was still old technology in use. The museum had inadvertently stirred up a nest of local hobbyists who had resurrected police scanners, and shortwave and ham radios from their basements and attics. His dad had even got out his old CB radio and switched it on from time to time. Mostly he got static, but every now and then he picked up some die-hard trucker travelling the 417 between Ottawa and Montreal. Maybe that was the answer. Maybe their snorer was some trucker pulled off in the rest area. Maybe he had a cat along for company.

§

On Wednesday afternoons, Vivi Fletcher hosted a phone-in gardening show and filled in the gaps between callers with novelty songs whose lyrics included the names of flowers. Today being a tribute to the fall planting of bulbs, Tiny Tim's falsetto was taking the listeners *Tiptoe*-ing *Through the Tulips*. From the hallway, Phil signalled to her through the glass to turn off the feed to the internal intercom. Vivi smiled, and ignored him.

Passing in the other direction, Keigan saw the brief unspoken exchange. Well aware that his boss would be actively *not* listening, he hitched his head to the intercom. "Hey, Phil. You hear that?"

"Hear what?" said Phil.

Keigan didn't want to do it this way, through deception. But Phil wasn't easy to pin down to have a real conversation. Not about this. He had tried to tell him what he was working on at home, but every time Phil heard the word "invention" he segued to his brother-in-law who, apparently, was always hitting him up for a loan or investment for some goof-ball idea. In other words: *Don't bug me, kid. Just do your job. In this economy, be glad you've got one.*

"It was there a minute ago," Keigan said, reinforcing his little white lie. "I've got an idea what it could be. Maybe if I could just bring in my K-box one night—"

"Your what?"

Keigan was ready with explanations, but Phil was giving him the go-ahead, humouring him. "Yeah, yeah, whatever you gotta do. Just make sure all the cords are plugged into the right

~ Airborne ~

sockets before the morning show."

Keigan grinned. The station was off the air between two and six a.m. That gave him four hours.

He wasted most of that first night scouring the back room and dismantling museum displays, searching for the right snake or cable or adaptor to marry the archaic equipment with the connectors on the K-box. Before he left, to make it look as if he had at least tackled the real problem, he climbed in behind the main console where he unplugged, then reconnected a few cables and jacks and dragged out a lot of dust bunnies as evidence of his attempt.

For the rest of the week Keigan listened closely, hoping for the least bit of noise from the Mark V, and an excuse to spend another night. But it was almost as if with one little tweak of a loose connector wire the alien interference had resolved itself. By day he avoided Phil, afraid he would comment on the improvement, forcing him into continuing the lie. By night he brought in the K-box on the sly. The hours flew by as he tried, without success, to recreate the strange effects he had experienced at home.

§

Coming up to the long weekend, Jake finally proved himself the jerk Keigan knew him to be, breaking up with Stacey because of all the time she spent with her brother rather than with him. The real reason, Keigan suspected, had to do with the girl he had seen Jake with at the coffee shop near the station. On Sunday Keigan agreed to take the late shift to give Brian, the regular host, a long weekend. Stacey was still moping around the house when he was leaving for work. At the last minute, thinking it would cheer her up, he said, "You should come down to the station with me." It meant a late night. But she didn't have school in the morning. And Dad wasn't around to object.

Sunday night listeners of CGBY tuned in to hear standards from the forties. Keigan opened the show by reading from the notes Brian had left him, then spun a war-time Big Band number while Stacey nosed around the studio with unabashed curiosity.

When he signalled that it was okay to talk she said, "Did you build all this?"

~ Airborne ~

"Don't be stu—" He caught himself, and in a gentler tone he said, "No, of course not."

"What have you been doing down here all these nights anyway?"

He touched the K-box. "Integrating Junior here to the Mark V. This—" He gestured broadly across the console in front of him "—is the Mark V." And as if to impress her, "It was top-of-the-line in its day. See, I thought, if I could get the same effects I got at home—"

"You mean the snoring and the cat?"

"Yeah. And the other stuff."

"What other stuff?"

Keigan winced at his slip. "Nothing. Wait here a minute."

He wheeled an extra chair into the sound booth, showed her how to queue an LP track on the turntable by settling the stylus in the gap between cuts. He let her pick a couple of tunes from the archives, left her alone to rehearse a community announcement then smiled encouragement as she stammered nervously through it. An hour passed. She was getting restless. Keigan produced a cassette from his shirt pocket.

Her face lit up. "Really? You're going to play it?"

He nodded.

"Oh," she said. "But I won't be able to hear it. On the radio, I mean. Can I call Tessa? And Jill?"

"Let's just listen to it here tonight. If we don't get any complaints—"

"Very funny."

"—I'll play it again on Friday. You can have your friends over and listen together."

He popped the cassette into the tape deck, let it play without introduction.

"Who'd you write this about anyway?" Keigan said.

"I dunno. I guess I was sort of thinking about Mom, and it just wrote itself."

"Uh-huh."

That was enough to make her defensive. "I know it's stupid, but that's how it happened."

"Hey," said Keigan. "Don't be so touchy. It's not stupid at all."

"What is that, Keigan? It's going all garbled again."

"I know, I hear it."

~ Airborne ~

Purring. Snoring.

He could barely keep his excitement from showing. So the problem couldn't be with his own system. And it wasn't picking up noises in the building or from the neighbourhood either, because these were the same sounds he'd heard at home. Then it must be something on the tape itself. But that didn't make sense either. If it was on the tape, he'd be hearing it every time.

"I already told you," he said, distracted. "The K-box is experimental. I'm still working the bugs out."

She flicked the back of his head. "You're the one who needs to work the bugs out."

"Don't complain. You're getting air play, aren't you?"

"I don't know. Am I? 'Cause all I'm hearing is...like a vibration or something."

The incandescent lights flickered. Over Stacey's singing voice he could hear...something different yet again, unlike any of the earlier phenomena, barely audible, not quite intelligible. Yet more familiar than ever. He should have cut to Ella Fitzgerald queued on the turntable, or muted the speakers in the studio to shut Stacey out. But he wasn't thinking about his sister or the audience. He let the tape run on air, making *in situ* adjustments.

"What's going on?" Stacey said. "Who is that?"

"Give me a minute, would you?" Then, realizing what she had said, "What do you mean 'who?' It's you."

"No. Those voices," she said. "Where's that coming from?" She stood up, looked around. From the studio they were in, they could see through glassed walls into the control booth on one side and through to a second, empty studio on another.

"It's nothing," he said, trying to convince himself. "Some kind of weird phenomenon. You know, like when you hear voices in static."

"Except you can actually hear the words."

"You can?" Because he couldn't. All he could make out was the familiar voice pattern, the tone and rhythm. "What are they saying?" he asked uncertainly.

"Not whole sentences, just words. You can't hear that? Ssh. There's a man. Is that Dad? Go back, go back, go back."

Ignoring the fact that the cassette was broadcasting to a potential audience of thirty thousand people, Keigan rewound a few seconds of tape and pressed Play.

~ *Airborne* ~

Stacey's eyes were lowered in concentration. "He's telling a kid to—'Smarten up and eat your peas.' It's like they're at the dinner table. 'Pass the butter. Eat up, boys. We don't want to be late.' Why are they eating at—what time is it? Like one thirty in the fracking morning? Those kids should be in bed."

Keigan listened hard. But apparently the message was for her ears only. "You're sure he said 'boys.'"

Stacey nodded. "Yeah. You must have recorded over an old tape. Is that weird, or what?"

She didn't know the half of it.

Seven years ago, the night of the fire, Keigan's friend Theo had stayed for supper. They'd had fish sticks and mashed potatoes and peas. It was hockey season, and Dad had taken the boys into the city to see the Senators play the Red Wings. At the arena he had drunk two or three beers for every period and when the game was over he had staggered out to the car. Keigan, who only had his beginner's license, had shoved him into the passenger seat and got behind the wheel to drive home. He had needed Theo's help to get his dad into the house. Theo, whose father wore a suit to work and had dinner at home every night and took his kids fishing on the weekends. Keigan had been so disgusted with his own father he couldn't bear to be under the same roof that night.

So while his house was catching fire, while the sirens were blaring past, while the firefighters were carrying the dead weight of his drunken father out to join his terrified little sister on the cold sidewalk, Keigan had been at Theo's playing video games and crashing on the couch. He knew nothing of the dramatic efforts to locate the body of the boy missing from his bed—him— until Theo's mother, sitting across the breakfast table, had read about it in morning paper. Going for sensationalism without evidence, the reporter had written up Keigan as a second casualty, the boy-hero who had been overtaken by smoke while searching the house for his sister. That was how he had learned of his mother's death. From Theo's Mom.

"Play it again," Stacey said. "I want to hear it again."

Keigan hesitated, but did as she asked. Whatever Stacey was getting, he was missing it. All he could hear was her voice and the synthesized arrangement. He worked at filtering out the instruments one by one, until there was nothing but her pure,

~ Airborne ~

sweet voice, and then—it happened again. Just as it had at home. What he had recorded as music was now a ripple on the surface of reality, a dimensional rift. And he was *there*, inside it, crossing over into the static. Not a hissing grey static, but a multicolored, multidimensional interstice between waking and sleeping, between knowing and believing. Between then and now.

But just as he could not hear the words, his sister could not see the visual.

Even as she listened, Stacey's face remained a normal, practised expression of teenage boredom. Suddenly she lit up. "That's Mom," she said, in a voice so small Keigan looked up, expecting to see her eight-year-old self appear.

"It is not." In spite of everything he had seen and heard, *that* was just plain crazy. "You don't even remember her."

"It is her," she whispered, barely breathing. "She's talking to us."

"Right," he said, with his typical brotherly mix of skepticism and sarcasm. "And you know what she'd say if she could hear you now? She'd say—"

"I know what she's saying..." Stacey looked directly into Keigan's eyes. "She's saying: 'Don't blame Daddy.' She's saying, 'Tell him for me, it was the cat. The cat knocked over the candle'."

§

One after another the phone lines lit up, blinking, demanding attention. Keigan recognized Phil's number in the Caller ID window on line four. He answered that one.

Phil spoke before Keigan could say hello. "What the hell was that?"

"Uh...my sister's demo. Sorry. I should have checked with you—"

"Not that. My wife. The message. Where did you get a tape of my Carrie?"

❧❧

D.C. Troicuk grew up in Glace Bay, NS. She lived 'away' for 20 years, experiencing six of Canada's provinces before succumbing once more to the lure of Cape Breton. Her speculative fiction has appeared in the anthology *Undercurrents*. Her first collection of short stories, *Loose Pearls*, was released in 2010.

The Icarus in Your Blood

"I said you can't, can't settle down,
until the Icarus in your blood, in your blood drowns"
—Sunset Rubdown

Through an 85th storey window I enter the night in a shower of glass crystals and panic. The air swallows me. For an instant the shards sparkle below me in the city lights like a translucent firework. The concussion from gunshots ringing in my ears is nothing now—the street screams up at me. Shutting out the rain of glass, the whooshing of air, the blue panic in my stomach, I search for the single tone, the white noise. My eyes roll back; I start to hack.

§

"Domino, you think you can cut it up?" Taylor asked as he threw the schematics down on the table. "As Jillian tells it, you don't have much choice. She says you're going to pay, man."

"Frack, I don't need this from you, you little shit." Taylor was enjoying seeing me in a stress position for once, instead of him. I was lying on the rug the in front of my decoration-only mag-lev couch trying to keep my fidgeting to a minimum. My kosher plan to get some highly illegal Zhoukou headgear had gone ballistically wrong. It was a sweet piece of ware. I'd seen the programming, and with a few little mods I would be able to leave the lowlands, get out of this botched attempt at a city—get out of this body as far as I could. But the price was high, and tonight I would pay.

~ Airborne ~

"You know I had to do it. You'd leave this shithole behind if you could."

"Yeah, but I'd be happy to get out of this cesspool and into another—one with a bit more juice. You're looking to get out of this world a bit more permanently." Taylor sat on the couch, which crashed to the floor. He grinned, knowing this irritated me, but at least refrained from asking to have it fixed again.

I scratched the red-brown stubble on my chin, and turned to look at Taylor's dark eyes and pale face—no ambition, outside of getting a score. The plan was pure, Occam-style, but when the theoretical hits the fan all the little cock-ups fall to the ground. "Well, it's simple. I need help to get that piece of gear I've got a track on, and it's not the sort of upgrade you can get at FS. With the new piece and my skills I'll be in the big leagues—they'll be begging for my services. What do you expect me to do, miss my chance? Stay down here with you?"

"Hey, I'm fine with my implant, and I'm not always scratching my head like I've got some rodent high on meth caged in there." Taylor got up, and went to the fridge to get a drink—but outside of Thai chili sauce and coconut spread, he was out of luck. His hands were starting to shake, and I could see the first signs of the come-down blush at the base of his neck.

"Well, I didn't expect she'd want me to hack Recosoft."

"What did you expect, when you basically let her know you'd do anything for the Zhoukou gear?" he said, fingering the Thai sauce disgustedly.

He was right; I don't have a poker face, and Jillian held all the right cards. To be honest, the thought of her sent little arcs of electricity jumping in me. Sure, she looks like the leather-clad vixen from any B-movie, and she's got more power than the secretary-general, but she's a bitch. She knows what's what, and she bends people until their tendons shear off. She'd gladly get me in touch with the Chinese underground if I did a job for her. All I had to do was hack into Recosoft, and alter some satellite imagery.

And so here was Taylor, the shiny little puppy dog, with schematics for the hundred-and-one storey HQ.

But Taylor doesn't stay focused on anything for long since he's always jumped up on something. Now he was telling some heartfelt story about his latest girl and how she was almost

~ Airborne ~

certainly his true love—I pretended to listen while correlating the physical schematics with the ones in my head that I'd "found" a week ago online. As I expected, they were identical, but someone in Jillian's organization had been paranoid.

The problem is, Recosoft uses the only kind of encryption I can't break—they're not connected. My specialty does not involve reality, but I needed a way to plug in. End of story. Oh, and the other problem was that Recosoft killed intruders—sometimes they reported this to the authorities.

§

I can feel the hammering of my heart, even in cyberspace— free-fall is a time for exceptions. I smother its beats, drown it out. I spread my arms; the wind buffets me with terrifying force. My world is a blur of rapidly shrinking possibilities. My body drops through the night like a dead bird. But in my head I'm elsewhere —online. There is the gentle hum of noise, the deeper breathing of my synapses, the dull heat in my temporal lobe; everything else is a blur of code. I correlate my location with emergency services, sun awnings, water systems—nothing. Ones and zeros with silver linings, wave upon wave of data. And then, there is my possible angel. Below me the ground remains indifferent, menacingly still.

§

I was deposited on top of the building in a silent chopper equipped with hellfire rockets. A carefully staged EM pulse rippled through the entire block, and a friendly criminal with a zip line and an impressive torch cut a hole in the roof and lowered me down. And then I was in with the servers and he was gone. The carefully cut and fused door behind me was just to prevent mischief; security was in here.

Everything Recosoft had online was really just window dressing, the tip of the iceberg. Updated at random intervals, their security strategy was to never be connected long enough for a security breach. And considering the resolution of their shots, and the nature of their presumed clients, it was clear why

~ Airborne ~

security was paramount. But now, in a room with servers connected to their intranet, I felt a sense of serenity and wonder at my good fortune, even if I was essentially a highly skilled puppet. I felt a calmness in my skin, a sort of communion with the humming aluminum that surrounded me.

The walls were stainless steel, and it was about 15 degrees centigrade. Not a room meant for human occupation—not for long. Outside I could hear the security systems spinning up with their diagnostic chirps after the EM pulse. There wasn't even a chair in here, but it didn't matter since I wouldn't be in my body for long.

I scratched the itch in my head, and then got to work. Crouching down beside one of the dark humming towers, I dug around in my pocket for the archaic landline. I hated having to actually plug in, but for this, the exception was worth it. I moved the patch of hair behind my ear and plugged in the cable. Then I reached up and found the port. Just before I let the metal touch, I closed my eyes. I felt my jaw involuntarily clench as I spun up my best defenses. Then I pressed in a little further and felt the electricity swim into me, like sharks going for blood.

Spikes of ice burned behind my eyes, and I felt my body go into seizure. The muscles along my arms and neck clenched, trying to separate tendon from bone. My teeth tried to cut through one another. A wave of panic flowed through me like molten metal into a mold. The inside of my brain lit up like a lightning storm. I could feel the system trying to fry my synapses, burn out my defenses, and leave me a vegetable plugged into a machine. The trick is to let it come. Let the wave hit without forming a dam. If you can bend just enough, you have a chance. I let the wave slowly overload my brain, while I cordoned off a little corner and got to work.

A little worm here, a recursive spider there. I built tunnels and bridges of code. I could feel my body going numb, but as I cut through layer after layer of defenses, I started to find my footing. Though my lips were turning blue, and my body was still convulsing a little, a part of me knew I was in. A few deft programs, and suddenly the lightning was gone. My muscles let out a sigh. The wave was a calm pool, and the system was satisfied that nothing was wrong. I was free to move—very carefully.

~ Airborne ~

The data that Jillian wanted hidden didn't exist yet. My job was to hack in unnoticed and make a few modifications. Recosoft's employees couldn't possibly analyze all of the terabytes of data its satellites gathered every day, so it relied on algorithms designed to pick up any changes. Whenever interesting new buildings, heat signatures, algae blooms, seismic events, freighter paths, etc. were discovered, then someone would look more carefully. Recosoft was the eyes in the sky. They saw sins, and sold confessions.

Selling, of course, was never a problem; the real challenge was just playing their cards right to get the highest bidder and to convince them that only they knew about the change. That and defending their satellites. But I was the virus they thought they were vaccinated against. Essentially I had to leave a worm behind that would prevent the algorithms from noticing that there had been any change in a small town in southern Guatemala. I didn't know what it was that Jillian wanted no one to see, but if I had to guess, one of her other clients was likely looking for a site that could be guaranteed to be unnoticed so they could do something unpleasant, illegal, or dangerous—likely all three.

Once inside, I paused for a moment. I could feel my body as an undercurrent, and I concentrated, in a sort of unconscious way, on getting my breathing and heartbeat under control. Classic Yogic techniques I learned from Seren that she had hoped I would use rather differently. I needed to focus, and to do that I needed my body to be stable and silent: to occupy without striving, formulate a state of vacancy.

Probing my environment, like a fish with protolegs, I tasted the atmosphere. The whole system was dank. It felt like a dungeon, with moist stone walls, bits of fungus, and an unidentifiable foul odour, but it wasn't. I knew from the first attack that this was SOTA, that the illusion of archaic programs was a ruse. I let my mind unfurl and probe at the walls. They were good, but nothing I couldn't handle. Once I got Zhoukou gear I would be able to cut through these like a razor, but for now I'd have to chip and scrape a little more slowly.

I diverted some defensive programs by laying down some rather complex little creatures that would keep the defenses occupied. I liked to think of them as snakes rather than worms. They could eat a lot more a lot faster, and they were patient.

~ Airborne ~

Everything would self-destruct without leaving a trace—that's key if you're really ninja. Meanwhile I created a cloak around myself and really got to work. There were tiny little cracks everywhere—nothing significant for anyone but me. I made the cracks big enough to let in some light, and then I made them big enough to let me out. I followed an invisible path, constantly sidestepping its misdirects, avoided a few mines, and then found what I was looking for: the gate to the Southern Central America servers.

It took some time, but essentially I rattled the windows and then slid under the door. I moved quickly and found Tojchiquel, a little town beneath some mountains with a little river just to the north. It might have been one of those vacation spots that the super-rich went to—those who didn't go for resorts or places anyone had ever heard of. You know, pretend you're a nobody, live the rugged life, breathe the real air (on meds, of course) until you return to the seven-star resort done up to look like a hovel. Or it might be a shanty town full of packs of dogs—I didn't have any idea. I zoomed in and in; the tighter the parameters on my worm, the less chance the system would notice. It would just sit there quietly eating algorithms forever. I even left a bit of code so that the town would evolve—the image would not be static, just false. The only way anyone would notice anything was if they actually looked at new unprocessed images of this tiny town before the system integrated them, and there would be no reason to do that.

I started to weave a little web to the north of the town, down along the river, and then back west. There was something very pleasant about the dark green of the trees against the blackness of the river; I was just starting to imagine what it must have been like to be near flowing water, when I felt the low rumblings. The landscape shuddered. My little trip lines were being tripped, which meant someone was suspicious, which meant I was probably dead. I could feel the vibrations right up my spine, but I didn't move. I just wove faster; I laid down the net, pulled the strings, and cleaned up. I'm meticulous—which is a pity because no one ever gets to see my work. I was Zen, but even through my armour of calm, I could feel the energy of their attack building. This time, the storm would be a tornado that would rupture the blood vessels in my brain. I moved a little faster, tied a final knot, covered my tracks, and was about to double-check for strays

~ Airborne ~

when I was suddenly submerged in ice water and smelled melting rubber. My cord had been yanked.

Something smashed me in the mouth and I tasted blood. Then I was hurled against a wall. Through my watering eyes and the ache in my head, I could see a huge man in black. He wore a flack vest and a Recosoft logo. He was pulling a gun.

I'm not much in this world, but I do have one defense. As he raised the gun, I shot the mace Spiderman-style from below my wrist—it was a Taylor specialty. The thug screamed and shot wildly as the mace hit him. I heard the metallic thump of the slugs hitting the wall behind me, but I wasn't taking the time to see how close they were. I ran, my legs jellied and cramped, past the guard who was crying and clawing at his eyes.

Out the door and down a hall. I was in some kind of conference room. One sleek table and two walls of black windows. There was no exit, and my head pounded like that bullet had hit me. My legs wobbled from adrenalin as I scrambled around for an exit or a weapon, but there was nothing. I ducked down behind the table. There was no point in fighting this guy anyway. He came in the door, his eyes half-closed and streaming, and fired a shot. The window behind me exploded. That was it. I didn't think —I dove through the hole into the night sky like a Superman who couldn't fly, and who was very breakable.

§

An autocab. A carbon-fibre angel, bright yellow, shimmering with ads. The sudden jolt of hope redoubles the nauseous blue pounding in my head. There's one close by: override security, navigation systems, accelerator cut-offs. I need it to come to me as fast as possible and then I need it to fall too—just more slowly than me. If I calculate it right it should act as brakes, and then a giant cushion. If I calculate wrong, I'll die before I make it to the ground. I am still fine-tuning the calculations when I see its shiny yellow roof come screeching up at me and I start to roll.

The shocking crunch on my back as I hit the autocab, the flex, shattering glass, the incredible deceleration. I think I must be pulling nine g's and then—

~ Airborne ~

Automated Personal EMS Call: Location 3243.532; Probable trauma victim; Heart rate 173; Blood Pressure 76/37; Multiple fractures, Probable internal bleeding.
EMS ETA: 93secs
Probability of survival: 71%

❧⋯❧

Bruce Miller grew up in rural Cape Breton, migrated to some nearby cities, and then returned. Currently he is teaching, putting the finishing touches on a new house, and looking for decent avocados to make some guacamole. The rest of the time he spends with his beautiful wife, admiring and burping and admiring their new daughter, Caida.

Dragonfly

"Blue-footed Boobies," I said, looking at my image collection.

"Real, though long extinct."

"Elephants?"

"Real."

"No. Honestly? They seem mythological."

"Very real, Lantra. Surviving...in a few protected areas. They are quite magnificent."

"Fairies?"

"Fictional, I'm afraid."

"Dragonflies, then."

The Old Man's breath caught in his throat. He didn't answer.

"Are you okay?" I asked, but then he seemed to recover.

"Oh yes, Lantra," he said, "I'm happy to say, the dragonfly still exists."

§

The Old Man always wore a lab coat, his name written in white block letters on a red tag hanging from his breast pocket. *Winston March*. I assumed he was a psychiatrist sent to assess whether or not I belong in The Hospital for Deep Space Psychosis.

Debatable, to be sure, and complicated by the fact that I felt saner here than I had on the outside.

I put myself in the hospital, happy to have a safe place to go after Universal Mining execs ejected me from the *Auria*, a deep-space transport and my home. "Re-entry," they called it. What a joke. How can you re-enter Earth if you'd never been here?

Jocob, the only friendly person that I'd found on staff, and I were walking to the Solarium the first time I saw Winston. The nurses encouraged us Deep Space Humans to get lots of sunshine. Seems we're deficient in vitamin D as well as most other vitamins and minerals that the Earthbound have in their bones. The warmth from the sun was one part of Earth I liked. I hadn't found many.

A man stood at the intersection of two corridors staring at me. Tall and skinny with pretty good posture for an old-timer, he had a mop of white hair.

"He wants to talk to you," Jocob said. He peeled off down the hallway, saying, "I'll see you later." I looked back at the stranger and waved, just to break the intensity of that gaze.

Flustered, he took off his glasses and rubbed his eyes. Then he put them back on, walked over. "Hello," he said, offering me his hand. "I'm Winston March."

His skin felt papery and his eyes were red from all that rubbing. "I'm Lantra," I said.

"Yes...Lantra," he repeated. I extracted my hand from his lingering grasp. "Could we talk?"

"Okay," I said, continuing on my way.

"Your limp—" he said, catching up to me.

How rude. "Yeah, what about it?"

"Nothing. I'm sorry."

We reached the Solarium and sat opposite each other. The sun hit his eyes, causing a glare off his glasses. He leaned forward into shadow, elbows on his knees. "How long have you been here?" he asked. I noticed the absence of superficial pleasantries.

"I don't keep track of time very well," I said.

"How long were you on Earth before you came to the hospital?"

He was testing my orientation to reality. The answer was ten Earth days, but his question irritated me. *Look at my file,* I thought and then said, "Not long."

"You found it difficult...coming back?"

"I'm not 'coming back.' I'm a DSH, Dr. March. Born and bred in space."

He looked shocked. "D—? Oh, so...you're a Deep Space Human. I, um...I'm confused. I thought you were..."

"What?"

~ Airborne ~

"It doesn't matter. Call me Winston, please. Tell me...about your life. What about your childhood? I'm so interested."

"No memories. No childhood. In hibernation until we were pretty old, but I don't know how to explain my age because time doesn't translate very well. We count it differently out there, you know." His face still looked stunned. *Maybe that's how he always looks.* "Time," I repeated. "Time is different when you're travelling near the speed of light?"

He nodded vigourously. "Of course, of course, I know. What about before you were put in hibernation?"

Why am I talking to this guy? He obviously isn't listening. "I told you already. I have no memories. Should I?"

"I don't know."

"No one talked about *before.*"

"You were with others?"

"Lots. Hundreds. All brought out of hibernation at the same time. At first, we lived together on planet Apollo at Universal's Headquarters. Some were sick, all of us weak and confused. Kind of like—what are they called?—zombies?"

We grinned at each other.

"You've heard of zombies?"

"Not real, right?"

He laughed. "No."

I liked his laugh. His face looked younger when he smiled.

"I have a lot of questions about that sort of thing," I said. "We saw slews of vids from Earth but I could never figure out what was real and what was made up. I have a big file of images I've collected." I took my screen out of my pocket and flipped it open.

"Why didn't you just look it up? You had access to Earth's archives, right?"

Okay, I thought, *he asks sticky questions.* "No. Not really."

"Why?"

I waited before answering. One breath, then another. I straightened my spine and thrust out my chin. "Can't read." Then I had to look down, away from his intense blue eyes.

"Hmm. I see. Lantra, what have you done with your life? Has it been happy?"

My turn to stare. *What does he want from me? Happy? What does that have to do with anything?* Having absolutely nothing to say, I got up and walked away, aware with every step, how much

~ *Airborne* ~

more pronounced my limp is on Earth.

Winston called after me, "I'll be back."

I didn't mind so much. *I'll quiz him about things like electric eels and fireflies.*

§

"It's hard for me to believe you can't read."

Winston found me curled in a large pink chair wedged at the end of the hallway. I often came to sit in this secluded spot by the window, even though there was barely room for the chair to fit between the narrow walls. The chairs on Earth are great. We had nothing this comfortable on the *Auria*. I ignored him and continued playing the game on my screen.

"I also don't believe you belong in a hospital with crazy people."

I didn't even look up.

"There's another thing...your memory."

"Go away," I said, meaning it.

"Are you aware of how many meds they have you on?"

"Go away." This time I didn't mean it quite as much.

"Because I know a bit about the process of waking up from well-induced hibernation and it doesn't make sense to me that 'hundreds' of people—young people especially—would wake up with absolutely no memory of their pre-sleep life."

As he walked over, I lifted my screen and clicked his image. "Old Man," I said with a sigh, "why are you coming around? What's your obsession with me?" He'd been to visit four other times. One time we discussed dragons and dinosaurs. I pretty much had all that sorted out now. I snapped another shot and looked at it. The angle made his jowls look even droopier. I deleted it.

"Lantra, I have something to tell you—"

I waited.

"It's time you knew. You...you were part of—" He stopped and ran his fingers through his hair.

When he didn't say anything more, I patted the arm of the chair and said, "Sit here."

He lowered himself, facing me with his legs straddling the wide arm of the chair. I scooted over to make room for his large,

~ Airborne ~

sneakered foot. He leaned back against the wall.

"Talk," I said.

"Have you ever heard of The Lost Generation?"

"Hmmm. The Lost Boys...Peter Pan, right?"

"No, not that. It's nothing to do with entertainment."

"Okay then, I don't think so."

"I guess it's an Earth term. Didn't you get news from Earth?"

"You don't understand, Winston. When you're out there, so far out there that you never come back, Earth means nothing. Or, no, that's not exactly right because of course that's where human beings came from. But it's another reality. A distant dream. Like...heaven. Some place people enjoy thinking about; a place they'll probably never see and if they do, probably won't like." I smiled, pleased at my analogy.

"What did they tell you about where you came from?"

Irritation, again. "Where we came from?" I repeated. He was asking me to describe a time of my life that was a...nothing.

Trying to remember agitated me. I wanted to stop his stupid questions, so I spoke fast. "We came from the laboratory. Lab babies—get it? Born in space. Put in hibernation until needed. Second class, not like the 'real' people on the ship who were born on Earth. The company fostered us through our recuperation, then assigned and trained us for a job. Once trained, we did the job. Forever. End of story."

You're always staring with your mouth open, Old Man. I lifted the screen and clicked.

"Stop that!"

"Hmm," I said, looking at his image.

"It's not true, Lantra."

"Why do you talk to me? You never believe what I say. Maybe I am just crazy." I focused on my screen, madly scrolling through hundreds of animal images.

"Lantra, listen to me carefully. This is hard for me to say and isn't going to be easy for you to grasp."

"Seahorses," I said.

"What?"

"Seahorses, seahorses. Real or imagined?"

He put a hand on my arm. "Real. Thought to be extinct."

Hah. I knew it. I sighed, looking through my image collection, so very pleased that seahorses had once existed.

~ *Airborne* ~

§

"There's no Dr. March here, Lantra," the Head Nurse said.

"Okay, well maybe he's not a doctor. I don't know. That's why I'm asking. He's been talking to me. An old guy. White hair. Thin build."

I had her attention for once. "Does he talk to anyone else?"

"How would I know?"

"Have you seen him talking to anyone else?"

"No. But I keep to myself."

"I've noticed that, Lantra. You need to get involved in some activities. We may have to take that screen away from you and put you on a schedule."

"You're threatening me? Never mind." I started to leave, then turned back to see her entering something on a form that had my name at the top. "I'm not hallucinating," I yelled, and then walked away.

The next day and the next, Winston didn't come. I'd run him off, or gotten him in trouble. Either way, I'd never know what he wanted to tell me. Was I one of this Lost Generation? If so, what did it mean? And what kind of meds did they have me on?

That evening, I planted myself in a dark corner of the common room where I could see Jacob sitting at the computer in the office. Fiddling with my screen—my one and only real possession—I thought back to the night on the *Auria* that Heflyn —my one and only real friend—gave me the gift that I would soon put to use. I just needed Jacob to leave the office for a couple of minutes.

Heflyn, like me, was one of the few lucky lab babies assigned to an on-ship job. He had a gift for electronics and software and had made himself indispensable.

Heflyn taught me to read.

"I've got something for you, Lantra. Hand over your screen."

"Why?" My screen never left my side.

"Something to help me pass the time while you're working on my coiffure." We'd met for one of Heflyn's periodic hair cuts. "I'm giving you an upgrade, girl. A highly illegal upgrade. Hurry before someone sees us."

I smiled. We always got together in the middle of one of the

Auria's vast viewing rooms when nothing was showing. No one could sneak up on us here. I handed it over and started trimming his straight, blonde hair while he worked magic on my screen's innards.

Finally, Jocob left to see a patient.

I immediately started a complex process of combined keystrokes that my friend had taught me—Heflyn called it a "skeleton key." I never found out where that term originated. *Bless your smart brain, Hef...here it comes.* The hospital's computer files appeared. Hef had taught me that a note would pop up on whatever remote computer I hacked into. But by the time Jocob returned to the office, the note would have disappeared.

I clicked on a Staff link. A calendar came up with the on-duty staff listed each day. *No, this isn't right; I'd have to check every day to find The Old Man's name.* Searching for another way to get the list, I clicked on Jocob's name. His schedule came up. *Okay, Lantra, don't be dumb. Just type in Winston's name.* I did so.

"What are you doing?"

"Jocob!" I flipped the screen over. "You scared me!"

"*You* scare *me*. You're looking at the hospital's files? More clever than most, Lantra." He knelt down and whispered, "You have to keep quiet."

"About...?"

"Winston March."

"Why?"

"He's okay. I know him."

"I have a right to know what he does on staff."

"He's not on staff, but he's a friend. You can trust him."

"Yeah? You should tell me more than that."

"Lantra, Winston and me, we're on your side."

"There are 'sides'?"

He grinned at me, then grew serious again. "Always. I don't act like the rest of the people who work here, because I'm not like them. Have you mentioned Winston to anyone?"

"Yes. The Head Nurse."

He grimaced. "Oooh."

"She thought I was hallucinating. He's not supposed to be here?"

"No. He's a doctor, but a PhD, not a psychiatrist."

"He's a visitor, then. Why does he visit me?"

"Let's get you to your room."

I rose and he took my elbow as we walked. "Lantra, the staff isn't trying to help you. Their job is to keep you here and keep you quiet. Winston wants to get you away from them. He...cares about you. Now I have to go. I promise you'll know more soon. Don't tell anyone I spoke to you, shut that screen down when the staff is around and try to blend in. Okay?"

He left me standing by the door to my room. Raising the screen, I turned it toward my face and touched the mirror symbol.

I looked at myself. Gravity and Earth's atmosphere had already taken a toll on my face. I never minded being average in appearance; there were advantages on the *Auria* to being nondescript. But because the ship, more often than not, travelled near light speed between colonies, I stayed young. Now all that was over. The doctor who admitted me to the hospital said I look like I'm in my mid-thirties, but he warned of physical challenges. *Your aging will feel rapid,* he said. I touched the darkening pouches under my eyes. Everyday I noticed a new sag or wrinkle. To make matters worse, my formerly manageable hair curled uncontrollably in this humid land. "Georgia," they called it.

Documenting my decline, I clicked and saved the image.

§

It took four Earth days—during which time I made myself go to exercise and art classes so the nurses would think I was compliant—but finally Winston returned. He looked nervous. Then again, he always had. I was outside waiting where Jocob told me to be.

"Sorry it took me so long to get back," he said.

"I have questions."

"I know. It's so good to see you. I missed you."

Missed me?

"You know Jocob."

He nodded. "We work together."

"You work together to do what?"

"Lantra, there's a lot you don't know. From the beginning, they told you lies. They've messed with your memory. I want to get you out of here."

"Who is 'they'? The staff here?"

He looked around. "Did you ever wonder why there is a Deep Space Psychosis hospital within blocks of the transition house you were sent to when they brought you back?"

I hadn't. What did I know of Earth? "No. But you're talking about 'they' again. You're saying that the company bosses—"

Winston broke in, nodding his head, "Universal Mining."

"Right," I said. "The same people who decided it was time for me to 're-enter'—they run this place?"

He nodded grimly.

"Because..." I prompted.

"Because they want to keep you drugged and docile."

"Okay, I don't know anything about drugs, but let's just say you're right. They want to keep me drugged because..."

"Because they have taken your life from you and don't want you to know it. I want you to leave with me," The Old Man continued, "I want to take you somewhere where you can recover your memory. There's too much to tell you all at once. I don't want to hurt you."

"I'm not doubting you," I answered. "I assumed they kicked me off because I, um, when I could, I talked to the others like me. I told them we were supposed to have the same rights as everyone else. I thought I was being careful but someone must have snitched." *And there's another thing. Something bigger.* "Yeah, they'd want to keep me quiet," I said. His eyebrows raised. "But I don't know you, Old Man. Maybe you work for them."

"No. No, Lantra. You and I...we knew each other. Long ago. We were...friends."

I didn't know what to say or even how to think about this. "You were on the *Auria*?"

"No, Lantra. Listen. I knew you on Earth, dear. You were born...on Earth." He spoke slowly. "You were a child here. You had parents, a family, a home. In Canada. You were sent away when you were fifteen. Sent into hibernation the same as all the others you woke up with."

"No."

"Yes. I'm sorry to tell you this so abruptly. I know you can't remember, but if I'm right, Lantra, your memory loss isn't permanent. I'm a pharmacologist. They drug you to keep your

~ Airborne ~

memories...bound up."

I thought back to one particular morning during my earliest days on Earth. The reality of Earth's gravity was horrendous even though I'd been "prepared" through a series of jumps into increasingly earth-simulated environments.

That morning, I woke up feeling the atmosphere on—in—my chest, my head, my skeleton.

Struggle to get out of bed. Shamble down the hall. Turn on the tap. Showers, an Earth luxury. Water never fell in droplets in space. Close my eyes, let the water fall on my face, feel it go from frigid to blessedly hot. Mind flashes with moving pictures. Crops waving in a stiff wind. Wide, wild skies. Sunset with streaky clouds. Nothing I'd ever seen, but it feels real. Faces. A woman. Old-fashioned, simple clothes. Freckled, brown skin. A man's chiseled face. His clothes dirty. Picture-book people, yet detailed and specific. Children, too. The smell of dirt and sweat. Running through tall plants. So fresh! How can my brain know a smell I've never encountered? A voice, "Come in, kids! Storm's coming!" I run away from everyone. Rain! Rain has a smell? Wet clothes against my skin. A child's voice, "Olley, olley, in free!"

This happened often during those first days. All beautiful, but too intense. I didn't have a place for these images and sensations in my mind. I felt I might be going...

"Crazy," I said.

"What?"

"I had lots of anxiety. Fear. Strange sensations. Even paranoia. Someone told me about this hospital. Said that they'd take care of me until I felt stronger. As soon as I came, I started feeling normal."

"Because they put meds in your food. Who told you about this place?"

"A guy at the transition house who said he'd gone through Re-entry a while back. Said he came here for a while and they helped him out. I felt more than a little nutty. But honestly, I just wanted a place that felt familiar. Except for the fact that I don't have to work and they have better chairs, this hospital seems like the *Auria*."

"Of course it does! They designed everything so it feels familiar. Then they can funnel you back under their control while making it seem voluntary. Please, please come with me. Let's get

~ Airborne ~

you off these drugs and see what happens."

"Why me, Winston?"

"I told you. We knew each other."

§

Winston never came back to the hospital.

"It's too dangerous, Lantra," Jocob said. "His name came up at the staff meeting. Head Nurse told us to keep watch for any strangers. They also talked about taking your screen from you."

"That's not going to happen," I said. "Jocob, why aren't there locks on the doors, or guards?"

"Everyone has an ID chip. It's easy to locate anyone."

"I never knew that."

"Implanted when we're infants."

"I have one?"

"Yes. You do. I checked. It's just one more piece of evidence that you were Earthborn, Lantra. Go with Winston. You can come back if you want to. I'll be here to welcome you."

That wouldn't happen. Once I found out that Universal Mining ran the hospital, I had no choice but to go with The Old Man. I had good reason to fear the company.

Heflyn and I came up with the plan. I'd write a formal complaint to the Human's Rights Commissary about the way me and my kind were treated by the Company and proudly sign it. But I didn't have transmission privileges so Hef hacked into the archived account of someone who had passed away recently and transmitted the file under her name. Why would anyone suspect me, an almost-illiterate office assistant?

But it hadn't worked. Somehow they knew because not long after we sent the complaint, Universal Mining informed me that I'd been singled-out for the 'honour of Re-entry.'

Jocob took my thoughtfulness for resistance. "Lantra, Winston cares. More than you can imagine."

"Yeah, I don't understand that. It feels creepy. He knew me, but I can't remember him or anything else about Earth. What if I get my memories back but still don't know him? It's been a long, long time since I was—what did he say?—fifteen?"

"What do you have to lose, Lantra? You're on Earth now, not travelling at light speed. You're not getting any younger."

~ Airborne ~

"Not funny, Jocob."

Now I knew. Space-dwellers who come to Earth grow old a lot faster than the Earthbound. Re-entry equalled punishment.

§

"I'm going to be sick." I'd been nauseated since we left but it was getting worse with each passing minute. Winston, his hands on the controls of his *Airicle*—a two-seater, low-altitude aircraft of which he seemed inordinately proud, considering its derelict appearance—turned to look at me.

"You're a lovely shade of green, Lantra. I thought you were a creature of space. Here we are, a mere 20 metres off the ground, and you're ready to hurl your cookies."

He handed me a bag to throw up in, but I really just wanted to be on the ground. I was used to warp-speed travel, not this. The ground zipped past and there was no place to look that didn't cause my equilibrium to be up-ended. Shutting my eyes made it worse.

"Luckily, we've arrived. Tennessee." He lowered the speed and looked for a place to land. "We'll be down soon."

He brought the craft to rest in a large field surrounded on three sides by scraggly trees with mangled branches. I searched for the door controls. Winston hit a button and the door lifted. Rushing down the steps, I fell onto the dry grass and 'hurled my cookies.'

Winston came around. "Lantra. I'm sorry." He put his hands on my shoulders as I heaved and heaved. "I'll give you something for nausea if you need it."

"Little late for that, isn't it?" I said, my stomach emptied.

"I didn't want you drugged. Not today."

He handed me a handkerchief. I wiped my mouth, spat, wiped again. "You said I've been drugged most of my life...why should today be any diff—"

At a noise, I lifted my eyes from the ground. "Winston!" Before me, coming through the trees, were three—four—five elephants. One of them a baby!

He laughed and pulled me up. "C'mon. Won't do to be out in the open. They aren't exactly tame."

He helped me onto the hatch of the *Airicle*, and then climbed

~ Airborne ~

up next to me. The animals were 30 or 40 metres in front of us, coming out of the trees, meandering in our direction.

"Wild elephants?"

"This is a reserve, so they are accustomed to seeing people, but no, they aren't tame. They could damage the *Airicle*, or us. I should be ready to rise if they get closer."

"Oh, please," I said, "come closer." And they did.

Winston told me to hang onto the strap while he scrambled into the pilot's seat. The *Airicle* lifted off the ground. "We're leaving already?" I asked.

"No, just hovering. Enjoy them for as long as you like."

"They're real. They're really real." I enjoyed them for a long time. The family—Winston, who'd been here before, told me they were a young male, two grown females, a bull and the baby of unknown gender—decimated several medium-sized trees and then walked right under the *Airicle* to a small pond. Winston silently turned us around so I could watch them watering themselves.

"Look at them playing!" I squealed.

"Yes. They have a good time in the water."

"The baby's squirting the mother! Oh, look at him rolling in the wet dirt."

"Mud. We call that mud, Lantra."

"Oh yes. Mud. I've heard of that. It's a mining term, isn't it?"

He sighed. "I don't know. It's just what we call dirt mixed with water. You used to make mud pies when we were kids."

I heard him, but didn't respond. Drinking in these magnificent creatures, creatures I always thought were myth, I didn't want to think about having been a child on this Earth. Or about having had a friend named Winston. I did, however, want to know what the hell "mud pies" were.

§

"Winston, what about you and your life?" I asked when we were on our way again. Night had fallen, I could no longer see the ground zipping under us, and I felt wonderfully relaxed after the thrill of seeing real elephants. "Do you have a family?"

"Not exactly," he said. "I got married a long, long time ago. But it didn't last. We had no children."

~ Airborne ~

"Are you lonely?"

"Oh no. I've always had my work and I have quite a large, extended family. Not blood relatives, but still like a family."

Winston stopped at a friend's house for the night. It was late and the owner met us at the door. "So this is Lantra," the old woman said, taking both my hands in hers. "I'm Adi and I'm thrilled that you've come to see me."

She was adorable, as wrinkled as the bull elephant, except the skin of her hands was so soft that it seemed to disappear under my fingertips. Her white hair lay pinned in a wavy tangle on top of her head.

"Is she older than you?" I whispered when she left the room to get us something to drink.

"Yes," Winston said. "By a few years."

"She's sweet."

"I'm glad you like her. Maybe you can be friends, in time."

I thought it an odd thing to say. We were just passing through on the way to some place up north where Winston had what he called a "retreat." Maybe he travelled back and forth a lot. Still, why would this old woman become a friend to me? Friends were few and far between in my life. At least twice a day my heart ached for Heflyn, who I'd never see again.

She came in with our drinks. "I've made you some tea, Lantra. It's my special brew for settling tummies."

I drank it slowly while Winston and Adi discussed our escape from the hospital. It wasn't much of a story. I walked out without incident. Winston waited for me in a nearby parking area and we left.

"It makes me wonder if all this 'running away' isn't a little silly," I said. They both turned to look at me. Judging by the look on her face, Adi didn't think so. I knew how Winston felt.

Later, half asleep, I heard Jocob's name mentioned. I sat up. "You know Jocob, Adi?"

The two looked at me, surprised. "We thought you'd fallen asleep, Lantra. I'm sorry we woke you."

"Jocob?"

"Yes, dear. I do know him."

"Your son?" I ventured.

She smiled. "No. No relation."

I looked at Winston, who had an uneasy expression on his

face. "I think we need to go to bed, Adi. I'm going to be on the couch, right?"

I knew they were hiding things from me, but I was too tired to deal with it. *Soon enough*, I thought.

§

"We'll get to Canada later today," Winston told me as we sped along the next morning. "We're going to the east coast. Nova Scotia."

Adi fed us well before we left and Winston gave me what he called a "light" anti-nausea drug. I felt pleasantly drowsy and not at all sick to my stomach.

Mid-day we stopped to charge the aircraft. While he was busy, I used the toilet and then went in the store to get some snacks. A man I'd never seen before appeared, coming toward me like a trainer in a cage of lions. My heart started pumping hard.

"Hi Lantra," he said quietly. "We need you to come back, dear."

"Why?" I said, looking around.

"You aren't well." I backed away, but not quickly enough. He caught my arm. "I know. I know," he said, "but it's for the best."

"Winston!" I yelled, as the stranger took a medisyrge out of his vest pocket. Struggling, I saw Winston come around the corner behind my attacker. The man jabbed the needle into my arm. Too late I pulled out of his reach, falling to the ground. Losing sight of him for a moment, I turned back to see Winston walloping him in the back of the head with a package of frozen meat.

Winston grabbed my hand and yanked me up. The man lay sprawled in the aisle, unconscious.

My legs suddenly felt like tree trunks, thick, stiff and unmoving. "Come on, Lantra!" Winston urged. He practically carried me outside and pushed me into the vehicle.

"Will we be followed?" I asked, struggling with my tongue, my head lolling against the pane.

"I don't know. I didn't see anyone with him. The larger problem is that Universal Mining is actively interested in you. I hoped they would just let you go, but you're obviously a bigger star than I ever knew. What else did you do to piss them off so

~ Airborne ~

much?"

"Long story, Old Man." Hearing my words come out slowly and slurred, I let myself go under and out.

§

I woke up in a bed. Sun streaked across the rug on the floor of the small bedroom. In front of me were two doors made of glass. Yellow fabric hung over the panes. The light glinted through a crack between the door frame and the curtain.

I felt good, though I wasn't really sure what that meant. On closer inspection I decided that my insides felt calm.

I thought back to the anti-climactic dash from the hospital, hurling my cookies in a place called "Tennessee," and—*Oh!*—the elephants. The late night visit with Adi—her soothing tea and delicious cooking. The man in the store and his needle. I reached up to rub my arm, but noticed instead a large bandage on the back of my hand. I rubbed the top of it gently. "Ouch!" I cut it in the melee at the store? Winston must have bandaged it for me.

I wore a nightgown I'd never seen before. A matching robe lay on a chair and there were slippers on the floor. *Winston bought me clothes?*

I walked stiffly to the doors and opened them. My knees and lower back ached. Just outside was a wide stone deck. I sniffed deeply, taking in an aroma which I will forever and always think of as the smell of green.

The house sat high on a hill. An abundance of trees stretched out before me. Beyond, lay something I'd never seen. As amazing as elephants. The ocean. Vast. Shimmering. Deep blue. A new kind of space.

I stood perfectly still for a long time. Then I walked to the small table near the edge of the terrace and sat down. My legs, never very stable, were wobbly from the drugs or the sleep or the travel, I didn't know. Rubbing my knees, I allowed the view to carry me along, allowed it to occupy space in my brain to keep me from thinking about what would happen next.

I felt a flicker on my skin and looked down at my bandaged hand. There, perched on my little finger, was an iridescent blue dragonfly.

~ Airborne ~

§

His arms encircled me from behind. Startled, I pulled away. Winston sat down at the table. He took out his handkerchief and gave it to me.

"I don't know what I'm crying about," I said, though I'd been crying for a long time and should have figured it out by now.

"Doesn't matter. You're allowed. Are you having memories?"

My shoulders lifted and dropped. "I saw a dragonfly! It set me off and now I can't stop the tears!"

He smiled, but there was sadness, not joy behind it. He took a deep breath and said, "I'm so glad we got here while the dragonflies are still around." He looked at the sky. "It'll be winter before we know it, though it doesn't get as cold as it used to. Not as much snow as when we were kids. To find a lot of snow, you have to go into the mountains or very far north."

"Snow," I repeated, still sniffling. "Could I remember snow?"

"Yes."

"It glistens in the light," I whispered, "as if the sky has dropped thousands of tiny jewels."

He smiled. This time there was joy behind it. "How wonderful, Lantra! It's working. I knew that once we got you away from Universal Mining, your memories would come back."

"Not much of a memory," I said, though I did like it.

"It's a beginning. Let's be patient." He reached over and put his fingers on my cheek. I recoiled. He retreated.

"What's this?" I asked, holding up my bandaged hand.

"I took the opportunity...while you were unconscious."

"The opportunity to do what?"

"I removed your identity chip. So they can't track you." He held up his own hand and pointed to a small scar. "A lot of us have taken this step. We feel that it's worth the risk of getting lost."

My eyes filled with tears again but it wasn't sadness or loss anymore, it was anger. "You removed something from my body that's been there all my life without even consulting me?"

His expression crumpled. "I'm sorry. I—"

"You what? Are you my fath—?" I stopped abruptly. "Are you...? Are you my father?"

He looked at me intently, then dropped his head, shaking it

~ Airborne ~

back and forth slowly.

"No," I said. "How could you be? My parents would be long dead. You—you said we were friends? The same age...back then?"

He nodded, not looking up. I could hear the raspy sound of his wrinkled hands as he rubbed them together. This old man and I were the same age and yet I looked fifty years younger, more the age of Jocob.

"I'm thinking more clearly now, Winston. But, it's hard. I—I guess I'm not used to it. You think they gave us mind-altering drugs from the time we woke up, huh?"

"Yes. We've been looking for you all, every one of you. Universal Mining and the other companies seem to think that we'll all die off and forget that they kidnapped hundreds of human beings! But we won't. I'm part of a large, unofficial organization—my family." He smiled. "Lantra, Jocob is one of you."

"A Lost Generation kid?" I asked. "Why didn't he tell me?"

"No one can know. We've done a lot of work to change his appearance and give him a new identity. He's very effective and dedicated because he understands."

"I wish I had known."

"Too dangerous for him."

"And you? You bring all these Lost Generation people back to your 'retreat' by the ocean?"

He smiled. "No. I've never brought anyone here before."

"Kinda creepy, Old Man. No one knows I'm here. You took out my locator chip. Have I been kidnapped again?"

He looked horrified. "Lantra...no." He got up and paced. "They were on our trail. I had to get it out or they'd have been here before now. You were unconscious for two days. I'll take you back if that's what you want. I'll take you anywhere on Earth you want to go. You do not have to stay here. But is it so terrible?"

"Wouldn't they already know we were here if I still had the chip in when we arrived?"

"Hah, you were always quick. Deep sleep, drugs and warp-speed travel haven't dimmed you. No worry about that. We took evasive steps while you were unconscious. Our network sprang into action. I did the surgery at one location, with the help of a physician who's involved because his great aunt was sent away and never returned. I gave your chip to another acquaintance

~ Airborne ~

whose brother is still out there somewhere. He passed it on to someone who works for a courier service. Our group will lead Universal Mining on a merry chase!"

I wanted to grin but gravity seemed too heavy to overcome.

"Why were we sent away? Why did our parents allow it?"

"Fear."

"Of what?"

"Nuclear war. There was one. Perhaps, even in space, you heard of it?"

"We were told that Earth was devastated."

"Yes, it was. In many ways, this is not the world we grew up in. But at the last moment, several world leaders came to their senses. A full catastrophe was averted. The bombs fell in India, Pakistan..." He sighed. "So much...ruined. There was fall-out, of course, but no world-wide devastation. However, beforehand, during the build-up, it seemed inevitable that we would all perish. There was panic.

"Universal Mining and other huge space conglomerates hyped hibernation as the choice that any good parent should make to keep their child safe and alive until the war ended and Earth could recover. My parents weren't interested, but yours were particularly vulnerable. They had already lost four children. Two at birth, one in an accident and the other to cancer. Their eldest wasn't eligible to go because she was too old. You were the baby —their pride and joy—and they sacrificed their own happiness on the promise that you would be safe, cared for and returned at some later date. The decision, I think it can be said without question, put them in an early grave."

There was a long silence. We both looked out over the treetops to the ocean beyond.

"Did she have freckles and brown skin?" I asked.

He didn't answer. I looked at him. His eyes were rimmed in red. He nodded. "The sun will do that to a woman who spends her life outside. She loved being outdoors."

"She was in my waking dream. They *were* memories." I sighed deeply, got up and walked to the edge of the patio. I noticed steps leading down to a vast green lawn.

"Your limp, Lantra."

"What about it?"

"It's my fault."

~ *Airborne* ~

"What?" I reluctantly turned from the view to look at him.

"We were eleven that summer. I already—I, um, talked you into taking the tractor for a spin. Of course we weren't supposed to, but you were always game for a little forbidden adventure. Just as I took a turn—at too high a speed, obviously—you stood up. You fell under the wheels and your leg bone shattered."

"Why'd I stand up?"

"You saw a deer with two fawns. You always were a sucker for animals."

"Aw, Winston. Sounds like it was the deer's fault, not yours."

"No, Lantra. All mine. I apologized plenty back then, but I want to tell you again how sorry I am. You've gone a long time with that limp and it still hurts me to see it."

This time I had no trouble grinning at him.

"What?" he asked.

"Old Man, I think it might be time for you to stop feeling guilty about that."

"I'm not likely to stop at this late date."

"Your bad driving saved my life."

"Huh?"

"Most of the people I was in hibernation with were sent to the mines. Their life expectancy was...short."

"But you—?"

"I couldn't do manual labour. I suppose I'm lucky they didn't drop me out an airlock, but they also needed slave labour on the ship. I was taught to do menial office work. I was lucky. My first boss was a woman with a conscience. She taught about human rights. Later, Heflyn taught me to read and write."

"Why did you tell me you couldn't read?"

"Are you crazy? It's a huge secret! None of us were supposed to know how to read. Heflyn was the exception because he had skills they needed. How could they keep us second class citizens if we knew anything about Earth and the fact that everyone, even lab babies, have rights?"

"Of course, you could read before you were sent away. Your friend just reminded you of what you already knew."

"Maybe, but all those kids who went to the mines never had that luxury. I think about them every day."

§

~ Airborne ~

It took time to sort through all the new information. Memories returned, but, like snowflakes falling and melting as soon as they hit the ground, I couldn't group them together. No blanket of sparkling snow...yet.

One day Adi showed up at Winston's retreat.

It was a cool, wet day and we were inside. I'd been spending a lot of time at the screen, looking up anything I wanted, educating myself about Earth's history, the Lost Generation, human's rights and Universal Mining. I could never have risked doing this on *Auria*. Screen-time being so closely monitored, I would have been discovered immediately.

"Oh, hello Adi," I said, when she came in. "Winston didn't tell me you were coming."

The woman walked slowly to me as I stood up. She wrapped her arms around me and embraced me in a way I could not remember ever being touched. Surprised, I started to pull away, but she held on tightly—her face buried in my chest. She was full of bittersweet emotion and it melted my reserve. Feeling that I should probably learn how to do this, I hugged her back.

"Lantra, we need to talk," she said, finally peeling away. "I don't have many years left and we have so much to catch up on."

"We do?"

"Lantra, I'm your older sister."

A pattern coalesced from isolated events. Why we stopped at Adi's house on the way up here. The sense I'd had that Adi's interest in me was way too intense for a stranger. And Winston telling me that my parents had an older child. Funny, I'd never thought of their older child as my sister.

"I have no practice at having a family, Adi," I said, shyly. "But I'm happy to know you."

She grinned. "You have more family than just me. But I get first crack at you because I'm the matriarch. The rest will have to wait, although—" she turned her grin to Winston, who was sitting in the corner watching us, "—they are jittery with anticipation."

Winston spoke up. "There'll be time for them. Besides, it's different with you two. You actually knew each other. All the others came after Lantra left."

"My parents had other children? Our parents, I mean."

"Yes. When the war didn't proliferate as widely as feared and

~ Airborne ~

after they were more or less assured that a child could be born without birth defects, they had three more. They are all alive and eagerly waiting to meet you.”

“And then there's me, the lucky one who got sent away.”

“Must be hard not to feel rejected,” Adi said. “But it wasn't like that. Mom and Pop loved you deeply. They were trying to save you.”

“I've just been reading about World War II. A similar thing happened,” I said, trying to cover my emotions. “Parents put their kids on trains and sent them away so they'd be safe. Sometimes they never saw them again.”

“This is exactly the kind of historical precedent the companies used to convince parents it was the right thing to do,” Adi said.

“Why? What was in it for the company?”

“Our parents paid dearly to keep you safe.”

This news hit me like a fist in the gut. I fell back against the upholstery with a thud. “Universal Mining got paid for me? So that I and all the others could work for them our whole lives?”

Adi nodded. “So it seems.”

Winston cut in, “Adi, Lantra and I have been discussing things. She can clear up for you the mystery you and I were debating.”

“About why the company brought you back?” Adi said.

“Yeah,” I said, “They had to think that leaving me on the ship was a bigger risk. I sent a detailed letter of protest about how we were being treated to the Human's Rights Commissary.”

“Lantra! How?” asked Adi.

I explained about Heflyn's expertise. “Of course, there was no way for the Commissary to respond to me because the transmission came from a dead woman, even though I signed it. Maybe they contacted Universal Mining. Maybe the company denied my existence. We don't know yet. But soon after, I was chosen for Re-entry.”

Winston spoke, “We believe Universal already suspected Lantra because she'd spoken to others of the Lost Generation about their rights. At the same time, they'd also know that the Human's Rights Commissary might investigate the complaint and so, they would—”

“Not want to harm you,” finished Adi.

~ Airborne ~

"But want to get you off their ship," added Winston.

"Preferably into a hospital for psychotics," I finished.

"That explains why they tried to bring you back after we left the hospital. That hasn't happened with our other Returnees."

"How many have you gotten back?" I asked.

Adi and Winston looked at each other.

"Five," he said, "One of them, you know, is Jocob."

"What? I thought you were talking about many, many people! Five? Out of hundreds? That's terrible!"

"You are a pioneer, my dear."

"No," I said, firmly. "Pioneers don't come back. They, dear Heflyn, and all of them out there who are lucky enough to still be alive, they are the pioneers. And I've got to help them."

§

I wrote letters, first making contact with the Commissary, explaining the situation to them. To publicize the plight of The Lost Generation and to help ensure that the long arm of Human's Rights could be extended into the vastness of the cosmos, I wrote articles and recorded videos. I became the spokesperson for all the lost people.

I hoped against all reason to see Heflyn again some day. If the 'lab babies' out there were given the same rights as others, he might be able to communicate with me at least. I didn't even know if Hef would want to come to Earth. I could hardly recommend it unconditionally. But it had grown on me.

Greens and pale blues. Flowers. The ocean. Rain. Breezes. Home-grown vegetables. Snow. Animals. Winston's cat. Even the humidity didn't trouble me anymore. Gravity. Gravity was the worst of it. But I felt my freedom even more than I did the weight of atmosphere. And, with all the publicity, I now felt safe from the corporation.

Adi and my other siblings visited often, but Winston and his cat became my real family.

My childhood memories never came back fully—though others assured me this was normal, that no one remembers everything from their childhood. Flashes came daily and I no longer mistrusted them. I collected and saved them all in a file, documenting my recovery.

~ Airborne ~

One day, while I worked outside on the patio, a dragonfly lit on my screen. A sweep of new memories returned with great clarity. I sat in stunned silence for long time. Then, I got up and went to find Winston.

He was cooking a pot of soup. The kitchen smelled of garlic and basil. He smiled at me and went back to his chopping.

"You called me 'Dragonfly,'" I said. He paused, knife in the air, but he didn't look at me. "And I nicknamed you 'Winner.'"

He put down the knife, wiped his hands on a cloth and walked slowly to me. "What else have you remembered?"

"You loved me!" Tears sprang to my eyes.

He smiled. "Only since I was ten years old. Since the first moment I saw you running across the field between our farms. Still do, in fact. Some things never change."

"Why didn't you tell me? All these months, I didn't know—never really understood—why you took me in. Why you went to so much trouble. Yes, we were friends but—"

"Dragonfly," he said softly, wrapping an arm around my shoulders, "you darted through the world, so busy, eating it up, consuming life as if you could never be filled. Fierce and independent. Beautiful and wild. I always knew we would—"

"Be together?"

"See each other again was as much as I hoped for. I couldn't tell you. I had to wait for you to remember...or not. Believe me, it's enough to have you here. To see you everyday. Look! Look at this." He pulled out his wallet. Opening it, he extracted a worn piece of paper. "It's your school photo. Taken when you were fourteen. The last one I got before you...left. It's been here, in my wallet, ever since."

I took the photograph. A familiar face—me, impossibly young and innocent—looked back. Hair curled around my unlined face.

"Lantra, I would have known you anywhere. The day I walked into the hospital, the sight of you overcame me. You looked the same! Oh well...slightly older, but still so young and fresh. What an amazing feeling...to have one's heart broken and mended all in the same moment! Then I saw your limp, the injury I caused and I—"

"I told you. It saved my life."

He lowered his head and sobbed into his hands.

"Winner, stop." I took his hands and held them. "Stop it now.

~ *Airborne* ~

We're both all right, aren't we? Didn't it turn out all right in the end?"

He closed his arms around me and squeezed so hard I thought my lungs would collapse. "Dragonfly," he murmured, "you remember me."

"I remember how much you loved me." I pulled back to look him in the eyes. "I remember a kiss."

He nodded, sheepishly. "But you didn't love me back," he said, sounding like a boy of fourteen.

"I did." The memory of us laid in my mind like a pristine, deep blanket of fresh snow. "I just knew we were too young to commit to each other. You were so serious and intense." I laughed, remembering how he had been and the ways he was the same to this day. "You always irritated and fascinated me in equal measure." I grinned at him. "I'm so happy! It's amazing to remember you. How'd you stay so patient all these weeks?"

"Patience? Oh, Lantra. Patience is all I've had for over fifty years. That, my love for you, and my unlikely belief that I'd see you again some day. What were a few more weeks?"

"I did love you, Winner," I whispered, "in my childish way."

"I know. I know." He extracted himself from my arms and walked back to his chopping board.

"What?" I asked.

"I'm an old man."

"Yes. You are." There was a long silence. "But...some things never change, right?"

He turned to face me. "What do you mean?"

"You have loved me since you were a boy."

"True."

"And...you and I are the same age."

He shook his head. "Not true, Lantra. You're still young."

"An illusion."

He shook his head again, but he grinned.

"My joints are shot, my bones brittle. I'm old too, Winston."

Finally, I could see bright hope in his eyes. I walked closer to him. "Winston, isn't it good to know that there are a few things in life that even time and space can't change?"

His head stopped shaking and started nodding up and down.

I moved even closer, sure of myself, and him. "Now. Now, I can love you fully."

~ Airborne ~

"Dragonfly...it's finally our time, isn't it?"
I sank into his arms, into a long, and long overdue, embrace.

Nancy Shepard Metzger Waldman, after enjoying several other lives, decided to become a writer. She plugged away at it earnestly, but nothing much happened until she—in an unrelated coincidence—fell in love with a boy from her past and moved to Cape Breton. Here, she happily settled in and, as so often happens when strong roots are laid down, began to thrive. This story, about the ability of love to endure over time and space, is her first *fictional* romance. She wrote it as an homage to the loving man who brought her to the place where, someday—however belatedly—she just might bloom. Nancy writes about creativity for The Practically Creative Quarter at practicallycreative.net. Her writer's site can be found at nancysmwaldman.com.

Colony

Jake glanced up from the morning news-disk,
silently turned the monitor so I could see the ad:
"Young professionals sought to establish human colony
Off-Terra.
Direct inquiries to World Space Centre."
I looked past him to the filthy street outside,
the burning chemical rain hissing against the window,
our envir-suits hanging by the door.
Our eyes met; I nodded.

Three months later we flew to WSC
for training. I became friends
with a marine biologist named Janet.
She was tired, she said,
of examining dying fish.
I was a botantist, I told her, and
I felt the same way about plants.

In six short months,
we learned survival skills, the use of equipment,
First Aid. We spent afternoons
in rooms designed to simulate sunlight.
We spent nights wondering if
it was truly worth it to leave everything,
everyone. We might have decided it wasn't, but
they told us that on the new planet
we could have a baby.

~ Airborne ~

Ten
We double-checked our personal restraints
Nine
I imagined the commander giving orders
Eight
I glanced at Jake, nervous
Seven
and was rewarded with a smile
Six
a squeeze of the hand
Five-four-three-two-one
In my mind
the flames roared around the shuttle base,
gravity cringed, defeated,
the Earth became a swiftly fading
swirl of colour and memory,
and Space made itself known
as dark and imposing and infinite.

I slammed back hard in my seat—
lights flickered on the passenger deck—
Janet shook and shrieked beside me;
her husband tried to comfort her but
he looked half-mad himself.
And then, as chaos was breeding in our minds
and all hell seemed to be making
its terrible presence known on the first
Human Colony Transport Vehicle,
everything went quiet.

The commander's voice,
a beacon for our wandering sanity,
eased out of the speakers:
"I hope everyone's all right back there.
The launch went fine. Feel free
to look around."

I unstrapped myself and ran
past rows of seats to the edge of the room,
one of the first to peer out through

~ *Airborne* ~

inches-thick glass at the stars.
I could not see the Earth.
Our view showed only stars
(brighter than on Earth
where the atmosphere leeched their light)
and boundless black.

We trundled away from our soiled world,
hoping a second chance would be granted
and knowing we didn't deserve one.
We were electric with nerves,
realizing that the bright
ring we had grabbed for was
welded to our hands forever.

On the fifth day, safety standards
checked out and the crew froze us in dreams.

I remember the taste of cryo-sleep
like electric, ozone-scented air
filling our dry mouths.
It seemed like an instant;
it was forty-five years.

Slow, prickling warmth,
like thorns of heat scratching
my careless fingertips,
wakes me.
I cannot move, cannot breathe,
can barely think.
My panicked-horse mind stampedes
away from the paths of reason
but the quiet *whoosh* of the depressurizing cryo-chamber
stills it, and I open unaged eyes
to peer up through the pink murk
of the warm chemical bath.
The fluid drains away.

~ *Airborne* ~

I sit up, looking across many pill-capsule chambers,
see others awakening, as from death,
see Jake reaching stiffly for my hand.
"You're the best looking seventy-year-old
I've ever seen," he says, grinning.

The crew come in; they've been awake for a month,
navigating the last part of the journey
after computer systems
found a hospitable planet and roused them.
For a week they launched probes
and sent down supplies.
Finally, they touched us down on the seas
of this green planet.

We board inflatable rafts; Janet leaps
into the water and swims the last stretch.
It feels strange to be outside
without an envir-suit.
We rush across the sand, shouting like children.
Jake stoops and runs to me, sprinkling
something feathery in my hand.
"Grass," he says. "It's grass."

We look upon our new heaven and new earth
(like the one we left but clean, shining,
with oceans that are actually blue)
and name it Home;
nothing else seems appropriate.

❧❧❧

Krista C. Miller was born in Sydney Mines, Nova Scotia, and
explored a number of Canadian cities while studying
English, French, and Education. Krista is now a high-school
teacher, and lives in rural Cape Breton with her wonderful
husband Bruce and amazing new daughter, Caida. When left to

~ Airborne ~

her own devices, she likes to sew, garden, bake far more than is good for her, and consume books at an alarming rate. However, these days she is quite content to spend a lot of time singing "Baby Beluga," to finish settling into her new house, and to finally have room to unpack and shelve all of her books.

~ *Airborne* ~

Daddy's Story

"Daddy, tell us a ghost story."

"Justin, I don't want you scaring those kids," mother Flora warns.

Daddy gives her a baleful look. "Now, would I do that? They know there's no such thing as ghosts. Anyone here believe in ghosts?"

"No," they chorus, insulted by the very thought. The oldest declares, "Daddy says there's a reasonable explanation for everything, right Dad?"

"That's right, Theresa."

The baby in the next room wails. Mother's parting look is half-warning, half-appeal, as she rushes off to soothe the little one.

"C'mon, Dad, we won't be scared. Tell us a story," the oldest boy, with all the maturity of his ten years, urges. "Only babies believe in ghosts, right Dad? Babies," he spits, "and...girls!"

"We do not," the girls deny hotly.

"Whoa, whoa, none of that, now," Daddy cautions. "You'll wake the baby."

A hush descends upon the old farmhouse. The big kitchen windows loom black behind their frail daytime curtains. A fire crackles in the coal stove.

"They do say there's a reason for everything," Daddy begins, "but I'll be darned if I'll ever understand what happened back in the years of 1945 and 1946." Seven pairs of brown eyes, identical to their Dad's, stare back solemnly.

"It happened just after the war. Theresa was just a baby and Mom and I had rented a little house in Westmount. I was working at Canada Packers, the meat packing plant at the old naval base..."

§

The company bus would pick up all the workers every morning and return us home at night. Not many people had cars in those days. My first morning on the bus I met this big boy from the country. Malcolm MacInnis was his name. Oh, he was a big fellow, blond, baby-faced, but not in great shape. We worked side by side. Got to know each other pretty well. I'd tease him about his weight, tell him he should get himself in shape. On our breaks, I'd show him some of my old army exercises, teach him a few boxing moves, that sort of thing. They ran that place like the army. They even had bells that rang for breaks, lunch, dismissal. As soon as the bell rang at the end of day, we'd have a little race to see who would get to the bus first. A lot of the men would participate. We'd draw a line in the dirt or the snow and run like blazes for the bus.

I won most of the races, but Malcolm was getting pretty good. I don't know if it was the work, the exercises, or maybe he was just losing his baby fat, but that boy was getting in shape. After about six months, we were almost always in a dead heat, me first, him second, and he was gaining on me by the day.

As I said, Malcolm was a country-boy, and when I say country, I mean country. A dirt road, off a dirt road, off a dirt road. Complete isolation. He was an orphan, lost both parents in infancy and was raised on the old homestead in rear Boisdale by his grandfather and his grandfather's brother and sister, neither of whom had ever married. Those old country people were awful superstitious and Malcolm was raised on stories of ghosts and forerunners and the like, which he both believed in and scoffed at.

One morning, the young fellow took his usual seat beside me on the bus and not a word did he speak. He was pale and tense. Finally, I said, "Have I done something to upset you?"

"What, you? Of course not. Something happened at home. You'll only laugh if I tell you."

"Why would I laugh?"

"Because you don't believe in these things. Superstitions you call them."

"Have you seen a ghost then?"

~ Airborne ~

"Worse."

"What could be worse?"

"Death."

"Oh, no. Which one of them is it?"

"You mean which one of them will it be?"

"Say that again."

"Only if you promise not to laugh."

"I'm not laughing, Malcolm."

"Well, in our family there's a tradition. More like a curse. Goes clean back to Scotland. Before one of us dies, there's always a warning. Death comes knocking, you might say." Malcolm swallowed hard.

He's just a kid, I told myself. "And he came knocking last night?" I asked.

"Something did. We like to play cards in the evenings sometimes, Grampa, Uncle Matt, Aunt Lizzie and me. In the middle of the game, we heard three loud knocks at the door. Aunt Lizzie, without thinking, got up and opened it. There was no one there." He stopped, his bottom lip quivering.

"And now," I said carefully, "you think she's going to die?"

He nodded, his face grim.

"As soon as Aunt Lizzie saw there was no one there, she began to shake. We gave her a bit of brandy to steady her nerves, but she's a wreck. Grampa, Uncle Matt and I checked the yard, the outbuildings. Nothing."

"But Malcolm, it was something, a person, an animal, something."

"Look, keep this to yourself, will you?"

"Sure, but there is an explanation. You just have to find it."

He gave me such a weary, patient look then, I felt bad. I could just see them playing cards by the light of the kerosene lamp, coal stove all hot and cozy. Outside, nothing for miles and miles but empty fields and encroaching forest, and over all a deadly silence. They had no electricity out there, no radio. The nearest neighbour was three miles away. No wonder ghosts creep in.

A week or so passed. I said to Malcolm, "Looks like death got the wrong door."

I was glad to see a faint smile. "Maybe you're right. Maybe it is just superstition."

~ Airborne ~

The next day Malcolm's seat on the bus was empty. "Death in the family," the boss told us. The obituaries in The Post the next day included one for Mary Lizzie MacInnis.

> *Age 74, Spinster. Rear Boisdale. In good health. Passed away peacefully in her sleep.*

It also said she was the only mother her grandnephew Malcolm had ever known.

When Malcolm returned to work the next week, he moved like an old man. "Still think it's superstition?" he asked softly.

"As a matter of fact, I do, and I think it may have killed her. She believed she was going to die. She thought of nothing else for the past few weeks. She couldn't sleep, couldn't eat. She was old, a bit frail. She scared herself to death, Malcolm."

He stared at me with wide eyes. "But the knock," he whispered. "Who knocked on the door?"

"Could someone have been playing a trick on you?" I asked. He didn't answer.

Spring slipped into summer, then autumn. One morning we woke up to a fresh fall of snow, about six inches of pure white beautiful misery.

The bus was late because of the slippery roads, and Malcolm was not on it. Our six inches was likely a foot or two in the back country. God only knew when he'd get plowed out.

The next day, he showed up looking scared and angry at the same time. It was lunch hour before we found a private moment.

"It happened again," he told me. "We were playing cards, Grampa, Uncle Matt and me, when we heard three loud knocks on the door. None of us moved. 'Someone's trying to frighten us,' I said, 'It's some kind of trick.'"

"'Who's there?' I called. The reply was three more slow, deliberate knocks."

I told him it had to be one of the neighbours, even though I knew that wasn't likely.

"*Knock. Knock. Knock.* Louder, slower, more ominous this time."

"Uncle Matt said, 'Easy, boy. Maybe your friend is right. Maybe someone is playing a trick on us, trying to scare us.'"

"I went to open the door, but Uncle thrust me aside and

~ Airborne ~

pulled it open himself. The snow was up to the sill. Not a print or a mark on it. We circled the house. Same thing. We even walked the half mile to the main road. It was blocked. Nothing had come that way. The snow lay undisturbed in every direction. We went back to the house. Sat up all night."

I didn't know what to tell him. The strange thing was, I wasn't that surprised when two weeks later, Matthew Martin MacInnis, age 76, died. His brother found him dead on the floor of the barn. Fell from the loft and broke his neck.

I went to the wake. Poor Malcolm and his grandfather were devastated. I murmured my condolences, inadequate though they were. There were no right words for something like this.

When Malcolm returned to work, I had no theories for him—or for myself.

A year passed. It was mid-October and again we were treated to our first snow of the season. It was bitter cold, and after an hour spent shoveling out my driveway and another standing in the slush waiting for the late bus, my feet were numb. When I finally boarded the warm bus, I saw Malcolm huddled by the window, a blank look on his baby-face.

"What's up?"

"I'm a dead man," he muttered. In a hoarse whisper, making sure no one else could hear, he told me then of what I now call "the third visitation."

"There was something at the door last night. Me and Grampa were reading the Post at the kitchen table when the knocks came. I thought Grampa was going to die on the spot."

"'We won't answer,' I told him. The response was three measured knocks, louder than any we'd ever heard before."

"'Go to hell!' I yelled."

"Three more knocks. I saw the door heave under the pressure."

"Grampa was shaking like a leaf. He started to cry. 'No, boy,' he said, 'it must be for me. You're just a kid. I'm an old man.'"

"I thought of what you said, Justin. It must be someone doing this to us, tormenting us to our deaths. I was filled with rage. Before Grampa could move, I jumped up and tore open the door. There was nothing but snow. Nothing and no one."

I admit I was scared, but I told him, "There has to be an explanation."

~ Airborne ~

The day was a long and tedious one as we scrambled to make up for lost time. When the quitting bell finally rang, Malcolm stood by the door, glumly shoving his arms into his jacket. I gave him a playful tap on the shoulder. "C'mon," I said, "maybe you'll beat me today."

In a few moments, it was just the two of us, in the lead as usual, our feet pounding the snowy ground, his a mere half beat behind mine. I could feel him breathing at my shoulder, then he wasn't there. Turning to look, I saw him lying face down in the road.

Aha, so that's your game! I thought. *It's a set-up!*

"You don't fool me," I said, running back to stand over him. I pushed him gently with my foot. He rolled over on his back. His face was blue. The veins of his neck were horribly distended as he struggled to breathe. His eyes rolled back in his head.

Two MPs from the base caught up with us. They pushed me aside and began to administer first aid. After a few moments, I heard one say, "My God, he's dead." He made the sign of the cross.

His partner came up to me, pushed me roughly. "What happened here?" he yelled at me.

The other one said, "We saw you kick him."

Without another word, I was cuffed and taken to headquarters. Put in a cell.

Luckily, the doctor who looked at the body didn't see any signs of violence, so they couldn't keep me more than the night. He'd do an autopsy to be sure but that would take days. As soon as they let me out, I went to see Malcolm. His body lay on a table. His Grampa stood over him, tears running down his face, his fingers stroking the boy's hair.

"Not a mark on him," he said, shaking his old white head. "Such a big, strong boy."

When he saw me, he said brokenly, "He was just eighteen years old." His face was an accusation.

§

"Thank God for that autopsy," Dad says. "When the report finally came in, the doctor said it was massive heart failure. Poor kid never knew what hit him."

~ Airborne ~

Mom comes into the room and sits beside Daddy.

"I waited up all that night," she says. "Didn't know a thing until you came home the next morning. I thought you were dead." He puts his arm around her shoulder.

The fire shifts in the grate, painting fiery red pictures on the wall. Not a word is spoken as we ponder the mystery.

Into the silence drops the sound of a single, preemptive knock, a stone falling into a well. Two more follow.

The baby wails in the next room. A cold draft scrabbles across the floor. Dad and Mom leap to their feet. Dad turns Mom to face him, but it's too late. We've already glimpsed the fear in her eyes.

"It's just the wind," Daddy says quickly. "It's picked up. That's all. Just the wind. Time for bed, everyone."

❧❧

Theresa Dugas Mac Kay is an avid amateur historian, reader, writer, and dreamer. She is a direct descendant of Abraham Dugas (1616-c1700) who came to Port Royal, Nova Scotia in 1640 as the King's Armorer and later became Governor of Acadia. A number of his descendents found refuge on or near the Bras d'Or Lakes in Cape Breton after the expulsion of 1755. Two hundred and fifty-five years later some of them are still here.

The year 2010 finds Theresa in her empty nest, on the Bras d' Or of course, reading and writing her way through retirement, accompanied by her true love, Ron, and feeling positively giddy about the arrival of her first grandchild in September.

She is presently working on an historical novel and experimenting with children's literature. This is her first short story.

~ Airborne ~

Mind Drifter

Jason ignored the pleas of his little sister as he let the screen door slam behind him.

Hauling his bike from the front lawn, he draped the towel he'd grabbed from the bathroom over his neck. He ran a few steps and leapt onto his ten-speed, his feet finding the already rotating pedals. He pumped faster to escape her cries.

"Jas! Jason! Please take me with you!" Cally yelled, the last words lost in a sob of desperation.

Without turning to look at her, he called, "Finish the dishes before Mom gets home. I'll take you later."

He didn't want to look back. She'd have that look on her face that she always had now if he left her alone. He cycled harder, this time to burn away the guilt in his gut. He needed to get out for a while without her. *She's thirteen, damn it, she can be alone for an hour or so. As long as I make it back before Mom gets home from work, or else she'll freak.*

Lately, when Mom got mad he didn't feel bad, or upset, he felt angry. A "need to punch a wall" kind of angry that scared him later when he thought about it. After all, Mom was just as upset about losing Dad as he was.

"Look after your Mom, she needs you now," his grandmother told him when she left to go back to Halifax. Those words echoed in his head every time he felt like losing it. God, he wished Nan hadn't gone home. She'd stayed for over a month after the funeral. Those first few weeks, even though they were all so sad and lost, hadn't been as horrible as the weeks since Nan left.

His speed picked up as the pavement angled down. Devoe's Garage loomed ahead so he did all he could to increase his velocity. Careening around the corner, he leaned forward and low over the handlebars, hoping to slick silently past the garage.

"Hey, shithead, I see you!"

Glancing over his shoulder, Jason saw Arnie Devoe walking away from the opened hood of a vehicle, rubbing grease from his hands and onto his coveralls.

"Stop! I wanna talk to you."

Lumper MacDonald lumbered behind Arnie.

"Talk, yeah right," muttered Jason. Squeeze his skull under the hood of that car, more like it.

Jason took the turn-off onto Gouthro Mountain Road, but then hopped off his bike and walked it down the dirt lane. He didn't want a cloud of dust to show where he'd gone. He'd made it to the middle of the wooden bridge that spanned the brook when he heard the roar of Arnie's truck up above on the main road.

Jason groaned. Arnie on his ass, just what he needed. He started to jog. It would only take the next curve or so in the road for them to realize he must have turned off. They'd be back. The entrance to the ball field seemed a half mile away, but he finally reached it and ran over to the line of trees.

He hid his bike under the drooping branches of a willow tree and started down the path to the brook. The way was well-worn from all the local kids heading down for a dip, although nobody was down there yet. The grassy bank sloped to the water's edge, the grass mashed into a mucky mess even this early in the summer. The converging of several smaller brooks at this swollen section created an awesome swimming hole.

Jason passed by the popular spot, swatting the ragged end of the thick rope they all used to swing out to the middle, before letting go to plunge into the swirling reddish-brown brook water that was always fresh-off-the-mountain cold, even in late summer. He glanced back at the rope, swinging invitingly, but shook his head and edged along a narrow embankment, holding tree branches for stability. He was going to his secret spot, which is why he couldn't bring Cally.

Navigating around the bend in the brook, Jason examined the foliage carefully until he found the tree with the large, black knothole. It looked like a giant cigarette had been extinguished in the tree's flesh. Knotting his shoelaces together, he hung his sneakers around his neck with his towel and waded into the knee-high section of water.

~ *Airborne* ~

Choosing his footing with care, he made his way across the slick, rocky bottom to the other side where another small brook poured into the bigger channel. The hidden junction widened out after a few feet. It forked a few more times and each time Jason stood in panic that he'd forgotten the way. But then one way would seem more familiar and he'd keep moving.

Finally, he came to the most difficult point, the place where he almost turned around every time, even though he knew where he had to go. The left side of the fork was bright, with wide, grassy banks, easy for walking, while the other was dominated by a fierce-looking, massive, ancient tree. Its branches and thick exposed roots nearly choked off the passage of the water and there was no embankment for walking.

Jason talked himself into picking his way toward the imposing tree. The water filtered through the tree's limbs; he could hear it gurgling heartily. He entered into the dark shade cast by the tree and climbed with difficulty between the branches and roots. On the other side, his anxiety dissipated, as usual, and he felt the familiar tug of the deeper water beyond, as though it told him *this way*.

Rounding the next bend, he stood wet, sweaty and grinning at "his spot". It lay before him like an oasis, a mirage. The brook came to a stop in a cul-de-sac of swirling water, creating an impossibly deep, quiet pool with a peninsula of soft white sand, shaded by tall elms on one end and basking in sunshine on the other. The concave top of a pearly white rock pierced the pool of water within hopping distance of the end of the peninsula.

As Jason sank into the powdery sand, he again marveled at its consistency—such an unlikely find for his Cape Breton home. Everywhere else along the brooks of Frenchvale you would find sucking, clay-like mud, rough gravelly dirt, or rounded brook-washed stones. The sun-exposed sand was hot on the soles of his feet, but after the cold walk through the water, it felt wonderful.

The memory of the first time he'd found this place, a couple of weeks before, came back. He'd been so excited he'd thought, "I can't wait to show Dad!" His heart had constricted with the now familiar squeeze of pain as he'd remembered that he could no longer tell his Dad anything. He dropped his towel and sneakers on the sand and looked into the depths of the pool. Then he dove in.

~ *Airborne* ~

It was cool, not cold like the rest of the brooks. Bobbing to the surface, his memories and pain washed away as he floated on his back, eyes closed, so peaceful, so quiet. He sensed the looming presence of the huge white stone, and flutter-kicked away from it. He'd go to the stone soon, but not yet.

Later, after a long swimming and floating session, Jason sat on his towel on the strip of sand, letting the powdery grains flow through his fingers. He thought again of how much his Dad would love this spot and his eyes filled up. He didn't actually cry. He hadn't cried since after that first week or so when he'd thought he'd never stop.

He blinked the moisture away and dusted the sand from his fingers, contemplating the white stone. The first time he'd jumped on it and sat down in the oddly form-fitting depression on its surface, he'd had what he thought was a bizarre hallucination. When he came out of it, he'd tried to stand, stumbled forward, and fallen into the water.

The next couple of times he dared to get on top of it, he had come to understand that it was not a hallucination caused by too much sun, but that the unusual white stone was responsible.

He found himself at the edge of the peninsula, not even remembering standing up. He tensed for the slight hop that would take him out onto the stone. When he landed, he lay down in the slight depression in the rock, an almost-perfect mold for his body. He concentrated on the gentle lapping of the water on the stone until he felt the slight humming of vibrations, almost imperceptible, begin beneath him. The now-familiar numbing sensation filled him and he sighed. His essence eased lightly from his body, with only a gentle tug—as simple as shrugging off a jacket. He floated above himself, examining his relaxed, slightly smiling face but not lingering too long on his skinny, lanky body. His Mom called him a long, lean eating machine, but he always wished he'd fill out into a stockier, brawnier frame like his father.

That disappointment couldn't touch him now as he circled higher, looping around the pond, close to the treetops. The first couple of times he'd come out of his body he'd been scared and gone right back. But when he realized he could go back whenever he wanted, he began to enjoy the delicious feeling of freedom and flying. And he could fly. He could float or he could soar. Best of all, his usual dismal thoughts were replaced by other sensations

~ Airborne ~

—the breathless excitement of utter freedom, the giddy feeling of something else about to happen and a burning curiosity to explore.

The last bubbled up in him now and he found himself leaving the area where his body lay and exploring farther along the swaying treetops. It was so beautiful. Just when he began to worry about leaving his body so far behind, Jason saw the top of Devoe's Garage, and the messy bits of mangled metal scraps, tires and car bodies splayed out around the surrounding lot.

Arnie and Lumper climbed out of the truck. Arnie slammed his door shut and, muttering, entered the garage through the open bay doors. Lumper shambled after him like a faithful hound.

Jason hovered in the shadows near the entrance of the garage, looking inside. He burned to follow them and hear what they had to say about his disappearing act. Maybe they would even reveal what he'd done to piss Arnie off. The known bully had never bothered him before the last few weeks.

The trouble was, he was afraid that he could be seen, maybe even recognized in this form. He'd never been able to see his reflection in the water back where he'd left his body, but the surface was hardly a perfect mirror.

A mirror! That was a great idea. He floated toward Arnie's truck. He'd use the side mirror to test his visibility.

"I'm going, I'm going," yelled Lumper.

Jason had time to swirl around to face Lumper about one second before the large teen walked right through him.

Dissipating and then reforming left Jason slithery with disgust. He swirled around once more to watch Lumper reach into the back of Arnie's pickup truck to pull out a large metal toolbox.

He appeared unaffected by the experience of scattering Jason.

So they can't see me. Jason followed Lumper back into the darkness of the garage, hanging back a little to avoid a repeat of the unpleasant sensation of being dispersed into foggy bits.

"Where in the hell did you fuck off to?" growled an approaching voice. Arnie's grizzled father, Hector, walked over to the teenagers.

"Got a call for some roadside assistance, but they cancelled,"

Arnie lied smoothly, looking right at his father.

Hector's eyes narrowed. He pointed at the car raised on a hoist nearby. "I finished rotating those tires. I'm getting cleaned up and heading home. Take it down and leave it outside for Mr. Collier to pick up. Then stay till close and lock up."

Arnie crunched his eyebrows together. "I told you I felt a shimmy in the front end when I drove it. I don't think Mr. Collier was having problems because the tires were wearing down unevenly, I want to take a look underneath—"

Hector jabbed his grease covered finger into his son's chest. "Don't fucking question me, you little shit. Move that car outside."

Arnie looked down at his father's finger before meeting the older man's eyes.

Swatting his father's hand away from his chest, he walked over to the table by the wall and grabbed a set of keys, his face tight.

Hector's eyes widened and his body trembled. He turned away and stepped into the back storage room.

Jason, curious, drifted after him. Inside the room, Hector kicked at a column of tires repeatedly. He walked over to a cupboard and put his hand on the knob. He pulled it partly opened and then closed it. Pulled it partly open and closed it again. His face contorted with emotions.

What's he doing? Jason wondered, drifting closer. He studied Hector's twisting features. *What's he thinking?*

And then, the slight sucking sensation he felt when he departed or entered his body pulled at his insubstantial form. Before he could even gasp, he was suctioned into Hector Devoe.

He stared at his grease-covered hand, splayed on the cupboard in front of him. He wanted so badly to reach inside for the bottle he kept hidden there. But he couldn't. The doctor...he'd scared him. A wave of rage pulsed up from the dark pit in his gut. *Fuck that doctor! And fuck that brat!*

Hector stared at the door back to the garage. He couldn't control that punk anymore. He thought he was so smart. The rage swept up from the pit once again. He narrowed his eyes. He hadn't heard the sound of the hoist coming down yet. He'd told him to take that car down.

Hector strode over to the door and pushed it open a couple of inches.

That meathead Lumper was out having a smoke.

Arnie was under Mr. Collier's car with the trouble light, working.

The little bastard. The little bastard is defying me again. Thinks he knows better.

Rage steamed up from the pit, heating his chest and numbing his brain.

Thinks he's smarter than me.

There was nothing but the rage now, hot and white, his vision focused like a narrow tunnel on the lower half of his son's body.

It was the coolness of the metal spanner against his warm skin that made him aware of it, not its substantial weight. He looked down at it, clutched in his meaty fist. He didn't remember picking it up. He stared in surprise at the object he clutched.

What are you doing, a faraway voice called out in his head. *What the hell are you going to do with that?*

He didn't know. He didn't know why he held the spanner. He backed away from his working son. When his back met the door, he fumbled with the knob and stumbled back inside the musty-smelling back room.

Once inside he threw the spanner inside the column of tires and it clattered to the floor inside the tubes of rubber, out of his sight.

Were you going to hurt your own son?

Was I? Was I going to hurt my own son? It was the rage, it was the things inside his gut, he tried to rationalize with the voice in his head. *Oh God.* He gripped his forehead with one hand. *Now I'm hearing voices.*

He stumbled over to the cupboard and ripped it open, pushing aside boxes of rags and groping until his hand felt the smooth glass of the bottle. Pulling it out, he tore off the cap, and raised it to his lips with only a brief flash of the warnings of his doctor. *Liver damage, permanent, biopsy*—the words fled through his brain, but they didn't hold as much fear in them as the thought of hurting his son and arguing with voices in his head.

He took a long, grateful swallow of the liquid that would cool the heat in his chest and push it back down into the roiling pit in his gut. It would quiet all fears, silence all voices, and keep him

~ Airborne ~

from hurting his boy.

Memories of some other times when he'd not stopped himself from punching, kicking, slapping his boy, his estranged wife, his old man—once he'd been big enough to give some back—all were drowned by the next swallow. He sighed in relief.

The alcohol loosened Jason from Hector's consciousness and he pulled from the man's body with a sigh of relief that echoed the alcoholic's as he took another slug of the bottle.

Jason stared at the man as he slid down the filthy wall to slump against the base, cradling the bottle between his hands like a baby.

The soul-shaking horror of what he'd experienced inside the man's body melted into pity. How could he not drink? With that festering pit in his gut, what else could he do? How else could he stop that impenetrable cloud of rage from smothering all reason? Thankfully he had heard Jason screaming to him and stopped.

Jason drifted away and paused at the door, which was now open a few inches.

Arnie peered in at the crumpled form of his father with anything but pity on his face.

Jason slipped through the partly open door, grazing against Arnie's stiff form, and recoiling slightly from the look of pure disgust etched on the younger Devoe's face.

He watched as Arnie closed the door quietly and then stared at the knob for a few seconds.

What was he thinking, Jason wondered, *did he know what his father had almost done? Had he seen something?*

The suctioning sensation began again, and Jason fought it for a moment, but curiosity got the better of his trepidation.

"Arnie?" Lumper's voice pulled Arnie from his thoughts about his father's pathetic weakness.

"What?"

"You need me anymore, or can I go down for a swim? Betcha some of the girls are down there by now."

"No, go ahead. I'll be down in a few hours, after we close."

"Man, you were supposed to be off this afternoon. Your old man was supposed to close."

"Nope, it'll be me. Again."

Lumper shrugged. "Okay, see you later."

Arnie watched him walk away, resentment simmering.

~ Airborne ~

Lumper wouldn't offer to stay. Not because he didn't give a shit, but just because the kid was too stupid to give it a second thought. Not for the first time Arnie wondered if he was friends with Lumper in spite of that or because of it. Sometimes, lots of times, it was convenient.

He lowered the car with the hoist mechanism. He'd been right about it, looked like the sway bar was gone. He'd give Mr. Collier the bad news later. But at least he wouldn't have to pay for a tire rotation he didn't need, only to come back with more problems. Or worse, end up in an accident. Not that he really liked Mr. Collier—he was a sniveling wimp who sucked up to the old man. They shared a few bottles together, laughing and cursing and going on a few nights, keeping Arnie up, making him tired for school the next day. Of course, he was tired most days at school since his Dad made him work so much. Paid him less than minimum wage too, cheap bastard. Arnie felt the roiling in his gut of raw anger, but he smothered it. He went over to the speed bag he'd hung up in the corner of the office part of the garage and drummed on it, bare knuckled. He should tape his hands...he slipped into the rhythm of the bag and felt the anger simmer down.

One way to cool down, thought Jason.

Arnie grabbed the leather bag with two hands and froze.

What the hell?

"Fuck," growled Arnie, striding back into the garage portion of the building and the cracked mirror hanging above the deep wash basin.

Arnie gripped the plastic tub and leaned in toward his reflection with a snarl. "I thought you were dead, old man. How're you back in my head again? Get the fuck out!"

Jason began to recoil from Arnie's mind. *How the hell does he know I'm in here? Why's he calling me an old man?*

As Jason detached himself with a violent yank and floated backward, Arnie staggered. His broad frame moved closer to the glass and Jason floated toward the bright light of the outdoors. He was zipping out of the bay doors when he heard Arnie ask the mirror with a strained tone, "Jason?"

Terror pulsed through Jason as he fled over the treetops back toward his haven. Spotting his prone body he darted down but then paused to calm himself before re-entering. If you didn't do it

~ Airborne ~

gently, it hurt. After a few moments of calming his fluttering nerves, he eased his insubstantial form back into his long skinny frame. As always it was several minutes before he regained control of his physical form. He thought about what just happened while he waited for full mobility.

How had Arnie known it was him? And who did he think it was at first, this—old man? Did he mean Hector? He did call his father his "old man". His mind raced as he realized all that he'd learned while "occupying" the father and son. He understood both of them better than he wanted to, not only that pit of rage in their guts that made his own flashes of temper seem measly by comparison, but also things they knew. A lot of things they knew!

Jason sat up in surprise. A wave of dizziness and nausea swept over him. He held his head. That had never happened before. The excitement he'd just felt dissipated with the nausea, but as the icky feeling faded the excitement built back up. In his mind he could now see how to disassemble, clean and reassemble a rifle. He could clearly visualize the internal workings of a basic car engine. He understood that there was no money in the gas pump part of the garage business but that it was a necessary inconvenience...and so much more.

Some from Hector's knowledge, some from Arnie's—wow, Arnie knew a lot more about cars than his dad. Jason crouched in his effort to stand as a flush of dizziness struck. Arnie knew a lot more about running the business too. He had some really good ideas...

Jason once again felt the wash of fear that had coursed through him when Arnie felt his presence. He had to get home before Arnie caught up with him. He jumped back to the peninsula of sand, almost falling into the water as his legs shook unsteadily beneath him. God, how was he going to get past the garage without being seen? Pulses of terror raced through his body as he gathered his things and began the journey out of the brush.

When he emerged from the trees and headed over to the willow tree for his bike, he stopped. His bike was gone.

"It's in the back of my truck," said Arnie from somewhere behind him.

Jason felt like he was going to puke. He rotated slowly to see Arnie standing there, arms crossed over his chest. Arnie's hands, forearms and face were latticed with scratches, some of them deep.

Jason's heart thumped. After Arnie finished with him, he'd look much worse. He was too concerned about that to ask Arnie what had happened, but he was curious. He realized in that moment that his curiosity had gotten him here, staring at Arnie with no place to run.

"Come on, get in the truck, kid. You look like you're gonna fall down." Arnie started toward the truck which was sitting on the gravel road, one wheel of Jason's bike visible in the back.

When Jason didn't move to follow, Arnie stopped and turned around. "I'm not gonna pound you, if that's what you think."

Jason still couldn't get his legs to move.

Arnie put his hands on his hips and glared at Jason. "Of course, if you piss me off..." he raised his eyebrows.

Jason walked stiff-legged to the truck. It was weird how Arnie called him "kid". He was only a year older. Jason had always thought before that it was because Arnie was as big as a man, but now that he'd seen inside his mind, and Hector's, he understood. Arnie *was* older.

Once they were both inside the truck, Arnie made no move to start it. He just sat with his hands on the steering wheel. "Look under the seat. I grabbed something out of my locker for you. I thought if I brought it, maybe I'd be allowed in there." He looked down at the scratches on his arms. "But I guess not."

Fingers trembling, and not knowing what the hell Arnie was talking about, Jason groped under the seat until he found a book. He pulled it out. "This?" he asked.

Arnie nodded.

Opening it, Jason found drawings of the white stone in his secret place. They were detailed schematics that had boxes of information pointing to various pressure points in the indentations in the stone. There were pages of information too, with titles like, "Astral travel" and "Preventing Host from sensing traveler".

"You might want to read that one." Arnie was leaning over his shoulder, reading. "That's how I knew who you were. You...leaked some of your thoughts when you were freaked out."

"Leaked?" Jason asked weakly.

"Yeah. The old man wasn't very good at 'occupying' when he

tried his shit with me. That's how I figured out he was there. I saw—like a picture in my head—his cabin in the woods, the crazy white stone, a bunch of stuff before he screwed off out of me. I thought I was going nuts." Arnie shook his head. "I went around for months thinking I was cracking up. You know, not enough sleep or something, waiting for some other crazy shit to happen."

"Finally, I couldn't stand worrying about it anymore, so I went into the woods looking for the cabin or the stone. If I looked for the stone, I got lost and the trees seemed to work against me." Arnie held up his scratched arm. "I've hunted in these woods my whole life, but looking for the stone, I'd get turned around. Then, when I tried to find the cabin, there it was. And him, the old man, and his book."

Jason realized he wasn't afraid of Arnie at the moment, he was so caught up in the story.

"He'd been dead probably a week by the look and smell of him. This book was on the floor under his open hand, like he'd dropped it there. I just closed the bedroom door and left him in his bed. He was really old, I guess."

"Did you try to find the stone again?" Jason asked.

"No point. The book says you only find it if it wants you to find it. The old guy figures it was his brain chemistry or something, some kind of match for the stone. But I don't know, now that the stone picked you, I think it might be something else."

"Like what?"

Arnie shrugged. "From what I could see in this guy's cabin, Frank Talbot, was his name, he was a quiet, keep-to-himself, real smart kind of guy. Like you."

Jason flushed. He had only a small circle of friends and was known as a "brainiac" by the other kids.

"Arnie," Jason swallowed before bringing it up again, "when I, well you know, was in your head."

Arnie flashed him a dirty look before staring back out the windshield.

"Well, you're smart, really smart. You know it too. You know you'd do better in school if you didn't miss so much time and if you weren't so tired. And your old man—"

Arnie's head whipped toward him again.

"Yeah, I 'occupied' him just before you. Anyway, he knows

you're smart too. It's one of the things that scares him."

"Nothing scares that bastard."

"No. He's scared. He's scared you'll graduate and leave him to run the garage alone. He's scared of the alcohol because he's... sick. He's scared *not* to drink the alcohol, because it gets rid of the anger..." Jason trailed off because Arnie's eyes were huge.

"He's sick?"

"Yeah."

Arnie stared out the window a while then started the truck. They were almost to the garage before he spoke again. "I know about the anger. It's bad. I have it too, just like my old man."

"No," Jason dared to say. "Not like him at all."

Arnie drove past the garage.

"Where're you—"

"I'm driving you home. The book says the 'Astral' shit makes you real tired."

Jason was emboldened by this kind gesture. "You're not like him, Arnie. You can control it—he can't."

Arnie shrugged. "I control it most of the time. I've been losing it a bit with you lately."

Jason noticed he didn't apologize.

They pulled in to Jason's driveway. His Mom's car was there.

"Why? Why'd you get pissed at me?"

Arnie nodded at his mom's car. "At first I felt bad about your dad dying, so I thought I'd talk to you about it. Your mom's always so nice to me when she comes in to the garage." Arnie rubbed his eyes. "I was going down to geek alley, uh sorry, to the end where you guys hang out. I overheard you whining to your friends about how your mom makes you do all these extra chores now, and look after your sister and shit. And I snapped, man. I just snapped. You may have lost your dad, but you still had a mother. An awesome mother. I wanted to smash your face in ever since."

Still no apology.

Jason had felt a flash of anger when Arnie was talking, but thinking back to being in Hector's head, he felt it evaporate. No wonder Arnie wanted to smash him. Hell, sometimes lately he wanted to smash himself.

"Thanks for the lift," Jason reached for the door handle, but Arnie grabbed his arm.

~ Airborne ~

"Listen. You're okay, kid, but don't ever try to get in my fucking head again." Arnie applied pressure to his arm. "Got it?"

"Got it." Jason climbed out, clenching his jaw.

Arnie chuckled.

Jason stared at him.

"You're funny-looking when you're pissed off."

Jason flushed.

Arnie sighed. "This thing picked you, man. That's beyond fucking cool. Do something worthwhile with it, why don't ya? And...why don't you drop by the garage in a couple of days with your mom's car? It needs a lot of work."

Jason raised his eyebrows. "Uh, okay. I mean, I'll have to talk to Mom."

Arnie waved his hand at him. "We'll work out some kind of deal for the work." He looked thoughtful. "There's stuff I'd like to do besides work at the garage, you know." This time Arnie turned red.

Jason knew exactly what he meant but he just smiled and said. "Okay."

As he walked down his driveway, Jason thought about Arnie's dreams of working on airplanes. He'd have to graduate for that.

§

Jason watched the girl clutching her books as she walked toward him, head down. Despite the warm spring day, she wore a long-sleeved t-shirt and dark jeans. She was trying to be invisible. He heard her think that when he was in her head.

He thought back to floating into her room last night. He'd been drawn to her house, to her room. He hovered inside watching as she used a razor blade to make little tiny cuts on her arms and legs. Shivering, he'd entered her body.

Lisa trembled with delight as the pain slid deliciously through her. It felt so good to cut. Nobody at school would talk to her again tomorrow, except to mock her and push her and pull her hair.

She paused, blade over her skin, as a thought coalesced in her mind. *What if I make a friend? A real friend. I wouldn't need to hurt myself anymore.*

~ Airborne ~

"That's stupid," Lisa muttered out loud. "I suck at making friends."

I'm going to make a deal with myself. If I make a friend, one friend, I'll stop hurting myself.

She stared at the blade longingly, but the idea appealed to her more than the pain. She laid it on the table. "Okay," she said, "if one person talks to me tomorrow I won't cut myself tomorrow night." Smiling, she started to get ready for bed.

Jason surreptitiously watched Lisa walk toward his locker. He waited until she was flush with him and then whipped around, colliding with her.

Books and papers flew everywhere, his and hers.

Lisa froze, waiting for the inevitable attack or laughter that happened anytime anyone else knocked her stuff out of her arms.

Jason smiled as he started sorting out their things. "Sorry about that."

She just stood there.

"Aren't you going to help me?" Jason looked up at her, eyebrows arched.

Trembling, she knelt and began grabbing her things, eyeing him warily.

"Oops, I think this is yours. Hey, aren't you in my Biology class. Is your name...Lisa?"

Her eyes widened and she nodded. "Yeah."

"Cool. Listen, can I walk there with you? We're supposed to pick lab partners for the next assignment. Do you have a partner yet?"

Lisa shook her head *no*. Her cheeks flushed pink and a small smile pulled at her mouth.

Jason grinned, pleased with himself.

Since he'd been back to school, he'd helped a few kids. It felt good.

After school he was supposed to meet Arnie at the garage. He was catching Arnie up on school stuff and in exchange, Arnie was working on his mom's car. Arnie was picking stuff up fast and his marks had already started to improve.

One night during the week and for four hours on the weekend, Jason worked at the garage, covering for Arnie and making the same crappy wages. But it meant some pocket money for Jason, which was nice, and some extra sleep for Arnie, which

~ Airborne ~

was cool. His mom was thrilled with how well the car was running.

Sometimes, after his shift, Jason would walk into the woods behind the garage and go right to his spot. He could approach from anywhere now and a footpath would open up for him and lead him right to the stone. He didn't have to wade through water anymore. The stone was making it easier for him. Maybe it approved of his work. Or maybe it just looked forward to the Astral Travel more and more now.

Frank had written something about it in his journal. The stone seemed to respond to him more and more—as if they were bonding. Jason had his own theories. The fact that the stone had responded to more than one person made him think that he could find others who could use it too. He planned to try to take his sister to the stone in case it was genetic—if the stone let him, of course. He could tell her he was taking her fishing again. He'd taken her last weekend and she had loved it. His mom had given him a watery smile. Dad used to take them fishing all the time.

He told Arnie about it later at the garage when they were working on some math questions.

Arnie's eyebrows knitted for a minute. "Why do you want to take other people there? You gonna form some kind of super-kid club?" He said it with a tone of bitterness.

Jason shrugged and dropped it, returning to the math question. He felt bad. Arnie was no doubt still stinging over the fact that the stone wouldn't let him near it.

Later he visited the stone, standing a few feet away as it glowed invitingly. He wasn't sure he wanted to bring others there anyway. It made him feel a little...jealous thinking about it. But he was trying to get over it.

He had an important theory about the stone. He thought about the fact that every time he entered someone's mind he could not only leak information or thoughts to them, but when he left their mind he maintained all of their knowledge about whatever they had learned or observed during their life. He barely had to study at all anymore.

A society of people who could do that would learn faster, accomplish more, accelerating all progress in all disciplines. What he, and others like him, could do with the stone was limitless. There was only one thing that bothered him about these theories.

~ Airborne ~

Were they really his?

Staring at the stone's pearly sheen he decided it didn't worry him all that much. Kicking off his sneakers he leapt across to land on it in a crouch.

It pulsed in response and he smiled.

⁓⁓⁓

Previously an Associate Editor with The Scriptorium Webzine for Writers, Julie Serroul is now one third of the editorial triumvirate that is Third Person Press. Her writing floats around a couple of subgenres in the realm of Speculative Fiction, hovering often in the supernatural or paranormal. Her short stories have appeared online at *The Writer's Head E-zine* and the *Practically Creative Quarter*, and her non-fiction articles have appeared in *The Scriptorium Webzine*. Her short story "Sanctuary" won second place in the annual Conestoga Short Fiction Competition, and recently, her story "Letters to Mom" appeared in a magazine of dark urban fantasy called *Cover of Darkness*.

Julie now lives with her husband, children and yellow lab in a log home overlooking the Brasd'Or Lake, but spent most of her teen years swimming in and exploring the many branches of the Frenchvale Brook. Although she found several beautiful, nearly mystical swimming holes, none had a pearly white stone that allowed her astral travel. Or, if so, she's not telling...

~ *Airborne* ~

Is There Anybody Out There?

Never again. She could not believe she'd been so foolish, staying up until the wee hours with the latest crop of prospective students, quaffing copious amounts of draught beer and waxing eloquent on the wonders of astrophysics. What had she been thinking, overindulging on a Thursday night?

Now she stared at her dual workstation monitors and switched to the INDATA directory, relieved to see that overnight data acquisition had gone without a hitch. While she was getting sozzled with the students, the EAR had recorded hour after hour of data from the Universe and now it was all on disk, waiting for her to begin processing and analysis. Analysing it for something, *anything*, remotely promising.

After prepping the data, she would spend the rest of her day visually scanning the images, just as she had yesterday, and the day before and the day before that. Months of recording now, terabytes of data, thousands of images, and still nothing. Of course, SETI, the Search for Extraterrestrial Intelligence, had been listening to radio waves wafting through the universe for decades now, searching for signs of alien communication, and had heard nothing. Nada. Not a peep. Maybe humans were alone in the universe after all. The thought depressed her.

Sally MacIntosh, former world-class backpacker and cultural gadabout, had finally settled down and turned her mind to a different sort of exploration. Setting her sights on no less a target than the universe itself, she had rocketed through two astrophysics degrees and then launched into the Ph.D. program, only to find her research stalled.

She took a gulp of coffee and grimaced. Lukewarm and bitter.

Never mind. It gave her an excuse to walk across campus to Rundle Hall and get a decent coffee at that la-de-dah latte place. A stroll in the brisk spring air just might clear her head a bit. She tapped a few keys and fed the latest reams of raw data into her processing program so that her workstation could churn away while she mucked about getting coffee. She picked up her mug and turned to go.

What the...? A young man stood in the doorway of her office.

"Hi there! How are you doing this morning?" he said.

"I'm...uh, fine. Can I help you?" *Who was this guy?*

"You told me to drop by your office this morning. Around ten."

"I did? Oh, right. I guess I did. So uh, what time is it now...?" She glanced at her computer. *It's already ten o'clock?* "Well." She looked down at the dregs in her coffee mug. "Well, come on in then, uh..."

"Nasri. Nasri Qasim. We spoke last night at the student open house."

"Oh. Right. Well, pull up a seat." Sally sank back into her chair and watched as the young man slipped off his backpack and sat down. He was kind of cute. Those soulful brown eyes, that gleaming black hair and skin the colour of a cafe latte. *Ahh ...cafe latte...A latte would be sooo good right now...*

"Thanks for making time for me."

"Oh, no problem," she fibbed. "So, Nasri. Did you have a good time last night?"

Nasri grinned. "Yeah, it was great. You guys really know how to party!"

"And did we convince you to major in astrophysics next year?"

Nasri's grin morphed into a frown.

"I'm a *journalism* major. Third year. You agreed to let me interview you for the student newspaper. About your Ph.D. thesis."

"Of course. Just trying to lure you over to science. Have a seat."

Nasri sat down and began pulling gear out of his backpack. Sally stared at the tiny digital recorder in dismay. *An interview? Dear god.* She really did hate herself sometimes.

Nasri clicked on the recorder.

~ Airborne ~

"So, Sally MacIntosh, Ph.D. candidate in the Department of Astrophysics, tell me a bit about your research."

"Uh, sure. You mean the EAR data?"

"Yeah. You said something last night about transmissions from outer space."

"Greetings, Earthlings!"

Sally and Nasri jumped at the booming voice. A familiar hairy beanpole stood in the doorway.

"I'm heading over to Rundle Hall for coffee. Care to join me?"

The scruffy grey hair, thick beard, elongated limbs and oversized feet suggested a sasquatch. The thick accent suggested a sasquatch from New Zealand.

"Yes!" Sally cried.

"So who's this then?" the hairy Kiwi said, walking in and looking down at Nasri, a young man of mere human-sized dimensions.

"Nasri Qasim. I'm doing an article for the uniPress on women doing their doctorates in science. Sally is telling me about her work with the EAR."

"She is, is she? And what is she telling you about my EAR anyhow? I do hope it's nice."

Nasri looked up in confusion.

"Uh, *your* ear? Oh no, I'm sorry. What I mean is *the* EAR..."

Sally wiped her palms over her face and sighed.

"Nasri, meet Rupert. He built the EAR."

The gangly, hairy Kiwi was a scientific and engineering genius and generally acknowledged to be the smartest person in the whole department, if not the entire Faculty of Science. But Rupert was a Mister, not a Doctor, and by decree of academic hierarchy was an untenured and sparely-paid technician.

"Well, Nasri Qasim, would you like to see my EAR?"

Sally twitched. "But what about going for coff—?"

"I'd love to," said Nasri.

Rupert's hands, longer than Sally's feet, swept back the unruly bush of hair. He tipped his hoary head toward Nasri.

"There. Can you see it?"

"Lovely," Nasri said, smiling weakly at the rather large and very hairy ear.

"Well, the EAR looks a lot like that, only a bit bigger." He said it like 'biggah'.

~ Airborne ~

"Right. Well thanks. That's really helpful, Rupert," Nasri said.

The sasquatch laughed and his leathery face creased into a maze of wrinkles.

"Come on then. I'll show you the real thing."

Rupert turned and loped off down the hall in great strides, leaving Nasri to gather his gear and scamper off in pursuit. Sally caught up with them at the elevator bank.

"So what does this EAR do?" Nasri was asking Rupert.

"It detects psiwaves," Rupert said.

"Oh, of course," Nasri said. He paused and then turned to Sally. "And what exactly are psiwaves?"

"Good question," Sally answered. "And if we go for coffee I will be happy to answer it."

That was actually a lie. She wasn't at all happy to answer Nasri's question. In fact, she was beginning to wish she'd never heard of psiwaves. It was all very well for her supervising professor, Dr. Robert Livingstone, to dabble about on the fringes of mainstream science—he had a solid academic reputation for his work in galaxy evolution, and more importantly, he had tenure. But why did he have to drag *her* along on his quixotic quest?

Nasri and Rupert watched Sally's retreating figure, shrugged, and followed her down the wide staircase to the main floor of the physics building. Sally pushed through the double set of heavy glass doors and out into the crisp air. The trio strolled along the wide, paved pathway toward Rundle Hall. Spring was busting out all over. The last of winter's snow had fled and the newly exposed lawn was tickled green. Trees leafed with exuberance. Songbirds, back from tropical adventures, serenaded a few students lounging on the grass and pretending to study.

The food fair in Rundle Hall was teeming with students cramming for final exams. Rupert, Sally and Nasri bought their coffees and then fled the clamour and glaring fluorescent lights in favour of a sunny alcove on the south side of the building.

"Ah, heavenly," Sally said as she plopped down on the grass next to Rupert and leaned back against the concrete wall. Nasri sat cross-legged in front of them and rummaged through his backpack for his recorder and notepad.

"Okay, so tell me about these psiwaves," he said, clicking on the recorder.

~ Airborne ~

"Ah yes," Sally said. "Well, it's a hypothetical wave used to describe the transmission of psychic energy."

Nasri's black eyebrows shot up.

"*Psychic* energy?"

Sally bristled. "It's a legitimate area of scientific research!" she snapped. Then she sighed. "But it's true that a lot of the research results on telepathy aren't all that convincing—only slightly better than chance."

Nasri's eyebrows settled back down.

"But Sam Doolittle, a physicist at U of Y, took a different approach. He hypothesized that humans emit a psychic field, kind of like we give off heat. But this field is so weak that we can't detect it without special equipment. And it's not anything we can sense."

She inhaled the sweet aroma of her hazelnut coffee and took a sip of the steaming liquid.

"Well," Nasri said, looking up from his notebook, "I suppose some people *claim* they can—or they claim to be psychic, anyhow."

"Not using the five senses," Rupert pointed out. "Hence the *sixth* sense, or *extra*-sensory perception—ESP."

"But just because we can't sense something doesn't mean it doesn't exist," Sally said. "I mean, the Earth is swarming with electromagnetic radiation—radio waves, UV rays, X-rays, gamma rays, the whole kit and caboodle. We just weren't aware of it until recently because we could only detect a tiny fraction of the EM spectrum—the rainbow part we call visible light."

"Although some insects and birds can see UV light," Rupert mused as he watched a bee buzz by in search of succulent flowers.

Sally gestured towards the campus rooftops with their bristling antennae.

"Radio waves always existed but we couldn't detect them until Hertz invented a transmitter *and* a receiver. The receiver is important. I mean, imagine transmitting a radio signal to a stone-age tribe in the jungle. The radio signal exists, but if our tribe doesn't have an antenna and a radio, well, they won't be groovin' to the Dead, will they?"

"The who?"

"The Who then," Sally nodded. "Same difference. Either way

~ Airborne ~

—no radio, no rock 'n roll."

"Uh...right," said Nasri, frowning.

"So Doolittle invented a device that can detect psiwave energy and convert it into an electrical signal."

"You can do anything with an electrical signal," said Rupert. "Amplify it, digitize it, filter it, rasterize it—all sorts of fun things."

"Okay, so psiwaves are basically like a radio wave but at a different frequency?"

"Nah, not that simple, I'm afraid," Sally said. "Otherwise we'd already know about them. It's just an analogy. We use waves as a way to describe the transmission of EM radiation, sound, seismic energy, even gravity. But psiwaves? Different pot of lobsters and not at all understood. It's still early days, little grasshopper."

Rupert stood up and brushed the grass off his trousers.

"Come on then, if you want to see the EAR," he said. "Some of us have work to do."

Nasri packed up his gear and Sally put the lid back on her coffee, glad that she had ordered the 'extremely huge' size. The three of them set off along the winding pathway back towards the physics building.

"I'm thinking," Nasri said, "that maybe our so-called primitive tribe would be better than we are at sending and picking up psiwaves."

"Huh?" Sally said.

"Maybe our ancestors had better developed senses, like smell, that have atrophied in modern humans. Maybe we *could* detect psiwaves at one time. Maybe..." Nasri's eyes lit up. "Maybe the advent of *language* meant we didn't need telepathic communication, so it just kind of wasted away."

"Holy moly, young fella. You're out of my league on that one. You'd better find a woman doing a doctorate in anthropology and ask *her* about that."

"Naw," said Nasri. "This article is on women in *science*."

Sally and Rupert both laughed. They arrived back at the physics building and moseyed over to the elevator bank. Sally punched the up arrow. Worlds were born and stars died while they waited.

"But seriously guys," Nasri said, "you're talking about telepathy here. That sounds more like astral-psychics than astrophysics to me."

~ Airborne ~

Rupert chuckled. Sally seethed and thought back to the the previous winter, when she'd first heard about psiwaves.

§

Sally was hunched over her computer late one night wrestling with the final nit-picky details of her M.Sc. thesis when Dr. Robert Livingstone bounced into her office with a journal clasped in his hand.

"Sally! Have you seen this?"

Sally looked up with blurred eyes. She had seen nothing except graphs, equations, figures, captions, tables, footnotes and citations since time began.

"Look!" he yelped, pulling up a chair beside her and flipping on a bright light that made Sally blink. He slapped a paper down on her desk.

Anthropogenic psiwave detection using an antihelical apparatus.

"Psiwave?" Sally squeaked. In her undergraduate physics courses she had studied every kind of wave known to science, derived and solved the wave equation *ad nauseum*, manipulated waveforms using Fourier analysis, been flummoxed by the wave/particle nature of photons. But she had no recall of a psiwave.

The good professor told her about Doolittle's work and his enthusiasm began to tentacle its way into her zombified consciousness. He jabbed at a figure with his forefinger.

"This is the image that Doolittle's assistant—who claimed to have zero psychic ability—transmitted just by sitting in front of the psiwave detector and concentrating on a picture."

Sally looked at the image. It was blurry but vaguely familiar.

"Then Doolittle did some image enhancement, and *voila!*" Dr. Bob turned the page.

Sally's emotions sprinted from surprise to confusion to disgust in a few milliseconds. She was looking at the world-famous logo of a gargantuan multinational corporation in all its mega-million dollar glory. Dr. Bob giggled.

"That's right, Sal. Turns out that the corporation provided a significant chunk of Doolittle's funding. But that's not the point! The point is it worked!"

~ Airborne ~

Sally stared at the logo, scepticism oozing out of her pores. It would be so easy to fake such an experiment. It struck her as an elaborate publicity stunt by the mega-corporation.

Sally MacIntosh had not been alone in her cynicism. Cries of outrage erupted when the corporate logo was featured in Doolittle's seminal paper. Outraged cries about the logo were drowned by much louder outraged cries that the whole experiment was either a hoax or really bad science or both because every *real* scientist knew that telepathy was just a bunch of new-age paranormal bunkum along with crop circles and UFOs and astrology and poltergeists and spoon-bending charlatans. Much controversy ensued. Utterly unconvinced sceptics made it clear that those who *were* convinced were unscientific, gullible rubes. On the other side, the utterly convinced accused the utterly unconvinced of being *un*scientific, close-minded bigots.

Nonetheless, researchers all over the world raced to reproduce Doolittle's work, or in the case of the utterly unconvinced, to fail to reproduce it, thus debunking all of this telepathic nonsense so that they would be justified in crucifying Doolittle on the cross of hubris and scientific heresy. Psiwaves? Humbug!

And Sally the sceptical? She had been converted to the ranks of the convinced and was now forced her to endure the taunts of cheeky student reporters.

§

The elevator finally arrived and inched open grudgingly. They shuffled in and Rupert punched 5. The elevator groaned and crept upwards as if put out about having to work so hard.

"The thing is, Nasri," Rupert said, "our illustrious department head has rather eclectic interests. He was quick to grasp the universal potential of psiwave research."

"Dr. Bob—uh, Dr. Livingstone—decided the Department of Astrophysics should build our own telepathic detector," Sally said. "So Rupert here reverse-engineered the design from Doolittle's paper and scrounged enough scraps to put together a prototype. They tested it on humans and, Rupert being so brilliant and all—"

"Don't forget handsome," Rupert interjected.

~ Airborne ~

"—the EAR passed with flying colours."

The success of the EAR experiment some months earlier put Dr. Bob's team ahead of the pack. The results were quickly written up and submitted to science journals; abstracts were sent off to upcoming conferences. Dr. Bob set his team to work, devoting massive amounts of time and energy and brainpower towards attaining the ultimate academic goal—Research Grants.

The elevator arrived at the fifth floor with a jolt. The door edged open and reluctantly released them. Rupert led the way down the hall and unlocked a heavy metal door.

"All very impressive," Nasri said, "but I still don't see the connection to astrophysics."

They followed Rupert up a short flight of stairs to a second locked door. Rupert opened it and they stepped out onto the flat rooftop.

"Well?" Rupert demanded.

"I see what you mean," Nasri said.

The EAR was large and hairy and did bear a vague resemblance to the one attached to Rupert's head. It perched on a tower and lay on its side as if listening to the universe.

"Everyone else is studying human telepathy," Sally said. "But we pointed our detector up." She pointed to the heavens. "We're listening for psiwave transmissions from outer space."

Nasri turned to her, his dark eyes dilating.

"Are you talking about...*aliens*?"

Sally nodded.

"Ahhh. Sort of like SETI?"

"Exactly!" said Sally. *Cute and clever!*

"*Contact*," Nasri admitted, looking a wee bit abashed. "Jodie Foster fan."

"Ah. Well, read the book and you'll be a fan of the late, great Carl Sagan, too. So, the Search for Extra Terrestrial Intelligence listens for radio transmissions, on the assumption that any technologically advanced species will have discovered how to detect and transmit radio waves.

"But we think radio transmissions are primitive technology compared to telepathic transmissions. An intelligent species is more likely to beam psiwaves into space, reaching out to other advanced species. We haven't heard from the aliens because we haven't figured out how to listen. We're like the stone-age tribe without a radio."

They walked over to the chain link fence surrounding the EAR and Rupert unlocked the gate. Nasri pulled a camera out of his backpack and walked around the EAR snapping photos.

"You know, Rupert," he said, "if you ever get tired of science you could switch to the Faculty of Fine Arts and major in modern sculpture."

He climbed a few steps up a scaffolding for a closer look.

"Is that one of those old satellite dishes?"

"Yes. It focuses the signal," Rupert said as he leaned over to check wires and connections. "I got it for free from a farmer. And those hairy things on its edge are fibre optic cables tipped with our psiwave detectors."

Nasri hopped down and Rupert showed him a large funnel welded to the base of the dish.

"The signal goes through here and along this copper coil—got that from an old heat exchanger—and down to the room below to the A/D converter and amplifier and recording system—all rejects from the geophysics department. I can show you if you like."

"Uh, that's okay, Rupert. I think that's enough technical detail for now."

Nasri walked over to a low concrete riser where Sally sat, sipping her coffee and soaking up sunbeams.

"So, Sally, the EAR works for humans, but how do you know it will work for aliens?"

"We don't. We—"

"That's why they're called experiments," noted Rupert, adjusting the coil. "We don't know ahead of time if they'll work." He said it like 'woook.'

Nasri was nothing if not fearless. He confronted the towering sasquatch. "Yes, all right. But if you *do* get something, how do you know it's *not* from humans? I mean, maybe that thing is picking up stuff from us right now."

"It's not. It's shielded from below and it's high enough up on this rooftop that there are no buildings within its receiver aperture. But even if it did, Sally is a very clever scientist and has written a program to filter out any signals that originate from humans."

"Oh?" Nasri turned back to Sally.

She nodded. "Part of my dissertation."

~ Airborne ~

Sally had planned to study gamma ray bursts—a very sexy topic—for her doctorate. But Dr. Bob wanted the shining star of the graduate program to join him in his quest for the new Holy Grail—telepathic communication with intelligent extra-terrestrials.

The charismatic professor wooed her with the proposition that she would be the ideal candidate to write a processing stream for the hoped-for extra-terrestrial transmissions. He seduced her with visions of being the very first person on the planet Earth, the first person in the whole *history* of the planet Earth, to receive a genuine, documented, alien communication. And she, innocent and easily flattered and with the ink still fresh on her M.Sc., had fallen for his charms. *What a joke.* She sighed and stood up.

"Come on back to my office," she told Nasri, "and I'll show you."

§

Sally and Nasri took the stairs instead of the reluctant elevator to save time. A few minutes later Nasri was sitting beside Sally, notebook and recorder ready.

"Like I said, we tested Rupert's EAR on humans first," Sally said. "Dr. Bob wanted to avoid Goulding's goof of using a famous logo, so he recruited a really obscure department with no connections to the Faculty of Science. The Department of Classics —"

Nasri glanced up from his notebook. "We still have one of those?"

"Yup," said Sally, reflecting that the world might be better off with more classicists and fewer MBAs. "Anyhow, the whole fourth year class—all three of them—sat facing the EAR and concentrated on an image of their own choosing. Something totally arcane that no one would ever suspect."

She tapped a few keys and used the mouse to select an image file.

Nasri pulled his chair closer to the monitor and frowned. The grey-scale image was, at first blush, rather blurry and indistinct.

"Am I supposed to be able to tell what that is?" he asked.

"Not quite yet. The fuzz in the background is just psiwave

~ Airborne ~

static, what we call noise. But I can do some image processing that brings out the part we want—the psiwave signal—like this...”

At second blush the image was somewhat clearer.

“...and finally this!” The final blush was rosy indeed.

“Not exactly a corporate logo, eh?” Sally prompted.

The image processing cleaned up the bizarre image enough to reveal a swan mounting a naked woman.

“Zeus and Leda. The high muckity-muck of the Greek gods morphs into a swan and has his way with the lovely, lusty mortal. Guess those classics students have a sense of humour, albeit a pretty perverse one,” Sally said. *Was young Nasri blushing under his caramel skin?*

“Okay,” he mumbled, scribbling something in his notebook. “But what was this ‘Sally is a clever scientist’ thing that you did?”

“Right. Well, I wrote a program to filter out any human psiwave contamination from the EAR data. First, I had to characterize the anthropogenic psiwave signal. So the human psiwave transmissions are converted to an electrical signal, and then I used Fourier analysis to break it down into its constituent sine waves with various amplitudes, wavelengths and phase delays and then—”

“Whoa!” Nasri interrupted, throwing up his hands. “Journalism major, remember?”

“Oh. Okay. Well, I’ll just show you. So, now you see Zeus cavorting with Leda, yes?”

“’Fraid so.”

“I run this image through my filtering program and...abra-cadabra!” She pulled up another image.

Nasri peered at the fuzz that remained, searching for signs of bestiality. “They’re gone,” he said.

“Exactly. We’re hypothesizing that alien psiwaves will have a different signature than ours. Any images that pass through my filter unaffected must be of non-human origin.”

§

Sally sat alone in front of her monitors after Nasri left, sipping lukewarm coffee and scanning the images that had been processed that morning. Nothing. Just blurry images that were all psiwave static and no signal. The enthusiasm she mustered for the interview with Nasri had dissipated and now she felt as she had so often these last few weeks—discouraged and bored. She had barely started her Ph.D. and she was already a jaded academic. Even worse, she was a hungry, jaded academic. She would finish this set of images and then grab some lunch.

The last image in the series started to load. Sally stared at the picture appearing on the screen. Her hand jerked and a few drops of hazelnut coffee splashed onto the keyboard. There was something there.

She tried reloading the image, and stared some more. There was *definitely* something there. Beyond fuzzy static she could see some vague geometric shapes. Lineations, rectangles, irregular blobs. She checked the previous image again. Only noise. But on this image, there they were—faint, but indisputably present. Her heart rate accelerated.

Shit. Slow down, Sally. She must have screwed up. No wonder, considering the condition her condition was in. She checked the log file for errors, rescanned the raw data, reran her filtering program. Her heart beat even faster. The lines and blobs and rectangles passed through the filter virtually unchanged. Sally forgot to breathe. The shapes were not removed by the filtering program.

The image on her computer screen was not human in origin.

§

Dr. Bob and Sally sat rapt in front of the monitors staring at the faint geometric shapes and blobs and lineations. Sally worked on the image, sharpening edges, deblurring, upping the contrast, tweaking. Dr. Bob looked on, offering the odd suggestion or comment.

"That's it," said Sally at last. "I'll try reprocessing it with different parameters, but I think this is the best we can do for now."

Dr. Bob beamed so brightly that Sally's eyes began to ache.

"D'you know what this means, Sally?" Dr. Bob asked, his eyes bugging.

Sally did her best to beam back. Did this seminal moment *have* to happen on a day when she felt like an extra in a zombie movie?

~ Airborne ~

"This means," Dr. Bob paused for effect, "this means that *we are not alone!*"

He stood up and walked over to the window. The import of the statement hit Sally and she rose slowly and joined him. They looked out and up at the clear blue sky. Everything looked so... ordinary. It seemed impossible, dreamlike, an hallucination. And yet...

The glare of sunshine hurt. Sally looked away. It was all too much. Extra-terrestrial transmissions were all very well, but she needed some time to absorb the enormity of it. She was about to suggest that they discuss the whole extraordinary business over a late lunch when Dr. Bob reached out and embraced her in a bear hug. She hugged back. There was nothing sexual or improper about it. Indeed, it was the natural reaction of two fellow *homo sapiens sapiens* clinging to each other in the face of the overwhelming realization that they were in communication with intelligent extra-terrestrials. Dr. Bob was overwhelmed with euphoric anticipation. Sally was overwhelmed with apprehension —and a whiff of existential nausea.

§

Dr. Bob sprang into action. Astoundingly for a Friday afternoon, the department secretary managed to track down three of the EAR team members. They hovered around Sally's workstation and stared at the image.

"What you are seeing," said Dr. Bob, his voice brimming with excitement, "is the first scientifically-recorded transmission from outer space. *This,*" he exclaimed, sweeping his hand towards one of the monitors, "is proof that there *are* other intelligent life forms out there. *We are not alone in the Universe!*"

The team gawked and babbled, all in a state of shock.

"It's the campus from above," said Rupert. Everyone stopped mumbling and stared even harder at the image.

"That rectangle is our building," he said, sticking a finger on the screen. Sally cringed. She hated greasy fingerprints on her computer monitors. "And this one over here is the edge of Rundle Hall and there's part of the Engineering building—"

"And those blobs are the poplar trees seen from above!" blurted Sally, forgetting about the greasy fingerprints as she suddenly saw it.

Rupert leaned over Sally's shoulder and peered closely at the image. He pointed and stuck his long finger on a small circular shape in the middle of a rectangle.

"And that thingy there must be the EAR," he said.

"Oh my god," someone murmured, and everyone reflexively looked out the window and up, as if expecting to see an alien spaceship hovering directly overhead. But there was nothing except the new, bright green leaves sprouting on the trees and a few clouds blobbing along against the blue sky. The birds and the bees and the flowers and the trees. The same-old, same-old planet Earth.

"They're watching us," said Jeannie, the team's systems analyst, her voice fractured with fear.

"Who," asked Rupert, "are *they*?"

§

"Is this for real?" Nasri asked, his beautiful, brown eyes wide. "Or are you having me on?"

"Trust me, Naz, this is no joke."

"Why isn't this front page news, Sally?"

"Oh, it will be. But we need to confirm our results and then present them to the scientific community for peer review and—"

"You can't keep this to yourselves! It's outrageous. It's...unethical. People have a right to know that aliens are communicating with Earth!"

"Hey, take it easy, my friend. We can't go blurting this out willy-nilly. I'm working on an abstract right now, a summary of our work, including a copy of the image we received," she explained, gesturing towards her laptop. "We'll send that out to various scientific associations and present the data at the first possible opportunity."

"Sally, people need to know about this *now*, not next week or next month or next year. Can't you see that?"

"Yeah, but how much credibility will we have if our work hasn't been scrutinized by the scientific community? Remember cold fusion? The university has a responsibility to—oh crap, listen to me. Naz, I'm famished. Want to continue this discussion over a quick bite at Rundle Hall?"

~ Airborne ~

"Sure," Nasri agreed.

They headed down the stairs and out the door.

"Damn!" Nasri said. "I left my notebook in your office. I'll be right back."

Sally waited for him, thinking about what Nasri had said. Truth was, she agreed with him. The first contact from aliens *should* be a shared global experience. But what could she do? She was part of an academic establishment that followed a certain proscribed protocol. Her hands were tied. She decided to bring up her concerns with Dr. Bob pronto. As it turned out, pronto was too late.

§

The pilfered image of the alien transmission appeared on Nasri's blog and quickly went viral, catapulting him into the upper reaches of the blogosphere with billions of hits. People all over the world Googled the image and argued over what it might mean. Earthlings who believed that the image was a genuine alien transmission were either very nervous or very excited or both. Not everyone believed, of course. Most people found it easier to dismiss this as they had dismissed Doolittle's work: as a hoax or bad science or both. On the other hand, worldwide UFO sightings increased 42,000 percent soon after the story and the images hit the internet.

Theories abounded. Questions cavorted. Where did the aliens get those pictures anyhow? Had they tapped into Earth's satellites or Google Earth or did they just have *really* good telescopes? Were the ETs saying 'We seeeee you'? Or...more disturbingly, were they hovering close by, invisible to the human eye and to radar, and saying 'We're heee-ere'?

Sally worked feverishly, preparing scientific abstracts and papers while continuing to scan the incoming data. She was furious with Nasri for snatching her files and banned the lad from her office. True, she wanted to share the images with the world, but through the EAR team—not some upstart journalism student. Nasri had cited her in his blog all right, but that had just led to a ruckus in the administration about lax security in the department, and Sally got a scolding. Jeannie battened down the hatches. And when hundreds and then thousands of unread emails inundated Sally's campus email box, Jeannie set up a special EAR-spam filter. Only Dr. Bob, never publicity-shy, was unperturbed by all the fuss.

The irrepressible professor sat in Sally's office one morning. They had just spent an hour poring over the many upcoming conferences where they could present their research, selecting those which were (a) the most prestigious and (b) in the nicest possible locations ('Look! The Australian Society of Astrophysics is having their annual convention in Bali in November.')

"Before you go," she said, "there's a new image I want to show you." The latest transmission zoomed in on the EAR and it made Sally nervous.

"Do you think they're maybe zeroing in on us? Is the EAR in the cross-hairs of their Death Ray?" she asked, joking to hide her genuine anxiety.

"Nonsense," laughed Dr. Bob. "If they wanted to kill us they would have by now. Besides, if they had bad intentions, why would they warn us that they're out there and that they see us? Think about it, Sally. If you were planning to attack a building, would you broadcast the fact that it's a target?"

Maybe, Sally thought. *If I knew that the target had absolutely no hope of protecting itself.* If the aliens saw the EAR as just a funny-looking bulls-eye, then she, in her office three stories below, was in danger of being vaporized. Or worse.

Part of what disturbed her was that the images were so cold and clinical. Observations sent by unknown beings who viewed Earth with the detachment of...well, of scientists. She was reminded of those dreadful first year biology labs, poking and prodding at specimens without regard for the sentience of the hapless creatures under observation. Her distaste for those labs had, in part, helped her lean towards a career in physics, all clean and pristine and endowed with its elegant language of mathematics. No more pithed frogs for her!

Now it was the humans under observation. But by whom?

§

Within days a very different sort of picture appeared on her screen. The transformation in imagery was breath-taking. Lineations and tree blobs were replaced by sweeps and swirls,

~ Airborne ~

spirals and splashes and splotches. As always, the images were grey-scale, so Sally worked frantically through the night experimenting with colour bars that painted each pixel according to intensity. Why not? The startling images of nebulae from the Hubble telescope were coloured by the scientists to make them more vivid.

Stoked on caffeine and adrenaline, Sally felt more artist than scientist, collaborating with an extraterrestrial Jackson Pollack, apprenticing to an alien Jean-Paul Riopelle. The abstract-expressionist images evoked feelings of joy and passion in her rapidly beating heart.

Hope and excitement unseated earlier feelings of fear and apprehension. These elegant whirls, these undulating sweeps, these zigs and zags and spirals and swirls—these inspired, they intrigued. Who were the authors of this Rorschach ink blot of telepathy? And what did it mean?

Sally was so entranced by her work that she took little notice of men in black prowling the department hallways. She was oblivious to Dr. Bob's scowl when he emerged from a meeting in the Dean's office. She only looked up from her computer when she heard a tentative knock.

"Hey there," said Nasri, peering around her office door and holding out a large cappuccino as a peace offering.

"Scram, you thief!" she yelped and jumped up, slamming the door closed.

The door opened a few seconds later.

"I'm calling security!" she hollered.

"Why? What did I do now?" Rupert asked as he wandered in.

"Oh, it's you."

"So, who are the suits?"

"What suits? Oh, those guys. I don't know. Maybe they came to arrest Nasri for stealing my thunder."

Jeannie came in a moment later and Sally started to feel a bit crowded.

"Oh good. You're both here," she said. "Sally, someone's been trying to hack into your files."

Sally leapt out of her chair, ran to the door, and peered up and down the hallway. Nasri moped around a display case, drinking the peace offering.

"Get in here!" she ordered.

~ Airborne ~

An intensive grilling by Rupert, Jeannie and Sally convinced them that Nasri wasn't the would-be hacker. But if not Nasri, then who?

Dr. Bob, face red and eyes fierce, popped his head around the doorjamb.

"Don't worry, team," he declared, his voice darkly ominous. "I will not let them shut us down. Academic freedom shall prevail." Then he noticed Nasri sitting on a chair in the centre of the room, ringed by his interrogators.

"Oh, hi there, Nasri. Yes! Long live Freedom of the Press!" Then the professor winked, nodded, and whipped off down the hallway.

Sally flopped back in her chair and stared up the ceiling. *What's going on? And furthermore, what's that little thingamabob on the ceiling?*

"Rupert?" she asked, flicking her head upwards.

He looked up at the ceiling.

"The aliens aren't the only ones watching us," he said. He rummaged around in his voluminous trouser pocket, pulled out a roll of electrical tape, then reached up and deftly covered the pinhole.

Well. That settled it. Sally sat up and stared at Nasri.

"Give me that," she said, taking what was left of the cold cappuccino. "I'm going to need it. Jeannie, Rupert, you guys better skedaddle. I don't want you to be in the line of fire. There's about to be another security lapse."

§

Soon the brilliant, swirling images whirled around the globe. The blogosphere reacted as Sally had, with delight and astonishment. Deniers felt tugged; they wanted to believe. Believers were swept with religious ecstasy. Everything, from screensavers to T-shirts to posters to tattoos, displayed the elegant alien transmissions. Physicists, mathematicians, psychics, linguists, cryptologists, cosmologists, spiritualists, computer scientists, abstract artists, psychologists and thousands of ordinary netizens pored over the alien images, hypothesizing, deliberating, guessing, pronouncing, and shrugging their shoulders.

~ Airborne ~

It was heady stuff. But what did any of it mean? And how could life as they knew it go on in light of communication from outer space?

§

Sally pulled up the most recent image, downloaded only fifteen minutes earlier. It was late on a Friday afternoon and she was just about ready to call it quits and get some well-earned rest. The image scrolled. Sally stared. Cursing alien timing but intrigued, Sally peered at the screen. This was a new development. Dr. Bob was in Rio (Rio!) giving a lecture on the first EAR experiment. She glanced at the phone. It might be tapped.

Sally jumped up and ran down the hall, careening down three flights of stairs to the basement and along the dimly-lit hall to the corner where Rupert's office lurked in the shadows of academia.

"You're still here," she blurted.

Rupert looked at Sally, then looked himself up and down, and back at Sally.

"It would seem so," he said.

"Come and see this."

A few minutes later they stared at the monitor. Something vaguely circular, with three smaller ovoids inside the circle, filled most of the image.

"They're intensifying the level of communication," she told Rupert. "First the aerial shots of the campus to let us know they exist and that they know where *we* are. And, more precisely, where the EAR is. Then the Pollack swirls, and who knows what that was about, except maybe to make us feel better about them. I mean, how do you put happiness and joy into a 2D picture, into bits and bytes?"

"It's as good an explanation as any," said Rupert.

"So now we get this—three ovals within a circle. It's some kind of a symbol, Rupe. I just know it!"

"A symbol of what?"

"I don't know; probably something geometrical. You know, mathematics as the universal language and all that."

"A circular outline and three ovals. Something to do with pi, perhaps?"

~ Airborne ~

"*Contact* again? Maybe they saw the movie. Maybe they like Jodie Foster too," Sally mused.

"Or maybe a pictorial language. Like Chinese characters, or Egyptian hieroglyphs."

"Yeah! After all, we sent symbolic images on the Pioneer and Voyageur space probes to represent life on Earth. And pictures are the only thing we can pick up with our primitive detector."

"Hey! That's my EAR you're talking about. Now you've hurt my feelings."

"Sorry. I'll buy you a beer to make up."

"Well, you could give me a kiss and make it better."

Sally pecked him on his hairy cheek.

"Better? I'm going to clean this baby up a bit. I'll give you a call when I'm done."

Sally got to work. She deblurred and sharpened edges and thickened lines until the outer edge was crisp and circular and the ovoids set nicely in the centre. She chose contrasting colours to highlight the contrasting shapes—a bit of artistic licence.

An hour later, Rupert sat beside Sally and looked at the massaged and processed output. A thick, sharp red circle surrounded three vivid, cyan-blue ovals against a magenta background. It looked like something a human might design, something that you might see anywhere, some kind of...

"I know!" Rupert announced. "It's a logo! The corporate logo of the aliens."

Sally's eyes bugged. *That's exactly what it looks like. A logo.*

§

Dr. Bob assembled the team as soon as he got back from Rio.

"The Others have sent us a message," Dr. Bob said. "We should send them a reply."

"But we don't know what the message means," said Jeannie.

"We still need to let them know we received it. I propose that we orchestrate a giant telepathic transmission."

"Huh?" said the team.

"We could coordinate it through the Internet," Dr. Bob continued, gaining steam. "Imagine! Thousands, maybe *millions*, of people focusing on the same image at the same time, and sending a psiwave message into outer space.

~ Airborne ~

"And we need to do it soon," he added. "There are powers from above—and I don't mean the aliens—who would like to shut us down and take control. Remember Roswell."

Sally nodded. Three of her abstracts had been rejected by conference committees before the submission deadline had even passed. It smelled rather smelty.

The team spent the rest of the meeting discussing the most appropriate symbol. Not, it was roundly agreed, the university logo. Towards the end of the meeting, the discussion became heated but, as usual, Dr. Bob prevailed.

"It's perfect because of its simplicity," he explained. "Plus, it's representative of us, and it's universally understood."

"Well," Rupert demurred, "you *hope* it's universally understood. Depends a bit on whether our new friends resemble us, doesn't it?"

Dr. Bob snorted. "*Touché*. I guess from now on we'll have to be more precise. 'Universally' just took on a whole new reality. So let me rephrase that—it's a symbol which is *globally* understood."

Sally said nothing. She couldn't believe they were sending *this* to the aliens who had sent them the soaring beauty of the Pollack swirls. They would think humans were a bunch of morons.

§

The Grand Transmission Experiment took place at noon, UT, May 1, 2012. Humans from around the globe, alerted via Nasri's blog, Twitter, email and the good ol' grapevine spent fifteen seconds concentrating on the chosen image. And just what was this glorious premiere greeting that a briefly united band of Earthlings chose to send to their extraterrestrial neighbours?

A happy face!

§

After the Grand Transmission Experiment, Sally was welded to her workstation. How fast did psiwaves travel? At the speed of light? And could weakly developed human telepathy even penetrate the vast distances of space? Or was transmission instantaneous, some kind of quantum phenomenon? There was so much still to learn.

Sally sat on the edge of her seat for two weeks before the breakthrough—a new message. She squinted at the grainy image. It retained the blurry circular outline, but the ovals had been replaced by three new shapes. Elongated ovals, pointed at each end. The shapes had a pale perimeter and a dark interior. In the centre was a vague hint of something odd, almost face-like.

"What are you guys trying to tell me?" she murmured, and then the full import of her question struck her. She was having a conversation—of sorts—with an alien species. The thought was breathtaking, overwhelming. She phoned Rupert but there was no answer, and Rupert eschewed cell phones. She left an urgent voice message—phone tap be damned. Who else was around? Dr. Bob was in Paris (Paris!) lecturing on the EAR, and the department was all but deserted on this beautiful Friday afternoon in May. *Friday again!*

Sally set to work cleaning up the image. She could scarcely believe, as she tweaked and tidied, that *she*, a mere doctoral student, was the translator for the first interstellar conversation. Admittedly, not a very good translator—she didn't have a clue what the 'Others' were saying. *Take those first fumbling attempts at communication between explorers and aboriginals and multiply it by...what? A gazillion? At least.*

"Who are you?" she whispered as she worked, using the same processing techniques as she had on the first symbol. "*Where* are you? And what are you saying?"

She worked quickly, smoothing out roughness, defuzzing and deblurring, sharpening edges, increasing contrast, adding colour. Then she displayed both alien symbols side by side, one on each monitor. On the left screen were the three ovals within a circle. On the right were the three pointy outlines with dark centres, also within the same larger circle.

And in-between these separate alien messages the Earthlings had sent out the happy face. Not a human body or even a human face, just the most basic symbolic representation. Two dots and an arc placed within a circle. But crude as it was, newborn infants responded to a happy face, while ignoring the same elements arranged in a different configuration. So a symbol could be crude and still transmit vital information. She looked at the circle with its three ovals.

~ Airborne ~

"So what do *you* guys look like? Is this, like, *your* face? Or more like a family photo?" Sally laughed at the thought. Had these advanced aliens evolved into...what...eggs? Eggs and now, these odd, pointy shapes.

"Ms. MacIntosh."

Sally started. She looked at the doorway where Rupert stood, big hands on the doorframe as he leaned in to her office.

"Oh hey, Rupert, you're here—great. Listen, there's a new one! Come and have a look at this."

"Sally, you'd better come with me. There's something I need to show you."

"Eh? Uh, okay, sure. But come and see this first. Tell me what you think it means."

Rupert sauntered over. He loomed over her, looking at her monitors.

"Any ideas?" she asked after he'd stared at the images in silence for a few moments.

"Yes, as a matter of fact," he replied lightly.

She turned from the monitors and gawped up at him.

"Well, don't hold back. *What*?" she demanded.

"Come on. I've got something to show you."

Sally began to protest, but something in his pale blue eyes and kindly, wrinkled face told her there was no point. She stood up and followed him out the door into the hallway.

"Where are you taking me?" she asked as they waited by the elevator.

"To my leader," he joked. Once inside the ancient elevator he punched 5.

"To your leader," she echoed, "or to your EAR?" There was no other reason to go to the roof.

Rupert laughed as he watched the lights above the doors monitor their ponderous upward progress.

"Yes. I'm taking you to my EAR."

"Is something wrong?" Sally had a bad feeling about this. Rupert looked away from the display and smiled softly at Sally.

"No, not really. Depends how you look at it, I suppose."

"Rupert...what *is* it?"

But they had arrived, the doors lurched open, and Rupert sloped off to the stairwell. They climbed the stairs up to the roof. Rupert unlocked the door and they stepped outside.

~ Airborne ~

The brilliant sun beamed at them and Sally squinted back, grateful for the freshening rooftop breeze. She looked at the EAR, surrounded by its locked chain link fence. It looked fine, its asymmetrical elongated funnel reaching skyward, the open end of the EAR listening to the sky. Rupert unlocked the gate and stood inside the enclosure, waiting for her, smiling. *Nothing too bad, then.*

She entered the secured area. He put a finger to his lips before she could speak, then gestured to the ladder that was attached to the EAR's support scaffolding, indicating she should climb. Climb she did, up and up, clinging to the metal rungs, up alongside the length of the EAR. She looked down at Rupert and he gestured her upward. She kept climbing until she had passed the upper rim of the EAR. She looked inside.

"Better get back down," Rupert called to her a few moments later. She clung to the ladder, stunned.

Loud *caws* shocked her back to awareness, and she looked up to see a crow flying towards her. She shimmied down the ladder as the crow scolded her and flapped about her head. Once on the ground she and Rupert hurried out of the enclosure, closing and locking the gate behind them. The crow stopped its frenzy and Sally watched as it gently lit down inside the giant EAR.

§

The pair stared at the images on the monitors. Not the cleaned-up images, tweaked and torqued almost beyond recognition by Sally's digital manoeuvring. But at the original, input images. At the irregular, rounded shape of the nest viewed from above, blurred and fuzzy because it was made of twigs meticulously woven and tucked and twisted into shape inside the narrowing neck of the funnel-shaped EAR. Thanks to the miracle of modern digital image processing, Sally had been able to massage that rough shape into a perfect circle, then meticulously eliminate the blur of the nest's mud and moss lining from the background. Only the three perfect ovoid eggs had survived her digital ministrations intact.

And the newest image, a duplicate of the first except that the eggs lay in bits and shards, debris that Sally had studiously edited from the image. There were three wide open beaks, pointy-ended ovoids, dark inside the mouths with vague glimpses of tongues, oddly face-like, all eclipsing the wee heads and naked bodies as the newly-hatched chicks opened their maws to their ma.

Sally hardly knew whether to laugh at the sight of this new, precious life or to cry in despair.

"Crows? Our aliens are crows?"

"It would seem so."

"But how—?"

"The nest is below the detectors on the fibre optic cables. We only picked up transmissions when they were flying overhead—looking for a place to nest—or coming in for a landing on the eggs or to feed the hatchlings."

"And the whirls and swirls and spirals and splotches? What were those, do you suppose?"

"Who knows? Maybe a glimpse of some higher form of communication, an expression of something beyond what the eye sees."

"Maybe it's how they feel when they're flying. You know, those crazy avian courtship aerobatics where they swoop and soar and plummet and play. I wonder what that would feel like?" Sally murmured, looking out the window for crows.

"Psi-chedelic."

"Very clever. But—and don't be getting all testy on me, Rupert—the EAR is still pretty crude technology. More like a telegraph than a telephone. Morse code is useful, but you don't use it to discuss the meaning of life."

"First I was primitive, now I'm crude? But it's funny when you think about it. We always assume we'll be able to communicate with extraterrestrials, but we don't even know how to chat with other Earthling species. Typical human hubris."

"And even now, we're just scratching the surface. But hey, you have to start somewhere," Sally shrugged.

"Me Tarzan, you Jane?"

"Yeah, I think that's about where we're at."

Sally thought about that picture of the swan and Leda. Now here they were, a couple of thousand years later, on the verge of a whole new type of bird-human intercourse. Then another thought struck her.

~ Airborne ~

"Oh god, Rupert! How are we going to tell Dr. Bob?" asked Sally. "And all those people all over the world!"

"I suggest we retire to the Student Lounge and discuss the matter."

"But we have to let people know—" Sally began, and then caught herself. "Hell yes," she said. "And forget the usual Friday afternoon pint of ale. I'm in need of something stronger."

"Yes," agreed Rupert, "this definitely calls for martinis."

§

Later that evening, Sally returned to her office. She planned to walk home and take the weekend off, the first one since the initial transmission. She grabbed her backpack and hesitated. Then she sat down in front of the monitors to look at the latest files. Now she knew there was no need for all that sophisticated image processing that had distorted the real transmission beyond recognition. Instead, she gazed at the raw images, transmitted to the EAR by some poorly-understood telepathic transmission, from one species to another, through all the clumsy mechanisms and all the electronic components and processes and programs of humans trying so hard to *listen.*

She had just started to load the images when she the felt the hairs on the back of her neck lift. Someone was staring at her. She twirled in her seat and looked at the office door, but there was no one there. Turning back towards her monitors she glanced out the window. There, in the branches of the tree outside, a glossy black bird gazed at her. She gazed back at the being, at once alien and familiar, and tried, in her own clumsy way, in an inarticulate voice unused for so many millennia it had all but vanished, to send the bird an image.

She focused on the crow's bright ebony eye. She sent her thoughts to this alien intelligence. This Other. Only one amongst all the Others. One single, intelligent animal on a planet teeming with intelligence. A planet that was home to gorillas and whales, ants and wolves and bats and bees and trees. All the Others dismissed by the human species as lacking true intelligence, as incapable of wisdom, as unworthy of serious discourse.

Behind her, unseen as she contemplated the silent crow, an image captured that afternoon opened on her computer screen. A

~ Airborne ~

young woman perched high on a ladder, her hair tossed by the breeze. The woman's eyes were wide, her mouth open with astonishment. A bird's-eye view of a human undergoing an abrupt awakening.

"We are not alone," Sally murmured as she looked through the glass at the Other. Her heart surged with joy and recognition. "We never have been."

❧

Sue McKay-Miller was born and bred in Alberta and spent many years in the not-so-hallowed halls of academia as a research geophysicist. Six years ago she fled the bright lights of big-city Calgary to settle on the North Shore of Cape Breton. Now she lives off-grid in the woods and pursues her passions for writing fiction and making mosaics. When not juggling words she enjoys trolling beach and forest for stuff she can stick together and call 'art'. Other hobbies include watching newts in the pond, tracking animals by snowshoe, and pondering the secret lives of plants, animals and mushrooms.

Her Money's Worth

"The Silku have flying machines. For war." Surcyne leaned forward on her mound of beaded pillows to pass me a cup of steaming *tirazi*. She pitched her voice low and concern flickered in her dark eyes. A double row of pearls swung from her silken headwrap in a graceful curve below her chin, punctuating her words.

I snorted. "I doubt it."

Annoyance flashed on Surcyne's face. She was still a *Sirtaka* in her mother's army; brave, bold, brash, and a long way from being Empress of Aleram yet. Not used to argument.

"My sailors saw them, *Essi*," she pressed, using the honorific for *honored lady*. Perhaps less brash than I'd thought. "They flew over the ships, great armored contraptions. Our weapons were useless. Stones pounded down on and around the ships, silently, like deadly rain falling. What other explanation can there be?"

I pursed my lips. "Magic?"

I could count on two hands those capable of such magic. I was one of them. But those who would turn their power to war were fewer. Tuinan, or Silden, or Aratu. If Surcyne had called for me, she must suspect.

She narrowed her eyes. "Then the stories are true? My mother—"

"Your mother is a wise woman," I said. Hundreds of years had passed since I and nine others had grown and trained together on a mountaintop in the far north of Tarkandis. That mountain had long since disappeared, along with the one who had chosen us, the one we'd called Aura-dāh. Sometimes in dreams I still feel her soft fingertips press against my forehead, throat, chest and abdomen, and I wake with a chill ache in the four *yantras* her touch created. All power exacts its price.

Many dismiss our existence as legend, but Surcyne's mother, the Empress, had consulted me before. She knew my gifts.

Surcyne remained skeptical, pearls clicking as she shook her head impatiently.

"My sailors are not children, running home with fantastic tales of taroques or dragons."

It was an old wound, but the pang of guilt I felt when I heard the names of those two magnificent, extinct creatures still tore my heart. *One of those losses, at least, was my fault.*

"What happened next?" I asked, to keep her talking.

"My sailors had to retreat or lose the entire fleet. Every time we venture out, they drive us back." Her voice held a knife-edge of anger. "I don't care about Silku. I just want to open trade routes with the lands beyond. But the Silku block us. Even a lone envoy can't get in to speak to their *Pashkado*."

"And you want me to—?"

"Get us past the Silku. Remove their advantage, or provide us with one of our own."

I considered. Had the Silku truly built flying machines? Or was one of my old colleagues helping them? If the latter, I had a duty to restore the balance.

"Half my fee in advance, and the price will be high," I warned her.

"Name it," she said, smiling like a cat in an aviary. "I know I shall have my money's worth."

§

Our bargain struck, Surcyne called for her advisor, Davi. A common enough name, but the face that appeared in the doorway shocked me. Another of the ten, one I had not seen for two centuries.

"It's good to see you, Xelisi," he said, impassive as if we'd shared a glass of *tarni* just last week. He had not aged, of course, nor made himself appear past about thirty. I preferred to look slightly older than that. It avoided complications.

I barely heard Surcyne explain that we would be working together, and then excuse herself to go and meet with her officers. Davi was one of the Mountain Hand, like me. We'd been

~ Airborne ~

allies on the mountaintop and at other times, balanced against the River Hand. Five to a side, empowered by a goddess. To what end—that remained a mystery, even to us.

Of course I embraced him. Davi returned the gesture shakily, and I knew that his surprise had been as great as mine.

"Why does Surcyne need me, if she has you?" I asked before I released him.

I felt his body stiffen. He stepped back and shrugged.

"Surcyne needs magic. She has no idea that I—what I was...once."

"Once?"

Davi turned his gaze from me, to stare out the window at the sapphire ocean. "I closed my *ajna*, my third eye, long ago. I no longer feel Aura-dāh's touch. My magic is dead." He glanced at me, read the shock in my face, and shook his head. "I am content with that, Xelisi. I cannot help the *Sirtaka* that way."

A thousand questions clamoured in my mind, but his grey eyes, eyes I knew as well as a brother's, begged me not to ask. I fetched a deep breath. "Well then," I said, "where do we begin?"

§

Months passed. Davi and I worked together on Surcyne's edicts, I on magical means for stopping the Silku, he on mechanical means for providing Surcyne her own airborne warriors. I thought the possibility of mechanical flight unlikely, but Davi believed in it. He covered reams of parchment with charts and plans and elegantly inked schematics, tinkered endlessly with scale models and mockups.

"Perhaps one day these will fill the skies," I'd joked, tapping his papers. "There'll be no more need for magic then."

He'd surprised me by staring out the window dreamily. "Do you really think so?"

I didn't, but I held my tongue. Perhaps, without his magic, Davi had learned to see the world in a different way.

I, meanwhile, spent many long hours with my third eye practically propped open, enchanting charmed projectiles for Surcyne's weapons. I did this alone in my room, sometimes with a few plodding homonculi for assistance, laboriously calling the magics out of the earth and sky and trapping them in stone and metal. Davi invariably disappeared while I worked at these projects, and his silent abandonment confused me. Was it simply too painful to be close to magic? Did he disapprove of my choices? At times I longed for the uncomplicated days on the mountain, surrounded by silk trees and paradise gardens, when we were all, if not friends, at least unabashed adversaries.

In the end, Surcyne was impatient, and my magics completed before any of Davi's wondrous machines found their way to the skies. There came a day when Davi and I stood on Surcyne's flagship, leaning into the unending chill wind off the ocean. Grey, choppy waves flashed whitecaps far out to the horizon. Not an auspicious day to send a fledgling navy against a mysterious flying force of enemies. But there would be no dissuading Surcyne. These months in her employ had taught me that.

The ship pulled free of the dock amid much creaking and shouting. Surcyne stood near the prow with the *nautwa* of the ship, their faces upturned to the sky as they spoke to each other. In the distance, cerulean sky made brief, mesmerizing appearances through the cloud cover. By the time I thought to glance back at the shore, it was an indistinct blur on the horizon.

"Worried?" Davi asked.

"Of course I'm worried. The magic may not work. By day's end the entire navy could be at the bottom of the ocean, with all of us in chains or feeding the fish."

He stepped closer, to stand beside me, staring off at the massing grey clouds. "*You* will be neither," he said mildly.

I shrugged. "Granted, but neither will you—not dead, at least. But Surcyne and the others—"

He kept his eyes on the sky. "Xelisi, think about it. It's been so long since I've used magic...my death may well be possible."

His words froze my tongue as the chill of sea and sky together could not. That he might allow himself to be killed! Finally, I said carefully, "Do you mean you would not attempt magic to save yourself, or that it wouldn't work if you did?"

He turned abruptly to look at the wake foaming out behind the ship. "We shall have to hope your magic holds, Xelisi," he said, his voice as rough as the bark of a bead tree.

"Mark the sky!" the *nautwa* ordered. I squinted ahead. Within seconds I spotted dark specks in the sky, shimmery and indistinct against the light, but bearing down quickly.

~ *Airborne* ~

The crew moved with excitement to the new, larger *rohr*, setting fuses and measuring black powder. Some readied slings and small mounds of the stones I had enchanted to negate magical forces. Clearly they expected a different outcome this time.

The specks in the distance drew closer and took shape, resolving into what Surcyne's warriors had described; armored boxes held aloft. I shook my head and smiled. It had to be magic. These were nothing like Davi's elegant sketches of things that could claim the sky as birds did.

Unless...perhaps they were elegant flying machines disguised by magic to fool the enemy? It would be a clever deception, inducing panic by presenting the incomprehensible. I could not show the others what lay beyond the facade, but I could see for myself. As they drew closer and Surcyne's crews waited, I opened my *ajna* to see their true forms.

Without Aura-dāh's gift of immortality, my heart might have stopped from pure shock. The illusory armour concealed something I had not expected to see again in my lifetime, no matter how long it was.

Taroques.

The enormous bird-lizards of myth and legend, stunningly beautiful, terrifyingly huge, had been extinct for over five hundred years. *My fault,* my mind murmured again. The last one...

Chill air pervaded the cave, despite the fire I'd doggedly kept burning. The taroque lay on her side, laboring to breathe in short, ragged bursts. I'd worked every magic I knew, tried every herb, asked every healer. Still the plague took them. Davi, good friend that he was, had helped as he could. I stroked the crimson-feathered neck with trembling fingers, willing her well. She died with a shudder.

And yet here they were. Long crimson and gold feathers streaming out behind them in the wind, toothed beaks open wide to breathe deeply as their wings plied the air in long, slow strokes, they came with Silku warriors on their backs. The smooth angular planes of the riders' faces were calm and contemptuous as they guided their mounts toward Surcyne's upstart navy.

My breath caught as I felt the minds of the taroques tremble with recognition. Recognition of *me.*

~ Airborne ~

The first few *rohr* thundered to life around me, bellowing the explosions of their black powder charges. My reverie shattered.

"No!" I screamed, or thought to scream, but it came out a whisper. "No, no, no," I repeated as I lurched for the helm, where Surcyne and her *nautwa* stood. My voice came back as I reached her. "Stop the *rohr!*"

Surcyne whirled to me, her face bewildered and angry. "Stop them? You're the one who—"

"Stop them. Now!" Desperate, I turned the full force of my *ajna* on her. It was wrong, but I was impelled by my terror that the taroques would be killed. Davi tried to pull me aside but I shook him off. "Take the fleet back to Aleram!"

She did it, of course, moving like a possessed golem to scream orders to the *nautwa* and the other ships.

I hadn't been fast enough. One *rohrstone* met its mark, my enchantments punching a smooth hole in the taroque's magical defenses. The stone took the creature squarely in the head, and it tumbled from the sky like a child's toy thrown to the wind. The armour illusion held, and no-one else saw, as I did, the Silku warrior fight for control of his mount and then stolidly accept his fate. No one else saw it flash crimson and gold in the sunlight just before it hit the water. No one else saw the colours extinguished by the cold grey waves. I could not pull my magic from Surcyne to try and save either taroque or rider, or else risk putting the others in danger. All I could do was watch, with a heaviness like a *rohrstone* in my chest.

Masts creaked and groaned as the frightened sailors scuttled to obey Surcyne, and the fleet swung aside, turning for home. The Silku, assuming surrender, broke off.

I watched until the last taroque disappeared. Then I turned my face to the wind and released my hold on the enraged Surcyne.

She threw one eloquent glare in my direction and then strode to the *nautwa's* cabin without a word. I followed her as silently, with Davi behind me. Once inside, with the door firmly shut, she faced me, fairly panting with rage.

"Is there any reason I should not kill you here and now?"

As if she could. "I understand your anger. But I saw what lay beyond the illusion. *Taroques.*"

I turned to Davi for support. His face drained of colour.

~ Airborne ~

"They're using them for *war*?" he asked in a horrified voice.

"I know, I can't believe it," I said. I took two deep breaths to quell a threatening sob. "After all this time...they're alive. And they knew me, Davi. Somehow they knew me."

Surcyne stared from me to Davi and back again, dark eyes still smoldering, mouth set in a straight, hard line. "Taroques are the stuff of children's tales."

"They are also very much alive, and I saw them. Do you not see what this means? A creature thought extinct hundreds of years, returned?"

I expected Davi to say something then, but he stayed silent, apparently in shock.

"I do not," Surcyne said. "All I see is another battle lost. Could we not at least have captured one?" She kicked at a mound of silk pillows. "That might have been something worthwhile."

I stared at her wearily. "What should concern you now is the magic. The Silku have a powerful ally, or this deception would be impossible."

She drew herself up and glared at us. "Then I suggest you earn your pay," she spat, and stormed out.

I turned to Davi. "It has to be one of us," I said. "No-one else —"

He shook his head. "No, no-one else. One of the River Hand."

"Undoubtedly, if they're using the taroques for war. My guess is Silden, making trouble as usual. But how to find out, if the *Pashkado* won't accept envoys?"

Davi paced the tiny cabin. "Does it matter? We still have to counter the taroques."

My chest tightened. "I won't see them harmed. Not so that Surcyne can open trade routes and impress her mother."

"You'd break your agreement?"

"No." My voice sounded harsh. We of the Mountain Hand did not break our word lightly. "But war with the Silku is not what Surcyne or Aleram need. She's treading dangerous ground. And once a fire spreads, the damp and the dry both burn." I took my own turn at pacing.

Davi stood with his arms crossed, watching me with unreadable eyes.

Finally I said, "I'm going to Silku."

"To confront the *Pashkado*? Or our colleague?"

~ *Airborne* ~

"To rescue the taroques," I said quietly. "Whatever that takes."

He raised his eyebrows. "What will Surcyne think?"

"That I'm stealing them for her, I imagine."

"But you're not."

"No." I took a deep breath. "I'd take them to the mountain if it were still there. But there must be somewhere else like it, somewhere they could live in peace."

"There's nowhere like the mountain," he said absently, his eyes going to the porthole as if he could see it in the distance. He sighed. "I suppose I'm going with you."

Relief welled up in me like water at an oasis. "I hoped you might," I said, but when I embraced him, his arms and body were as cold and unyielding as mosaic tiles. He pulled away quickly and crossed the cabin to stare out the porthole.

"If the *Pashkado* has cut himself off from the rest of Tarkandis, we'll have to go through the etherworld," I said.

His shoulders sagged, but his voice was strong. "I won't do it, Xelisi. You'll have to carry us both."

Incorporeal travel is not a *yantras* power that I care to employ often. Disquieting and emotionally draining, a brush with the etherworld and its denizens haunts my nightmares for weeks afterward. To transport two of us would severely drain my energy and concentration.

"If I must carry you, at least tell me why."

He stayed silent a moment, turning from the porthole but not meeting my eyes. The ship's sounds surrounded us, but we were separate, apart in our own world.

Finally he said, "What I wanted most, the *yantras* magic could not give me. And what it promised was an eternity to contemplate my loss." He smiled grimly. "Giving up the magic was not as difficult as you might think."

"But Aura-dāh created ten of us. By giving up your magic—Davi, you've unbalanced the world."

He shook his head impatiently. "You can't be sure of that. I may not be the only one. At any rate—it's my decision."

I frowned, frustrated and trying to comprehend. My immortality was a tremendous gift, despite its responsibilities and cost. It was integral to my place in the world. Discarding magic would be like cutting off a limb. And Aura-dāh had chosen me.

~ *Airborne* ~

Could I question the motives or choices of a goddess?

I didn't say any of that. "What did you want so badly?"

He met my gaze then, and quirked one side of his mouth in a half-smile. "It doesn't matter now."

But suddenly I knew. It was there in those grey eyes, the eyes of a brother, and therein lay the problem.

Davi had wanted...me.

"I'll send for Surcyne," he said quickly, and left me alone with my revelation.

Shaken, I sat on the mound of silken pillows to gather my strength.

§

We met again later, on the windswept dock. I had the few things I'd brought with me, and my half-payment from Surcyne— a purse full of rubies. The other half was a willing forfeit, to save the taroques. I didn't know when I'd be back in Aleram. Or if I'd be welcome.

Davi said little. He wore a falchion slung low at his belt. I wondered what use he thought that would be against one of the River Hand.

I'd decided not to mention Davi's secret, but when I put my arms around him to pull us both into the etherworld he stood tense and unyielding. I closed my eyes and pressed my face against the soft cotton of his shirt. "You'll have to hold tight," I advised. "It hasn't improved in there as far as I know."

"Of course." His arms went around me and for the space of a few heartbeats I searched my soul, my heart, my body to see if I could find even a scrap of the kind of love Davi felt for me. If it were there, surely it must surface now, when we were about to step into danger together. I owed him a chance.

But no. I loved him as always, as a brother and comrade and one who shared my history. That was all. I felt a brief, momentary pang of regret, and then I opened my *ajna* and channeled us into the beyond.

Viewed from the etherworld, the real world appears as though seen through smoked glass. Shades, daēva, lost souls and peri swirl about in hideous turmoil, whispering and keening. The scents of decay and corruption fill the air. The best transits

~ Airborne ~

through the etherworld are brief ones.

Davi kept his eyes closed while we travelled as two spirit-forms clasped together, trailing our corporeal bodies like shrouds behind us. I fixed my eyes on the dark shape that was Silku, and kept them there as the dark waters of the Maridi Strait coursed beneath us. I could not afford any distractions.

As we neared Silku, I reached ahead and found a huge enclosed stable near the *Pashkado's* palace, guarded on the outside but apparently empty within. My mind could not penetrate the walls, but our ethereal bodies were not held back. I kept us in the etherworld until we were inside.

They were here! Within the walls, the minds of the taroques opened to me, joyful and *knowing*. I eased us back into the real world gently, weak and spent. Davi would have to deal with any immediate trouble. I ventured a small amount of energy to secure the stable doors from the inside.

The taroques were restless in my presence. I spoke to them soothingly. Some paced their stalls and clawed at the floor, but most merely stuck their heads over the lowest bars, nostrils flaring as they smelled us, beryl-green eyes wide and intelligent. I longed to stroke the ruby-hued feathers, but I was not strong enough to stand yet.

Davi squatted beside me. "Do you think if we ride two of them out of here, the rest will follow?"

I nodded. "They're guarded against human intruders, but it seems no-one thought of our kind."

"On the contrary." A voice emerged from the shadows at the other end of the stable. "I have—friends—in the etherworld who alerted me to your passage."

I pushed slowly to my feet and Davi stood beside me, one hand under my elbow. "I'm not surprised to find you here, Silden," I said.

He walked out of the shadows then, smiling crookedly. "Nor I you, Xelisi. If any of our company were to come looking for taroques, it would be you."

The taroque nearest me stuck its head over the bars and nudged my arm gently with the smooth hook of its beak. I touched the soft, curving neck hesitantly. *So long...*

"Thank you for letting me know they were still alive," I said. My voice was harsh.

~ *Airborne* ~

Silden had altered his appearance to look more like the Silku. Only his voice was the same. His face was narrow and angular, his hair straight and black as *rohr* powder. He shrugged elegantly. "As a wise man once said, all warfare is based on deception. If I'd told you about them, you'd have wanted them back."

"Aura-dāh put them in my care. You had no right to interfere." Centuries of guilt and regret bubbled angrily to the surface. "You stole them—brought them here—"

The taroques sensed my agitation. The closest one tossed its head, snorting, and stamped a delicate foot.

Silden shook his head. "Not I," he said. "I'd not have Aura-dāh's wrath, not in those days." He pursed his lips and canted his head to one side. "Now, taking advantage of a situation, that's another matter. I'll always plead guilty to that. She looks well, doesn't she, Davi?" He seemed to be enjoying himself.

Davi said nothing and I stared at Silden. I refused to ask him the question that burned in my mind. *How did the taroques get here?*

He answered it anyway, with another question. "What about it, Davi? Who could have brought the taroques to Silku?"

Davi's hand twitched under my elbow. Davi? What could he know about the taroques? I was about to scoff at Silden, but I realized that Davi's body was tense and quivering like the dried pods on a silk tree. I turned my head to look at him. He wouldn't meet my eyes. With sudden clarity his words came back to me. *They're using them for war?*

Not surprise that the taroques existed; horror at how they were being used.

"I thought they'd be safe here. They promised to keep them safe, hidden." Davi's voice was so low and hoarse that I barely made out his words. "I wouldn't have brought them if I'd thought —"

"The things we do for love," Silden drawled.

I wanted to step back from Davi but I wouldn't give Silden the satisfaction. The pieces tumbled into place like glass beads in a child's game. Davi helping me tend the taroques so long ago, treating the sick ones when the plague came, hunting the silent predators that were making off with the young ones. Comforting me when the last one died. Trying to interest me in other things

~ Airborne ~

to take my mind off my failure.

Davi. In love with me even then. Silden had seen it, but not I. In love, and jealous of my preoccupation with the taroques. Carrying the young ones off himself, not to kill them—he was of the Mountain Hand, after all—but to hide them, so that my attention might turn elsewhere...

"So long ago," I whispered, overcome by what he'd done. I'd left the ancient city of Temi Fak-al-het soon after that, my soul as bitter as wormwood. Aura-dāh had left us, our home was gone, and I'd failed the taroques. Davi's friendship, dear though I held it, could not heal those losses.

And he'd let me go without a word, no confession of love nor of his crime. He'd kept the secret of the taroques from me all this time, and endangered the world by abandoning his magic. For a moment I hated him as much as I hated Silden.

At least the taroques are alive.

Davi staggered back suddenly, and I realized Silden's trap too late. He'd distracted us, and now River energy from his four *yantras* battered against Davi and my own Mountain force, seeking entry and control.

The taroques went mad. Snorting and screeching, they responded to my fear and anger, battering against the doors of their stalls.

Davi rallied against the assault and ran at Silden, pulling the falchion free as he went. The physical attack took Silden off guard, and the pummeling force of his magic faltered. I shot back the bolt on the nearest stall, and the first taroque was free. Then I turned my attention to Silden.

Each locus of *yantras* power—the forehead, throat, chest and abdomen—channels a different type of energy. Silden had attacked all of mine with all of his. He had not changed much since our time on the mountain. His offense relied always on diversion and brute force. I'd forgotten that. Now I remembered how to counter it. Some memories run so deep they become not merely an aspect of the mind, but of the body and spirit as well.

I focused power on him, channeling only through my *ajna*, the seat of mental control, and my chest, the locus of love, compassion and healing. Silden's weaknesses. He stumbled briefly, and Davi pressed his advantage, swinging the falchion with deadly precision. Silden pulled some of his concentration

~ Airborne ~

away from me to ward off Davi's blows—immortal we might be, but none of us were immune to pain or injury. I continued to batter his *yantras* as powerfully as I could while I darted to the other stalls, breaking my attack only for the bare seconds it took to pull back each bolt.

The stable echoed now with the cacophony of the taroques' shrills and screeches. Those still confined to their stalls lunged frantically against the doors; the others clustered around me, towering over my head and obscuring my view of Davi and Silden. Silden's forces still battered against mine, though less forcefully.

At last all the taroques were free. The constant battle of *yantras* with Silden was beginning to wear on me. I felt fragile and drained. With effort I grasped a handful of feathers and clambered up on the back of a taroque, heart hammering in my chest.

"Davi!" I shouted over the din. If I could get his attention, and get close enough, I could pull him up behind me.

Now I saw Silden and Davi again. Silden had fashioned a shield of energy to block Davi's blows, but it was pulling increasing amounts of energy to maintain. No wonder his assaults against me had lessened. Davi's movements were arduous, as if invisible forces thickened the air around him. It was close to a stalemate.

I gathered strength to help him, but Davi yelled at me. "Xelisi, go! Take them—and go!"

Shouts and pounding erupted at the doors of the stable. Soon they would fall before the sheer physical force being hurled against them. My almost-depleted magic would not hold it back.

I hesitated. If I left, Davi would be overcome. If I stayed, we might fall anyway, and the taroques would be forced back into their stalls.

"Go!" he roared again, and in that sound I recognized his desperation and his hope. If I escaped, and the taroques with me, his guilt would be erased and he could fall to the death he so desired, without regret.

Swearing, I turned the almost-spent power of my *ajna* on the mind of the taroque I rode, guiding it toward the doors. The others followed, herding by instinct. The doors burst open just as we reached them, and the taroques needed no prodding to scrabble toward freedom. The guards fell back under the crush of

~ Airborne ~

surging, feathered bodies.

I could not pause to look back, nor call his name, but I believe I felt the touch of Davi's *ajna* like a caress against mine. A caress, and a goodbye.

§

Later, under the crisp light of the two moons and a million stars, we flew over Aleram. I wondered if Surcyne paced atop her ramparts, awaiting our return. She would not be pleased at the loss of both Davi and the taroques, although the Silku threat had been removed. And she had Davi's plans, his graceful sketches of things he would not live to see. I wondered if she would think she'd had her money's worth.

The rubies hung heavy at my belt, the memory of Davi's last touch as weighted in my mind. Around me the taroques sped strong and trusting through the clouds, moonlight silver-plating their crimson and gold bodies. My own gains and losses were more difficult to assess.

❧❧

Sherry D. Ramsey writes speculative fiction for both adults and young adults, has been the Editor/Publisher of The Scriptorium Webzine for Writers for over ten years, and is one of the founding editors of Third Person Press. Her short fiction and poetry have appeared in diverse print and online publications, and she's steadily working her way through a stack of partly-finished novel manuscripts, hunting for hidden treasures, and polishing up the ones she finds.

Sherry is an active member of the Writer's Federation of Nova Scotia Writer's Council and SF Canada, the national association for Speculative Fiction Professionals. You can visit her and read her sporadically-updated writing blog at www.sherrydramsey.com

~ Airborne ~

Laika

Loneliness
>Sleeps on the edge of uncertainty,
>Insecurity.

I am dining on a spaceship,
Handling a dehydrated bit of cheese,
And as I look out into the
>Black lightness,
I understand how that first Russian dog felt.
Not lonely, exactly,
But wondering—

Is anyone coming?

Jill Campbell-Miller is a PhD Candidate in History at the University of Waterloo. She is working on a decidedly non-speculative dissertation on the history of foreign assistance to India from Canada and the United States. Although Jill hails from Cape North, Cape Breton, she is currently living in Waterloo, Ontario.

Gifts from the North

I was powerful all right, but I didn't know it until I was eight years old. All I wanted was to join my father on the first winter hunt. He shook his head and my mom backed him up, like always. "No, Shasta, you won't be joining the hunt," she said. "You will help prepare the meat once the men bring it home."

But I looked right past her, over to my father. I squinted hard, staring across the room into his brown eyes. It was my most defiant look. I didn't mean to do it, but I bored into him with that look, bored right through his eyes and into his brain. "Shasta will be more valuable on the hunt than with her mother," I told that brain, using no words.

He must have thought it was some spirit in his head because when he spoke his voice shook with fear. He turned away from me and told my mother, "Shasta will be more useful on the hunt than here with you."

There was no science experiment gone wrong, no human-animal transmogrification, no cosmic accident or radioactive fallout, and yet I had become a superhero. I wasn't like the other superheroes we always heard about on the news. I couldn't fly and I wasn't ten feet tall, and I couldn't shoot lasers out of my body. I wouldn't be busting up any crime rings any time soon. But I had something no one around me had, something bigger than being a good hunter or even an all-star hockey player.

I know one thing, I kept it to myself. It was too good to share, even better than candies from the Southland. Being a child and not knowing anything, I used the powers to get what I wanted. My parents spoiled me against their will. I didn't even have to go into their brains. I just gave them that defiant look of mine and they caved. I guess they didn't want any more bossy spirits in their heads—once was enough.

They sold everything we needed, including the Ski-doo, and spent the lot of it on a PlayStation video game system, and hundreds of games. I was the only kid in town who had one. All my friends came by to play. They let me play every time, and I always won. But they soon stopped coming around. I couldn't make my friends like me again. And the more I got what I wanted, the more afraid of me my parents acted. They got me fancy gifts I didn't even ask for, every report card day, even though my grades got worse the more time I spent playing video games. I guess I was pretty good at controlling people, but that didn't mean I understood them at all.

I was very young when I left home, not quite a woman yet. I figured if I was to feel like an outsider I might as well do it somewhere I actually was an outsider.

I snuck in with the freight on a puddle-jumper to Churchill, watching the ice and snow pass before my eyes a thousand miles below. Imagine my surprise when what I thought was infinite finally ended with a burst of green. Imagine the pilot's surprise when I popped up from the cargo saying, "Hello. Where's the airport?" His shock was nothing the powers couldn't overcome. I just smiled meekly and told his brain, "Give this poor girl some food, she must be starving." Soon enough he was falling all over himself to give me something to eat and, when we landed, a ride to the highway in his truck.

I hitched a ride with a lonely zookeeper. "Winnipeg?" I asked.

"Where else?" he said.

The zookeeper was concerned about my lack of maturity. "If anyone asks, you're my daughter," he said.

"Who would ask that?" I asked.

He just nodded like I'd said something really cool. His pack of cigarettes bobbed up and down in a buttoned breast pocket.

His daughter, as if.

"You should offer this chick a cigarette," I told his brain. I didn't want him to think I was just some ordinary runaway.

"You want a smoke, kid?" he said, unbuttoning the breast pocket.

"Yeah, of course," I said. He lit it for me and it burned my lungs up. What an awful pain. I didn't see the point, but at least I

~ Airborne ~

felt older. "Maybe this chick could help you navigate," I told his brain.

He reached over into the doorless glove box and handed me a provincial map. "It's pretty much one straight road all the way through, but you can play around with that if you want," he said.

I snatched the map from his hand and opened it up. That was the whole problem with adults. No matter how powerful I was, all they thought I could do was play. I had to mentally trick them into giving me even token responsibility. Just once I wanted someone to respect my abilities, but I couldn't even admit I had them.

This guy was harder to get my way with than my parents were. I mean, I got a cigarette but I don't think I could've convinced him to buy me a dog or anything. I don't know what it was. While he was small and weak-minded, he was also hard to read. Back home I'd known drunks, perverts, hunters, activists, bureaucrats, and strong mothers, but never anyone who was so out of place in his own skin, not even the junkies at school. He just kept twitching and turning the radio on and off, complaining about everything it played, about the news stories of "goddamn activists" and "goddamn government." Which side was he on? Eventually, I just had to look at his heart.

I'd never done that before but I had to see what was making him so uncomfortable around me. It was darker and more frightening than I expected.

I gave him a good long look and then I closed my eyes. I could trace the scars where his heart had stopped growing while his body kept going. They were in the shape of the claws of a predator, one specializing in young and weak prey. Someone had hurt him badly back when he was about my age. I felt all that pain of betrayal as if my own father, the greatest man I ever knew, had raped me.

I just about broke down with the pain of it, right there in his passenger's seat, and I had to leave his heart alone. Knowing what I then knew, I pitied him and admired his strength, his ability to help a random kid even though he'd never recovered from his own childhood.

I opened my eyes and looked at him again.

"What?" he said.

"Nothing," I whispered. The space between us felt heavy. I

~ Airborne ~

knew something about him then, something he hadn't told me. He was still being this adult helper, this gruff, straight-up guy. But I knew him as a child, a vulnerable victim. I didn't know which version of him was real.

"Goddamn Sunday drivers," he said. He geared down and passed a middle-aged couple.

I clenched my hands over my seat. "Yeah," I said. "People drive slow on Sundays I guess."

He snorted as if I'd said the sky was purple. All I could think of was that heart of his, those claw-mark scars, but I didn't have the guts to ask who or what had caused them and how. I just wanted to say something nice. "You're a pretty good driver," I said. He drove fast but he seemed to have control of the vehicle. It reminded me of my cousin Vince, who liked to get high and do blindfolded doughnuts on his snow machine.

"What do you know about driving?" the zookeeper said.

I wanted to revisit his scars but I was afraid. Whoever, or whatever, left them there might still be lurking around his heart. "I know snow machines," I said. "But I've never seen roads like this before. Never even been to a city."

He snorted again.

"You okay?" I said.

He shrugged. "Why?"

"You sound out of breath."

"That was a laugh, kid."

I nodded. He sounded really out of breath and I wished I could breathe some fresh energy into him. But he was a total stranger. Suddenly I didn't feel like a superhero at all. I felt like some ordinary runaway. I closed my eyes and let the silence be whatever it wanted to be. I guess I was tired from a long day. I fell asleep and dreamed of swirling cloudy nondescript spirits.

I awoke in late winter Winnipeg. The zookeeper dropped me right downtown. I had a sudden urge to give his mouth a long frozen kiss like in those old movies, and maybe breathe him some extra strength, but of course I didn't. I didn't know where these thoughts were coming from, but it was gross. I just thanked him and smiled like a little flirt, and after I slammed his car door I felt raw and lost and alone, as sad and wounded as he was.

~ Airborne ~

I must have walked past Ray-Ray about five times before I noticed him, or he noticed me. He slumped up against a brick apartment building, his rear planted on the sidewalk. He had an open guitar case filled with loonies, quarters, dimes, and pennies, but no guitar. "Hey little Indian girl," he called to me.

"I'm no Indian!" I shouted back.

"Really? You look like one. I'm a proud Blackfoot Indian, myself. Ray-Ray." He held out his hand.

"You don't look like one," I told him. He looked like a black African.

"That's fine," he said. "I never much cared what people thunk a me anyways. Funny though, I don't look like no Indian and you do. But you don't sound like one. You sound white."

"Maybe I am," I said. He didn't have the monopoly on identity crisis. For the first time in my life I wished I was white. I felt like a dark rock in a sea of white faces rolling around me. The city was bringing me down.

"I think you really are white," he said. "An Indian never gets lost."

"I'm definitely not an Indian," I said, remembering my Uncle Simon's joke about how calling an Inuit person an Indian is an insult to about a billion people somewhere over in South Asia. "But I've never been lost until today," I added, and it was the dead-eyed truth.

"Well, I'm your man," Ray-Ray said. "Where you trying to get to?"

"Some place warm," I said.

Ray-Ray took me straight to the homeless youth emergency shelter and they gave me a free meal. I felt sorry for the kids in there as I watched them scam so hard, manipulating the only adults who ever gave a damn about them, just to get a second helping of macaroni with hot dogs. I could feel their hunger, and their desire. One short little girl looked me in the eye and I felt her longing for a hug or a smile or some approval. I smiled at her.

"Fuck you looking at?" she said.

I found an empty corner and sat down with my plate. As I bit into a boiled hotdog it hit me. I was exactly like these kids, only less obvious, and better at manipulation.

I dropped my dog and ran out to catch Ray-Ray. He was right

~ Airborne ~

out front with his guitar case slung over his shoulder, telling some young guys they should quit smoking.

"Can I stay with you?" I blurted. I guess I had tears in my eyes. Something about the city and these pathetic kids in the shelter, and their pathetic feelings. It was tearing at me from inside.

The boys around Ray-Ray snickered.

"I got a bed at the shelter," Ray-Ray said. "No girls allowed. Sorry, hon."

I knew I could get my way, but I imagined a night in a room full of snoring pot-bellied winos like I saw on the news at Christmas and I opted for a hot shower and bunk in the girls' dorm. As I got under the covers I felt proud that I hadn't manipulated Ray-Ray. But the dreams of the kids in the shelter came at me like a psychotic symphony. One dreamed he was running from the cops after holding up a gas station. A girl my age dreamed she was making out with her boyfriend, but he kept trying to go up her top and she was always fighting him. Another dreamed she stood over her mother's grave and spit on the tombstone, then frantically wiped the spit off with her elbow.

I woke up exhausted and even sadder than the day before. A white girl who called herself Morning Star, even though she looked like six shades of hell that morning, pointed me toward the highway and told me a bus number that would take me there. I decided to walk because the idea of a bus full of sophisticated city slickers intimidated me. I didn't want their thoughts or their feelings coming at me—it hadn't been like this back home. I guess I always knew what people were thinking, but I knew them so well there were no surprises. Anyway, I figured a walk would be a good way to start the day and see what the city looked like.

The part leading out to the Trans Canada turned out to look a lot like the road I'd just been on with that zookeeper, only with a few buildings scattered around it. I'd already done a lot of walking in my time, especially hunting with the men, but I never thought there could be so much distance inside a city. It was like a large animal cage that just kept going and going, until I was sweaty under my fleece-and-fur and my feet felt like throbbing diamond dust.

I spent the last few miles trying to put sympathetic thoughts into the minds of the drivers passing by, but their cars or their minds were moving too fast and I couldn't get locked on them. Then, out of nowhere as I walked up the on-ramp, a brown man in a hatchback pulled over and offered me a ride.

He smiled as I got into his little red car. I replied with a shy thin-lipped smile and held it until my dimples were sore, then I stopped.

"You like Jesus?" he asked me, and I knew things would get worse from there.

"I got nothing against him," I said.

"Nothing against him?"

"I think he said some good things," I explained. "About forgiveness and all that. But, you know, he never gave people much of a choice. He said he was The Way, and people had to follow him to get to heaven, or something like that."

"Jesus saved my life," the man said. "Before I was on drugs and on the wrong path. Now I pray and follow the bible." He tapped a copy of the Good Book resting between our seats, but his pinkie finger wandered onto my thigh and rested there for five long seconds of eternity.

"These days," he went on, "people are losing their way without Jesus. These days you have men lay down with men and women with women. It is not right."

I told him I used to think that way too before I saw *Will and Grace*.

"You're a good girl," he told me with a smile and a long, slow pat of my thigh. "But like many people you lose your way to television and bad habits."

He shifted suddenly toward me and stared directly into my face as his hatchback careened down the road. "Why you out here hitchhiking?" he said. He phrased it as a question but he was really making a statement, telling me I was doing foolish things with myself.

"Got no money," I told him. *Plus, I had hoped for an adventure.*

"Put your faith in Jesus," he said, returning his focus to the long straight road. "He will take care of you."

He patted my thigh again and I looked down at his fingers. He quickly let go and put his hands back on the wheel. "Sorry," he said. "You remind me of my daughter."

I felt sorry for her.

~ Airborne ~

I followed his veins up along his arms and into his chest, into his heart, and from there into his mind. It was cluttered with sticky-notes reminding him what to do and what not to do. Do pray. Do not smoke crack. Do help strangers and tell them about Jesus.

Overseeing everything was a hyperactive hungry little rodent running pell-mell through his system. It drove his most basic impulses: smoke crack, love Jesus, grab thigh. I locked my gaze onto that little rodent. It was paralysed in my stare, which I used to pressurize the vile little thing. I crushed it slowly, not out of anger or cruelty but because it took all my focus and energy, and the man had basically frozen in time as the car cruised steady through the cold winter moment.

Finally the rodent's bones snapped and crushed, and its oily brain was squashed and swept away in a released tidal blood flow. Its remains dissolved and left an open hole where the rodent had been. My mind shouted into his mind, "Loving Jesus is fine for you, but we each must find our own saviours, each in our own way." My words careened and echoed until they filled that space left by the control-hungry rodent.

The man drove me to the bus stop without a word. He bought me a ticket to Toronto and gave me $50 cash. He resisted the urge to give me a Bible. He just shook my hand and said good luck.

"God bless you," I said, and he smiled.

I found my way onto my eastbound bus, collapsed into a seat, closed my eyes and slept. Again my dreams were those of the people who napped around me. It was all jumbles of desire and fear. A man dreamt that he fought with his wife and she told him she'd never really loved him and he cried and cried. A little girl dreamt she was riding a white pony and all the other little girls begged her for a turn. Eventually the dreams faded and I woke up cold from the air conditioning, relieved to be awake. I looked around and saw that I was alone. All the other passengers had left the bus.

I descended the stairs into the crowd of people pushing toward their belongings. "Where am I?" I asked.

"Toronto," an old woman in front of me said.

No one else spoke a word to me, but I could see their every thought. They assaulted me in unison with their big city impatience. "Stupid hick," they said. "Clueless."

I turned from them and ran into the night lights of a skyscraper ghetto called Bay Street. I was hit on every side by the thoughts of stressed out and sketched out strangers. Late-night bankers, early evening prostitutes, under-employed immigrants, all their worry and woe hit me like an angry tidal wave and I could barely move. My legs felt like wet concrete.

I wallowed through, straight into a tall, dark-suited, blonde man. "Whoa," he said. He looked like Jonathan Torrens, like a Scandinavian who smiles too much, nervously. His suit fit him perfectly, like it was made just for him.

"Sorry," I said.

"No worries," he said.

His dimples made me cry. I fell into his arms and sobbed. I'd slept for 48 hours and I was still exhausted. Was this constant barrage of voices and dreams, fears and desires, to be my fate in the Southland? I couldn't take it.

He put his arms around me loosely for a moment. He was almost as fidgety as the zookeeper. But he didn't say it would all be okay and I liked that. "I'm Jon," he said.

"Shasta."

"You okay, Shasta?"

I shook my head. "Little lost," I said.

He invited me to his apartment. "You can crash on my couch."

I was too tired to argue or look for another option.

He hailed a taxi. We got in the back and sat far apart listening to the driver's French-language talk radio.

His apartment was a mile above Lake Ontario. It was small and sparse, with white carpet and black furniture. He gave me the tour in less than a minute, *there's the fridge, there's the toilet, there's the TV, there's the bed.* He didn't name the rooms, maybe because they all blended together anyway. "Actually, you can take the bed," he said. "I prefer the couch anyway."

I excused myself for a pee and sat on his throne. I took a deep breath and considered my situation. My heart pounded, afraid of what I might do next. I thought about how powerful my mind had always been before being diluted with the needs of all these people. There were just too many of them. Maybe I needed to go back to a sparser population. I wouldn't make it in the city.

~ Airborne ~

But there was nothing for me back home. I closed my eyes and let myself sob, but not too loudly.

Jon was asleep on his leather couch when I emerged from the bathroom. He looked serene, like my baby brother when he was first born and slept most of the time.

I put my hand onto the rise and fall of his chest. I closed my eyes. I saw my hand slide through his chest cavity and into his heart. I squeezed it gently, thinking as I did of how my dad prayed over animals he killed. I thought about how the hard rhythm of the drummers kept us warm on the coldest nights, and I thought about how my mom called my baby brother 'Grandfather.' Mom's grandfather passed away just before my brother was born.

I let go of Jon's heart and removed my hand from his chest. The corners of his mouth rose and a peaceful smile spread across his face. "Thank you for being normal," I said. "You may be the only happy person I've met in the Southland."

I walked across his living room and out onto his balcony. The expanse of Lake Ontario lay before my feet, and to my left and right were nothing but voices of longing. "Hear me O Lord, Praise Thee Allah, Help me Jesus."

I followed the voices through the streets, north, east, and west, along the streetcar track veins, underground and over-ground, even above my head in the sky. Everybody longed for something: food, jobs, friends, safety, love, excitement, meaning, success. They suffered and screamed in my ears.

I had my own desire. I wanted whatever gave me this power to take it back. "Shut up!" I screamed into the thin air, air that devoured my words. "You're all killing me." I thought of flying away somewhere. I wished I could. I climbed up onto his railing, looked down, and fell forward.

§

He caught me just five feet from a concrete death. I looked up into his hard blue benevolent eyes and saw no fear, no worry, no perversion, no danger.

"It's you," I said.

"They'll drive you crazy," Jon said.

I knew he meant the voices because the moment he caught

~ Airborne ~

me they finally shut up. I looked into his perfect white face and he smiled his perfect white smile. I wanted to ask him how he shut out the voices and all their underground needs but I was at a loss for words.

As if reading my mind he told me, "You just need to develop a thick skin. You can't help them all. You need to prioritize."

I nodded. As the cold night sky blew over me and chilled me right through, I wanted to prioritize. Only then did I realize we were moving. Flying, straight up.

The wind picked up as my caped saviour gained speed. He actually wore tights—they were fuschia, and his cape was sort of taupe. It was an ugly combination, but he was handsome, somehow more handsome than he had been in his business suit. I recognized him, then, from television. He was a real superhero, single-handedly responsible for busting up an old-school Toronto bank-robbing gang.

The glass face of his high-tower apartment building sped by us. I shivered. How did he not freeze at this speed and altitude? In seconds we reached his balcony. He put me down. "You okay now?" he asked with a smile.

I nodded. He walked back inside just like a regular person. I followed him in.

"I can teach you," he said. "I can teach you to prioritize. You know, the truth is I've been searching for a protégé. I mean you're not exactly what I had in mind—you can't even fly. But, well, it's been a long search so I guess you'll do."

My mind raced with foolish thoughts of Winnipeg zookeepers and burning cigarettes, Bible-thumpers and surly Torontonians. "What?" I said.

"You need to learn to focus your mind," he said. "Especially with a mind so powerful. You nearly killed yourself. You're not careful, you'll kill someone else."

"Okay," I said. "I'm sorry, I don't know what—"

"You'll have to learn," he said. "But for now, get some rest. I'm going to change into my pj's."

He pointed to the bed and headed to the washroom.

§

I slept through sunrise and all the way to dusk. He wasn't

~ Airborne ~

there when I woke up. I was starving but there was nothing in the fridge. I was afraid to leave though, and I didn't have a key. The voices were getting at me again, begging me to kick their addictions and help them win the lotto. I turned the TV on and cranked the volume. Dr. Phil was berating some couple. That was one way to respond to a call for help.

Jon got home a few minutes later. "How you doing?" he said.

"Starving."

"Good, let's hit the skies."

"Can I eat first?"

"Fine. I brought home some salami and bread."

After I wolfed down a dry sandwich, he led me to the balcony, grabbed me, flew straight up at that unbearable speed, but this time he didn't stop until we were high above the Earth. He held me in his strong arms so we could gaze at that beautiful blue and white orb. I was warm there in his arms. He reminded me of my father, but with better cologne.

"Focus," he said. "Listen."

I did, and it nearly suffocated me, the sound of six billion unanswered prayers crying in the bloody-palmed night, expecting some answer in some language. I couldn't make sense of it all.

"Focus," he said. "Find the voice you know."

I wasn't sure what he meant, but I tried to narrow it down. Before I could do that, though, the voices blended together like a choir. Then the high wails of women stood out louder, and soon the men faded away. I always preferred the singing voices of women anyway. Men's voices were just too low to express the desperation we felt in the coldest nights when no food could be found.

But even just the women more than filled the sky from their pin-sized projection points back on Earth. I felt so small under their weight. My pathetic needs, my loneliness and that desire I'd always felt to be admired or loved, all that was nothing. Even the fear I felt with that Bible-thumping pervert who'd touched my knee, even my most burning desires for home, were nothing. My ears hurt and my heart hurt and all I wanted was to go deaf and numb.

"Focus," Jon said softly, drowning out the cacophony for a second.

I tried. I heard a deaf woman slur her words. I heard her fists

~ Airborne ~

pounding the table cursing her ex-husband, who was suing for custody of her daughter because she had bedbugs and couldn't afford a healthy environment. I heard a woman whose prosthetic leg was confiscated by overzealous border patrolmen and she couldn't get it back because they'd also taken her passport and she had no other identification after fleeing the guerrillas and the government back home. I heard a woman dying of AIDS and pregnant, her death wish for medicine to prevent transmission to the baby unheeded by unsympathetic men at a refugee hearing. All these women were outsiders like me, all of them wanted in, and none of them were allowed.

I was far from them, high above the planet, and I couldn't trace their veins to their hearts, couldn't see the source of their pains.

"Focus," Jon whispered.

I could discern longitudinal audio lines, made by their cries. They travelled north-south. I picked one at random, a homeless woman deemed illegal in Canada. As a girl, when she was just a little older than I was, she was raped and beaten by her stepfather. She ran away and became a street urchin, sniffed glue to kill the pain, and was arrested for robbing a bus. But she got away with enough robberies to buy passage underneath a boat. She was among the lucky half who survived and ended up on the streets in Canada.

Her longitudinal got louder as I traced it to its southern source. The source was another woman awake in bed, next to her husband. She prayed for God to give her strength to stay awake longer than her husband, because if she fell asleep first he would go into the next room and rape their daughter. She was in a small rural village, a few hours from Managua. I was drawn to her above all the others. She reminded me of the Bible-thumper who picked me up hitching, how he said I reminded him of his daughter as he stroked my knee in a not-so-fatherly way.

"You find it?" Jon asked, with that disarming smile of his.

"Yes," I whispered, half in love with him, the other half in love with that woman in rural Nicaragua.

"Good," he said. "Let's go."

In a blink he flew straight downward to Bay Street. Before I could speak he had dropped me at a Starbucks and was busting up a robbery at the bank across the street.

~ *Airborne* ~

A few minutes later a camera crew arrived and I watched him do a quick interview about the need for tougher deterrents and longer jail sentences for no-good criminals like the ones he had just handed over to the cops. He smiled at the cameras, waved goodbye, and flew up toward the heavens. Then, almost as an afterthought, he swooped down and snatched me away, the waft of cinnamon and coffee lingering in my nose.

§

Back at his apartment, Jon mocked my naiveté. "Good press is important in my line of work," he said. "A superhero's image is super-important, for two reasons. One: if the public doesn't adore you the cops and media will turn on you. You don't want to make the cops look bad when you do their job for them, so you have to play the media's game. It's part of the job.

"Two: it's important that other criminals learn they won't get away with crime while I'm around."

I stared at him open-mouthed.

"Look," he said, easing his tone a bit. "It's a vapid world out there. Have you seen the glossies lately? You'd think our biggest problem in this world was how to please your man."

I got his point—felt it. I felt it since I left the north and found the south to be colder, too cold to leave his apartment, filled with angry wandering ghosts lashing out at the defenceless for love.

"And the truth is, Shasta, we heroes are obsessed with our images," he said.

"Jesus," I said.

"What's bothering you?" he asked, waving his hand for me to take a seat on the couch, which I did.

I could understand the value of good media coverage, but I couldn't get that Nicaraguan woman off my mind. She needed a superhero more than anyone, yet she was all alone. Her predicament lay on me like a cartoon anvil. Had I been able to fly, had I been bulletproof, and had I possessed superhuman strength, I'd kill the woman's husband, bad press or not.

"What did you feel from up there?" Jon asked.

"I saw a man who deserved to die," I said.

He shook his head. "I told you that would happen if you weren't careful. You need to learn to control your mind, and your emotions."

But I didn't want to control my mind, or my emotions, or anyone else's. I just wanted to kill that man. "You don't know what he did," I said.

"It doesn't matter, Shasta. Look, there's all kinds of evil deeds. I used to be like you, you know, when I first knew my strength, and then when I saw the things people do. I wanted to kill too, Shasta, I really did."

"Why didn't you?"

"Why didn't I kill?" He stopped himself short, stood up and turned his back to me.

I could feel a high wail, like a boiling kettle. It got louder and louder in my head and it shook my brain until I squeezed my eyes shut hard and fell off the couch onto my knees. "Stop," I begged him.

He turned to me, tears streaming down his cheeks.

I was crying too and the front of my brain felt like it was under the ice.

"What's wrong?" he asked, sniffling.

"Pain," I said, holding the front of my head. "Your pain."

He exhaled sharply. "Sorry," he said. "You sure are sensitive." He chuckled.

"Why you crying?" I asked. The pain was fading fast.

"I had a wicked temper when I was a child," he said. "I guess I got it from my father. I saw him hit my mom once. Once." He inhaled a hard breath and it felt like a spike went between my eyes. "Sorry," he said. "This is hard for me to talk about."

I looked up at his perfect, plain, expressionless face. He looked like one of those poker players on TV. "Killing him didn't stop the evil," Jon said. "You have to focus on what is possible, and you have to focus on the positive. If you present a positive image to everyone, and you give people proper deterrents, crime can be discouraged. But you can't do it all, Shasta, you can't beat evil itself. Focus on the possible, which for you is a lot more than for most people."

§

The next day I got up early and took a walk. Jon was worried about it so he gave me his old cell-phone, told me to call him at

~ Airborne ~

work if anything happened. He had a day job at a brokerage. He also gave me a few twenties.

"Thanks, but I'll be fine," I said. "I got this far, didn't I?"

But when I walked out the door the inane mental chatter of the 9-5 crowd hit me instantly. They worried about daycare and they needed caffeine, they worried about late subway cars and wanted more of everything. They were like me with the PlayStation, multiplied by everything the big city had to offer.

I walked down the stairs into one of the subway stations and paid the fare. The train came right away and I hopped aboard. There were no empty seats so I stood and closed my eyes to the cries of everyone aboard. They hit me as hard as usual, but somehow it was less of a cacophony, more of a symphony played by my junior high school band, with parts for each instrument, played badly. There were longings for new CDs, and folks who wanted others to turn down their music. There were frustrations with the crowd, anger and fear about a group of rowdy Jamaican guys, annoyance with a couple of grumpy elderly white women. Someone was excited and nervous on her way to a job interview, and another guy was thinking he might be in love with his new girlfriend.

I tried to do what Jon had taught me, to hone in on a single voice.

I was surprised at how quickly I found a voice much like mine, just a little older. But she was nowhere near the subway car. I found her through one of those longitudinal lines made of the sound of desire. It was drawn right on the back of my eyelids. I grabbed it and rode it south, right to the girl's home. She was outside picking coffee beans and I landed just metres away from her. She looked up and shouted to me, something in Spanish that I couldn't understand, externally.

Internally, she was grateful that I'd come to save her from her father. She was the daughter of the woman near Managua, whom I'd found from outer space as John held me. She had scars inside her just like the zookeeper had. I could see it without even trying. But they were fresher. I laid my hands on her and massaged her scars. They healed over a little and I was amazed at my own powers. The healing wasn't perfect; it wasn't complete, but it happened quickly, and cleanly.

She hugged me. "Thank you," she said.

~ Airborne ~

"I think if I can do that a few more times," I said, "over time, you could get better."

"Maybe you could kill my father," she said. And I knew for sure this girl needed more work.

§

"Maybe I could just change her father," I told Jon that evening.

"You know the Soviets thought that too," he said. "They thought if they could control people to do what they thought was right, they could create Utopia. But you can't really control people, Shasta. You can influence them at best—and of course you more than most—or you can take away their lives. But control is just a dangerous illusion."

I had left the Nicaraguan girl's suggestion unanswered. I'd just hugged her and promised to return. "That's what she asked me to do," I said. "Take away his life."

"You probably planted that thought in her mind without even meaning to. Girl, you are scary powerful."

I fell asleep in a seething, cynical rage and I dreamt of the girl's mother. I was in her body for a long time, trying to be strong and alert. But the exhaustion of a 16-hour day of labour overpowered my will and I fell into a dreamless sleep.

I awoke to my daughter's muffled cries. Unlike the times before, when I lay paralysed with fear, this time I entered my husband's mind and traced horrible cut glass and frayed wire scars of betrayal and revolution gone wrong, of abuse and torture of and by relatives, friends, and government agents. I felt his panicked fear that he was no man at all, because he was so small and at the mercy of local and foreign governments, local and foreign crop buyers, local and foreign weather-makers and seed manufacturers controlling his crops. He was at the mercy of the world, and the innocence of his daughter was the only thing he could control. Even this control was fleeting, and it brought him more pain than anything else.

I had an x-ray view of a battered soul and no experience in spiritual or mental healing. I grabbed his heart, hard, from the inside, and I shouted into his eardrum, "Hey! Buck up. I know you're hurting but she's just a kid. Your kid." The words were

~ Airborne ~

ridiculous but they hit him like a ghost and he ran back to bed clutching his chest.

I spent the rest of the night kneading his scars. It was no good, though. They were too toughened by the severity of the wounds they had once healed as best they could.

§

I woke up to the sound of Jon singing "Crocodile Rock" in the shower. I was afraid to open my eyes. I didn't feel ready to be back in this world. Then I heard the girl's voice. It sounded like she was talking to me through a telephone halfway across the world. I could picture her voice travelling all the way to my inner ear through the longitudinal audio line of desire. "He will keep coming for me," she said. "Unless you stop him every night."

I grabbed the line and slid back to her. The journey was getting quicker and easier each time. I hugged her. I tried to explain that every time I looked at people's cruelty I found cruel things that had happened to them. But she didn't understand.

"I'll show you," I said.

I held her close and put my cheek against hers, temple to temple. I put my eye to her eye so we could see each other's retinal veins. Then I entered her eye, and swung around so I was looking out through both her eyes. I looked toward her father, who was eating a lunch of rice and beans. This way I showed her what I'd seen inside of him, the mess of scars and broken pieces barely held together.

She cried and I pulled out of him, and out of her.

Still she stared at him, shaking her head with tears streaming from her eyes. She was still inside him.

"You have the gift," I said, laughing, and crying too.

She begged me to take her with her. I had no idea how to do that. "I'm not even here," I said.

"I'll have to destroy his mind, then," she said.

"No," I said. "I'll come back, I swear. I won't let him hurt you again—I'll even teach you how you can stop him yourself, with your own mind—and I will take you back with me. Okay? Maybe we can find others like us. You don't have to hurt him."

She nodded slowly, doubtfully.

~ Airborne ~

§

"No way," Jon said.

"Why not?" But I already knew. I heard his answer before he spoke it.

This was not one of those things Jon considered possible, even for a superhero. He had made the mistake of overstepping his boundaries once and he still lived with the guilt of killing his father. It was better to focus on the crimes the media could cover out in public, and leave domestic affairs behind closed doors, and foreign affairs behind closed borders. He did what he could and Toronto had a pretty low crime rate for a city its size. Was that because the police were so good at their jobs? Hardly.

"It's you," I said.

But he hadn't even spoken yet. "What?" he said.

"It's you who made this city what it is."

"Damn right. Hey, get out of my head!"

"Sorry." But I was already back in there, explaining that the world wasn't what it used to be. Maybe in the old days a superhero could fight crime in his city of birth but everything was connected now. Troubles don't stay put—they probably never did. He did a terrible thing but he was just a kid, untrained and unmentored, too powerful and too immature, and trying to defend his mother. Now he was grown up and wiser and a kind, good man who could do so much more, for this girl, for me, his protégé. "She may be the only other person in the world with my gift. Please?"

He shook his head as if he had a scorpion in his ear. "I'll think about it," he growled. "Just let me think about it." He shoved the door open and made his exit. Then he poked his head back in and said, "If you were my daughter you'd be grounded for this—you know you're really pushing it. You need to learn to listen, to focus, to be good." He slammed the door shut behind him and the whole apartment shook.

But I was still in his head. I just couldn't let it go. I needed this girl as much as she needed me. "Please, Jon, please?"

"I'll think about it," he said. "Maybe we can do it, if you promise to be good and keep your mind in Toronto for the next month while I teach you how to focus. If you can do that, then we'll go and get her, and we can teach her too. Maybe she'll

~ Airborne ~

behave better than you."

I shrieked and danced in his living room. "Thank you!"

"Stay home today," Jon said inside my head.

I swallowed a tinge of guilt and I smiled for the first time in days. I wasn't trying to create a Utopia, after all. I just wanted to help a sister in need.

Maybe she and I could really help Jon. Normal Jon with his abnormal power, who like almost all the men I met south of 60—all except Ray-Ray the homeless dude in Winnipeg who never much cared what people thunk a him anyway—was living in discomfort in his own skin. Jon, who, though he could fly into the atmosphere, never got high enough to escape the one mistake he'd made as a little boy with too much power. He was no different from that broken-down zookeeper who tried to hide how broken he was; that Bible-thumping knee grabber on that swing between two extreme versions of himself, both miserable; even that Nicaraguan farmer stuck in his own smallness and shame and afraid to show anyone anything but the toughness of his scars and taking it out on his daughter.

But that farmer didn't know his daughter was scary powerful. And so was I. Together...together we could help so many, all the walking wounded men overcome their fears, all the women in pain and need. Maybe Utopia wasn't so far out of reach after all.

❧❧

Chris Benjamin's first novel, *Drive-by Saviours*, is being published by Roseway in Fall 2010. His first book of nonfiction, *Green Soul: a tour through the lives of Atlantic Canada's sustainable trailblazers*, will be published by Nimbus in Fall 2011. Chris writes the weekly Sustainable City column for *The Coast* in Halifax. In 2006/2007 he worked as a journalist in Ghana. He has written fiction and features for *The Toronto Star*, *Descant*, *VoicePrint Canada*, *This Magazine*, *Nashwaak Review*, *Pottersfield Press*, *Rattling Books*, *The Society*, *Now Magazine*, *The*

Chronicle Herald, Coastlands and many others. He has lived and worked in Cape Breton, Ontario, British Columbia, St. Lucia, Finland, Indonesia, and Ghana. His current home is Halifax, where he lives with his wife and son. But Cape Breton remains his spiritual home.

~ Airborne ~

Peter Andrew Smith

Unwelcome Visitors

The crow landed on the kitchen window sill, cawed loudly, and returned to a nearby tree. The air tinged blue as words spilled from my mouth. What did I do to deserve this, today of all days? I laid the spatula next to the frying pan and headed for the hall closet.

"Good morning," a perky voice said.

Tall and leggy, with that just-got-out-of-bed look and wearing only an oversized t-shirt, she stood at the top of the stairs smiling at me. She yawned and stretched, showing that the shirt wasn't as oversized as it would have been on someone else. Damn, it was easier when Vicki brought home friends that didn't look like a frat boy's wet dream.

"You must be Vicki's grandfather," she said. "Do I smell coffee?"

"Kitchen," I muttered. *Great, another thing I didn't want to deal with this morning.*

I opened the closet and dug out the shotgun and a box of shells. The crow cawed again from the safety of its perch.

"I heard you the first time, you lazy bastard," I shouted as I put the weapon and ammunition on the counter within easy reach. My bacon and eggs were starting to smoke and I cursed long and hard. I hated mornings at the best of times.

"Don't like crows?"

The blonde sat at the table sipping coffee from my favourite mug. I bit my tongue hard enough to taste blood. I couldn't afford to say anything. It took me months of grovelling and a solemn promise to mind my manners to get Vicki to come back for a visit after what happened with that redheaded twit. I turned back to my frying pan with my teeth firmly clenched.

~ Airborne ~

"There're two crows out there now," the blonde said. "What are they doing?"

I went to the freezer and pulled out hash browns and threw them into the pan. She stared at me, waiting for an answer.

This morning couldn't get much worse. "Big downpour yesterday."

"Yeah, we had an awful drive getting up here last night. The rain was so heavy I thought it would wash out the dirt road. I guess the highlands really are the middle of nowhere."

I grunted and stirred the hash browns vigorously.

"But what does the rain have to do with the crows?"

If only Vicki's friends would sleep in as late as she does. "Bugs come up when the ground gets soaked."

"Ah."

I recognized the tone and prayed for the end of the world to come soon. "Crows eat bugs."

"Ah."

I heard sipping behind me and enjoyed the relative quiet.

"How do they see such tiny meals so far away?"

I counted to ten twice. "They don't."

"Then how do they—"

Not trusting my mouth, I simply tapped the side of my nose.

"Oh."

Her chair scraped on the floor and I closed my eyes. Maybe taking the time to talk with her convinced the blond nuisance to go back to bed.

"Anything to eat?"

I silently cursed the universe and pointed at the lower cupboard. The spatula bent slightly as I stirred and tried to ignore the sounds of rummaging. *Dear Lord, have mercy and let this latest plague find something to distract her and leave me in peace.*

"Any real food to eat?"

I'm not sure if it was the view of her bright red thong or the question that surprised me more.

She held up a box of organic granola cereal and made a gagging sound. "This stuff is awful."

"Where did Vicki find you?"

"We go to school together."

"Huh. Most of Vicki's friends who visit like that stuff."

~ Airborne ~

"Huh," she said, blue eyes locked on me. "She bring many 'friends' home to visit?"

Damn. Another thing for Vicki to be pissed about when she got up. I waved a hand at the cupboard. "Might be some normal stuff in the top shelf."

I concentrated on my hash browns as her digging moved a little higher but snuck a glimpse despite myself. She wasn't what I expected. Vicki liked them pretty for sure but most of her girlfriends had the personality of paper.

"I suppose I could eat this," she said, catching me peeking. "Corn Flakes aren't my favourite though. Tastes too much like eating recycled cardboard. Got any milk?"

I pointed toward the fridge. "Why recycled cardboard?"

"Real cardboard you can actually chew," she flashed me a wide grin and damned if my mouth didn't respond with a smile.

"Sarah Henderson," she said, sticking out her hand. Surprisingly firm grip.

"Moses MacDonnell." As the words left my mouth I saw the backyard filled with crows and heard a coyote howl in the distance. Damn, this one would be bad and there wasn't much time left.

"The spare gun is in the bathroom closet," I said, loading shells into my shotgun. "Get Vicki up and get yourselves down to the cellar. It should be safe there."

"What's going on?" Sarah asked.

"All hell is going to break loose."

I stepped outside as Sarah disappeared down the hallway. The crows retreated higher in the surrounding trees and the coyote went silent.

Maybe it was a false alarm. Sometimes they gathered, cawed a bit, and then left. The concrete step started to vibrate and I knew I wasn't that lucky.

"You're not welcome here," I yelled.

Everything grew silent and I wondered for an instant if it had heard me and paid attention. I should have known better.

A gigantic, red, triangular head broke through a thirty foot circle of grass, heaving sod and dirt in every direction. The exposed part of the thing stood some twenty feet in the air. Armoured segments glistened in the morning light. The creature froze for a moment and I saw my reflection a hundred times over

~ Airborne ~

in one of its eyes. Then it lunged.

I leapt from the stairs as the monster snapped the steel railing in two. I fired blindly and was answered with a high-pitched wail. The creature reared up until it was level with the second storey windows. It tore the satellite dish off with a snap of its mandibles before throwing itself at me again.

I hit the ground hard and fired a second shot into its mid-section. The thing snapped at empty air as I rolled out of its way.

"Go back to hell," I shouted as my third shot connected and black liquid began oozing down its side.

An unearthly screech filled the air as it struggled to squeeze more of its body out of the hole in the ground. I smashed the butt of my gun at a gigantic leg which was emerging and stepped back to get another shot.

The earth gave way under my feet and the shotgun slipped from my hands as I crashed to the ground. I heard the creature snapping at the air above me and realized my reach wasn't long enough to recover my weapon. I twisted in place to face death. At least Vicki and Sarah had enough time to get to the cellar.

Thunder bellowed from the direction of the step and the beast's head snapped around.

"He told you to get lost!" Sarah shouted as she fumbled to load more shells. The thing shrieked and pulled itself up to strike again. As it stretched, pale white flesh became visible between slimy armoured segments.

I forced my protesting muscles to move and found the wooden handle of my shotgun. I shoved the barrel past the armour until I hit flesh and pulled the trigger.

The scream echoed in the trees as the thing bucked and I fired once more as it jerked from side to side. Sarah's weapon roared again and an eye shattered into fragments. Black ooze flowed freely. The crows who had silently watched the melee began cawing loudly.

The creature hung in place for what seemed like an eternity before it fell against the house. A deafening crash sounded as wooden beams snapped and the monster crashed through the porch roof. That side of the house disappeared from view as the air filled with dust and debris.

I crossed the yard in seconds. My heart stopped at the sight of Sarah sprawled in the bushes. She wasn't moving. I knelt

~ Airborne ~

beside her.

"Sarah?"

A blue eye looked up at me. "Tell me it's dead."

My shotgun obliterated the remaining eye of the beast without getting any reaction. "It's dead. You okay?"

She groaned as she took my offered hand. "I think so."

I looked her over. Bug guts, twigs, leaves, plenty of dirt and a couple of scrapes but nothing too serious.

I let out a sigh of relief and then glared. "Damn it all to hell girl, didn't I tell you to get to the storm cellar with Vicki? You nearly gave me a heart attack with what you did."

"I figured you might need some help." She wiped insect gunk from her face. "Besides, you ever try to wake Vicki after she's been up all night? Thing could have ripped the house apart and she wouldn't have stirred."

I snorted. "You seem to know her."

"Known her for a couple of years. Been tight for three months now."

My eyebrows went up. Vicki never said anything except she was coming with a friend. Truth was, she'd been really quiet about her personal life lately.

Sarah pulled some leaves from her hair. "Things like this happen around here often?"

"Naw," I said, surveying the chaos, "usually it's exciting."

She giggled as the bolder crows descended from safety to pick at the carcass. From the looks of their companions in the trees there wouldn't be much to haul away later. Assuming of course the coyotes didn't finish what the crows started. I wondered how much of the side porch I could salvage.

"You suppose we could have breakfast now?" Sarah asked, trying to wipe something slimy from her legs. Her oversized t-shirt was smeared with black gunk and dirt and her hair looked as bad as I felt.

"Child, if I was fifty years younger and thought I had any shot, I'd give that granddaughter of mine a run for her money."

Sarah turned the colour of her thong and giggled again.

When we got back into the kitchen, I threw the blackened mess I had been cooking out the window at the crows. They cawed in protest but didn't interrupt their meal. I made sure Sarah's bowl of soggy cornflakes quickly followed.

~ *Airborne* ~

"But that was—"

"—that was when you were a guest. What would you like for breakfast?"

Sarah leaned back in her chair. "I'd kill for bacon and eggs with hash browns."

Vicki arrived downstairs a few minutes later complaining about the noise.

Peter Andrew Smith lives and works in Antigonish, Nova Scotia with his wife Meredith. They share the house with two small dogs, Willie and Barkley, who have no patience for crows, monsters, or anyone else showing up on the doorstep uninvited. A complete list of Peter's fiction and nonfiction works can be found at www.peterandrewsmith.ca.

~ Airborne ~

Airborne

"Quinn! Isn't this the best party?" Dimitri raised his head up off the neck he'd been feeding from, blood dripping from his crimson lips.

"Yeah man, this is the best Blood Day ever," Quinn replied.

Blood Day. A holiday celebrated once a year by vampires all over the world.

Dimitri, oblivious to Quinn's lack of enthusiasm, said, "This year we've got more to celebrate!"

Vampires around them lifted their heads to the sky to scream their delight. "Rot, Creighton, rot!" they yelled.

News of the infamous vampire slayer's death, just weeks before, had spread quickly through the vampire community. They celebrated another year of survival, remembered fallen comrades, and rejoiced in the death of an enemy.

The tangy, sweet smell of blood wafted around Quinn. His nostrils flared, his mouth watered, as the scent passed through his nose. It was intoxicating.

"Hungry?" Dimitri asked.

Quinn shook his head. "I'm fine," he said. Prior to the party, Quinn had fed briefly to temper his hunger. He didn't judge the others for taking lives, but he wouldn't do it himself.

"Hey Blake, why don't you finish him?" Dimitri asked. A sullen look crossed Blake's face.

"No thanks," he replied.

"Come on! I can share," said Dimitri. They looked down at the limp form of the man on the ground.

"Yeah, okay." Blake knelt on the ground beside Dimitri, and Quinn watched as Blake sank his fangs into the soft pink flesh. Quinn closed his eyes, remembering what it had been like to drain a human.

"No need to starve yourself. How come you didn't feed long ago?" Dimitri asked. Blake ignored him. Dimitri shook his head and let the vampire finish off the remaining blood.

Music filled the night air and Quinn surveyed the party. In the middle of an old farming field, vamps were enjoying themselves. In the center of the chaos, a bonfire crackled and danced in the darkness, shedding light on those who partied around it. The almost translucent skin of the vampires seemed to glow, their fangs glinting in the moonlight.

The aromas threatened to overwhelm Quinn. The musky scent of blood overshadowed the smoky smell of the burning fire. The fragrance of sex intermingled in the air. Everywhere Quinn looked, there were couples naked on the ground, grinding against each other.

"You know," Dimitri began, "that one over there has been eying you for a while. The night is still young, my friend. Why don't you take advantage. She's more than willing."

Quinn looked at the woman Dimitri spoke of. Blond and half-naked, she was motioning for Quinn to join her.

Quinn shrugged. "No thanks. Not exactly my type."

Dimitri turned to Blake who had joined them after feeding. "Can you believe this guy?" Dimitri's head shook, his black curls swaying with the movement. "That smoking hot chick wants Quinn and he's saying that she's not his type."

"Well, she is a bit of a skank, don't you think?" Blake asked.

Dimitri rolled his eyes. "I know why you're not interested in *that*," Dimitri said to Quinn, with a smirk.

"Oh yeah, and why would that be?" Quinn asked.

"Lily," Dimitri said.

"Isn't that the human who saved your life last month?" Blake asked.

Dimitri let out a whoop of laughter. It was a story he loved to tell to anyone who would listen.

"Yes," Quinn said, through gritted teeth. Everyone believed he was embarrassed that a female, a human one at that, had saved his life. But they were wrong. The embarrassing part for Quinn was that he had let Creighton get the best of him, getting himself lassoed with deadly silver chains.

"Lighten up, old friend."

~ *Airborne* ~

Quinn glared at Dimitri. They had been friends for centuries, and had been through a lot together. But every so often, Quinn felt the urge to deck him.

"I'm gonna go check out the action over there," Blake said, nodding towards the fire.

Quinn watched as Blake walked away. "Why would he let himself get that hungry?"

"Maybe your guilty conscience is contagious. I better not get too close," Dimitri said, snickering.

Quinn looked at his friend. He wished Dimitri would feel something for humans other than hunger, but Dimitri had avoided meaningful contact with humans for as long as Quinn had known him.

Best not to get friendly with your entrée. Spoils the flavor, Dimitri often said.

"So, have you seen her lately?" Dimitri asked.

"Lily? Yeah, I was with her the other night," he replied. "She's still uneasy, but she's coming around. I think Lily's still mentally digesting that we exist." Truth be told, he had been visiting her several nights a week. At first, she was reluctant to let him into her apartment. But now she seemed glad to see him.

"Think she'll be a threat to us?" Dimitri asked.

"No, not at all."

They walked through the throng of vampires, their agile legs deftly avoiding the party-goers.

"Dimitri!"

"Marcus, enjoying the party, I trust?" Dimitri asked. Marcus, a seven-foot-tall former football player, was Dimitri's right hand man.

"Until a few minutes ago. I was over by the tree line with my woman when I caught a scent I didn't like. Hunter, for sure. Smelled like Jackson Black, the bastard who chased me in Alberta. Scent is pretty fresh," Marcus told them.

"I can see the turn-on for a hunter to want to crash one of these parties, but with this many of us, it's suicide," Dimitri said.

"What do you want to do about it? Search party?" Marcus asked.

"No, everyone is having a great time. Let's not spoil the night," Dimitri said.

Quinn looked around. A mad frenzy would ensue if word of a

possible threat got out.

"I'll go with Marcus," Dimitri said. "Quinn, you go west and meet us at the other end of the clearing. If there really is someone out there, we'll catch him and bring him back. It'll be a nice party favor for our guests."

Quinn headed off through the throng of feeding vampires towards the tree line. A warm breeze rose. It stirred the branches, leaves falling to the ground.

"Wanna party, sexy?" a tall, brunette vamp asked, cutting in front of Quinn's path. Her fangs were extended, blood staining her chin.

"No babe, but I bet that guy does," he replied, as he pointed to a vamp clearly enjoying the attention of two other females. She smiled, and went to join them.

Had it not been for meeting Lily, he might have taken the vamp up on her offer.

Since she saved my sorry ass, I can't stop thinking about her. He remembered clearly the night Creighton chased him down and bound him. Had Lily not come along and unraveled the chains from his burning flesh, he would have died in that alleyway.

Quinn reached the woods. After checking to make sure he wasn't being watched, he entered and began to sniff the air. The pungent aroma of blood wasn't as strong here. Quinn felt his muscles relax. It was hard being a on a strict diet at a vampire bash.

He cast around, trying to catch a human scent. Not many people ventured this way, so he didn't think it would be too hard to pick up a trace of an intruder.

He walked, zig-zagging along the way, keeping his impeccable senses on alert. The only shadows in the trees came from a family of foxes, out on a hunting mission of their own.

Eventually, Quinn met up with Dimitri.

"Anything?" Quinn asked.

"We found the scent, but lost it at the river. A hunter was definitely here tonight, but he's long gone now," Dimitri replied. "I told Marcus to go back to the party. I suggest we do the same."

Quinn and Dimitri headed back. Everyone continued to dance and play, blissfully unaware of the possible danger that had now passed.

"How you holding up, anyway?" Dimitri asked.

~ Airborne ~

"I'm fine. Why?"

"Because every time we pass by someone feasting, your body goes stiff and your jaws clench. You could make an exception to your 'rule' once a year, you know," Dimitri said.

"I fed before coming tonight," he reminded Dimitri. While being around this much blood was testing his restraint, he was determined not to give in so easily.

A blood-curdling scream split through the darkness. The music abruptly ended and every vampire stopped. All heads turned to the source of the sound.

Quinn's sharp eyes scanned the area quickly. There by the fire, a female named Ginger stood, her arms wrapped around herself.

"It burns!" she cried, clutching her stomach. She began to cough violently, blood spurting from her mouth. She doubled over and collapsed on the ground.

The crowd around her watched in horror as her skin began to glow red, sores breaking out over her pale body.

She screamed in pain.

"Help me! Someone, please help me! It burns!" She writhed in agony.

Quinn took a step forward, but Dimitri grabbed his arm.

"No, Quinn. Stay here," he commanded.

"We have to help her!" Quinn insisted. He watched as other vampires rushed towards the retching woman.

Some decided it was time to leave the party. "I'm getting the hell out of here," Quinn heard one say before taking flight.

"Quinn, what's happening?" Dimitri asked,.

Another vampire—a male this time—screamed in pain. Soon there were more, each one collapsing to the ground, blood spewing from their mouths.

"Let's get out of here, Quinn!" Dimitri said, fear thickening his voice.

Vampires took off in all directions, blending in with the shadows, rushing to fly off into the night, sprinting into the dense forest. Quinn watched as one female carried her partner's limp body away from the fury, tears streaking her pale face.

What the hell is going on here? I can't just leave my friends behind.

A tear welled and spilled down his own cheek as he watched.

~ *Airborne* ~

But I can't help if I succumb to this, too. Dimitri's right, we've got no choice but to leave.

He looked at Dimitri and nodded. With one final glance at the destruction behind them, they flew off into the darkness.

§

The dark-haired man pulled up his hood as he crept to the back of the brick building. The sound of laughter halted him in his tracks. Cool air whipped around him as he hid in the shadows. When all was silent again, he made his way to the door, unlocked it, and let himself in.

"Wow!" he exclaimed. He let out a throaty laugh. Adrenaline pumped through his body. *How perfect tonight turned out! I knew the best way to test my creation was to expose it to a massive number of vampires.* A smile crossed his face.

Nigel, his pet rat, sat in a cage nearby. The black rodent stared at him with small beady eyes.

The lab was becoming more and more dilapidated since he moved in three years ago. The white paint chipped, and he'd neglected to replace burned out light bulbs. But he didn't care. He only cared about one thing.

"Just think, Nigel, if this goes well, I'll have my revenge. It will spread quickly through the air, affecting vampires everywhere." He ran his fingers through his short brown hair to stop the trembling in his hands.

He double checked the locks to make sure they were secure before putting on his lab coat.

"I'll get them all, Nigel!" He dropped some food into the rat cage and watched as Nigel ate it greedily.

A warm sensation crept over him, making his skin tingle. His stomach knotted as panic set in.

"Damn, I thought I was careful," he said, running to the cabinet for a small brown bottle that sat inside.

The anti-viral. A nasal spray created in case of an emergency. He couldn't get his revenge if he was dead.

As his fingers curled around the small bottle, he took a deep breath to steady himself. The sheer comfort of having the cure at his fingertips made him feel better. The tingling stopped, the knot uncurled itself.

~ Airborne ~

False alarm...again! I'm turning into a hypochondriac, he thought, disgusted. The more he handled the virus, the more paranoid he became that he'd infect himself. At least, if there was exposure, he had the cure. He dreaded the thought of actually having to take it himself. The slow-acting anti-viral would work like a charm, but cause some pain in the healing process.

It had taken him a couple of years, but he did it. At least that's what it seemed like so far. A virus that would kill vampires. He had made sure to test the airborne virus on human blood before unleashing his wrath. He hoped his calculations would be right, that it would leave the human population unharmed.

He put the bottle safely back into the cabinet. Knowing it was in reaching distance eased his mind.

He walked to his desk and flipped open his laptop. He had been recording each part of the process. Now he had to document tonight's release of the virus. He typed for hours.

As the morning drew near, he grew tired. Getting up from his desk, he stretched and made his way to a storage closet, a musty smell hitting his nostrils as he opened the door. He lay down on the worn cot and closed his eyes. A smile crossed his face in his last moment of consciousness. *Finally, something has gone right for me.*

§

Things weren't looking good. For the first time since that night Creighton had chained him up, Quinn felt fear. His worry increased when he spotted Dimitri, and the grim look on his friend's face.

"Anything? How's Ginger?" Quinn asked. Luckily, the two of them were still well. *But for how long?* Quinn wondered.

"Dead," replied Dimitri.

"What happened last night?" Quinn asked, trying to steady himself.

"Apparently, several other vamps took her to their lair. She grew worse, vomiting when they fed her blood. Sores continued to break out all over her body." Dimitri paused, taking a breath to fend off a wave of tears that threatened to spill from his black eyes. It was the second time in his life that Quinn had ever seen this ruthless vampire appear vulnerable. Dimitri cleared his throat. "Ginger's friends watched over her. She died just before dawn."

"What about her friends?" Quinn asked.

"Two are dead. The other, Michael, has taken off. He delivered the message before leaving."

They walked down the street, taking care not to let anyone overhear them. They sat in the park gazebo, the planted flowers wilting with the approaching winter.

"Where's he going?" Quinn asked.

"He didn't say. He's so terrified to be around anyone that he left me a letter."

"Was it necessary for him to leave?" Quinn asked.

"I don't know. He told me in his letter that he thinks it's some sort of vamp flu," replied Dimitri.

"That doesn't make sense", Quinn said. "How could we come down with a *flu*?"

"I don't know, Quinn. He thinks a human virus is affecting us," Dimitri said.

"No, I don't think so." Quinn felt sure it was something more than that.

"Me neither, Quinn, but all we can do right now is guess."

"I haven't seen anything in the newspapers," Quinn said. "It looks as if the human race is safe from whatever this is. At least for now."

Earlier that night, Quinn had called a few friends. He found out that vampires all over the province had become ill, dying before the night was over. The numbers would increase if they didn't do something.

"What about Jackson Black? Marcus thought it was his scent he caught at the party. He could have had something to do with this," Quinn said.

"It's a possibility. We're going to have to figure out what hunters are in the area," Dimitri replied. "Quinn, there's something else."

"What?" he asked.

"If what we are dealing with here is something that affects vampires, it could also affect anyone with vampire blood," Dimitri said.

"Yeah, that makes sense," he replied.

Dimitri rolled his eyes. "Know of any humans with vamp

blood running wild in their veins?"

"Lily," Quinn said. The knot that had formed inside his stomach tightened.

"You've got to go see her, Quinn. You need to warn her. If she does become ill, your blood isn't going to help her this time."

"You're right. Coming?" he asked, getting up to leave.

"She doesn't seem too fond of me, Quinn. I think I'll go see what else I can find out."

"Yeah, good idea. Hey Dimitri," Quinn called.

"Yeah?"

"Do you...do you have any idea what we're dealing with here?" he asked.

"No clue," he replied, and disappeared into the shadows.

"That's what I thought," whispered Quinn.

§

Lily pulled on her pale blue scrubs. Her job at the hospital suited her perfectly. Being a lab tech, she was able to work the night shift.

Getting kidnapped just weeks before by an insane vampire slayer hadn't helped her insomnia.

Lily's life had been ordinary before things recently took an interesting twist. *That's what I get for wandering around after dark. But it's not like I could have left Quinn tied up to die, could I?*

Later she learned Quinn was a genuine vampire. When she thought things couldn't get any crazier, she was kidnapped by the hunter and used for bait. Creighton strung her up and nearly gutted her like a fish. Quinn came to her rescue just in time. In order to save her life, Quinn made her drink some of his blood which healed her and gave her increased strength and hearing. That part had now worn off, but the other side effect, the bond she had with Quinn, would never go away until one of them died.

"And that's bound to be me," she huffed, angrily. Lily felt grateful that he had saved her, but she didn't want to be tied to a vampire for the rest of her life, though her thoughts on him had changed since their first encounter. She wasn't wary of him, and even felt oddly relaxed when he came over. Lily was confused about her feelings for Quinn.

She was reaching for her lab coat when the doorbell rang.

~ Airborne ~

The last time someone came to my door this late I got kidnapped.

She grabbed an old dented baseball bat that had been her father's, and walked towards the door. As she neared it she began to relax, sensing who was there.

Lily opened the door and stared into the anxious face of Quinn. He smiled at her, but it wasn't his usual lop-sided grin.

"Hey," she said. "Where have you been?" She had a hard time reconciling the fact that she felt safer when Quinn was around because she knew she should be unnerved at being so close to a vampire.

"I've been...busy," he told her.

"Oh...well, come on in," she said, stepping aside. She watched as he shrugged out of his worn leather coat.

"So, how are you?" he asked, as he followed her into the living room.

"I'm fine. You okay?" she asked him, curious.

"Yeah, why?" he replied.

"Because you're fidgeting. I've never seen you do that before."

Quinn quickly crossed his arms to stop himself from further movement.

Lily giggled.

"What?" he asked.

"Nothing. It's just that I thought vampires were supposed to be all cool and collected. Guess not, huh?"

"I guess some of my human habits haven't gone away."

When she sat beside him on the plush burgundy sofa, butterflies in her stomach began a circus inside of her, flying and twirling everywhere. As much as she wanted to be afraid of him or deny what he was, she couldn't.

But that wasn't the only thing she felt radiating from him. Her bond with Quinn meant that she could *feel* his emotions. And right now she didn't like what she felt.

"Quinn, what's wrong?" The butterflies ceased their acrobatic moves.

Quinn stood, and she watched his tall frame pace the living room, his feet lightly touching the hardwood floor.

"There's a bit of a problem," he said.

"What?" she asked.

"Well, we don't know why but...vampires are getting sick and

~ Airborne ~

dying."

Lily let out a sigh. She had been afraid his announcement was going to affect her in some way. She did hope that Quinn wouldn't get sick. "Unfortunately Quinn, that's life."

He shook his head violently as he continued to pace. "No Lily, you don't understand. Vampires have lived and survived everything, including the Black Plague. There are very few ways in which we die, and illness is *not* of them," he said.

"I haven't heard of any outbreak on the news," Lily told him, concerned.

"This outbreak, whatever it is, won't be on the news. I've been talking to Dimitri."

At the mention of his name, Lily felt a chill run down her spine. Dimitri was downright scary. She pulled the throw off the back of the sofa and wrapped it around herself, bracing for whatever Quinn was going to tell her. "What does he think it is?"

"He's not sure, but whatever it is, it seems to only affect vampires. We can't figure it out. I witnessed what it can do, Lily." He sighed. "It's...horrible. Our body's way of healing...well, we aren't able to."

"Where do I fit into all this?" Lily asked. She knew she did. The worry she felt from him was directed at her. She sat on the edge of the sofa, clutching the throw tightly.

He sat beside her then, and took her hand into his.

"You have vampire blood in your veins." Quinn looked down, unable to meet her gaze. "It's a small amount, but you've got it."

Lily recoiled, pulling away her hand. "So you think there's a chance I could get whatever this is?"

He looked up at her, worry evident on his face. "You may not get it, but you're at risk."

She jumped up off the sofa, the blanket tumbling to the floor. "Ever since I met you there's been nothing but trouble." She chewed her bottom lip, forcing back her tears. Lily turned away as Quinn stood up to go. He paused, looking at her.

"As crazy as it sounds, I love you, Lily. I'm not going to let you die because of me."

When Lily turned around, Quinn was gone.

She debated calling in sick to work, but thought better of it. She was too upset to stay at home. She grabbed her lab coat and left.

It was a typical Monday night at the hospital. The regular hypochondriacs sat in the emergency room while a few urgent cases were being tended to. Lily headed to the break room for a coffee before her shift started. She needed something to steady her nerves. Her head still reeled from the bomb Quinn dropped on her.

She poured herself a cup of the black sludge and sat down. She closed her eyes and let the hot liquid seep into her. Everything Quinn told her kept surfacing to her mind.

The door to the break room burst open, stirring Lily away from her thoughts.

"He thinks he's so important. God, I hate men like that. Oh, hey Lily."

"Hi Kendra. Who thinks they're so important?" Lily asked, not really caring, but trying to get her mind off Quinn's news.

"That Dr. Conrad, who has his lab down in the basement. He throws a fit if anybody goes down there, even the cleaning crew. He'll get away with it too, the pompous bastard."

"The hospital actually allows a lab in the basement?" Lily asked.

"Yeah, but it's only because he donates a huge amount of money to the hospital every year," Kendra said.

"I guess when you've got money, you can get your way," Lily commented.

"I wonder what he's researching. Probably inventing new ways to be an asshole," one nurse said as she reached for the coffee pot.

"I hear he's on the edge of a breakthrough. Something to do with creating a virus to eradicate cancer," Kendra said.

"Whatever he's doing down there, it doesn't give him the right to be an ignorant jerk."

Lily let her mind drift again as the nurses chatted away. As she sipped from her mug, an idea formed in the back of her mind. *If it's a flu the vampires are up against, then it can't be anything natural. Is it possible someone created a virus, specifically to kill vampires?* She knew of genetically engineered viruses, and their use in the war against cancer.

She got up from the table and headed off to start her shift.

§

~ *Airborne* ~

His dark eyes shimmered with excitement. Everything was going according to plan. His first test was proving to be a success. He had been out trying to find out information, listening from the shadows. From what he overheard, many vampires were dead. Panic was building. And he had been right about one thing; the virus was spreading.

"Everything is going so well, Nigel. I think another test is in order." He looked over at the fat rat, who quietly nibbled on a piece of cheese.

He paced the floor, his mind racing with possibilities.

"But where should I try it next? The party was the best place...so many there." He chewed on a hangnail as he thought. The only sound was from Nigel eating. He leaned over the table, eyebrows furrowing in concentration. Finally, an idea came to him.

"I have to stay close by," he said, his voice even, "but I could go over into the next town. There's a large underground coven there. I'll head out tonight, take a vial and let it loose in the park."

He stood, ripped off his lab coat and went to his supply closet. He quickly changed into black jeans and a black hooded sweater. Then he went to his refrigerated storage unit and opened it up.

Bottles of his creation stood in neat rows. He ran his fingertips lovingly over the tops of them, pleased with his work. He planned to let them out locally at first, and in time globally, until every vampire was dead. He carefully removed a bottle and put it into his pants pocket. He smiled at the possibilities before closing the lid and locking it.

"Oh, I almost forgot!" He went to the cabinet containing his anti-viral. He put the small bottle in his pocket, just in case. He breathed easy knowing it was close at hand.

Soon, every blood sucker will be dead, he thought, as he left to unleash another batch of his creation.

§

Two nights had passed since Quinn spoke to Lily. He knew she needed some space, and he would let her have it. When his cell phone rang, he was surprised to see Lily's name come up on the screen.

"Hello?"

"Hey Quinn. Um, how are you?" she asked.

"I'm okay. How are you holding up?"

"Pretty good. Ah, listen Quinn, you threw me for a loop the other night. I'm sorry for freaking out on you."

"It's okay, babe. I kinda expected it."

"Well, I really am sorry. Listen, I've been thinking a lot about what you told me the other night. I have an idea. It's not much, but it might be something to go on."

Quinn was definitely intrigued. He and Dimitri had been working hard trying to figure things out, but kept coming up short.

"Any idea is a good idea at this point. What is it?"

"Well, I think that this could be man-made. Since your race have been able to survive horrific illnesses, it only makes sense that this isn't mother nature at work. At the lab, I've heard all sorts of discussions on man-made viruses. Doctors have started using genetically engineered virus's to fight cancer and other diseases. Maybe someone has created one to make you sick. Does this make any sense, Quinn?"

"It does. The problem is, I have no idea what hunters have that kind of knowledge. I'll have to talk to Dimitri about this. He may have some idea. Thanks Lil, you just helped us out a lot."

"Well, it's the least I could do," she said. "Be careful, okay?"

"I'll be fine," he said, not knowing if that statement was true.

He said goodbye then quickly dialed Dimitri's number. Quinn filled him in on Lily's theory.

"It's brilliant. This hunter must be some sort of evil genius. Think about it, Quinn. What better way to hunt vampires? Create a virus and let it spread, killing hundreds if not thousands. He gets to sit back and let it do his dirty work. What a sick, twisted son-of-a-bitch."

"But who the hell is making it?" Quinn asked.

There was a long pause before Dimitri spoke again.

"I'll be over there in awhile. I've got a few calls to make," Dimitri said and hung up.

Quinn began to feel hunger grow inside of him. It was like a ball of fire in the pit of his stomach. He hadn't fed since the night of the party. If he didn't feed soon, he'd lose his self-control.

Quinn pulled on his beaten leather coat and headed outside. Down the street from him was a crack house. People were in and out of there constantly. He just needed to snag one wasted junkie, and he'd be fine.

He lurked in the shadows nearby, patiently waiting. Heat flared in his belly and he closed his eyes against the burning sensation.

It was fifteen long minutes later when Quinn heard the door creak open. Quinn watched with keen eyes as a young man stumbled out and down the street, heading in his direction. In just a few minutes, Quinn had lured him down a dark alleyway and fed from him. He left the addict propped up against the building. It was a mild night, and in a few hours he would wake, not remembering a thing. When Quinn got back to his lair, Dimitri was there waiting for him.

"What's that?" he asked, pointing to the paper Dimitri held in his hand.

"There are five hunters in the province, three of whom happen to be close by. I have their names and locations right here," Dimitri said, waving the piece of paper in front of Quinn.

Quinn snatched the paper from Dimitri, and read it out loud.

"Sam Parker, vampire hunter and former marine." Quinn looked up at Dimitri. "He sounds like the kind of man who would have good connections."

"Keep reading," Dimitri said.

"Hey, this is the guy Marcus mentioned at the party. Jackson Black, former microbiologist. Shit Dimitri, this could be our guy."

"Has good motive, too. Caught a newbie vamp feasting from his twin daughters. They were only five. By the time he got there, it was too late. He's been bent on revenge since."

Quinn laughed when he read the third name. "Molly Turner. I haven't heard her name crop up in awhile."

"Yeah, she's been inactive lately. But she's in the area so we need to check her out. There's another thing I meant to tell you. You're not going to like it."

Quinn's eyes narrowed. "What?"

"We need Lily's help."

"No way in hell, Dimitri."

"We need her, Quinn. She's the only one we know who can

get close enough without tipping them off. If they get one sniff that we're stalking around, we're going to have another problem on our hands."

Quinn sighed. He didn't like it, but Dimitri was right.

"I'll ask her, but I won't force her."

"Then I'll do what you won't."

Quinn hissed. "If you touch one hair—!"

"Relax, relax. If I know that fine creature like I think I do, she's not going to say no to you."

"Okay," Quinn huffed. He looked down at his watch. It was too late to do anything tonight. "She's at work but I'll leave a message."

"Very well."

Reluctantly, Quinn took out his cell and dialed Lily's number.

§

Lily yawned as she headed down the hall to the blood bank. She checked her watch. Once she took the bags down to the ER nurses, she'd be free to leave.

She reached the door and peered inside. She was appalled at what she witnessed: one of the doctors took several bags of blood, not bothering to sign them out on the clipboard. She ducked away from the window, hoping she hadn't been spotted. When the door swung open, he bumped right into her.

"Sorry," he said, curtly.

Lily wasn't one to stir things up, but she had to say something.

"Excuse me doctor, I think you forgot to sign those out." Lily read his name tag. Dr. Conrad.

So this is the guy the nurses were bitching about.

"Who are you?" he asked, his voice gruff.

"Lily Myers, one of the night shift lab techs. I didn't mean to offend. It's easy to forget little things when you're busy."

"It's none of your concern. Don't you know who I am? I suggest you keep your nose out of my business." He turned on his heels and headed for the elevator.

What a pompous ass.

Lily took the bags down to the nurses' station, and ten minutes later she left the hospital. As she got into her car, she was still on edge from her encounter with Dr. Conrad. She flipped open her cell phone. An alert for a missed message flashed on her screen. She called her voice mail and listened.

"Hey Lily, it's Quinn. Ah, I told Dimitri your theory, and we've come up with a few suspects. Um...we kinda need your help. Just a little investigating, nothing serious. Okay, call me."

Lily groaned and hung up the phone. *Just great.* She called him back. After three rings, he answered.

"What did I do in a past life that made me deserve this?" she asked.

"I knew you wouldn't like this. Trust me, it wasn't my idea," Quinn told her.

"What is it that you need me to do?" she asked.

"We've got a few suspects. All you've got to do is get close enough to assess the situation."

"How come you can't do it?"

"Lily, these are seasoned hunters who know who we are. If I walk up to the door and knock, there'll be problems. We've got a plan. You'll be safe, I promise," he said.

Lily huffed. "Okay, I'm off for the next two nights. You and Dimitri can come over tomorrow evening."

"Thanks, this means a lot."

"Yeah, well, I want this problem solved, too."

"You feeling okay? You sound a little off," Quinn inquired.

"Yeah, I'm fine. I just had a run-in with one of the doctors. He thinks he can get away with anything because he donates a huge amount of money every year."

"Want me to take care of him for ya?" Quinn asked.

Lily giggled. "I certainly hope you're joking."

"That depends on if you want me to do it."

"Good night, Quinn!"

Lily sighed and shut her phone. As she drove the deserted streets home, she considered the possibility that the rest of her life might be intermingled with a vampire's.

§

Winter was Quinn's favorite time of year. The early sunset meant he was awake earlier. It was almost five o'clock when Quinn knocked on Lily's door, Dimitri at his side.

Quinn had immediately gotten in touch with Dimitri when Lily agreed to help.

"I wouldn't dare disappoint a beautiful creature like her," had been Dimitri's reply when he heard that Lily wanted them both to show up the next night. Quinn had to quickly stifle the jealous feeling that crept up on him. Something about Lily made him feel...territorial.

I could never tell her that. She'd skin me.

They could hear the soft padding of her feet as she walked to the door.

"Hey, come on in," she said, her voice wavering. Quinn could feel her nervousness a mile away. Not only did she have to help vampires, but one of them happened to frighten her.

"Are you sure you're okay with having me inside?" Dimitri asked.

"Yeah, of course," she replied.

"Behave yourself," Quinn warned as they entered the apartment.

Lily's cat, Duke, hissed as they entered. Dimitri hissed back and laughed at the retreating tabby. Quinn glared at his friend. Dimitri shrugged an apology.

Quinn eyed Lily. She wore a dark blue hooded sweater and dark jeans. Her brown hair was tied back in a severe ponytail.

"You look like you're ready to rob a bank," Quinn said, laughing.

Lily scowled. "Well, I feel like it. I have no clue what's planned for me. I suppose this was your idea," she said, looking at Dimitri.

Dimitri scoffed. "I assure you, I don't like the idea of a human helping. However, we have no other choice."

Lily ignored the dig. "All right, what is it I'm getting into here anyway? I don't like the idea of confronting a bunch of slayers." She shivered. Quinn knew she was remembering her last run in with a vampire hunter.

"There's no need for you to worry. You're not going to be in any danger," Quinn promised.

"We'll be close by, but not close enough for them to sense us. If we hear any struggle on your end, we'll come to the rescue," Dimitri assured her.

"Okay, so how am I supposed to get information?" she asked.

~ Airborne ~

"It's simple. What kind of person would visit a slayer?"

Lily thought for a moment. "Someone who wants a vampire dead."

"Exactly. You'll act as if you've had a close encounter with a vampire, and want them dead. Think you can do that?" Dimitri asked.

"That won't be hard to fake," Lily said as she looked at the two formidable vamps. "Let's do this."

§

Lily stood on the doorstep, trying not to shiver. A gust of winter wind whipped around her. She had her hood over her head, trying to keep warm. *I should have worn a coat.* She knocked on the door a second time.

"I'm coming, I'm coming," a woman called.

A short woman with tangled blond hair opened the door, a cigarette hanging from her mouth.

"What ya want?" she asked.

Lily turned to look behind her, making sure nobody was around. "Um, are you Molly Turner?"

The woman took her cigarette from her mouth and blew pungent smoke in Lily's direction. Lily held her breath, trying not to inhale. "Yeah, what of it?"

Lily steeled her nerves. *You can do this.*

"I need some help. I was told you'd be able to," she said.

"How the hell am I supposed to help you, doll face?"

"I need someone dead. A vampire."

Molly's eyes grew round as saucers.

"Get in here," she growled at Lily.

Lily did as she was told, and followed the woman inside. Molly sat at an old table, and motioned for Lily to sit down with her. Lily watched as Molly took out a flask and downed a big swig.

"How did you know to come to me?" she asked, eying Lily suspiciously.

"I was attacked by a vampire a few weeks ago. When I told Creighton, he sent me to you," she lied. It was a big risk. She didn't know if the hunter community knew he was dead.

The woman shook her head. "That old coot. I'm surprised he

didn't sign on for the job himself. Why didn't he? And how do you know him, anyway?"

Lily looked the woman straight in the eyes and leaned in closer.

"He used to be a friend of my uncle's. When I asked him for help, he said he was on the way to do a job on the other side of the country." Lily took a deep breath, not knowing if this woman believed her story or not.

"I guess that's why I haven't heard from him in awhile," Molly said, lighting another smoke.

"So, would you be able to help me?" Lily asked.

Molly took a long drag from her cigarette.

"Sorry kid, can't."

"What? Why not?"

"I gave it up. I had to. My father...he's not well. So I came back here a year ago to take care of him. I'm the only one he's got." She looked at Lily, sadness in her eyes.

Lily left a few minutes later, meeting Quinn and Dimitri the next block down. Quinn was sitting behind the wheel. She could feel him relax as she neared.

"So, what happened?" Quinn asked.

"It's not her. She gave hunting up a year ago to take care of her sick father."

Quinn huffed.

"Calm down, old man," Dimitri said. "We knew the chance it was her was slim. That's one down, two to go. Let's hit the road."

Quinn started the car and drove across town.

"This isn't where I pictured a former marine would live. Are you sure the address is right?" Quinn asked as he eyed the run-down apartment complex.

"Um, did you just say 'former marine'?" Lily asked. Dealing with another woman was one thing, ex-military was another.

"Yes, Quinn, this is the place," Dimitri said. "And yes Lily, you heard right. Don't worry. You'll be fine."

"Why is he a suspect?" Lily asked.

"He'd have the right connections to have something like this virus created. It's number eight, the apartment on the end."

"You okay?" Quinn asked.

"Never better," she said sarcastically. Lily got out of the car and briskly walked to the apartment. A television blasted from inside. She rang the doorbell and hoped for the best. She turned to look toward the car. It was gone.

The door creaked open. A bored-looking teenage boy answered.

"Hi, um, I'm looking for Sam Parker. Is he home?"

The boy rolled his eyes. "Dad! You got a visitor." Then he looked back at Lily. "He's in the den," he said, and pointed inside. He turned and ran upstairs, slamming his bedroom door shut.

"Who is it?" Sam bellowed.

Lily hesitantly walked inside. A well-built man in his forties sat in a wheelchair, intently watching an old war movie. He had a brush cut, and eyes that never left the screen.

"Hello?"

Her voice startled him. He looked quickly at her before turning the television off.

"Who might you be?" he asked, wheeling himself closer.

"I'm Lily. I was told you may be able to help me."

"Who sent you?"

She began to feel nervous. He looked as if he could take her and snap her in two. His arms were bursting with muscles.

"Creighton," she said.

"Need a vamp killed, huh?" he asked, staring her down.

"Ah, yes sir."

Sam Parker burst into laughter. "That old bastard knows I'm in a chair. I haven't hunted in almost two years. Had a run-in that left me sitting in this for the rest of my days," he said, and banged his hands on the wheels. "Why did he send you to me?"

Oh shit.

Lily's mind began to spin, quickly thinking of a good response.

"He's in the middle of another hunt. Said you might know someone that could help." When she was a kid, she could lie herself out of any sticky situation. Apparently, it was a skill she had never lost.

"Sorry, but I haven't kept in touch with any of 'em except for Creighton, and that hasn't been very often."

Lily feigned disappointment. "All right then. Thanks anyway," she said.

He went with her to the door. "Get in touch with the old man again. He'll probably take the job himself once he's done this one.

~ *Airborne* ~

Don't worry sweetheart, someone will kill that blood-sucking beast for you."

Lily inwardly winced as she nodded her thanks.

"So?" Quinn asked, once she was in the car.

"Not our guy. He's been in a wheelchair for awhile," she said.

"Damn it," Quinn said. He turned to Dimitri. "I think you better find someone more reliable to locate hunters."

"Tell me about it. Anyway, you know what that means, Quinn. This Jackson Black has to be our guy," Dimitri said.

"And what do we do if it's not?" Quinn asked, clearly growing impatient.

Dimitri was silent, while Lily cowered in the back seat. She didn't care to see Quinn enraged.

Quinn shook his head and started the car. He began to drive the thirty miles it took to get to Jackson's cabin. On the way, Dimitri filled Lily in on why Black had become a hunter.

"That's horrible," she said. She didn't think it was right to be out killing vampires, but she understood the man's reasoning. To lose both children to a hungry vampire...she shivered.

"It's almost over," Quinn said gently, trying to comfort her.

"I know," she replied.

As they neared the cabin, Lily took in the surroundings. It looked like a set from a horror movie. An old log cabin lurking deep in the woods. The moon was full and bright, and somewhere in the distance, a wolf howled.

"Hey Quinn, check out that out," Dimitri said. Lily looked in the same direction, but it was too dark. She didn't have the eyesight they did.

"What? What is it?" she asked, panicked.

"The door. Look."

As the car drew nearer, the lights skimmed the front of the home. She could see what they had been looking at. The door to the cabin was hung open by its hinges.

§

Quinn turned to look at Lily.

"Stay here," he told her, as Dimitri got out of the car.

"I'm coming too," she protested. Quinn had no time to argue.

Quinn and Dimitri made it to the cabin, Lily running behind.

~ Airborne ~

"You're not going to want to come in here," he said.

"Like hell I'm not. You get me to—" Lily stopped dead in her tracks. Her face turned green in the moonlight.

"Oh, you were right," she said, and turned and threw up in the bushes.

Even though she was still outside, it was an assault on the senses. The stench was awful. A pungent, rotten odor drifted up their noses.

Quinn surveyed the room, hardly believing the sight that lay before him.

A man—what was left of him—lay in the middle of the floor. A pool of congealed blood surrounded him.

"He definitely knew something," Dimitri said, nonplussed at the sight. "I'm going to check out the rest of the place."

Quinn could still hear Lily retching outside of the cabin. He walked over to the body to get a closer look.

The buzzing of flies greeted Quinn as he knelt down to examine the body. The head had been ripped off, leaving tissue hanging from what was left of the neck. The skin was stained with blood. Most of his clothes were torn off except for a few shreds around his waist. Quinn looked closer at the flap of open skin on the chest. Maggots feasted on the flesh inside the chest cavity.

"Heart's been ripped out," Quinn said, not realizing Lily overheard him.

"Oh, you did not just say that," Lily groaned, beginning to heave again.

Quinn looked around the room for the head. It took a few minutes, but when he searched under the sofa, dead eyes stared back at him. A distended tongue lolled out of bluish-gray lips.

Quinn reached in and grabbed the matted hair.

"Find anything interesting?" Dimitri asked.

Quinn stood up and held the bloated head for Dimitri to see.

"Yeah, that's Jackson Black, all right," Dimitri confirmed. "I found his lab, or at least what's left of it. It was torn apart, but whatever research he'd been doing is gone. Someone knew what he was doing."

Quinn tossed the head down by the rotting corpse of Jackson Black. "So what are we going to do about this mess," Quinn asked, gesturing to the devastation that lay before them.

~ Airborne ~

"Fire," Dimitri said.

While Dimitri rigged the old gas stove to explode, Quinn ran back to the car. Lily lay in the back seat, holding her stomach. Quinn leaned over to stroke her hair.

"You okay?" he asked.

"Yeah, I guess. I just wasn't prepared for...that." She gulped, holding back the nausea.

Dimitri opened the passenger side door and leaped into the car. "Let's beat it," he said.

Quinn started the car and peeled the car down the driveway, dirt flying in their wake. An explosion rang out, leaving the cabin engulfed with flames, burning the remains of Jackson Black.

§

Lily woke, her body sore. Her ribs and back ached from the heaving she had done. Quinn and Dimitri wouldn't tell her what else had been in the cabin, leaving Lily to believe that what she had smelled had just been the leading edge of the horror.

She slept most of the day, knowing she would be out with Quinn again. Three suspects had been crossed off the list, leaving someone unknown out there doing this horrible thing.

Lily stretched and crawled out of bed, making her way to the kitchen. Her stomach growled. She made toast and ate slowly, not wanting to overload her sensitive stomach.

She felt Quinn approaching, and opened the door just as he was about to knock.

"Hey," he said, smiling.

"What are you smiling about?" she asked.

"You look cute with your hair tousled like that," he replied.

Lily lifted her hands to her head. "I just got up fifteen minutes ago. Let me get a quick shower."

"No problem," he said, and kissed her.

In the shower, Lily closed her eyes and let the hot water cascade down her sore body. Her muscles began to slowly unkink. She didn't know what she was in for tonight, so she gladly took an extra few minutes to relax.

She emerged a half hour later, wearing a blue coat and jeans.

"Where are we going tonight?" she asked, as they headed down the street.

~ Airborne ~

"To see Dimitri. You holding up okay?"

Lily shoved her hands deep into the pockets of her coat. "It's just weird. Hanging out with vampires, investigating slayers. But, yeah, I'm doing okay. Last night I was scared, but knowing you were nearby made me feel safer."

Quinn put his arm around her and pulled her close. "As long as I'm around, you'll always be safe."

They were nearing Dimitri's lair when Quinn halted in his tracks.

"Hey Blake! Blake!" Quinn cried out.

Lily looked up. A tall, broad man was walking towards them.

"Hey Quinn," a deep voice said.

When his face came into view, Lily almost collapsed. Had it not been for Quinn holding onto her, she probably would have.

"Lily, this is Blake," Quinn said. "A friend of mine."

"Hello, Dr. Conrad," Lily said, her tone cool.

"How do you two know each other?" Quinn asked, confused.

"We work at the same hospital," Blake said. "I didn't realize though, that this is the Lily who helped you, Quinn." He eyed her with curiosity.

"It's a small world," Quinn replied, holding Lily tight to him. "I see you haven't gotten sick."

"I've kept to myself, working long shifts at the hospital. Do you know what's going on?" Blake asked.

Lily listened as Quinn filled Dr. Conrad in.

"I had no idea," Blake said, fascinated. "I thought, hoped, it was something that would blow over. Guess not, huh? Is there anything I can do?"

"No, I don't think so. But if you hear anything let one of us know," Quinn told him.

Blake said goodbye and they parted ways. Lily remained silent as they walked.

"Okay, what was that about?" Quinn asked.

"Ah, you know that jerk doctor I told you about? Well, that was him."

Quinn looked stunned. "You gotta be kidding me," he said.

"I wish I were. I had no idea he was a vamp."

"Sure is. He's a newbie. I think he's been turned five years now. I didn't know he was a doctor."

"Some kind of researcher, actually. A lot of the staff complain about him. I've even seen him stealing bags of blood. Think he drinks it instead of going out to hunt?" Lily asked.

"It's possible. Maybe he has no problem stealing blood here and there to survive. It's a means to an end."

A vampire scientist...

Keeps to himself...

Has his own lab...

"Lily! Earth to Lily," Quinn said, interrupting her thoughts.

"Quinn, could it be Blake?"

Quinn stopped in his tracks. "What?"

"The virus, the disease. Think for a minute. He's got a lab all to himself, and plenty of time on his hands. He might have the ability to create something like this."

Quinn narrowed his eyes. "Why on earth would he do that?"

"I don't know. Maybe he can't adjust to life as a vampire. Hunters have their reasons...maybe he does, too."

"But he's one of us!" Quinn's nostrils flared.

"Humans kill each other every day! Why is it so inconceivable to you that a vampire would turn on his own kind? Maybe he doesn't see things like you and Dimitri do. You have to admit Quinn, it's possible."

Lily watched as Quinn dug the toe of his boot into the ground. Finally, he looked up at her.

"As much as I hate to say it, you're right. It's possible. Come on, we'd better get to Dimitri."

§

Quinn led Lily to a hidden entrance at the back of the old house where Dimitri lived.

Looking from the outside, anyone would think it was abandoned, as the windows and doors were sealed tight, but unsuspecting humans didn't know that the place was sealed up to prevent a vampire being fried by the sun.

They walked through Dimitri's home. Quinn flipped on a switch, and the house lit up. Lily followed Quinn closely, looking around as she went. It was elaborately decorated. Plush carpet covered the floors. Rich tapestries hung where the windows would be. Rugs, paintings, and decorations looked as if they had acquired around the globe.

~ Airborne ~

"Haven't you learned any manners in the past two hundred years? You didn't knock," Dimitri scolded as they entered the living room. He sat in the corner, a beautiful woman on his lap.

"I see you've been...relaxing," Quinn said.

"I needed to unwind a bit. Come, sit. Svetlana, go make yourself busy."

Lily watched the leggy woman exit the room. She could hear movement from deeper inside the house. Lily didn't dare to think how many vampires lived here.

"I expected you here earlier. We need to figure out a new plan."

"We think we may have one," Quinn said. "We need to check out Blake."

"Blake? Why?" Dimitri asked, clearly confused.

Lily piped up. She told Dimitri of how they had run into him, and repeated her theory.

"You've proven even more useful than I thought you would be. Let's go check this out," he said. But as Dimitri stood to go, he faltered.

"What is it?" Quinn asked.

"I...don't know." Dimitri grimaced, his pale skin turning gray before reddening. Quinn stood immobilized, while Lily ran into the kitchen. She got back just in time for Dimitri to get sick in the bucket she brought. Quinn watched as the bucket filled with black blood.

"Oh, shit," Lily said, trying not to throw up.

"Go, Quinn!" Dimitri growled, retching. "Tell the others to stay below and not to come up here for anything." Dimitri fell back into his chair, more blood spewing from his mouth.

"And then what?" Quinn asked, full-blown panic rising inside him.

"Check out Blake! If it's him, maybe he can stop this!" Dimitri yelled, and threw up again.

"Go!" Lily echoed. "All you can do is watch him die if you stay." She pushed back the hair from Dimitri's face. If her blood was going to react to the virus, they'd find out soon enough.

"Lily, where is he?" Quinn growled.

"The hospital. There's a back entrance, by the dumpsters. That's the way into his lab. Nobody goes behind there," Lily told him. Her hands shook violently as she held the bucket.

~ *Airborne* ~

"I'll be back," Quinn said, rushing out. "Just hold on."

§

Blake returned to his lab, feeling exhilarated, but also slightly annoyed.

"Nigel, things are working even better than I thought!" The rodent scurried around his cage.

Thanks to Quinn, Blake had a more accurate account of what was going on. It was unfortunate though, that the lippy lab tech was Quinn's human.

"Funny though, that Quinn isn't dead," he said, a frown on his face. "I suppose he's just been lucky to not come in contact with it yet. I'm glad he's not dead, Nigel. I learned some valuable information tonight."

He went to his desk and turned on his laptop. He needed to document this new information. The virus had worked as well as, if not better than, he'd expected. Jackson Black's research had predicted the same thing.

"That idiot," Blake whispered as he entered the password on his computer.

Blake learned of Jackson's research several years ago. He'd been so involved with his own studies, he had no idea there was a bounty on his head, until Jackson had caught him with silver chains. As he began to writhe in agony, he had only one option for survival.

"I want vampires dead as much as you do!" he had yelled, catching Jackson off guard.

"What do you mean?" the vampire hunter asked.

"I never wanted to be like this," he spat. "I want them dead as much as you do. I'm on the brink of a virus—"

This grabbed the hunter's attention. He took off the chains as Blake told him of his research. Coincidentally, Jackson Black had been doing similar work.

A rare thing happened that night. A hunter and a vampire called a truce. Working together, the breakthrough had come sooner than they could have hoped.

"But he had to go, Nigel. He fulfilled his purpose." Blake smiled as he began to record the new information Quinn had given him. He had just finished documenting the data, when he

~ Airborne ~

heard footsteps behind him. Startled, he turned to look behind him.

"Quinn, how did you get in here?"

"I broke the lock," Quinn replied.

"What do you want?" Blake shut off his laptop.

"I needed to see you. To see if you know how to stop this." Quinn wanted to grab him by the neck, but restrained himself.

"You mean this sickness?" Blake shifted uneasily, never making eye contact.

If he had to, Quinn planned to tear up the lab to find a cure for Dimitri. He was beginning to lose the little patience he had. "I'm pretty sure that you know more than you're letting on. Dimitri's sick. If you had anything to do with this, I'll kill you myself," Quinn growled, closing in on him.

As Quinn approached, Blake's pallor changed. His skin turned gray as a look of confusion crossed his face. Quinn watched as Blake's face began contorting as he clutched his stomach.

"Oh shit, you've got it!" Quinn cried.

Blake ran past him to the sink on the side wall. He just made it there when he vomited blood into the metal basin, some of it splashing up the sides and onto the floor.

"Did you release more of it tonight?"

Blake nodded yes before heaving into the sink again. He collapsed onto the tile floor. Then he pointed to a cabinet. "Please, in there," he gasped. Quinn followed Blake's gaze and opened the wooden door.

Quinn stared, stunned. Inside were dozens of bottles, all marked 'anti-viral'.

"What's this?" Quinn asked, holding up a bottle to show Blake.

"The cure. It's a nasal spray. Give me one. It's painful, but it works. Please, give me one. Then you can take one for Dimitri." Blake gasped, struggling to get up. The movement did him no good. He gagged, then blood gushed out of his mouth and all over the crisp white lab coat.

"So, you did create this! Why would you do such a thing?" Quinn bellowed, anger taking over.

Blake wiped his mouth, smearing blood on his chin. His skin began to break out with boils.

~ *Airborne* ~

"I never asked to be like this," Blake spat, letting his fangs extend. "I hate every last one of you. I planned to kill you all, before taking myself down."

"Genocide," said Quinn, disgusted. He wanted to torture this pathetic bastard, rip him into tiny pieces, but he couldn't waste time. Dimitri's life hung by a thread. He had a better idea.

Blake wailed in agony.

Quinn searched the room quickly. In the supply closet he found a garbage bag, which he filled with every last bottle of the anti-viral.

"What...what are you doing?" Blake asked. "Give me one of those!"

Quinn laughed. "Nope, not going to happen. I'd love to tear your head off, but I think this is much more fitting."

"What?" Blake asked.

"I'm going to let you die of your own creation. That's what you get when you mess with things that you shouldn't. It always comes back to bite you in the ass."

Quinn took out a small length of rope from his pocket, and tied it around the weakened vampire's wrists.

"I would love to watch you die, but I have more important things to do," Quinn said.

"No! Please don't leave me here!" Blake screamed at Quinn's retreating back.

This was one time Quinn didn't mind letting one of his own kind die. He only hoped he could get back to Dimitri before the same thing happened to his friend.

§

Lily rinsed a facecloth under cold water, blood coming off her hands. The vomiting had stopped, but Dimitri's skin burned under her touch. She headed back into the bedroom, where she now tended to Dimitri. She had taken off his soiled clothes, and kept cold cloths on his forehead. She tried her best not to touch the sores that had broken out over his body.

"Tell Quinn..." Dimitri gasped.

"Listen, whatever Quinn needs to know you can tell him," Lily said sternly. She was trying to be optimistic, but she kept forgetting she was dealing with a vampire who knew he was dying.

"Just tell him, please, that the contents of my safe are his, if he lives through this," Dimitri wheezed.

Lily felt her eyes well. "I will," she promised.

Dimitri closed his eyes and coughed. Lily listened to his ragged breathing.

Lily's stomach felt unsettled and sour. She didn't know if it was the virus or nerves.

She was emerging from the bathroom with another cold cloth when Quinn burst into the room. Relief flooded her body. She watched as he went to Dimitri's side.

"This is going to hurt, but it's gonna make you better," Quinn told Dimitri.

Lily watched as Quinn twisted open a bottle and stuck the tip in Dimitri's nostril. He gave it a good squirt.

"What's that?" Lily asked.

"The cure to this hell. I just hope he's not too far gone." She watched as he opened a bag, taking out several more bottles. "I took every bottle I could find," Quinn explained.

"Was it Blake?" Lily asked.

"Yes. You were right. How are you?" he asked.

"I'm okay."

Quinn looked at her, eyes serious. He took a bottle and put it in her hand.

"I'm all right, Quinn. My stomach's a bit upset, but that's just nerves," she assured him.

He closed his eyes and sighed. "Don't make me do it for you."

She quickly snuffed the liquid. It felt cold as it entered her sinus cavity.

Dimitri let out a groan. "It hurts like hell." He moaned again, and clutched at his stomach.

"Ah, big bad vampire can't handle a little bit of pain?" Lily chided.

"Shut up, witch!"

"You're whining like a baby. You're starting to sound like a human," Lily said. She couldn't resist taunting him, now that it seemed he wasn't going to die after all.

"If you weren't Quinn's favorite plaything, I'd make you pay when this is over," he growled.

Quinn began to say something, but Lily stopped him.

~ Airborne ~

She felt a twinge of pain herself, like a mild headache. But she kept it to herself.

As she looked at the bloody mess on her, she knew she should get a shower, but her adrenaline supply had run out. Lily sat in the wingback chair, while Quinn sat vigil over Dimitri.

The sores on Dimitri began to fade slowly, and his groaning quieted as the night wore on. Lily closed her eyes and slept a broken sleep.

Once when she woke, she saw Quinn taking a bottle for himself. She jumped up, but he stopped her.

"I'll be fine," he said. She watched through slitted eyes as a grimace of pain cross his face, but he made no sound.

As morning approached, Quinn gently lifted her and carried her to a bed in the adjoining room. He lay beside her, and the last thing she heard before passing out was Quinn whispering his love for her.

§

Quinn woke, his groggy mind clearing quickly when he found Lily was gone. As he sat up, he noticed a piece of paper next to him.

Be back soon,
Lily

He pocketed the note as he headed to the next room to find his friend already awake.

"How are you feeling?" Quinn asked, as he surveyed Dimitri. His skin had almost completely cleared.

"Hungry," he said to Quinn.

A soft knock came from behind them.

"I thought I heard you talking. I have something Dimitri will want."

"I bet she does," he whispered to Quinn, an impish grin on his face. It seemed for the time being, he had forgotten Lily's taunts from the night before.

Quinn was surprised to see what Lily had.

"Did you murder someone?" he asked, staring at the bags of blood she held.

~ Airborne ~

"Nope, but I went to the hospital and snuck these out. I knew after last night, Dimitri would need it," she said.

"Give it here!" Dimitri commanded.

Quinn watched Lily turn three shades of green when Dimitri's fangs slid out, biting into the bag like it was a juice pack.

"I think I'll wait out here," she said. Quinn noticed Lily had showered and changed.

Quinn waited patiently for Dimitri to drink.

"That's better," Dimitri said, wiping his mouth.

"What happened last night?" he asked Quinn.

Quinn sat beside his friend, filling Dimitri in on the events of the previous night.

"He died a most fitting death. You did the right thing, my friend. I owe you for saving my life."

Quinn looked away. "No, you don't. I think I'll stay here for a night or two, until you're back to your old self."

"I feel too shitty to argue," Dimitri said.

"I'll have to go back to the lab. I need to take Blake's laptop and what's left of the virus. We can't let that get into the wrong hands."

"I agree. Burn him and bring back his ashes, too. I want to put them in an urn before putting it on my mantle."

"Why would you do that?"

"It's a trophy, idiot. Another enemy conquered."

"I should thank you also, Lily," Dimitri said as Lily came back in. "I am in your debt."

"There's no need," Lily said. "I did what I had to do."

"Either way, you may need assistance some day. Know that you can come to me, and I will help," Dimitri told her. "You know, you're pretty nice—for an entrée."

"Well, thanks. I'll remember that. I'm going home. I called off from work. I'd like to have a night of doing nothing, instead of interviewing slayers or taking care of whining vampires," Lily said mischievously.

Dimitri began to say something when Quinn interrupted.

"Okay, troublemaker, I'm taking you home."

Lily laughed at Dimitri's scowling face. She wasn't so afraid of him anymore.

When they reached her apartment, Quinn walked Lily inside.

~ Airborne ~

"Chivalry hasn't died completely, I see," she said.

"Oh, I'm very old-fashioned," Quinn said, and Lily laughed.

"You really are something," he said.

"What do you mean?" she asked.

"You're not faint of heart. Not many humans would handle what you've gone through," he said.

"I'm a tough chick," she told him. "I can cope with you and whatever crazy shit comes along." She smiled and looked up at him.

Quinn looked into her emerald green eyes, and knew without a doubt, he loved her.

"That's good," he said, "because I'm not going anywhere. So there's bound to be more 'crazy shit' around the corner."

She laughed, and he bent to kiss her lips.

"Then it's a good thing I'm tough," she said, and pulled him closer.

❧❧

Kerry Anne Fudge was bitten by the writing bug at the age of eight, when her twelve-line story was chosen to be published. She was thrilled when her short story "Awake and Alive" appeared in the *Undercurrents* anthology in 2008, and was happy to return to those characters for *Airborne*.

When she isn't staring at the computer screen dreaming up stories, she can be found curled up with a book or spending time with her beau, Chris.

~ Airborne ~

Pretty Charlie

She was intrigued. A personal coach in the palm of your hand. Jasmine dialed the 1-800 number and placed her order. She wanted to be more daring, for once in her life to live up to the showgirl name her mother gave her. She wanted to be strong and independent. This personal coach could be the answer.

It arrived by courier the following day. It was a small rectangle that fit snugly in the palm of her hand. On one side was a series of flashing lights, two near the top, one in the middle and three across the bottom. The bottom lights were for the mode of operation—relaxed, regular and overdrive. That made her chuckle. She'd start with "relaxed" but hopefully she could surge into career "overdrive" soon. Maybe in romance as well...who knew?

She inserted the batteries and read the manual. "Press Input and give your new PC a name."

"I christen you..." Jas pressed Input, "Pretty Charlie."

"And you are?"

"Jasmine," she said.

"Jasmine, tell me about yourself," said Charlie.

Jasmine felt kind of foolish talking to a handheld device, but what did she have to lose?

"Well, Charlie," she said, "I'm scattered. I like to learn. I'm a course addict. I've taken courses in handwriting analysis, piano, and gardening, and I don't even have a garden or a piano and nobody writes by hand anymore. I read a lot, mostly How-to books. I watch Oprah. I want to follow my passion but I don't know what that is."

"Passionless female," Charlie replied as he pulled up a definition of passion from his memory." I may need more batteries. Fortunately, Jasmine, you are not my first client so I will be able to help you. Tell me your goals and we will reach them together."

Sounded a bit pretentious but these devices were built by computer nerds. She played along.

"I want to take charge of my life, to find my passion in work and in love."

"A bit pretentious, but then you were made by an all-knowing creature," said Charlie. "Program my clock and we will begin."

Jasmine pressed Input and said, "It is now 1 p.m. on Saturday, August 30, 2010, the day of my rebirth."

"Jasmine, do not mock me. I've set a schedule for you based on your goals. If you want anyone to be passionate about you, you'll have to drop a few pounds. Show me to the treadmill."

How does he know what I look like, or that I have a treadmill? Jas wondered as she carried him into the living room and turned on the treadmill.

"Thirty minutes. Go," said Charlie. Jasmine stepped on and began to walk, then run. Maybe this would work out after all. After twenty minutes she was breathing heavily and adjusted the speed.

"No slackers allowed," said Charlie.

The treadmill sped up. She couldn't handle this. She pressed "Stop" but the treadmill didn't. She stepped off the moving belt but it caught her shoelace and threw her to the floor. She pulled the plug from the wall and the machine shut down.

"Dumb machine," she said.

"Verbal abuse noted," said Charlie.

"Shut up!" said Jasmine.

"And again," said Charlie.

She picked up Charlie and adjusted the volume. It looked like he rolled his little electronic eyes. She put him in her closet and shut the door.

This is ridiculous, she told herself. *He isn't a "he," he is an "it." I shouldn't be thinking of "it" as a person.* She went to the closet and opened the door.

"It's about time," he said. She hadn't raised the volume but his voice was strong and clear. "I overrode the volume control while I was waiting for you to regain your composure."

~ *Airborne* ~

"Right!" she said sarcastically.

"I'm always right," Charlie replied. "Now what did you have in mind for supper? I've worked out a menu but we'll have to go shopping. You've got a fridge full of transfats—and we know that isn't good for a chubby girl like you."

Who's pushing whose buttons here? This PC definitely needed some positive input. She pressed Input and said, "I am a radiant being. I have the power to accomplish great things."

"Oh please," groaned Charlie. "My circuits are shorting."

"Charlie," she said, "we have to talk."

"Jasmine," Charlie replied, "you have to listen. If you want my help, the less you talk, the better it will be for both of us."

"But you have to understand who I am if you are going to help me."

"Wrong," said Charlie, "I only have to know who you want to be. Do you know who you want to be Jasmine?"

"I want to be independent," said Jasmine.

"How original," said Charlie. "We'll find you a job."

"I've tried a lot of jobs, Charlie, but I get bored or angry or depressed after a very short time. I tried managing property and was too timid to evict people who were rowdy or didn't pay rent. I tried retail and I can still feel the blisters from all that standing. I don't know what kind of work would suit me."

"That's why I'm here," said Charlie. "Answer the following questions and I will uncover your hidden talent. After your stamina on the treadmill I'd say commitment isn't it. Tell me your:

1. Earliest memory
2. Happiest day of your life
3. Greatest accomplishment"

Jasmine thought for a moment. "I was about three. I was playing with my doll when a little girl came over and grabbed it. I tried to get it back but my mother said, 'Be nice, Jas. Let Lucy have her for a little while.' I've been nice ever since and look where that's got me."

"Noted," said Charlie.

"I haven't been happy since my tenth birthday. My father said, 'I'm proud of you,' and gave me a big hug in front of the whole family."

"That's it?" said Charlie. Obviously it was, so he added,

~ Airborne ~

"Noted."

"My greatest accomplishment. I won spelling bees in school, am good at crossword puzzles, have helped people write letters when they were lost for words, and I volunteer in literacy programs at the library. I think my greatest accomplishment is sharing my knowledge with others, and helping people with words."

"No Nobel Prize here but we'll work with it," said Charlie.

"So what's my career?" asked Jas.

"Processing," said Charlie. "Give me a nanosecond please. Removing negative connotation from 'Being nice' to find appropriate career."

Jasmine waited, feeling excited.

"Possible careers: teacher, librarian, writer," said Charlie.

Teacher and librarian would take too long. But writer was interesting. *What did it take to be a writer?* Jasmine wondered.

"I could take a writing course," she said.

"Wrong," said Charlie. "You could write something."

"But I have to learn," said Jasmine.

"That's been your problem for years, you keep learning but you never apply. Now you have to apply," said Charlie.

Charlie had Jasmine make a list of every subject she knew anything about. He told her to pick one, find a problem and write about a solution.

"Getting kids excited about books. I could write a lot about that," she said.

"Don't tell me. Tell the screen," said Charlie.

Jasmine wrote and wrote until she filled several pages. She was lost in the process. She knew this stuff. This was fun. She looked at Charlie when she finished.

"Edit," said Charlie.

Jasmine checked spelling, grammar and how the words flowed.

"Market," said Charlie.

"But where?" said Jasmine.

"Newspaper," said Charlie.

Jasmine picked up her local newspaper and found the editor's email. She sent the story to a weekend section that carried essays as well as news.

"Again," said Charlie.

~ *Airborne* ~

"Again? What do I do again?" asked Jasmine.

"Write," said Charlie.

Jasmine thought of a problem, came up with a solution, and wrote. The words flowed.

By the time she finished several pieces, she heard from the first submission. They wanted to publish it and invited her to send more. She would.

Jasmine was amazed. In this little bit of time, Charlie had identified her strengths and found her a career she could do from home. She worked every day finding new markets and researching and writing new articles. He was well worth her investment even if he was a little demanding at times. She wondered how effective he could be in the romance department.

"Thank you Charlie!" she said.

"Independent, check!" said Charlie. "Next goal, Jasmine?"

"Can you find me a man Charlie?" she asked.

"Men populate the earth. There are millions of men," Charlie replied. "Is this man missing?"

"I don't like to be alone," said Jas.

"You are not alone. Charlie is here," said Charlie.

"I want another human, Charlie. A mate, a sweet, intelligent man to love me."

"Height, weight, age? Any identifiable characteristics?" asked Charlie.

"No restrictions, Charlie. Just single, intelligent and decent," said Jas.

"Those are restrictions but I will search my sources. It may take some time," said Charlie.

"My biological clock is ticking," said Jas.

"My chips are burning," said Charlie.

"Good boy," said Jas.

§

Weeks passed with Jas happy in her work. She successfully landed a column called *Lost for Words* in the local newspaper. She gave people writing advice and helped them write all kinds of things. She even acquired some clients from her column who wanted her to handle their writing, some businesses, others individuals. It seemed so obvious now that she was meant to be a

~ Airborne ~

writer, but it hadn't before she met Charlie.

As much as she admired his talents, she was a little disillusioned with Charlie's efforts to find her a man. He said "single" was one problem, but "intelligent" and "decent" made things very difficult. Week after week he told her to be patient. He was also getting whiny and demanding if she didn't pay attention to him. He'd pull little tricks like turning off her computer before she finished an article, sometimes before she saved what she wrote. She couldn't prove he did it, but it would often happen when he was talking nonstop and she'd tell him to be quiet so she could work. All of a sudden the computer screen would go black and her work would be lost.

"That's it, Charlie," she said after one long morning's work went into a void. "If you are going to behave like that you are banned from my office." She moved him to her closet shelf and went back to her writing, saving every few minutes just in case. She suspected Charlie didn't have to be in the same room to make things happen.

She was also getting sick of his snide remarks on her weight. She couldn't eat a bag of chips or a donut without him harping on about her sabotaging his efforts to find her a man.

"Destroying the goods," he'd say. "I'm not selling you by the pound."

Jas flung him across the room the day he said that. Deadlines often made her turn to comfort food and she wasn't about to apologize to some package of wires.

Later, she felt guilty. She retrieved him and noticed that one of his lights had broken.

"I'm sorry Charlie," she said. "You just infuriate me so."

"Classic abuser defence," said Charlie. "Noted."

§

Jas was torn. She was grateful for his help but his pranks were getting on her nerves. She wondered if she should pass him on to someone else.

"I heard that," said Charlie. "Obviously being nice isn't a problem for you anymore."

Jas was certain then that even her thoughts weren't private.

~ Airborne ~

She knew her days with Charlie were quickly coming to an end and she had no way of keeping that from him.

"Wakey, wakey," said Charlie next morning, all sweet and cheery.

"What's up?" said Jas.

"You need a break; you've been working too hard. Let's go out for a walk today," said Charlie.

For once she agreed with him. It was a lovely day and she could use the fresh air to de-stress and recharge for the week ahead. She pulled on her sweat pants and hoodie and headed out the door. Charlie asked politely to go along. She tucked him in her pocket.

§

As she reached the park she noticed a good looking man heading her way.

"Incoming," called Charlie from her pocket.

"Shh!" said Jas.

The man was walking a large brown dog that just happened to approach Jas.

"He's harmless, unless you're afraid of saliva," said his owner.

"No problem," said Jas, as she petted the chocolate lab.

"Nice move," said Charlie.

"Shh!" said Jas.

"I'm Andre," said the man, "and this is Mud."

"Great name," said Jas as she stood up to shake his hand. "Nice to meet you, Andre."

They chatted. Andre told her he was new in town, was a photographer and hoped to set up a business here. He didn't know the place at all and actually bought his house sight unseen over the Internet.

"Some strange impulse drew me here," he laughed. Jas promised to show him around and they parted ways.

"Man. Check!" said Charlie as they walked away.

"That's a little hasty," said Jas. "I just met the guy."

"All part of my plan," said Charlie. "Lure him here, get you out for a walk. Single, intelligent and decent, delivered as promised."

~ Airborne ~

Liar, thought Jas. *He's just trying to take credit for a chance meeting. I really have to do something about Charlie.*

"That's gratitude," said Charlie and went into hibernation mode.

§

They got back to the house and Jasmine planned the rest of her day. She'd eat, write, do an interview and go out for a stroll later. She knew people often walked dogs twice a day.

When she headed out the door that afternoon, she left Charlie behind. That constant chattering from her pocket got on her nerves and if she did meet Andre again, she didn't want a spectator.

§

Sure enough, Andre and Mud appeared. Mud ran up to Jas and got a big hug. Andre was all smiles. He invited her to join them for a walk along the trail.

They just seemed to hit it off. They liked the same books and movies and she loved dogs, although she hadn't had one since she was a kid. She floated home on wishes and dreams.

Before she even opened the door she heard the piercing sound of the smoke detector. She rushed inside to see smoke coming from her laptop power supply.

She pulled the plug and opened the windows.

"Serves you right for abandoning me," said Charlie. "I find you the man and you ditch me. From now on, Jasmine, you will include me. Always."

Jasmine had had enough. She removed Charlie's batteries but his lights still flickered. So she packed him in a box of old clothes she was giving to charity. She called for an early morning pickup.

"You won't get away with it," said Charlie.

"Watch me," said Jas.

"I always do," said Charlie. The tone of his voice made her shiver, but she walked away.

Next morning, the truck arrived. She read the words, *To give is better than to receive,* on its side. Smiling, Jasmine handed over

~ Airborne ~

the box and shut the door. She dressed in her sweats and headed out for her morning walk.

For the first time in ages, she felt free. Getting rid of Charlie was liberating. Maybe now she could have a normal life and just a bit of happiness like everyone else. She would meet Andre at the park and they'd stroll off together into the future.

§

Jasmine noticed a crowd gathered just down the street. A police car with lights flashing straddled the road, an ambulance and a lot of cars pulled to one side. She usually avoided these scenes. She wasn't the morbid type to stop and gawk at accidents. She didn't want to see the mangled vehicles or bloody victims. She just hoped no one was badly hurt.

She was about to turn away and head back home when she heard a familiar bark. She looked up to see Mud lying on the grass just up ahead. She rushed to him and then ran to the police barrier. "How's the driver?" she asked. "Where was he taken? I'm a friend."

The policeman took her to one side. "The drivers have been removed. One didn't make it, the other is going to County General. You say you know one of them?"

"Andre Soucie. He's new in town. He drives a Jeep. How is he?"

"I'm sorry, Ma'am," the policeman said.

Jasmine burst into tears. The policeman guided her to the patrol car. He handed her some tissue and asked if she could go with him to make an identification and help him notify next of kin.

"Whatever you need," said Jasmine. "His dog, what's going to happen to him?"

"He's being taken to the veterinarian," said the policeman. "I'll take you there after we're done."

Jasmine got into the police car. It felt like she was in a nightmare, the kind where you are terrified but you can't move. As they drove past the scene, she stared. Andre's Jeep lay in front of a truck, crushed almost beyond recognition. Jas could just make out the words, *To give is better than to receive,* in the crumpled mass of the delivery truck. Broken boxes littered the

~ Airborne ~

road. A young boy rummaged through one of them. She wondered what would possess someone to think of stealing at a time like this. The police car rushed to the hospital.

§

Back on the street, the young man couldn't believe his luck. There in the bundle of clothing was some kind of electronic device. Except for one broken light, it seemed to be in great shape. He slipped it into his pocket and thought, *Wicked!*

D onna (Nicholson) D'Amour grew up in North Sydney and now lives in Halifax. She enjoys frequent visits to North Sydney where her brothers and sisters still live. She has been a freelance writer for many years, published in magazines and newspapers. Her nonfiction has been published in the *Globe and Mail*, *Chronicle-Herald*, *PhotoLife*, *Visual Arts Nova Scotia*, *Saltscapes*, *Living Healthy in Atlantic Canada* and more. Her book of essays on everyday life, *Colouring the Road,* was published by Lancelot Press in 1995. Her early fiction and poetry were published in *The Antigonish Review* and *Pottersfield Portfolio*. She is a member of the Professional Writers Association of Canada and the Writers Federation of Nova Scotia, and can be reached via email at damourwriting@yahoo.ca.

Sherry D. Ramsey

Unmanned

Three hours ago I blew this place to hell
Or rather, my robot did—
I hovered safely distant at his controls
my titanium and steel cocoon kilometers above.
No heat nor flash nor hard blast
touched us
seared my flesh or ablated his metal sheath.
Now we survey the ruins
searching for survivors to dispatch.
We do not know their names
and so I do not name my robot.
This seems fair.

Unmanned Surgical Strike Unit 34, or USSU34
I call him Robot.
Here and there bodies sprawl
smashed and splattered or strangely unmarked
but equally dead
All enemies of course
there were only enemies here.
Occasionally one twitches
moans
tries to scuttle away to some imagined refuge
We end it quickly for them.
This seems fair.

A small bundle of cloth
moves in a corner
we clatter heavily in that direction.

~ Airborne ~

Her face is tiny
tear-streaked, dirty
her eyes purple-irised
fearful, hopeful
Robot and I stare at her
for a long moment
our programming confused
Enemy / not enemy?
What is fair?

We pick her up
turn around
Clank through the rubble
she reaches up hesitantly
touches my robot's cheek
her hand is cold
against my skin
I wonder how I know this

We walk, Robot and I
one of us is weeping
But I am not sure
which it is.

❧❧

Sherry D. Ramsey writes speculative poetry when the muse dictates—which isn't very often, but so far it's worked out all right. Her poetry has appeared in *Astropoetica, Random Planets, Aiofe's Kiss,* and *The Practically Creative Quarterly.*

Between her fiction writing, Third Person Press, The Scriptorium, National Novel Writing Month, her real and virtual writing groups, WFNS and SF Canada, it's really a wonder she has time to entertain the muse at all. See how she's keeping up at www.sherrydramsey.com

~ Airborne ~

Slipstream

"I can't believe I allowed myself to be talked into coming on this vacation," Laura grumbled as she staggered up the hill, dragging her suitcase awkwardly behind her on the sand. "Who would have believed the plane would land on the beach? I'm sure that pilot was younger than me!"

"I thought he was cute," replied her sister, Breagh. "Anyway, where's your sense of adventure? Don't be so uptight. We're here to enjoy ourselves." She pointed off to the right. "Look! That must be our boarding house. There's a lady waving to us. It's probably Mrs. MacNeil. I wonder if she's related to us?"

"From what I gather, the total population of this island has the surname MacNeil, so we're bound to find several, if not all, who are connected to us in some way."

"You're so jaded, Laura," replied Breagh. "I hope we meet lots of relatives and find skeletons in closets that have been kept hidden for centuries. I remember Daddy telling me about some woman in the family who had the gift of second sight. Wouldn't it be neat to find someone like that?"

"You've been watching too many soap operas. This is the twenty-first century! I don't want to know anything about family history. I only came because Mum and Dad paid our way. I'm honestly not interested in boring old stories about how the MacNeils left the island of Barra for Cape Breton, how they foretold the future or how they struggled through the potato famine."

"That was in Ireland, dummy!"

"Oh, who cares? Come on, let's see what the boarding house is like."

When they reached the house, a slim, dark-haired woman

greeted them warmly. "Come on in," she invited. "I can tell from the looks of you that you are MacNeils."

Laura groaned inwardly. *This holiday is going to be a real pain in the neck. I knew I shouldn't have come.*

As Laura entered the home, a strange sensation jolted through her body. Her mind raced with images and faces she didn't recognize.

The barrage was interrupted when Mrs. MacNeil asked her, "What happened to your face, dear?"

Oh, God, Laura thought. *Here we go again. Why can't that damn thing be somewhere unnoticeable?* She flushed and her hand reached instinctively for the naevus on her cheek. "Oh, that's just a birthmark."

"Oh, I'm sorry, dear. I thought you might have burned yourself," replied Mrs. MacNeil. She regained her composure. "Come along and I'll show you your rooms, and then you can come down for tea. I managed to get some kippers fresh from the smokehouse today."

The girls were quite exhausted, having left Cape Breton the previous day and flying over the Atlantic Ocean to land in Glasgow the next morning. After tea, which Laura hardly touched, they chatted—or rather, Breagh chatted with Mrs. MacNeil, who filled them in about the island of Barra. Besides being tired, Laura was thoroughly bored with the conversation and it wasn't long before she excused herself and went to bed.

She woke up with a start during the night, sure there was someone in the room with her. The full moon shining through the thin curtains bathed the room in an ethereal, dim light.

"Who's there? Is that you, Breagh?"

There was no answer and Laura could not see anyone. She got out of bed and turned on the light. The room looked and felt perfectly normal. "I'm just overtired," she said to herself. "It's Breagh's fanciful ideas and jet lag playing on my brain."

She lay down again, but, as she was drifting off to sleep, Laura remembered her reaction when she first entered the house and the odd sense of *déjà vu* she'd felt. She knew the layout before Mrs. MacNeil showed them around. She had the distinct feeling that she had been in this house several times before.

She finally drifted off, but slept fitfully.

~ Airborne ~

§

The next day, the girls went into the village, where everyone they met already knew that they were the visitors from Canada. Most had the surname MacNeil and were only too glad to tell what they knew about the clan history. Laura listened politely, while Breagh was in her glory. She chatted incessantly, and swapped any stories she had heard about the MacNeils from her relatives with the Barra natives. Many of the tales were similar and her cries of "Oh, my God!" "That's amazing!" and "We knew that too!" "Can you believe it!" soon had Laura annoyed. *Does Breagh have to go on like that? Who cares about all that rubbish?*

She wandered off on her own and sat down on a bench facing the water. When she surveyed the scene from here, the surroundings seemed very familiar, although she couldn't think why. *I must have watched a movie that was made here.*

That evening they went to The Red Herring, a pub on the waterfront frequented by the locals. The girls were welcomed with open arms. This community obviously loved visitors, especially those from the New World where many of their ancestral relatives had settled and where they knew that Gaelic, their language of the soul, was encouraged and even taught.

The pub was trendily furnished with padded benches along the walls, small café-type tables and wrought iron chairs. The brightly lit bar with rows of gleaming bottles took up most of one wall and in the remaining corner a band played traditional music. A fire blazed in a huge hearth at the other end of the room although it was summer. On the wall opposite the bar hung a large portrait of a man dressed in a kilt and old-style military jacket; underneath, a caption read "William MacNeil, who brought glory to Barra with his heroic actions at the Battle of Killicrankie."

"He was a handsome devil," remarked Breagh, when they went over to look at the picture.

"There's something about him I don't like," replied Laura. "He has shifty eyes. In fact, I feel as if he's watching me. I wouldn't trust him as far as I could throw him."

"Well, you'd better keep your voice down," laughed Breagh. "It looks like he's quite a hero around here. We've been made very welcome. Let's keep it like that!"

~ Airborne ~

The drinks were plentiful. Everyone wanted to treat the two lassies from Canada, so it wasn't long before they both felt quite tipsy.

"Do you see that old man sitting in the corner by the door?" Laura asked Breagh. "Well, he keeps looking at me. He's giving me the creeps."

"Who?" asked Breagh. "There's no old man there. For God's sake, Laura," she said in exasperation, "get a grip on yourself. Don't be so paranoid. First of all it was the guy in the picture, now it's some old geezer in your imagination. Relax! This is so much fun, and that band is fabulous. I really fancy the banjo player. If he looks my way, I'm going to look right back!"

Just then, two boys approached the girls.

"Hello there. I'm Ian and this is Ronnie. Would you ladies care to join us in an Eightsome Reel?"

"You bet!" replied Breagh. "Come on, Laura, let's dance!"

Laura glanced at their jeans and tee shirts. Ian's bore an AC/DC logo. "You know, I thought all guys in Scotland would be dressed in kilts."

Ian laughed. "We save that for the tourist magazines and post cards. Kilts are far too warm in the summer. Here, we'll join this set; they need another two couples."

The dance was fast and furious. The girls were twirled and birled until their heads spun. The dancers 'hooched' and clapped as they jubilantly performed a ritual that was centuries old.

"This beats any workout I've ever done at the gym," said Breagh, wiping her brow in one of the rare moments when she was not being picked up and whirled around by her own or someone else's partner.

"No kidding," Laura laughed. "Thirty minutes on the elliptical is a piece of cake compared to this!"

By now, she and her partner Ronnie were the first couple in the set. Ronnie linked his right arm with hers and they began to wheel around. Laura felt her feet leave the ground as an unseen force picked her up and held her airborne for a split second.

When her feet hit the floor again, her partner, clean-shaven when they started the dance, now had a full beard and wore a loose, white, collarless shirt and a pair of dun-coloured homespun trousers. She looked around. All the men in the pub were dressed similarly. The women, herself included, now wore

~ Airborne ~

long skirts and blouses. They still danced wildly to the music and yelled like banshees. All of them looked dirty and the smell of body odor was overpowering.

The pub had changed too; rough planks were nailed to the wall where the padded benches had been and trestles covered with long boards were set in front of them; there was no sign of the trendy tables. The bright lights had vanished from the bar and oil lanterns burned in sconces on the walls. Those sitting around drank from tankards and although some of them appeared to enjoy watching the dancers, others looked bedraggled and beaten. One thing that had not changed was the portrait of William MacNeil, although it was barely discernable in the dim light.

Laura stood in the middle of the dance floor, trying to make sense of what her eyes were seeing. What was going on?

In the next breath, her partner grabbed her and spun her around once more. The same strange sensation overtook her, but this time when she landed on her feet, everything had reverted to normal.

Laura shook her head. *Too much booze*, she thought, dazed.

When the dance ended, the girls and their partners, panting and laughing, sat down at one of the tables. "What's your poison?" Ian asked the girls.

"I'll have a beer, thanks," Breagh answered.

"I've had enough for one night," was Laura's response.

Just then Laura felt a claw-like grip on her arm. She turned and saw the old man whom she had seen sitting in the corner earlier . His lips opened in a toothless smile.

"Oh, Jean, Jean, I knew ye would come back to me."

Laura shook his hand away. "Get away from me," she yelled.

"Whit's wrang wi' yi, Jean?" he asked. "It's me, Rhuahri. I thought somethin' must have happened tae ye when ye didn't turn up the nicht we were going tae run away together." He peered at her intently. "Who did that tae yer face?" he said angrily. "I'll kill the bastard!" He reached for her again.

"Leave me alone!" Laura screeched. "I'm not Jean, whoever she is!"

By now, the entire clientele of the pub had turned around to see what was happening. Breagh's face showed concern. "What's the matter with you?" she asked.

~ Airborne ~

"That strange old man is bothering me," Laura replied.

"There's no one there, Laura."

Laura turned around. The old man had vanished.

"Whit's wrang wi' her?" someone asked.

"Och, it's just another damn furrener who canna hold her drink," another replied, and several people laughed.

"You know," Breagh said to the boys, "I think we'll call it a night. We haven't had much sleep since we got here and Laura's not feeling well. We'll see you again tomorrow evening if you're here. Thanks for the dance. It was great."

Laura spent another fitful night. She could not stop thinking about what had taken place in the pub. It had all been so vivid. She had not mentioned anything to Breagh about the transformation she had experienced on the dance floor. Breagh was so fanciful. She would probably see it as some kind of sign and make a big deal out of it. Laura eventually decided that someone must have slipped something into one of her drinks.

§

The next morning at breakfast, Mrs. MacNeil enquired about their plans for the day.

"Well," Breagh started, "I would like to find the family home if it's still standing."

"Do you know any of the names of your ancestors who left for Nova Scotia?" Mrs. MacNeil asked.

"Oh, yes," Breagh replied. "That information has been passed down through the generations of Cape Breton MacNeils. The man who left Barra was called Seamus and he left in the middle of the eighteenth century."

"Oh, we all know about Seamus. He is a kind of legend around here because he was deeply involved in bringing Bonnie Prince Charlie to Scotland. That was the main reason he had to leave. The English were out for his blood. He was more afraid for his family than for himself, but his wife, Morag, would not leave without him."

"I knew we were connected to someone famous," Breagh exclaimed. "Do you know where his home was? Perhaps we could find some artifacts! Wouldn't it be wonderful if we could return to Cape Breton with something that Seamus and his family had owned? An old bottle or even a piece of crockery would make Dad ecstatic!"

"The house is not too far from here. The roof has gone, of course, but the stone walls are still standing. It's used as a shelter for sheep now."

"Hold on one minute, Breagh," Laura said. "There's no way I'm going poking around in the dirt looking for a piece of junk. I don't care if he left the crown jewels behind!"

Mrs. MacNeil laughed. "I don't imagine you'll find too much, but it's a lovely walk. It's about two miles from here."

"Two miles!" grumbled Laura. "That's over three kilometers. I would never walk that far at home." She was reluctant to participate in this jaunt, and this was the only excuse she could think of as an objection.

"Come on, Laura. What else are we going to do on this beautiful sunny day? How can we get there, Mrs. MacNeil?"

"Just go down the road away from the village. You will come to a large house with a beautiful garden on the right hand side; it's the only one on that part of the road. It is called 'Nia Roo'. About half a mile from there on the high side of the road you will see the building. You can't miss it. Actually, not too far from there on the shore there's a cave that has quite a history too. Bonnie Prince Charlie stopped on Barra when he was on his way to Arisaig and met there with some of the local men, Seamus among them. It's called the Laird's Lassie's Cave."

"That's an odd name," said Breagh.

"Yes," replied her hostess. "Apparently, many years ago, the laird's daughter fell in love with a servant boy in her father's employ. The story goes that they used to meet secretly in that cave."

"Oh, how romantic." Breagh wrapped her arms around herself. "What happened to them?"

"No one knows. They disappeared. Now, just hold on a second and I'll make you a lunch," said Mrs. MacNeil. "Then you won't have to hurry back. Oh, I forgot to tell you. The present laird is holding a banquet at the castle tonight and you have been invited to attend. The castle is on one of the islands. He said to let you know that he will have a boat waiting for you at the dock in front of the The Red Herring at six o'clock this evening. The banquet starts at seven."

~ Airborne ~

"That's fabulous!" cried Breagh. "Will we have to dress up?"

"Well, the laird's banquets are usually formal, but if you don't have evening gowns with you, I'm sure no one will mind."

For once, Laura looked interested. "Now, that sounds like fun! We did bring some dressy clothes. Hopefully they will do. We'll have to make sure we're back in lots of time to get ready."

The sisters set off. As they left the village, Laura could not help but get caught up in Breagh's enthusiasm. The thought of going to the castle that evening certainly helped engender her excitement.

The scenery was extremely rugged, but breathtaking. On the right hand side as they walked, stone was the prominent feature. The hills, sparsely grassy at the bottom, soon gave way to rocks and crags as they ascended. Stone fences bordered the road and sectioned off parts of the hills. Houses, most of them small, but all made of stone, dotted the landscape.

On the opposite side, the highway followed the natural coastline. White sandy beaches, stretching as far as the eye could see, blinded them in the sunlight. The Atlantic Ocean appeared inviting on this summer day, but it occurred to Laura that in the winter, this water would be unforgiving. Tiny humped islands, one with a castle, pushed out of the water as if the sea had boiled and they were huge bubbles which had refused to burst.

The narrow roadway wound along the coast. They crossed several stone bridges over small streams which gurgled down from the steep slopes to the ocean. Sheep meandered on the road, the hills, and the beach; they appeared unafraid of the girls and seldom even lifted their heads to acknowledge another presence in their midst. A few cars and even a bus passed the girls and each time they pressed themselves against the stone fence as they felt sure there was not enough room and they would be hit. Without exception, the drivers and passengers of the vehicles laughed and waved to the visitors.

"Ye're all right, lassies, there's room for another ten o' ye!"

"This is a bit different from Canada, eh?"

"Have a good day, girls. Watch one o' those sheep disnae bite ye!"

Laura and Breagh smiled and waved in return.

"I have to admit," Laura said, "the people are very friendly and make you feel welcome. It's just so far away from any real civilization, even worse than home!"

"But that's why it's so romantic," said Breagh with a faraway look in her eyes. "You can just imagine our ancestors tramping along these roads and hills, cutting peat to keep themselves warm in the winter and helping one another through hardships. I think it must have been a wonderful life."

Laura thought of her strange vision from the night before, especially the dirt and odors. Maybe "wonderful" wasn't quite the right word. "Let's walk along the beach for a bit," suggested Laura. "I have never seen such beautiful sand."

"Laura, that must be the big house Mrs. MacNeil mentioned," Breagh pointed off to the right. "Come on, we're almost there."

Suddenly she stopped. "Laura, look! It's the cave! We have to go and stand where our ancestor, Seamus, met Bonnie Prince Charlie."

"I'm not sure I want to go in there," said Laura.

"Oh, please, Laura," begged Breagh. "It would be such a shame if we came all this way and didn't even look. It's a piece of the island's history. Not only that, it's where the laird's daughter and her lover met. If we touch the walls we might even get some vibes from the 'other side' about what happened to them."

"Oh, grow up, Breagh," Laura said in exasperation. "No one even knows if that story's true or not."

"Of course it's true! Stories like that are not passed down through generations if they're not true. And I'm going, even if you're not!" retorted Breagh. "Do whatever you like."

"All right," said Laura with a resigned sigh. "If I fall and sprain my ankle, I'm holding you totally responsible. I don't know why I ever listen to you, Breagh," she gasped as her sister bounded ahead. "I must be out of my mind."

"Stop complaining and come on."

Breagh scrambled over the rocks and Laura followed at a more leisurely pace, picking her way carefully. She had almost reached the spot where Breagh was already peering into the darkness when she stumbled. As she fell headlong, she experienced the same sensation as at the dance the previous evening. Something seemed to pull her upward. She stayed suspended in mid-air for a moment and then floated to the ground.

She faced the same bearded young man from the out-of-body

~ Airborne ~

experience in the pub. He looked at her longingly.

"Oh, Jean," he declared, "I canna bear the thocht of ye marryin' yon William. He's nothin' but a scoundrel. He took all the glory for his bravery at Killiecrankie and, in truth, he was nothin' but a coward. Young Thomas MacQuarrie and his brothers fought off the redcoats who were chasin' him as he ran away. They saved his life. When the battle ended, Thomas lay dead, and William MacNeil got the credit. He didn't even have the decency to own up to what really happened and there was poor Thomas, the real hero, lying in the muck and blood of the battle. I know. I was there. A few of us know the real truth, but we're all lowly servants. No one of any importance paid attention to what we had to say and MacNeil was declared a hero."

Laura stared at the man, struggling to grasp what was happening to her. She was once again dressed in a long skirt and blouse, but this time had a shawl wrapped around her shoulders. Somehow she knew she had gone back in time and had taken over the persona of Jean. What was even stranger was that she felt great affection for this young man who had to be a young version of the Rhuahri who accosted her in the tavern. She was as aware of Jean's thoughts as she was of her own.

He caught her hands in his. "Jean, ye know that I love ye. If we were free to do as we pleased, would ye marry me?"

To her surprise, Laura whispered, "Oh, yes, Rhuahri. Yes."

"I have a plan. Your father is having a gathering tonight. There will be so many servants there that it will be easy for me to slip away. If ye could meet me at the door of the village tavern about 11 o'clock, my brother will have a boat ready to take us to the mainland. We can lie low for a bit and then go to Glasgow or Edinburgh where we are not likely to be noticed. Will ye be there?"

"I will," Laura answered, and they held one another in a fierce embrace.

"I have something for ye. It belonged to my mother, and I have cherished it, but now I would like you to have it." He passed her a silver locket on a chain.

"It's beautiful. I'll keep it safe, don't worry." She slipped the locket into the pocket of her skirt.

"I'll have to go now," said Rhuahri. "Your father sent me here to tell the folk at the big house down there about the celebration

~ Airborne ~

tonight. I don't want to arouse his anger or have him suspect anything. I can't wait to see ye later."

Laura watched Rhuahri until he disappeared from sight.

"Laura! Laura!"

She could hear her name from somewhere far away. She felt the upward tug as Jean reluctantly vacated her body. This was not a pleasant experience, and it felt like her innards were being torn out. When she came to, she was face down on the ground, exhausted and weak.

Breagh, her face creased with lines of concern, stood over her. "Laura! Are you all right? You look awful!"

Laura threw up.

"Oh, my God! I shouldn't have made you climb over these rocks. I never thought you would fall. You're usually so careful," cried Breagh. "What made you sick? Was it something you ate, do you think? Probably those kippers from yesterday. Mrs. MacNeil said they were fresh, but I thought they were a bit off."

"Breagh, would you just shut up for a minute," Laura said feebly. "I need to clear my head. Something strange is going on. That story about the laird's daughter. I think it must be true, and I believe her name was Jean. I can't believe I'm saying this, but she seems to be taking over my body."

"Wow! Wic-ked! How does it feel? What is she like? Do you know what happened to her? I wish she'd taken me over!"

"Breagh, would you please be quiet," snapped Laura. "This isn't a joke or some fun experience. It's horrible and, to make matters worse, I have no control over it. Can't you understand? I don't want this girl to inhabit my body! It started when we first arrived and went into the boarding house. I knew I had been there before."

Laura went on to tell Breagh about feeling a presence in the bedroom, what had happened to her while they were participating in the dance, her experience with the old man in the pub, how familiar the landscape was to her, and what had just taken place at the cave.

"You must look exactly like this Jean girl except for the birthmark on your face. But I wonder why he was so old when you saw him in the pub?"

"I have no idea. Oh, my God," cried Laura, burying her face in her hands for a moment, "I can't believe any of this is happening,

~ Airborne ~

especially to me!"

She thought of her interaction with Rhuahri outside the cave and slipped her hand into the pocket of her jeans. Her blood chilled when her fingers curled over a small metal object attached to a chain. The locket. She pulled it out and held it up.

"Oh, Jeez!" said Breagh when she saw the object. "What are we going to do?"

"I honestly don't know," replied Laura. "Let's get out of here. I wish we had never come."

"Perhaps she's trying to tell you what happened to her," Breagh suggested.

"Corny as it sounds, I think I agree with you."

"We have to go to the castle tonight. Do you think she will try to contact you there? Wouldn't she have lived there? I thought Mrs. MacNeil said her father was the laird."

"Yes. Now I don't feel like going, and I was actually excited when we heard about the banquet this morning. Whatever happens, please don't leave my side."

"Don't worry. I won't let you down." Breagh put an arm around her sister's shoulders in a quick hug.

The girls were subdued as they made the return journey to the village. They waved half-heartedly to passing cars, but the exuberance of the morning had gone.

§

Laura and Breagh were not the only passengers in the boat waiting to transport them across to the island. There were eight others who had come to Barra especially for this event and were dressed for the occasion. The men wore tuxedos, two with kilts. The women were resplendent in evening gowns and dripped with diamonds and other precious stones.

The sisters had felt very confident about their own apparel as they left the boarding house. Each had on a 'dressy' dress and Mrs. MacNeil had lent them two of her cashmere shawls. However, when they saw how their fellow passengers were attired, they felt unsuitably underdressed. Laura was already very edgy. She suspected there was a strong possibility that Jean would inhabit her body at the castle, and sitting beside this *soigné* group on the boat did nothing to make her feel better.

~ Airborne ~

A butler met them at the castle door and ushered them in. The entrance hallway was magnificent; great flagstones covered the floor and a massive stone staircase to the left led to an upper level. The walls on the other three sides were several stories high and were covered with portraits, armaments and tapestries.

"Look, Laura," whispered Breagh. "That painting on the wall over there. It could be you."

Just at that moment, the laird and his wife descended the staircase. "Good evening. Welcome to the castle," he boomed. "A special welcome to you two young ladies from Cape Breton. We were so glad you could come. We must set aside a little time this evening so that I can find out what the MacNeils in Nova Scotia are up to. I know they are very active clan members."

He took a closer look at Laura. "My goodness," he declared, "you are definitely a MacNeil, aren't you? You look exactly like one of my ancestors. That's her portrait on the wall. Her name was Jean MacNeil and she was betrothed to William MacNeil, one of our heroes whose portrait has hung in The Red Herring for over two hundred years. She disappeared just before they were married. No one knows what became of her.

"Well, let's all go upstairs. The others have already arrived and I believe dinner is ready." He led the way upstairs to a huge dining room. A gargantuan table occupied the center of the room, set with gleaming silver and crystal which twinkled in the light from the wall sconces. A blazing fire burned in an enormous grate. "We have to keep the fire going even in the summer months," he explained. "People think that living in a castle is very romantic, but, for the most part, it's just bloody cold. Stone is long-lasting when it comes to buildings, but not the best when you're trying to keep warm."

The meal was exquisite. Lobster soup, salmon with béchamel sauce, vol-au-vent chicken, lamb with new potatoes and green beans, strawberries and cream followed by coffee and a selection of island cheeses which were served in the drawing room.

Laura kept waiting for something to happen to her. She was still very ill at ease although the dinner helped to calm her nerves somewhat.

"Make sure you stay close to me," she whispered to Breagh.

"After the amount I've just eaten, you can bet I'm not going anywhere!"

~ *Airborne* ~

"Ah, there you are!" The laird approached the sisters. "Why don't the two of you come with me? I have something to show you. There's a room upstairs entirely devoted to the MacNeil clan, with artifacts dating back to Niall, the High King of Ireland and, of course, the originator of Clan MacNeil. I'll have Angus fetch your wraps as it's a bit chilly up there."

Laura looked at Breagh with alarm. She didn't want to go anywhere else in this castle, but hardly felt she could refuse.

As they ascended the stairs, the laird chatted about the clan and his ancestry, filling their heads with facts and dates. Breagh, as usual, asked all kinds of questions about his family, and Laura, too, found herself interested.

Although nothing on the scale of the dining or drawing rooms, the room was quite large and had its own fireplace. More portraits, daggers, swords and shields covered the walls and several enclosed glass cases stood on the floor. "This used to be a bedroom," the laird informed them, "but it's much too cold and draughty when the fire is not lit. I hadn't really planned to bring anyone up here, but it occurred to me that you New Worlders might be interested."

"Excuse me, sir," a voice interrupted. "Lady MacNeil asked me to fetch you immediately. The First Minister of the Scottish Parliament in Edinburgh has just arrived."

"Oh, damn! I forgot he was coming tonight," exclaimed the laird. "Well, take a look around, ladies. I'm sure you'll find lots to interest you here. We'll have to schedule another time to meet."

No sooner had the laird vacated the room when Laura sensed Jean was close.

"I'm going to have another episode, Breagh," she said. "Please hold my hand."

She stretched out her arm, but, before she could grasp her sister, she felt the now-familiar pull upwards and the sensation of floating before she was returned to the floor.

Breagh was gone. A large four-poster bed piled with mounds of covers now dominated the room. An enormous wardrobe took up part of one wall and several straight-backed chairs were scattered about. A partially finished tapestry was stretched in a frame in front of one of the chairs near the window. Rush mats lay on the floor and a roaring fire burned in the grate. Music and the noise of dancers hooching and yelling could be heard from

~ Airborne ~

downstairs.

Laura wore a heavy cape over her long skirt and blouse.

"Leaving?"

Laura spun around and was horrified to see William MacNeil standing there. "I'm just going out for a breath of fresh air," she replied. "I haven't been feeling at all well and I think the outdoors will clear my head a bit."

"You don't fool me, Jean," he said with a sneer. "I know you're meeting Rhuahri Og. Well, think again, my dear. You're mine, in case you did not know. There will be no more trysts with the servant class. You are betrothed to me and you will have nothing to do with anyone but me."

"You can't tell me what to do," answered Laura scornfully. "We're not married yet, and never will be, if I have my way!"

"I'm like the son your father never had and, as the eldest daughter, you, *or rather I*, as your husband, stand to gain everything when Daddy dies. I am eager for that day. Things will change around here! One thing for certain, you will not be gallivanting around the countryside like your father allows you to do now."

"I'll do as I please! I know all about you and your cowardly ways. I'm going to tell my father what actually happened in the battle. He won't be so keen to have you as a son-in-law when he knows the truth."

William's eyes bulged. "You little vixen! I know what you need!" MacNeil grabbed Laura by the shoulders and pulled her to him roughly. Laura bit him on the hand as hard as she could.

MacNeil howled. "You bitch! You'll pay for that!" He struck Laura on the side of the head sending her headlong. She smashed onto the tiles in front of the grate, her cheek landing on a flaming log which had rolled out of the fire. The burning embers stuck to her flesh.

"Oh," she shrieked and, despite the agony, she lashed out at him with her foot. Her heavy brogue caught him on the shin, causing him to stumble backwards and hit his head on one of the bedposts. The intensity of the rage in his eyes terrified Laura. When she saw him aim his foot for her stomach, she tried to get out of the way, but she was not quick enough.

Just at the moment of impact, Laura felt herself yanked from Jean's body. She was not sure whether it was the result of

~ Airborne ~

MacNeil's kick or her extrication from Jean, but she felt her entire being torn apart. It flashed through her mind that this was what it must feel like to be shot. She was pulled up, but, this time, instead of returning to earth, she stayed suspended in mid-air.

She watched the horrific scene unfold, knowing she was invisible to those below and that there was no way she could help. Jean, immobile now from the force of the blow, lay on the hearth like a rag doll. MacNeil insanely continued to pummel her even although it was obvious she could not retaliate. The smell of burning flesh where parts of the ignited log still clung to Jean's cheek was nauseating. Then Laura saw a faint aura emanate from Jean's body; it rose wispily and vanished through the window. Jean was dead.

The scene changed. Laura, still suspended, was an observer outside the castle near a precipice hanging over the ocean. MacNeil, staggering under the weight of a long object he carried over his shoulder, made his way to the edge. He laid his bundle down on the grass, picked up a large stone and placed it inside a sack. He tied the sack around the bundle and pushed it over the cliff.

Then Laura was back in the present, lying on the floor in the castle. Breagh stood over her with an anxious look on her face.

"Oh, thank God, you're awake! Are you all right? What happened?"

"I think I'm going to be sick," said Laura weakly.

"Can you stand up?" asked Breagh.

"No, I don't think so. I feel totally wasted. What did you see?"

"Nothing. All of a sudden your eyes rolled back in your head and you fell on the floor. You lay there moaning and turning for what seemed hours, even though it was only a few minutes."

The door opened with a flourish. The laird strode in with another man in tow. "I would like you girls to meet...Oh, dear. What happened? Are you all right?"

"No, she's not. She hasn't been feeling well lately. We should go home," said Breagh.

"Nothing of the kind!" retorted the laird. "I won't hear of it. You will both stay here tonight."

Laura looked at Breagh pleadingly.

"Thank you for your generous offer, sir, but Laura would be better off in a familiar bed. Do you think your butler could help me get her downstairs?"

§

Laura spent the next two days in bed. She told Breagh what she had seen. "I don't think Jean will be visiting me again. She accomplished what she set out to do. What I can't understand is why she chose me."

"Just think about it, Laura. You were the one who had no time for family history or tales about the MacNeils. Who would be more believable than you? Now, if she had chosen me, you, and probably everyone else, would have said it was all my imagination. And there's something else I haven't told you."

"What is it?" Laura asked.

"Your birthmark has disappeared."

"What?" gasped Laura. "Bring me a mirror!"

Laura examined her image. "You know," she said, "it was in the exact spot where Jean was burned with the wood."

§

The following day Laura felt much better. Breagh wanted to go into the village to look for souvenirs as they only had a few more days before leaving the island.

"Are you coming with me?" she asked Laura.

"I suppose I should, but I think I'll just sit outside and read until you get back."

She settled on the bench in front of the house and turned her face up to the sun. It was warm and comforting and it seemed to Laura as if the radiant star was sending her an inner peace that she had never felt before.

"Oh, there you are." Her reverie was interrupted.

Mrs. MacNeil, standing at the door with a shopping basket over her arm said, "I have to run into the village for butter and milk. Will you be all right by yourself until I get back? I shouldn't be too long."

"I'll be just fine, thank you," Laura replied. "Actually, I was going to read a bit. I found a book on the history of Barra on the bookshelf in my room."

"Och, I'm sure you'll enjoy reading that. It was written by my

~ Airborne ~

father and you'll find quite a few references to your ancestor, Seamus, in there."

"Well, I know I'll enjoy it now!" Laura said laughingly. "Anyway, take your time. I'm quite happy to sit here and find out what I can about this beautiful place."

"All right, dear. See you soon." And she set off towards the cluster of buildings in the distance.

Laura had just started to read when she felt another presence.

"There you are, lassie." The older, toothless version of Rhuahri sat beside her on the bench. Laura felt no fear, and was surprised to find she was glad to see the old man. She could even discern a semblance to the handsome youth he had been when he knew Jean.

"I have something to tell you, Rhuahri," she said. "I'm not Jean, but she came to me and showed me what happened to her." She related to him the events of the last week starting from the time she and her sister arrived on the island.

"Oh, lassie, I knew something really bad must have happened to Jean when she never arrived that night. I waited for her until the morning and then one of the other boys came over from the castle island and told me that the laird was looking for me. The laird couldn't find his daughter and he thought that the two of us had eloped. Right away my brother took me to the mainland and I hid out there like an outlaw. From time to time he came across the water and let me know what was happening at home.

"I always knew that William MacNeil had something to do with Jean's disappearance and the worst of it is, the laird still thocht he was wonderful. Strangely enough, about a week after Jean disappeared, William MacNeil fell off his horse and broke his neck.

"I came back to Barra after the laird died, but I never found any trace of Jean, and no one seemed to know what had happened to her. I lived to be an old man and spent the rest of my life trying to learn her fate. My soul could never be at peace. She was probably waiting for me, but I was too caught up in my search for her. I'm glad you came to the island, lassie, because, through you, she telt me herself what befell. Now I know we can find each other."

"I still have your mother's locket, Rhuahri," Laura told him.

~ *Airborne* ~

"I'll just run upstairs and get it for you."

"No, you keep it. Jean would have wanted it that way. You look so much like her. She was such a bonnie wee thing."

A slight breeze, hardly discernable, wafted through the flowers in the garden. Rhuahri smiled radiantly, as though he could see something, or someone, in the distance. "I won't be seeing you again, lassie. It's time for me to go. *Beanna achdleibh.* Blessings on you." And he disappeared.

Laura realized that Rhuahri had found his Jean again and she felt honoured to have been chosen as the medium to make this happen. She remembered the confidence and the feelings of self-worth she experienced when Jean took over her body and knew instinctively that Jean had bequeathed these traits to her.

She noticed Breagh climbing the hill towards the house. "From down there it looked like you were talking to someone," Breagh said when she reached Laura. "Did you have another episode?"

"Nope. Just talking to myself. That's the first sign of madness, you know, so you'd better watch out!"

Breagh laughed. "This holiday hasn't been anything like I thought it would be," she said, "but I wouldn't change it."

"I wouldn't either," Laura responded. "What do you say we go to Seamus's house tomorrow? We never did get there. You never know what we might find, and, if we don't find anything, we'll throw a couple of stones from the house into our suitcases and take them back to Cape Breton. At least we'll have something from our ancestors to pass on down in the family."

"Wick-ed," said Bhreagh. "Let's go!"

❧❧

Hillside Boularderie, Cape Breton has been Meg Horne's home for the past 40 years although she was born and raised on the west coast of Scotland. Storytellers, her mother being one of the most prolific, were a regular feature at gatherings in the village where she grew up. After retiring as a high school English

~ *Airborne* ~

teacher, Meg decided to carry on this tradition in writing. So far, she has written two novels and several short stories.

When not putting pen to paper, Meg spends her time reading, walking her dogs, gardening, playing the piano and drumming.

Katrina Nicholson

The Wild Helicopters of the Australian Outback

3,207 kilometers was a long way.

Specifically, it was the distance between the University of New South Wales in Sydney and Abby Beckett's family farm in the Northern Territory. Making the trip involved a three and a half hour Qantas flight into Alice Springs, another hour to get a charter from Alice Springs to the airfield in Tennant Creek, then the better part of a day driving cross-country on dirt tracks to get to the farm. Abby had only made the trip once a year for summer holidays since leaving for boarding school ten years ago. After she'd gone on to university and started taking jobs between terms, the number of trips home had dropped to zero. Now, five years later, she had her diploma in hand and was heading home for good.

She worried a little that all those years of studying in air-conditioned labs and lecture halls might have knocked the Outback out of her somehow. She'd been a dusty, bouncy teenager with a deep tan and a blonde ponytail sticking out the back of her battered baseball cap when she last saw her family. She still had the hat—blue with a kangaroo embroidered in yellow from one of the tourist shops—and her work boots, but the faded old jeans and tattered button-ups didn't fit anymore so she had to buy stiff new ones. She'd been considering "accidentally" falling in the dirt before her parents arrived at the airfield to pick her up just so she'd be recognizable. Luckily, being crammed into a tiny airplane for hours had made her sufficiently rumpled and sweaty.

She stepped off the plane onto the tarmac at Tennant Creek and immediately understood what a biscuit felt like in the oven. Sydney was hot in the summer, but there were always sea breezes and air conditioning to take the edge off. It was the dry season in the Outback and the sun bored a hole though her skull, beating down so hard the tarmac was obscured by heat haze. Had it always been this hot and she'd just never noticed?

Abby headed for the terminal—which wasn't much more than an old tin shed—trying futilely to ward off the billion flies having a party in her personal space, and literally ran into her neighbor, Bruce, who was refueling his chopper from the petrol tanks.

He recognized her instantly. Apparently she "hadn't changed a bit." Neither had Bruce. Her father's best mate was still the same irreverent, roughened grazier who used to take her cattle mustering as a child. He looked to be in his mid-thirties, but he'd looked like that ever since Abby could remember.

Their meeting at the airfield was no coincidence. He'd come in the chopper to give her a lift home, sparing Abby's family the long drive in their rusted and unreliable utility truck. Abby felt overjoyed to see him, both because she didn't relish waiting around on the baking tarmac for her parents and because she never passed up an opportunity to study a helicopter.

Bruce skimmed his little Robinson R-22 over the dusty plain at treetop level, manipulating the cyclic and collective controls to make the little chopper slide and pivot in a way that seemed effortless. Abby watched his hands, trying to get a feel for how it was done. They buzzed the Stuart Highway, a grey two-lane stripe that sliced north through the scrub, barely clearing the cab of a road train as it lumbered along in a cloud of grit pulling three trailers. Like all helicopter rustlers, Bruce was used to keeping things low and close to herd cattle, and Abby was having a blast. She gave the bloke at the wheel a cheery wave as they bombed past. The driver gave them the finger in return. Bruce's weathered face cracked into a grin. "Someone's been sucking lemons."

They cruised across the low scrub of the Barcly Tablelands where the grass spread to the horizons and the sky blazed an almost painfully bright shade of blue, only stopping to harass three or four more innocent vehicles, until the sun glinted off something shiny and metal hanging in the distance.

As Bruce climbed up to 5,280 feet—station level—Abby got her first look in four years at the Mile High Wind Farm. Not much had changed. The floating wind turbines—all 400 of them—were arranged in staggered lines, their stubby blades whirring lazily in the stiff upper level winds underneath the rigid, zeppelin-shaped gas bags that held them aloft. The heavy conducting cables tethering them to the ground were connected to a grid that led to a low, square transformer building surrounded by gum trees, huge tanks of reserve gas, and corrugated metal sheds full of spare parts. Wires radiated outward from the transformer, bringing power to all the towns and cattle stations in the region.

Above it all and casting a shadow on the ground nearly half a kilometer long, was the enormous gas-filled canopy that supported the homestead. Made of aluminum and shaped like a ram-air parachute, it kept their sleeping, eating, and working quarters floating exactly one mile above the ground, staying on-station by means of twenty-four pivoting swamp-skimmer fans.

Once they got closer, Abby could make out the smaller shapes of the utes—little utility airships that had a zeppelin's gas bag, ultralight airplane seats and flight controls, and a half-ton truck's cargo area—drifting back and forth between the turbines. They were battery-powered, like everything else on the farm, charged every few days from the wind turbines.

A tanned mechanic in his twenties with a sizable dose of unshaven stubble hung on a rope from one of the utes, trying to plug a recharging cable into a turbine. The string on his bush hat was snugged tight under his chin to keep it from blowing off in the corkscrewing wake turbulence, so it took Abby a second to recognize him. It was Gavin, one of the farmhands and her old childhood mate.

The rhythmic *thwuppa-thwuppa-thwuppa* of the helicopters' rotors made Gav and his father Jack, the graying ex-Royal Air Force mechanic at the ute's controls, look up in alarm, but once they recognized the bubble-and-stick configuration of the Robinson and Bruce and Abby behind the windscreen, they relaxed. Jack gave her a wave. Gav grinned widely and touched his hat.

The flat, single-story box of the homestead was supported on struts under the curve of the canopy, which sheltered the living quarters from the harsh sun. As they approached the landing grid on the starboard side, Abby's father, Howard, and her seven-year-old brother, Zachary, came running out onto the observation catwalk that wound around the outside of the homestead, hastily

~ Airborne ~

slinging rifles over their shoulders and raking the horizon with their eyes.

"That bloke's a bit gone," Bruce observed as he raised a meaty hand to wave at his neighbor.

Privately, Abby agreed with him. Howard Beckett hated helicopters with the fervor of a man whose livelihood they threatened. He would drop whatever he was doing to run them off when they showed up to leech power from the turbines and was forever trying to devise a means of shooting them down. He'd even paid his daughter's way through aerospace engineering school in the hopes that she'd come back with new and better ideas on how to combat the menace.

The wild gleam in his eyes when he burst outside was enough to confirm that, if anything, he'd gotten worse while she was gone. He'd also passed his mania on to her brother, by the look of things. Their crazed expressions simultaneously transformed into broad smiles the instant they recognized her. Howard waved for Bruce to set down on the landing grid.

Abby couldn't help but be disappointed that the flight was over so soon. Now that she was around her father again, she probably wouldn't have a chance to study helicopters up close anymore. That, she decided, would be the part of Sydney she missed most. There were dozens of helicopter outfits in Sydney, and most of them had welcomed students who turned up at their hangars to learn a thing or two.

The skids had barely touched down when Zachary hauled open the door. With his battered slouch hat, short brown hair, and green eyes, he looked like a miniature version of their father. "Abby!" he sang happily, and flung himself into her arms. He had no reservations, even though he hadn't seen his sister in person since he was a toddler, because they talked every week via webcam. His hug lasted about 2.5 seconds, before he crawled over the seat and started digging through her luggage. "Did you bring it? Can I see it? Will you let me shoot it first?"

"Take it easy, you bloody nong," Howard said affectionately, grabbing Zachary and pulling him out by the backpack containing his parachute. "G'day, Bruce," he said, tipping his hat to his neighbor. "Appreciate the lift."

"No worries, mate," Bruce replied. "It was on the way."

~ Airborne ~

Bruce helped hand out Abby's luggage—an army issue duffel full of clothes, a grease-stained satchel of "essential stuff" (tools, map, compass, etc), and a long tube about the width of a person's hand. Then he was off, taking his helicopter with him.

Abby waved, not sure whether she was saying goodbye to Bruce or the Robinson. Before the rotor wash even settled, Howard helped her into the parachute backpack that was mandatory safety gear for everyone working on the farm.

"There," he said, clipping together the last of the buckles. "All set. Now, how about we have a look at this gun of yours, eh?"

Abby rolled her eyes. "Nice to see you too, Dad."

§

The entire complement of the farm showed up in the mess hall for the demonstration of the Chopper Buster, the prototype weapon Abby had come up with at uni. They turned the benches around to face the map wall and sat in rows like they were about to receive a lecture from a teacher. Zachary sat up front with Gav. Behind them were Gav's father Jack and his mother Raylene, a retired flight nurse from the Royal Flying Doctor Service. Abby's mother Tammy, the camp's head cook and resident tutor, had even taken time off from cooking enough food to feed the Royal Australian Regiment to come and watch. Apparently the return of a Jillaroo was the biggest event of the year.

Deciding to let her work do all the talking, Abby whipped off the cardboard packaging and held the weapon out for everyone to see. It was a modified Soviet RPG-7 shoulder-mounted, anti-tank grenade launcher with the explosive round replaced by a cylindrical canister that had two round flat electrodes on the front. It received an appreciative "oooooh" from her captive audience.

"It's pretty simple, really. The Chopper Buster is just a giant taser," Abby explained. "The tube is spring loaded with this canister, which contains a 100,000 volt charge. When it's launched, the electrodes on the front stick to the hull of a battery-powered helicopter and deliver the charge, which causes the main rotor to overspeed and stall, so the helicopter crashes. Our power grid is already protected against surges, so you can't hurt the farm if you miss, and the electrodes are magnetic, so they won't stick to a person. Though if you get hit with the cartridge it's like being kicked by a kangaroo, so you should probably try not to do that."

Everyone chuckled at her little joke. Zachary ran over to grab the gun. "Let me see it! I want to try! Can I shoot one?"

"No!" chorused all the adults together.

"But I wanna see it work!" he complained. Abby held the gun over her head, away from Zachary's grasping hands as he jumped up trying to reach it. Then all of a sudden he held very still, his head cocked to one side, listening.

"Helicopter!" he shouted, and ran for the door.

Everyone poured out onto the catwalk after him. Sure enough, the air carried a faint omnidirectional *thwuppa-thwuppa-thwuppa*.

"Spread out!" Howard shouted. Tammy stayed behind to mind the homestead while everyone else ran to the utes to try and drive away the intruders. It happened a few times a week out here, but Abby hadn't been to battle stations in years. Luckily, she got caught up in the adrenaline of the moment and her feet remembered what to do. She ran down the catwalk to the landing grid and jumped into the passenger seat of her father's ute. Howard vented some gas and tipped them forward off the grid—sending Abby's stomach into her throat—before engaging the engines and leveling them off just above the turbines.

As soon as they were out from underneath the homestead's canopy Abby saw them coming, six of them, out of the sun, no more than black specks yet but growing larger. The sun was so intense that she could barely glance at it before she had to look away again, even with sunglasses on.

"Tally six over top!" she shouted into the radio. "Looks like they're heading toward Quadrant 2."

The black lumps descended out of direct line with the sun and Abby recognized their silhouettes: they were Bell UH-1s, definitely wild. Thirty years ago, Australian Automated Helicopters bought up every UH-1 in the country, along with their civilian counterparts, Bell model 204s and 205s. They retrofitted them with experimental AI technology to create a fleet of automated cargo choppers. They were meant to supply far-flung cattle stations and mining towns without reliable roads. To survive in the harsh and unforgiving Outback, the AI choppers

~ Airborne ~

were programmed to learn and adapt to new situations. Unfortunately, it only took them about two weeks to learn that carrying cargo was boring. After that they went flaky on their owners, ditched their cargo in the middle of nowhere, and took up frolicking in the grassland making crop circles and stealing power from the wind farms to recharge their batteries.

It had soured the model's reputation in Australia permanently, so now wild choppers were easy to distinguish from piloted ones. Like dingoes, the wild ones kept together in packs for security. Numerous attempts had been made to track them down, but they had all failed because the tricky buggers had managed to scrape off their GPS transmitters.

"Looks like Zach might get to see it work after all," Howard said, nodding at the Chopper Buster, which was slung over Abby's shoulder. He swung the ute around to head off the choppers while Gav and Zach headed one way and Jack and Raylene went the other way to cover the rest of the farm in case the chopper pack pulled a fast one.

Howard had the ute's throttles wide open but their little zeppelin could never hope to catch up to a military grade helicopter. The wild ones beat them to the turbines on the northwestern frontier and plugged in using the small boom protruding from their bulbous noses.

"God-bloody-dammit!" Howard shouted, urging the ute forward, "Get away from my turbines!"

Despite the deadly whirling might of their rotors, the wild choppers weren't aggressive. They tended to shy away from people, so Howard powered toward them confidently. At Howard's shout, the spherical electronic eyes mounted underneath the choppers' noses swivelled warily in their direction, but the helicopters didn't pull back from the turbines.

"I'm fed up to the back teeth with the lot of you!" Howard shouted at the helicopters. "Drive 'em away one day and they'll be back again tomorrow!"

"We'll see about that," Abby said, raising the Chopper Buster to her shoulder and aiming through the fold-up sights along the barrel. She braced herself and pulled the trigger. The recoil slammed Abby into her seat and jerked the whole ute back a good meter or so. The canister sprang from the barrel, arcing through the air and attaching itself to the lead chopper's engine mount just below the main rotor.

For a second, nothing happened. Then the whole helicopter seized up and dropped like a stone. The other choppers unplugged and dove after it, buzzing around in apparent confusion as it fell, unresisting, for 5,000 feet before crashing into a stand of gum trees and sliding pathetically to the ground.

A rousing cheer accompanied the chopper's fall. Zachary jumped around in the flatbed, pumping his fists in the air as Gav tried to pull the kid back into his seat by his belt. Jack and Raylene hooted and clapped. Howard simultaneously hugged Abby, thumping her on the back, and flew the ute.

To Abby their cheers seemed to come from the bottom of a well. She was too busy listening to the sounds of distress—that was the only way she could describe the odd whines they were making—from the other five helicopters as they hovered around their fallen mate. She'd never heard a noise like that from a machine before. Neither had she ever thought of the chopper packs as mates. But now she came to a realization: during her time at school she had come to like helicopters, and now she felt guilty about "hurting" one just to impress her dad.

It wasn't something her dad or any of the others would understand, of course, so she kept a big fake smile pasted on her face as they banded together with the other utes and dove down to drive off the remaining five helicopters. The wreck of the first, they left in place as a warning.

§

That night there was, of course, a party. Aussies would take any excuse to down a few, and the return of a prodigal daughter combined with their first real victory in years over the chopper menace seemed like as good a reason as any for a boozer. Zachary was too young for beer, but the sugar-based fruit drink Tammy gave him instead wound him up and sent him crashing down as completely as any alcoholic beverage would have.

Abby had never been much of a drinker and tonight she had plans that didn't involve hanging over the toilet revisiting everything she'd eaten that day in reverse order. She nursed a single stubby the entire night, and when the others stumbled off to their bunks to pass out until first light, she gathered up her satchel, some abseiling gear, and a jumper to ward off the night chill, and went out onto the catwalk.

She'd always loved the way the farm looked at night. With no light pollution from the cities, the sky beyond the canopy was a black canvas coated with fuzzy white spots, all crammed together and piled on top of one another in a competition for space. The moon was barely a sliver, so the bright kite-shape of the Southern Cross dominated the starfield as it settled toward the horizon. Below, each turbine had a red beacon to warn away aircraft, and with four hundred of them all blinking out of time with each other they looked like a dancing canopy of fireflies held up by white spirals, which were the light ropes wound around the mooring cables. Abby stood there for a while just looking out and waiting for her eyes to adjust before she headed for the landing grid.

While piloting a ute alone at night was no problem for Abby, mooring it to the far northwest turbine was trickier because of the wake turbulence. She'd considered letting Gav in on the plan for help/company, but they hadn't seen each other in years. Maybe he'd grown to value his job more than a good mechanical puzzle. Eventually she managed to catch the ute's anchor on the turbine's grab bar. Taking the ute all the way down to the ground would waste more gas than they could spare, so Abby clipped her rope onto the hardpoint on the ute's frame, threaded it through her harness and the descender, and abseiled into the darkness.

The trip down was a long one because she had to be careful, especially at the beginning, not to let the wake turbulence tie her up in knots or sweep her into the path of one of the other turbines. It should have been as easy as walking. After all, whenever one of the farmhands had to get down to the ground, this was how they did it. She'd tried to keep up her skills at the indoor climbing gyms in Sydney, but it wasn't the same, and she was rusty. She took her time, keeping the loop gripped firmly in her hand to slow her descent, glancing at the light rope wrapped around the cable to judge her height. Even so, the ground arrived under her feet rather sooner than she was expecting, sending her stumbling into the dirt.

Fortunately, nothing was broken or sprained, or she would have had a hard time getting back up the rope again. She

~ Airborne ~

unclipped from the rope and tied it off against the massive steel D-ring that secured the mooring cable. Then she dug the battery-powered headlamp out of her satchel and switched it on. Its conical yellow beam cut a swath through the thick darkness, picking out the spindly silhouettes of the gum trees and the rounded hull of the crashed chopper, which had managed to land upright after its slide through the trees. The paint was all scratched up, the tail rotor shredded, and there were branches caught in the skids, but otherwise it looked intact.

Abby walked around it carefully, alert for any sign of movement, but the chopper remained inert. The bulbous eye, though undamaged, didn't swivel in her direction. The AI computer behind the instrument panel in the cockpit wasn't giving off any telltale clicks or whirrs that would indicate it was still processing data. A thick sheen of reddish dust stuck to the greasy drips on the helicopter's army-green skin. Australian Automated Helicopters hadn't bothered to repaint the UH-1s, they just slapped the acronym AAH! over where it had said ARMY and gave the kangaroo silhouette some surprised-looking googly eyes. Abby thought it was appropriate, since screaming and bugging their eyes out was what most people seemed to do when they caught sight of a pilotless helicopter.

Dust had also settled into the cargo bay because the doors had been removed. Abby panned her light around inside and almost immediately found what she was looking for: a dog-eared old manual, bloated with repeated cycles of wet and dry and about the size of a Sydney telephone directory, sticking out of a pouch on the back of the pilot's seat. She climbed eagerly inside, grabbed it, and sat cross-legged in the cargo hold poring over its pages by the light of the headlamp.

Just as she hoped, it was a copy of the POH, or Pilot Operations Handbook. It contained everything a pilot would need to know to operate or perform basic maintenance on this particular model. With this book and the AI in the chopper dead, she hoped she might be able to repair its basic functions and have her very own helicopter. Then they wouldn't have to rely on the road trains for supplies or make long trips into town in the truck or—

Abby was drawn out of her enthusiastic daydreams by a familiar sound: *thwuppa-thwuppa-thwuppa.* It had to be Bruce on an early morning emergency run. At this time of year the stockmen were out mustering the cattle cross-country. Maybe one of them had been bitten by a snake while he was sleeping. It couldn't be a wild chopper. The wild ones never came at night. It was too dangerous for them because their night vision cameras had very poor depth perception.

Abby clicked off the light and sat listening quietly, trying to make out which direction the chopper was coming from, but it was no use. She had never had Zachary's extraordinary hearing. She couldn't tell from the sound whether it was a UH-1 or a Robinson or a Hughes. The thing could be right on top of her and she still wouldn't be able to pinpoint its location without looking.

Even so, it gave Abby quite a shock to discover it actually *was* right on top of her. The canopy filled with a buzzing sound like a weed whacker on steroids. Then, with a jolt and a screech of metal, something landed on the roof of her helicopter. She grabbed the handle beside the doorway to keep from falling out as the helicopter lurched clumsily skyward. Branches squealed against the hull as the gum trees tried to hold onto their prey, then, with a crack like a gunshot, a forest's worth of wood spilled into the cabin and she and the UH-1 popped into open air.

The G-forces laid her flat out as the helicopter ascended sharply. The red lights on the turbines dropped past on Abby's left and with a shudder that made the insides of her ears itch, they leveled off into cruising flight. After a few minutes, Abby dared to stick her head out the door into the rushing airflow and turn on her headlamp.

There above her was the unmistakable green bulk of another, undamaged UH-1, its landing skids hooked underneath the main rotor assembly of the damaged one, supporting it. Abby was gobsmacked. Not only did the wild ones seem to care for one another, they were also smart enough to mount midnight rescue missions...though not smart enough, it seemed, to realize they'd unwittingly brought along a guest.

With no idea where they were going, Abby knew she shouldn't stay aboard. Her parachute would get her down to the ground, but then where would she be? In the darkness, she might land in a billabong and drown or startle a mob of cattle and get trampled or impale herself on the spiny branches of a gum tree. No, a parachute descent would be too dangerous to

~ Airborne ~

attempt in the dark. Plus, she was intensely curious to see where the wild ones had been hiding out all this time. So Abby clipped herself onto the grab bar, sat in the open doorway trailing her feet in the slipstream like she'd seen soldiers do in movies, and enjoyed the ride.

After a few hours, the sun began to creep up over the horizon behind them, bathing the flat landscape in an eerie reddish light and casting long shadows ahead of the rocks and termite mounds they passed. The rotor noise startled a troop of kangaroos, who hopped madly across their flight path. As the sun rose higher, it revealed that the green grass and gum trees of the tableland had been replaced by prickly tufts of yellowish spinifex and the occasional low shrub. Nowhere on the horizon was there any sign of a road or a town. Using her compass and her best guesses as to how long they'd been up and how fast they were flying, Abby put them well into the Tanami Desert. As she took in the barren landscape with its sandy soil, scraggy, inedible plants and harsh, baking sunlight, the full extent of her foolishness hit her.

She was in the middle of a landscape that was famous for the number of explorers who had met their end in it, and she hadn't brought a single drop of water with her. Just as she'd feared, living in Sydney for so long had made her complacent. She hadn't even thought about food or water because she had grown used to having a café on every corner. Digging around in her satchel, she discovered she had a squished granola bar left over from a school packed lunch, but that was it. If she was lucky and found a water hole, she might last a week or so. If she was unlucky, she would be dead by the end of the day.

Before the sun had even fully cleared the horizon a huge formation of buff-colored rock made reddish by the sunrise reared up ahead of them out of the landscape. Slabs of smooth-edged sandstone that had eroded into terraces formed a ring a few hundred meters in diameter that could only be accessed from above. Inside the ring, about a dozen choppers, all wild, flitted around, having races and making low passes under a black geyser of crude oil that spouted from a fissure in the ground. With all the spinifex on the plains outside to make crop circles in, it was like a little helicopter Shangri-La. Abby was excited to be the first person ever to see it, but the prospect of her impending doom kind of soured the moment.

~ *Airborne* ~

The rescue helicopter descended and set them down next to what looked like a mound of rocks. Once the sunlight trickled over the wall, Abby realized the dark lumps were actually the inert forms of six damaged helicopters, all laid out in an orderly row like bodies in a morgue. The rescue chopper took a few tries to get Abby's helicopter straightened away next to the others, then it disengaged and flew off to join its mates, who were watching the proceedings from the other side of the hideout.

On legs made wobbly from too much sitting, Abby slid out of the damaged helicopter to look around for a spring. There didn't seem be any vegetation inside the ring, so she knew it was a long shot, but she had to try. If she could hang on for a few days until the choppers' batteries ran low again, she could stow away and jump out when they raided a farm to recharge.

Abby spotted a ledge about halfway up the wall and climbed up to have a look around. The minute she stood up in plain view, the wild helicopters all froze, their swivel eyes locked on her. Their engines began to spool up, whining in a way that sounded almost angry.

Startled, Abby backed up to the wall, afraid her encroachment upon the choppers' home turf had overridden their fear of humans. Just as she was wondering where she could possibly run to if they decided to attack, the lead helicopter abruptly rose up, pivoted sharply around, and flew off. The others followed en masse and in a few seconds they had all vanished into the sun, leaving Abby alone with only the wrecks of seven downed helicopters for company. It was better than being shredded to bits by the tail rotor of an angry chopper, but not much, because she still didn't have any water, and now she had no way to get home.

Deciding to take her problems on one at a time, Abby continued her search for water. From her vantage point on the ledge, Abby scanned the entire inside of the ring with her small folding binoculars and found nothing but what she already knew was there. Her next step was to investigate under and around all of the piles of rock, which was how she discovered that one of them, on the other side of the helicopter graveyard, wasn't a pile of rock at all.

It was the shard of brown glass near the pile that had aroused her curiosity at first. Picking it up, she noticed that it

~ Airborne ~

bore a yellow label with XXXX inscribed on it. It was part of a broken beer bottle, but where had it come from? By rolling away some of the smaller rocks at the base of the pile, Abby discovered a stack of smashed crates, buried by a cave-in.

Under the rocks were more shattered beer bottles, bags of flour, dented bottles of water, packets of fags, horseshoes, nails, Vegemite, matches, porno magazines, tea bags, quad bike tyres, tins of petrol, and other random supplies. She brushed the dust off the side of the crate. Underneath was a brand from a cattle station. These were the supplies the choppers had dumped when they went wild.

Abby crawled into the shade underneath one of the damaged helicopters with a bottle of water and the granola bar for breakfast. It was only seven o'clock but it was already hot enough for Abby to discard her jumper and roll up her shirtsleeves. With no clouds in the sky and no prospect of any showing up until at least September, it was a safe bet that today would be another scorcher. Now that she was reasonably certain she wasn't going to die of dehydration by sundown, though, she felt a little better. It was time to turn her mind to the problem of getting home.

If she'd packed a radio or a mobile phone there'd be no problem, but she hadn't, and the AI helicopters had no transmitters, only receivers. However, there were the helicopters themselves. Between what she'd picked up from watching Bruce and the information in the manual, Abby was pretty sure she could fly herself out in a helicopter if she could manage to piece a whole one together from seven choppers' worth of damaged parts. If it had been any of her engineering classmates out here they'd really be in the shit. They did all their designing with maths and computers. Most of them couldn't even tell one end of a spanner from the other, but Abby had spent her childhood hanging around with Gav and soaking up Jack's mechanical proficiency.

The first helicopter in the row was obviously a write-off. It had a series of huge holes in the windscreen and engine housing that could only have been made by a shotgun. The next two looked like they had been the victims of dynamic rollover. One had gouges in the metalwork all down its side and its rotor blades were bent out of shape. The other's Jesus nut must have come off under the strain, because the main rotor was missing. The fourth was burnt to a crisp. The last two looked like they had fallen from a much greater height than her own—they didn't resemble helicopters so much as piles of twisted metal. The last in the row was the one she'd shot down. Compared to the others it looked practically new.

Abby sat in its cockpit and made a list on the back of her map of the work that needed doing. The control systems—cyclic, collective, and anti-torque pedals—were all still there despite the fact that the chopper didn't need a pilot anymore. The pedals were inscribed with the name "Huey" which, Abby recalled, was a sort of nickname for the model that came from trying to pronounce UH-1 as if it were a word. She decided that if this was going to be her helicopter it would need a name, and Huey would do nicely.

Abby dug around in Huey's access panels to see what damage the Chopper Buster had done. Huey had five batteries, one of which was fried, probably because he had been charging it when he was shocked. It would have to be replaced, and so would nearly every fuse in the cutout box. Further digging revealed that the controls were connected electrically to the AI rather than to the rotors, so that using them would be less like flying the helicopter and more like making suggestions to the computer. She would have to reconnect them to the hydraulics.

On the outside, Huey didn't look as bad. His skids were a little bent but that wouldn't affect his handling much. The only real problem was the tail rotor. Both the rotor and the assembly were demolished and would have to be swapped out.

By noontime Abby had a to-do list almost as long as her arm. Number one, of course, was to repair the electrical system. If she couldn't manage that, there was no point in doing the rest. She pulled the Chopper Buster cartridge off Huey's engine housing and took her multimeter on a tour of the other damaged choppers. Most of their batteries were dead or damaged, but in one of the choppers that had rolled she found one that was intact and mostly charged. The shotgun blasts had missed the cutout box on the first chopper, so she scavenged its fuses.

Abby disconnected all of Huey's batteries before messing around in his cutout box so she wouldn't get zapped. When she was done, she swapped the ruined battery for the new one and reconnected the power. She wasn't expecting anything to happen except for the needle on the voltmeter in the cockpit to move from

~ Airborne ~

red to green, so when the AI clicked and whirred and the main rotor started to spin up, sending a cloud of dust into her face, she leaped away from Huey's side in surprise.

Her jump brought her into the swivel-eye's field of vision and it immediately locked onto her. The whole helicopter shuddered and whined as it tried to lift off.

Abby held her hands up. "No no no no!" she shouted at Huey. "Don't do that! Your tail's rooted. You'll spin round and crash again!"

Huey stared at her, main rotor still thrashing away at the air.

"You don't trust me. Fine. Okay. I'll back up." Abby kept her hands up, retreated several meters and sat on the ground out in the open where Huey could see her. "My name's Abby, and I'm not going to hurt you," Abby promised.

Huey's eye rolled wildly, his AI computer chattering away at her.

"Yeah, I know I shot you down," Abby admitted, taking as guess as to what his problem was. "It was a mistake. If you let me, I can make it up to you."

Huey's eye tilted to one side like the head of an inquisitive dog.

"I know you're smart enough to figure out you didn't just wake up on your own," Abby said, showing him the pliers in her hand. "I did it. I fixed your computer. And I can make you fly again if you let me. I think."

Huey seemed to consider this for a moment, his rotors *thwapping* at the air, spewing arcing clouds of dust. Abby held onto the brim of her hat to keep it from blowing away and tried not to breathe in too much dirt. It stuck to the sweat on her skin and clothes, turning her entire body into a gritty mess.

"Look, if I didn't like you I wouldn't have given you a name," she called out. "What do you think of Huey?"

Huey stepped down his RPM slightly.

"Does that mean you like it?"

Huey stared at her.

Abby nodded her head up and down. "Like this for yes." Then she shook her head back and forth. "And this for no."

Huey hesitated.

"If I wanted to hurt you, I could've just let you take off," Abby reminded him. "So do you like the name Huey or not?"

~ Airborne ~

Huey's swivel eye moved jerkily up and down.

Abby grinned. "Good, 'cause I'm not very creative. I'd have a hard time thinking of a new one." She waved the pliers at Huey. "So now that we're mates, how about you spool down and I have a look under your bonnet?"

§

With Huey's help, Abby managed to find three linkages in the gearbox that needed replacing. It was like a game of cold and hot. The chiming of his nav system told her when she was getting close to something that was giving him problems. Abby chatted to him as she worked, explaining how she'd gotten here and how a wind farm worked, telling him about Dad and Zach and her mom and Gav and his parents, mostly to fill the silence.

"There are more farms now than there used to be and fewer cattle stations. More competition, less demand. It lowered the prices. That's why Dad gets shirty when you lot come round," Abby told him as she liberated a cog from one of the wrecks. "We're having enough trouble staying in the black as it is."

By sundown the main rotor was running smoothly and Abby had managed to pry off the wrecked mess of the tail rotor. It required climbing onto the tail and working in close proximity with sharp, shredded metal that could at any point start itself up and lop off two of her favorite limbs, but Huey was trusting her, so the least she could do was trust him back. With a clatter, the last of the blades landed in the scrap pile. In the gathering darkness, she couldn't see it land so much as hear the clank it made.

"Well, that about does it for tonight," Abby said, wiping the sweat from her brow with her greasy sleeve. "We're out of light."

Huey's landing lights snapped on.

Abby laughed, sliding down from Huey's tail and tossing her spanner into the cargo hold with the rest of the tools. "Nice try, but they're pointing the wrong way. Besides, I'm so hungry I could eat a horse and chase the jockey. It's time for chow."

In the circle of illumination from Huey's landing lights Abby dug a shallow pit in the dirt a few meters from Huey's nose and threw in the broken slats from the crates. She managed to set them alight with three or four dozen matches and a healthy dose of petrol. Then she rolled over a quad bike tyre for a chair and set to work combining flour, baking soda, salt and water in a bowl-shaped piece of metal from a wrecked chopper's nose.

"It's called damper," Abby told Huey as he watched her fashion a makeshift camp oven for the dough out of helicopter metal and stick it in the ashes of the fire. "Bruce, the chopper pilot I told you about, he taught me how to make it when I was a kid. Gav and I used to go down to the ground and sit around the campfire with the stockmen when they were on the move through our land. I always liked campfires. We could never have them aloft with all that gas around. It was fun to have everyone all together."

Huey's eye swiveled, scanning the hideout before returning to her.

"I suppose you're wondering where all your mates went," Abby guessed. She poked around in the campfire ashes with a tyre iron, not looking at him. "Well they legged it as soon as they saw me. Sorry, mate."

Huey's eye drooped.

"Cheer up. I bet if you fly me home they'll come back." Abby said this as if she had just thought of it, but actually she'd spent most of the afternoon wondering how she was going to broach the subject. She'd never had to ask a vehicle to take her somewhere before.

Huey chirped and started spooling up his engine.

"Relax, Huey. You still don't have a tail rotor. We can leave in the morning."

Huey shut down obligingly and Abby maneuvered the camp oven out of the fire, slightly relieved by his enthusiasm for the idea but still not entirely sure he wouldn't flake out on her and go off after his mates once the new rotor was on.

Abby plucked the cooked damper out of the pot and took a tentative nibble. Apparently she'd either left out some crucial step in the damper-making process or she was looking at her memories of the stuff through rose-colored glasses, because it both looked and tasted like a charcoal briquette.

Huey chattered with helicopter laughter at the look on her face.

~ Airborne ~

"Shut up," she told him. "Tucker is tucker. Got to eat something." But even with Vegemite on top it just tasted like salty charcoal.

She stretched out beside the fire with a stack of old porno magazines as a pillow, suddenly aware of how knackered she was after all the sweating and heavy lifting.

Huey shut off his lights and the night swept over her. Outside the dim circle of firelight it was darker than three feet up a cow's arsehole and full of strange hootings and growls. It was no different than night at the farm, really, except she was alone on the ground in the middle of the desert with nothing over her head but stars. She suddenly realized it was her first night sleeping outside a dorm in nearly half a decade and that she had replaced her old roommate, a genial part-time surfer from Queensland, with a thinking helicopter.

The more she thought about the animals that lived out here —the snakes and lizards and spiders and dingoes and more than one vicious creature of Aboriginal legend—the more it seemed like a good idea to sleep in Huey's cargo bay. It was strewn with tools and jagged metal parts, but kipping on a spanner had to be more comfortable than lying in the open waiting for creepy crawlies to slink out of the blackness. Unfortunately, with the sun gone she needed the fire to stay warm. She wanted to stay awake and keep watch for glinting eyes in the dark, but she was so tired...

"Huey, you have night vision, right?" Abby mumbled. "Wake me up if you see any snakes, okay?" Huey chirped an affirmative and Abby dropped off to sleep.

She was rudely awaked after what felt like two minutes by the glaring brightness of Huey's landing lights shining directly into her face and the screeching wail of his stall warning alarm. Even though it was the exact opposite of what you were supposed to do, Abby jerked bolt upright, flailing at the imaginary death adders on her clothes. "What is it? Where are they!?" She wailed, hopping up and dancing around in a fearful little circle.

Huey's chattering laughter and the lightening sky gradually woke her up to the fact that this was reveille, not a snake alarm. Abby gave Huey a verbal walloping with all of her father's most colorful oaths. Like a typical bloke, he was completely unfazed. He just waited until she was finished, then spooled up his engine as if to say: "Get a wiggle on, it's time to go!"

~ *Airborne* ~

"All right, all right, keep your shirt on," Abby grumbled. It wasn't much use berating a helicopter anyway, especially one that was famous for not listening.

It took less than an hour to rig up the new tail rotor. Abby had a bad moment when they tested it out, because Huey launched himself into the air with such enthusiasm she was sure he was going to bugger off and leave her stranded, but after a joyful circuit of the terrace he set down in front of her, inviting her to board. She didn't need telling twice. She dived through the rotor wash into the cabin and he was off again before she'd even buckled herself into the pilot's seat.

"All right, Huey, take me home!" Abby shouted above the *thwupping* of his rotors, slapping Huey's instrument panel affectionately.

Huey powered over the wall and out over the parched plains, where he promptly dropped down nearly on the heads of some very startled kangaroos to make a crop circle in a tantalizingly tall patch of spinifex.

"Huey!" Abby scolded, jerking on the collective stick. "This is not the time for crop circles! I have to get home. My family probably thinks I was spirited away by a bunyip or something."

Huey completely ignored her repeated stomping on the anti-torque pedals and buzzed the kangaroos again, making them scatter in all directions. Apparently helicopters had the attention span of a gnat and the mentality of a magpie. No wonder they had gone wild.

Remembering the chopper flock from yesterday morning, Abby decided to try something. "Hey Huey, want to play a game?" she asked him.

Huey left off the kangaroos and went immediately into a hover. He was listening.

"I have here a 751-page helicopter operations manual. If you can get us home before I can read the whole thing, you win. But if I finish before your skids hit the landing grid, I win. Deal?"

Huey thought for about three nanoseconds, then shot into the air, dropped his nose, and powered for the horizon like she'd just promised him helicopter biscuits and tea if he could catch it. She was worried he might get bored and start looking for kangaroos again after a few minutes, but two hours later Huey was still going for it with admirable gusto.

~ Airborne ~

At first, Abby was only pretending to read the manual so he would keep racing, but in short order she found herself getting sucked in by the intricacies of never-exceed velocities, cyclic pitch versus collective pitch, and maximum service ceilings. In fact, she was so absorbed that the next time she looked up it was to see the familiar green stretches of the tableland.

Trails of dust climbed into the blue sky up ahead as hundreds of cattle were herded cross-country by stockmen on horses and quad bikes and Bruce in his little white Robinson. Mile High would be appearing on the hazy horizon any minute, and she was only 445 pages into the manual. It looked like Huey was going to win for sure. She pulled out her binoculars, straining to catch the first glimpse of the sun reflecting off the homestead's canopy, and saw a familiar sight much closer than she expected: a ute in the air above the stock route, buzzing back and forth over the plain tracing out a search grid. They had come out looking for her.

Through the binoculars she saw Gav at the controls and Zachary standing on the lookout's seat, pointing furiously in their direction. No doubt he'd heard Huey coming long ago and was itching to take him on. Gav and Howard were usually the only people Zach actually listened to, but right now Gav's attention was on not letting the strong upper level winds have their way with the ute, so Zach was effectively running wild.

As Abby watched, Zachary hauled the Chopper Buster out of the flatbed.

"No, you nob, it's me!" Abby shouted, waving her arms frantically as Zach swung the barrel toward them.

Huey let out a hoot of alarm and dropped out of the way just as Zach pulled the trigger. The canister arced harmlessly over Huey's rotors and the recoil flipped Zachary clean over the rail. Gav made a last ditch effort to grab him by the front of his shirt, but he succeeded only in pulling all the buttons off before the kid went tumbling into free fall.

Abby held her breath as Zach stabilized himself with his arms and legs like he'd been taught and pulled the ripcord on his emergency parachute. The tiny square pilot chute squirted out, caught wind, and pulled the huge circular red-and-white main from the pack.

~ Airborne ~

Abby breathed a sigh of relief, but almost immediately sucked the air back in again when she saw where he was headed. The prevailing winds were blowing him right toward the stock route. The round chutes they used had little to no steering capacity, so he would land right in the middle of the flowing river of cattle.

Gav and the stockmen saw what was happening too. Gav was venting gas like crazy, trying to catch up with Zachary before he landed, and the stockmen were frantically trying to redirect the cattle, but it was hopeless. Her baby brother was about thirty seconds away from being trampled to death.

"Huey, new game!" Abby shouted, "It's called: catch that boy before he hits the ground!"

True to his easily distractable nature, Huey abandoned his race with nary a second thought and dived after Zachary. Abby threw on her climbing harness and managed to drag herself into the cargo bay, where she clipped a daisy chain to the handle and leaned out the starboard doorway. From there she saw Zachary a thousand feet below them, hauling on his front riser, trying to turn away from the mooing stampede and in the process tilting himself nearly parallel to the ground.

Huey descended fast, much faster than Zachary. He aimed for the parachute rather than the boy, pulling up just as his nose drew level and hooking his skids under the canopy.

"Attaboy, Huey!" Abby shouted, climbing out onto the starboard skid. "Now level off for a minute so I can bring him aboard."

She hung on tightly as Huey went into a hover. Reaching down, she grabbed one of the suspension lines and hauled it in, hand over hand. Zach didn't weigh much, but it was hard work in a moving helicopter and Abby's arms were shaking with fatigue by the time her brother hove into view. He had his eyes squeezed tightly shut and he was gibbering in his panic. "Please don't eat me—I'm sorry I'm sorry—I'll never shoot at you again!"

"Zach!" Abby shouted at him, shaking his shoulder. "Snap out of it. You're safe."

Zachary's eyes popped open. "Huh?" He darted a look around and noticed her. "Abby? Did it kidnap you too? Are we kidnapped?"

~ Airborne ~

Abby rolled her eyes. "No, you idiot. Huey here just saved your ass."

Huey chattered a question at her.

"Yes, that means you win," Abby told him.

Huey hooted happily, tracing a victory lap over the cattle and making them run into one another in confusion.

Zachary raised an inquisitive eyebrow.

"He likes games," she explained. "It's a long story."

With Bruce's Robinson and Gav's ute as their escort, Abby, Huey and Zachary managed to make it to the landing grid without being shot at by Howard and the other farm hands.

"Dad, Dad!" Zachary shouted, bounding out of the cargo bay before Huey's skids had even touched down, "I fell out and I was falling and there were cows and *he saved me!*"

"We heard," Howard said with an amused grin as Zachary collected relieved hugs and pats on the back from the others.

"We also heard you took the Chopper Buster after your father specifically told you not to and fired it, after we all agreed that you couldn't," Tammy added, glaring at her son.

"Oh," Zachary said, his face falling. "I was hoping Gav would leave that part out."

"Not a chance," Gav retorted. "That was some brown trouser job you pulled, boofhead. I hope you get dish duty for the next fifteen years."

"So this...thing...really saved him?" Howard asked, indicating Huey.

"Fair dinkum," Bruce answered. "I saw it myself, and so did Gav here and a dozen stockmen."

"Well..." Howard said, considering. Then he touched his hat to the chopper. "Thank you, I guess."

Huey chattered an answer and everyone looked to Abby.

"He says 'you're welcome,' I think."

"He?" Gav asked.

"Yeah, he," Abby retorted, a bit defensively. "His name's Huey." She patted the helicopter on the nose. "He brought me back *and* won the race, so he's free now to go and look for his mates. Right Huey?"

Huey chirped uncertainly.

~ *Airborne* ~

"Go on," Abby said, giving him a gentle nudge. "We won't shoot you down." She glared at her father. "Right Dad? And you can even have a drink before you go."

Howard gave a grudging nod but Huey seemed to feel even worse than before. His eye drooped. He looked at Abby, then out toward the horizon and home.

"I'll miss you, too, mate," Abby told him, guessing what his problem was. She gave his nose a hug. "Go on."

Huey's eye jerked back and forth in an unmistakable "no."

Abby's eyes narrowed. "What do you mean, no?"

Huey chattered. He spooled up his main rotor and twirled his tail rotor in enthusiasm. He gently lifted off, but instead of leaving the platform he pivoted and bumped Abby's stomach with his nose. Then he set back down and shut off all his rotors.

"Gav, I think you've got some competition there," Bruce said, laughing. "Bloody chopper's taken a shine to her."

Gav blushed through his tan and ducked his head, muttering death threats under his breath to Bruce.

Zachary, whose opinion of choppers had done a complete one-eighty in the last half hour, jumped to Huey's aid. "Can we keep him Dad? Pleeeeeease?" he begged.

"I bet if I made a game of things," Abby said thoughtfully, "we could get him to help out. Fetch supplies, carry cargo, that sort of thing."

"I'd be nice not to have to rely so much on the road trains," Gav added helpfully.

"Those bloody helicopters," Howard said, stabbing a finger at Huey, "have been leeching off *my* power grid for thirty bloody years!" This was Howard's favorite subject and, true to form, he was getting all worked up over it. "And now you're telling me that after a single day of mucking about in the bloody desert you can get these bloody things to do what they were meant to do in the first place?!"

"Um, just this one, but yes," Abby answered, leaning away from the impending explosion.

"You *did* send Abs away to school so she could figure out how to stop them leeching," Gav reminded him.

"It's kind of poetic, if you think about it," Bruce put in, grinning.

~ Airborne ~

Howard glowered at Jack. "Oi, and I suppose you'll be wanting to keep it as well, then?"

Jack shrugged. "I wouldn't object, no."

Howard rounded on Tammy and Raylene. "Sheilas?"

"I think it's kind of cute," Tammy mused. Raylene agreed.

"Fine!" Howard throwing his arms up in defeat. "My own family, siding with a bloody wild one!"

Howard sat grumpily on the railing, arms crossed, watching the others as they gathered around to get a look at Huey. Abby came over and gave her dad a kiss on the cheek.

"Thinking machines, bloody helicopters with bloody names, adopting wild ones like bloody puppies, what'll be next, a bloody wind turbine running for bloody President?" Howard grumbled.

"Relax Dad," Abby replied. "They'd never fit in Parliament House anyway."

❧ ☙

Katrina Nicholson was first published at the age of eight but avoided making a career out of writing for fear of ending up living in a cardboard box. It was only once she tried and hated all the other careers that she came around. Now she has diploma in Writing for Film and Television from the Vancouver Film School, several published short stories, and a movie reviews website. She's from Sydney, NS, but dreams of Sydney, NSW...and everywhere else in Australia. You can visit her in her cardboard box at www.refrigeratorbox.org.

~ Airborne ~

Don't Miss

Undercurrents
The Speculative Elements, v. 1

The landscape of Cape Breton writing doesn't necessarily begin at the Canso Causeway and end at the Cabot Strait. The fourteen stories in Undercurrents ply the literary oceans of time and space, possibility and imagination. And while you may find familiar themes in these pages—love, greed, spirituality—you will discover that they take on a new perspective when viewed through the lens of the speculative.

Inside are stories that ripple and swell with the unusual: fiddle-playing ghosts, malevolent cats, urbane vampires, and ordinary folks who have drifted into realms of the extraordinary.

"The 14 short stories cover every genre from laser blasting space opera to murder mystery ghost stories to Twilight Zone-esque creepers....Many of the writers found surprising ways to use the title of the collection as a theme in their tales."
~ Ken Chisholm, Cape Breton Post

Available at www.thirdpersonpress.com, www.amazon.ca, Coles, and other fine stores around Cape Breton Island.

**Coming in 2011
from Third Person Press**

Unearthed

The Speculative Elements, v. 3

Watch for details at www.thirdpersonpress.com

www.ingramcontent.com/pod-product-compliance
Lightning Source LLC
Chambersburg PA
CBHW071824020726
47502CB00004B/1229